Anna King was born in the East End of London and grew up in Hackney. She wrote ten novels before her death in 2003.

Maybe This Time

ANNA KING

SPHERE

First published in Great Britain by Warner in 2003
Reprinted by Warner in 2004
This paperback edition published in 2011 by Sphere

A CIP catalogue record for this book
is available from the British Library.

ISBN 978-0-7515-4836-5

Printed and bound in Great Britain by
Clays Ltd, St Ives plc

Papers used by Sphere are from well-managed forests
and other responsible sources.

MIX
Paper from
responsible sources
FSC® C104740
www.fsc.org

Sphere
An imprint of
Little, Brown Book Group
100 Victoria Embankment
London EC4Y 0DY

An Hachette UK Company
www.hachette.co.uk

www.littlebrown.co.uk

For Susan Bull who is always there when I need her. Thank you for being my friend, Sue.

ACKNOWLEDGEMENTS

My love and thanks to my niece, Hollie Masterson, for inspiring the title of this book. Keep singing, sweetheart, and don't forget your Auntie Anna when you're rich and famous.

I would also like to mention Mary Graham, a friend for over thirty years, and better known as the Hedda Hopper of the East End! Here's my latest effort, Mary, and all I can say is: 'Pick the bones out of this one!' Still love you lots anyway.

CHAPTER ONE

'Hello, Janie, you're looking lovely today, ain't she, boys?'

'Oh! Thanks, Barney . . . Ta. That's nice of you to say so.'

Even as the words left her mouth, Jane Flynn silently cursed herself for a fool and felt her cheeks grow hot under the earnest stares of the handsome young man looking at her – a man who was no friend of her family; especially her brother Rory. Never comfortable with people at the best of times, and knowing she was being made fun of, she found herself increasingly flustered by the presence of Barney Hobbs and his grinning companions. The men's sniggering only made her feel more uncomfortable. Keeping her face averted, she tried frantically to think of something witty or amusing to say. Better still, some cutting remark that would put Barney Hobbs at a disadvantage, but like always, no words came to mind. They would later, after she had replayed the scene over and over in her mind as she lay in the safety of her darkened bedroom, but not now, not now when she needed the quick repartee most girls of her age would find easy. But then most girls of her age weren't handicapped by a disfiguring strawberry birthmark that covered the left side of her face. The worst part of her affliction was that most people treated her with either embarrassment or pity, when all she had ever wanted was to be accepted for the person she was inside. But the sad fact was that the majority of people only looked at the appearance that was presented to the world; namely the face. Her only consolation was the fact that she lived in a close-knit community, and because of that the people in her street and the surrounding area had seen her grow up from a baby to the sixteen-year-old girl she was now. Those friends and neighbours accepted her just the way she was. The same kind people had long since looked past the ugly stain that had ruined what would have been a pretty face.

It was easy to spot strangers to the area, for they would stop and stare at the young girl as if she was some sort of freak. She should have been immune to it by now, but as often as it happened, Jane never ceased to feel a stomach-churning shame and embarrassment for her affliction. Then there were people like Barney Hobbs and his cronies. Cruel and indifferent to people's feelings, their only source of enjoyment was tormenting and inflicting hurt upon anyone who was different, for their own twisted amusement. And, to add insult to injury, bullies like these assumed that anyone not normal in their bigoted eyes must also be simple-minded. That thought brought Jane's head up proudly. If there were any ignorant people present, it certainly wasn't her. If she was given the opportunity to pit her wits against any one of the smirking, drunken men, she knew with absolute certainty that she could wipe the floor with the lot of them.

Yet this knowledge was of no use to her as Barney Hobbs and his friends formed a circle around her, pushing her against the wall of the closed shop on the corner of the street where she always waited for her brothers, thus blocking any chance of escape. She could feel the heat of the hot June day through her cotton dress, and the burning cobbled pavement was penetrating her thin sandals. Then she felt Barney's hand run over her buttocks, his face showing a cruel, sneering veneer, confident his prey would be too scared to make a fuss. And he was right in his arrogant assumption. For Jane, her heart pumping so violently she could hear the noise resounding in her ears, stayed rooted to the spot. Trembling from head to foot, she didn't think she could feel any further fear; until she looked directly into Barney's eyes and saw a new look enter them. Jane Flynn had led a sheltered life, protected as much as possible from the outside world by her parents and three older brothers, but even in her innocence she recognised the look of lust reflected in Barney's eyes as he stared down at her hungrily. He pulled her close to his chest, his hand undoing the ribbon fastened under her chin to keep in place the wide straw hat she always wore. His grin widened as he pushed the protective garment from her head, leaving her feeling vulnerable

3

and exposed in the bright sunlit day. People passed by the small group, but no one paid them any attention. To all intents and purposes Jane and the four men were merely larking about; it was a common enough sight on a Sunday afternoon. The sound of a tram approaching caught her attention, giving her a moment of hope. Surely someone sitting on the open-topped tram would notice her distress and come to her aid. But the tram rumbled by noisily on steel tracks, disappearing from view within seconds.

The fear that now gripped her had paralysed her voice, preventing her from calling out for help. If only her brothers would show up. They should have been here by now. They knew she would be waiting for them on the corner of Morning Lane, five minutes from the pub they frequented, just as she had done every Sunday lunchtime since she was twelve. This ritual had been instigated by her mother, sick of waiting for her three sons to arrive home on time for their Sunday dinner. She had threatened numerous times that if they were late just once more she would throw their meal to the first passing stray dog, adding that at least then her cooking would be appreciated, but the strapping young men would laugh and slap her rounded buttocks with affection as they left for their Sunday outing to the pub.

When the boys were younger they would all accompany her to church and watch with envy as their father disappeared into the pub on the journey home. Paddy Flynn still had a drink after Mass – just the one, though, and Annie didn't begrudge her husband his Sunday treat; she never had – but those times had long since gone. Her boys no longer attended Mass, but they never missed their Sunday pre-lunch drink. Even their father, who they loved dearly, wasn't able to get them out of the pub before closing time. Once, out of anger at seeing another roast dinner dry up, Annie had marched into the crowded pub and pulled her sons out by the scruff of their necks, giving them each a sound slap across the back of their heads for good measure, much to the amusement of the regulars. It was a sight no man had seen before; the Flynn brothers being given a sound thrashing, running from the irate woman who barely came up to her sons' chests as if the devil himself was snapping at their heels. But the following week she had waited in frustration while the dinner she had so carefully prepared grew cold. It was then she'd had an idea. They might ignore her and their father, but if they knew Jane was waiting in the street for them, then they would make sure to keep an eye on the time. Her ploy had worked. Since that first Sunday she had sent Jane to wait on the corner for her brothers, they had never been late. And Jane, who adored her big brothers, had been ecstatic at being allowed out on her own. For from the first moment she could remember, there had always been someone with her, guarding her against the world, against life itself, something they would never have done if she hadn't been born with the disfiguring facial blemish. She often thought her family worried more about her appearance than she did, but if that were true it was only because they loved her. And that unconditional love had seen her through the rare moments of self-pity and despondency that had sometimes threatened to overwhelm her.

Sunday had been her favourite day since then. She would attend Mass with her parents, then, when the joint of meat was ready to be carved by her father, her face would light up, for this was the signal for her to fetch her brothers. And though she loved all her brothers it was Rory who meant the most. He was always the first one to arrive, picking her up and twirling her round until she felt giddy. He would make her laugh until she felt sick and begged him to stop. Then Shaun and Pat would turn the corner and the four of them would walk home together. But it was those first few minutes when she had Rory to herself that she treasured.

'What's the matter, love? You waiting for yer brothers to turn up? Maybe they've forgotten yer. You know what the Irish are like when they've 'ad a few drinks. You're all the same, the lot of yer. All holy Joes ranting on about yer precious St Patrick and the Pope, then it's outta church an' into the nearest pub.' The sneering voice brought the young girl out of her reverie, and with it a rare flash of bravery. She would never have thought of sticking up for herself, but nobody talked about her family like that. Struggling wildly, she managed to free her hands and pushed hard against her tormentor's chest.

'Don't you make fun of my family, Barney Hobbs. You wouldn't be so brave if my brothers were here, would you? You're just a coward and a bully, so there,' she ended childishly, her eyes darting down the road as Barney's words echoed in her head. Surely they hadn't forgotten her! No! They would never do that. They would be here any moment now;

6

but every passing second seemed to the frightened girl like an hour.

'Listen to her, lads. That's something else the Irish have in common, a bad temper; 'specially those with red hair. Ooh, I'm shaking in me boots.' The derisory comment brought hoots of laughter from the drunken men, fuelling Jane's fear even further. 'Look, lads, she's blushing,' sneered Barney, his full lips spread in a cruel smile. 'Mind you, it's a bit hard ter tell with that face, ain't it?' He pressed his body closer to the terrified girl, his hand tightening on her buttocks. 'Like that, d'yer, love? I mean ter say, with a face like yours, yer ain't likely ter get many offers, are yer?' As Barney became more aggressive with the girl, the rest of the young men began to feel increasingly uneasy. It was one thing to have a bit of fun, but Barney was taking things a bit too far for their liking. They began to fall back, their initial amusement abating, along with the alcohol they had consumed, as they suddenly remembered who the girl was.

Then, seemingly out of nowhere, a red-headed man burst through their ranks. With a roar of outrage, he grabbed Barney by the scruff of the neck, turned him round and threw him up against the wall so hard that pieces of chalk and brick rained down on his head and shoulders. The unexpected attack knocked Barney senseless for a moment, but he quickly recovered. Growling, he launched himself at Rory Flynn with the fierceness of a wild animal; but the Irishman met his adversary head on. Jane began to cry as the two men exchanged blows, the sound of fists hitting bone making her squeeze her eyes tightly shut in an effort to blot out the scene being played before her. By this time, the remaining men had fallen well back, their eyes flickering up and down the street as if expecting more company, their expressions filled with mounting dread. They didn't have to wait long. Two men raced into view. It was Shaun and Pat Flynn. Recognising them immediately, Barney's friends turned to flee. No one in their right mind would pick a fight with any of the Flynn brothers, but to attempt to take on all three of them would be tantamount to suicide. Like the cowards they were, the men ran off, but they weren't quick enough. While Rory took care of the ringleader, Shaun and Pat quickly caught up with Barney's friends, and with a loud whoop of glee they proceeded to give the cowardly men a good hiding.

A passing policeman heard the commotion and walked towards the sound. Seeing the seven men brawling in the street brought the middle-aged sergeant's eyebrows together. There was no mistaking the Flynn brothers, not with the red hair that identified the youngest and eldest boys. And where they were, Pat Flynn would be close by. He was the only one to take after his mother in looks and colouring. Taking a closer look, the sergeant saw a well-built man with black hair land a heavy punch on one man's jaw while another clung to his back; but not for long. Pat looked over his shoulder and grinned before shrugging off his assailant with ease, sending him sprawling alongside his friend. The uniformed man smiled. That was Pat Flynn all right.

The police officer glanced from side to side to make sure no one had seen him before resuming his beat, his baton swinging idly in his sturdy hand. Once, many years ago, he would have launched into the fray, but he was getting too old for that kind of lark any more. Whistling cheerfully, he walked on, glad he had grown out of the idealism that had made him join the police force. The men back there were more than capable of looking after themselves.

By now Rory had Barney by the throat, and the man was making a stomach-turning gurgling sound.

'You filthy piece of scum,' Rory yelled. 'You wanna fight, come on then, I'm ready, or d'yer only pick on girls?'

'Rory! Rory! Let him go . . . Let him go, Rory, you're choking him.' Jane was pulling desperately at her brother's arm, but she could have been a fly for all the notice her brother took of her. Barney's hands beat Rory about the head in a frantic attempt to loosen the stranglehold, but his attacker took no heed. Sobbing with fear now, Jane called to Pat and Shaun, who were thoroughly enjoying giving the other three men a sound thrashing. Shaun, holding one of the men in a headlock, was the first to hear his sister's cries, and, knowing his eldest brother's temper, quickly released his hold, letting the bruised man fall with total indifference, and raced to Jane's side.

'That's enough, man . . . I said, that's enough,' he shouted, grabbing Rory by the arms. Shaun was a strong man, but it was only when Pat joined him that they were able to pull their enraged brother away from the choking man.

Barney Hobbs slumped down the wall, his breath coming in tortured gasps. Held firmly by his brothers, Rory, his eyes blazing, shouted at the slumped figure, 'You can count yerself lucky, Hobbs. Next time I catch yer near my sister, yer won't get off so lightly.' He managed one last kick at the prostrate body before being dragged away.

'Jasus, man, what's the matter with you?' Shaun was shouting at him. 'I've no time for Barney Hobbs either, an' he deserved a good hiding for frightening our Jane, but God Almighty, Rory, you nearly killed the man.'

But Rory wasn't listening. Instead his gaze was still focused on the bruised and bloodied man getting to his feet. Which was just as well, for if he had looked behind him all hell would have broken loose once more, and not even his brothers' combined strength could have held on to him. Barney was on his feet now, wiping the blood from his swollen lips – lips that were spread into a mocking grin. Shaun and Pat tentatively loosened their grip on Rory while at the same time following Barney's gaze. And what they saw brought a knowing look to their eyes and a muttered oath to their lips. For there, across the road, her face clearly showing her amusement beneath a fancy white parasol, was Cathy Meadows.

Seeing the three men watching her, Cathy arched her eyebrows mockingly, before walking slowly away, her hips swaying provocatively beneath her long blue dress, a dress that was designed to show off her voluptuous figure. Jane too had seen the woman who had turned their family upside down, and just managed to stop herself from drawing Rory's attention to the retreating figure. He mustn't see that woman, not now, not after all this time. Not now he was just beginning to get on with his life. Jane and the rest of the family had thought Rory had finally put behind him the memory of Cathy Meadows, and the cruel and public humiliation she had caused him by dumping him for Barney Hobbs.

Tears began to well behind Jane's eyes. Judging by the brutal attack Rory had let loose on Barney, it was obvious he still hadn't forgotten Cathy, or forgiven the man she had dumped him for. He would still have given Barney a good slap for what he had done to his sister, but what Jane had witnessed had gone much further than a simple act of brotherly loyalty. If Shaun and Pat hadn't been there, Rory could well have killed Barney Hobbs, and that awful thought brought a fresh burst of terror to her shaking body.

What she mustn't do was tell her brothers, or anyone else, that Cathy had appeared across the road just moments before her brothers, and hadn't lifted a finger to help her. Jane Flynn hadn't a spiteful bone in her body, which considering the cruel trick life had played on her was remarkable in itself, for many people in her circumstances used their infirmity to justify their surly attitude towards those who, to their mind, were normal. Yet Jane had never been one to feel animosity towards her fellow man, but in Cathy Meadows' case she was willing to make an exception. For that woman had done the unforgivable: she had hurt Rory and nearly driven a wedge between him and their mother. Please God, she prayed quietly, don't let her be back for good. Let it be that she's just home to visit her parents. Though that notion was unlikely. Cathy wasn't the type to have family ties, not unless it was to her advantage. A burst of hope rose in Jane's breast. Maybe that was it. Maybe she had come home to try and get some money out of her long-suffering parents before disappearing again. Oh! Please! Please let that be the case.

Taking the now calm Rory by the arm, she made sure she kept his attention on her and said softly, 'Come on, Rory, let's go home. Mum will be wondering where we are. And you know what she's like if we're late for our dinner.' Rory glanced down at his sister with a stab of guilt. He had almost forgotten about her, and she was the one who had suffered most from the unpleasant incident. Pulling her close to his chest, he hugged her tight.

'You all right, sweetheart?' he asked tenderly. Then, pushing her back so he could see her face, he asked, 'He didn't . . . I mean, he didn't hurt you in any way, did he? 'Cos if he did . . .'

Summoning up a smile, Jane answered quickly, 'No, Rory, he just scared me a bit, that's all . . . Honest.' Not for the world would she ever admit the full extent of the assault Barney Hobbs had subjected her to. For if she told, or Rory ever found out . . . Jane felt a ripple of fear pass through her body at the thought of what her brother would do if he were to discover the whole truth – and not just Rory, but the rest of the family as well.

On the way home, Jane kept up a constant stream of chatter, aided by Shaun and Pat, in an effort to restore her brother's natural good humour, for their mother was as sharp as a knife and none of them could ever keep anything from her. As they neared the house she looked to Shaun, saying over-brightly, 'I'll run on ahead and tell Mum you're coming.'

Sensing the reason behind Jane's words, Shaun and Pat both nodded. 'That's a grand idea, Jane. It'll give us time to cheer this miserable bugger up, 'cos we don't want Mum to see him like this. We're already gonna get it in the neck for fighting on a Sunday.' A knowing look passed between them, a look that spoke volumes.

Jane needed no more encouragement. Holding her hat in place with one hand, she picked up her skirt with the other, so as to not impede her movement, and ran on ahead, bursting into the terraced house out of breath and trembling as the full enormity of what she was about to tell her mother dawned on her.

'Jasus, girl, what ails ye?' Annie Flynn came out of the kitchen wiping her hands on a clean dishcloth. 'Sure ye look like the divil himself was after ye.'

Jane held her hand at her side as if she had a stitch from running. Gasping, she said, 'Where's Dad, Mum? I've got to tell you both something.'

As if conjured out of thin air, Paddy Flynn appeared behind his wife.

'Did I hear someone take me name in vain?' he quipped humorously. But the smile slipped from his face as Jane blurted out her news.

'Cathy Meadows is back. I saw her, Mum, and so did Shaun and Pat.'

At her daughter's words, the colour drained from Annie's face. Feeling behind her for a chair, she sank down unsteadily. She felt her husband's hand grip her shoulder and grabbed hold of it tightly, taking reassurance from the loving gesture.

'Now are ye sure, Jane?' Paddy asked, while knowing the question was futile. His daughter wasn't daft, and she'd said Shaun and Pat had seen Cathy too. So all that remained was to find out if Rory knew. For if he did, then God help them all. Paddy would never have believed any of his sons would have been so devastated on account of a woman, for none of them had ever had any trouble in that department. He had lost count of the girls they had taken up with. But that . . . that woman had left his eldest son's life in tatters.

'Holy Mary, mother of God.' Annie gripped her husband's hand tighter and asked the question that was hovering on his lips. 'Did our Rory see her, love?'

The question was more of a plea than a query, and Annie visibly slumped with relief when Jane, looking from her mother to her father, answered, 'No, Mum. He was too busy fighting with Barney Hobbs to notice . . .' She trailed off as she realised she had unwittingly dropped her brothers into trouble, but she needn't have worried. Her sons fighting was the furthest thought from Annie's mind at the moment.

'Right then,' said Paddy. 'We'll have to make sure it stays that way, for the time being at least.' As Paddy started to talk, Annie knew what her husband was going to say and quickly forestalled him.

Annie got to her feet, her chin jutting out determinedly. 'I know we can't keep it quiet for long; the gossipmongers will be having a field day once this gets out, so we'll say no more about it for the time being. For now we'll carry on as normal. It'll give me a chance to think of something to stop that trollop from getting her hooks into our Rory again.' Briskly now, she set about laying the table, banging down the plates so hard Jane was sure they would break, but she wasn't about to say anything – she'd had enough upset for the day.

When the three brothers came through the door, Annie told them to wash before coming to the table, cuffing them all around the head for fighting, especially on a Sunday. For even if Jane hadn't split on them, the state of their clothes and the minor cuts on their faces and hands would have given them away. Though if Annie had known what had provoked the fight she'd have gone round to Barney Hobbs' house and flattened him herself. At any other time she would have asked what it was about, but her mind was busy elsewhere.

When the family were seated at the table and Annie had said grace, they set about eating the roast beef and Yorkshire puddings, verbally sparring with each other as they always did. To anyone looking on it would have seemed like any other Sunday lunch. Only those seated at the table knew that the friendly banter was merely a façade to hide their true feelings.

Later, as she got into bed, Annie said to Paddy, 'I'll be off round to Shore Road first thing in the morning. I want to find out what that woman's up to.'

Paddy gathered her into his arms, murmuring, 'You do what ye feel is best, me darling, you always do. But ye can't be doing anything tonight, so try and get some sleep.'

An angry tut of annoyance spilled from her lips. 'Sleep, ye say! Mother of God. Sure an' how d'ye expect me to sleep with all this worry on me mind? But you go ahead, I wouldn't want to be depriving ye of your rest. Though how yer can even think about sleeping is a mystery to me.'

Knowing that whatever he said he would still be in the wrong, Paddy kept his own counsel and stayed silent.

It wasn't long before Annie heard Paddy's soft snores. She had a sudden irrational urge to prod him awake, but she resisted it and lay staring into the darkness, seething with anger and worry, her mind conjuring up the image of Cathy Meadows' brazen face. For what seemed like hours she tossed and turned, but Paddy didn't even stir. Gazing up into the darkness of the room, Annie thought back over the past year. Yet even as she worried over her son's reaction once he found out that Cathy Meadows was back, her mind turned to Josie Guntrip. Poor Josie.

There had been no one more delighted than Annie when Rory had first shown some interest in Josie. They had grown up together, started and left school together. Up until that time Rory had looked upon her as a sister, though to anyone with half an eye could see, the adoration shining from Josie's face whenever Rory was near her had been painfully obvious. Then one day he had started taking more notice of his childhood friend. For nearly six months they had courted, and Annie had prayed silently that things would eventually get serious, for there was nobody she would rather have as a daughter-in-law than Josie Guntrip; even if it meant taking her mother into the family. Annie's lips pursed at the thought of Elsie Guntrip, then she chided herself for letting her mind wander. Turning on to her side, she concentrated on the matter in hand. But first she had to be fair to her son, for though Josie had been in love with Rory for years, Rory had never led her to believe that there was a future for them.

A wry smile moved Annie's lips. Ever since he'd been in short trousers, Rory had had the girls after him. Shaun and Pat had had their share too, but Rory had that certain something that attracted the girls, something that was hard to define and impossible to put into words. And Josie, God love her, had been no different. Those six months with Rory had been the happiest time of Josie's life, even though she knew Rory wasn't in love with her. Just being with him had been enough for her. Annie had tried her best to encourage her son to make a commitment, but he had just laughed, declaring he was too young to settle down, adding cheerfully that he and Josie were just fine as they were. Then Cathy Meadows had appeared on the scene, and Rory had fallen head over heels in love. And poor, sweet Josie had quietly slipped into the background without a word of protest, leaving Rory free to take up with the girl who had shattered her dreams for the future.

Everyone had been furious with Rory for treating Josie in such a callous manner, but Rory hadn't seen it that way. He had genuinely believed that Josie shared his feelings, and couldn't see why everyone was making such a fuss. He had even asked Josie if she minded him ending their relationship, and of course Josie had made it easy for him, even though Annie had known the young woman was heart-broken at losing Rory to another woman.

Annie thumped her pillow, turning her face into its softness as her mind continued to wander. The affair with Cathy Meadows had lasted just four months, before the woman had turned her attention to Barney Hobbs, leaving Rory devastated. To make matters worse, he hadn't received any sympathy from anyone; his family included. Josie was well thought of, and there were many who believed Rory had got what he deserved for treating her so shabbily.

It was no secret that Cathy had left Rory for Barney Hobbs simply because he had his own business and wasn't short of a few bob. Barney and Rory had never got on, but Barney's glee at getting one over on the man he detested had been short-lived, for Cathy had soon moved on to her next victim. This time it was a middle-aged businessman, who could offer her not only a wealthy lifestyle, but also the opportunity to leave the East End to take up residence in his home in affluent Knightsbridge. Cathy had jumped at the chance. Barney Hobbs hadn't had a clue what was going on behind his back. He had learned the truth only when he'd gone to her home, to be told by Cathy's parents that their daughter had packed her belongings and left the previous night, accompanied by a man old enough to be her father. That had been nearly eighteen months ago. In fact Annie knew to the day when Cathy had left. It was the same day that the new king had come to the throne. So, for Annie at least, it had been a double celebration. Of course there had been much sadness following the death of the Queen, for she had been well loved by the people she had ruled over for so long. But Bertie, as he was affectionately known, had proved to be immensely popular, just as his mother had been before him.

No one had seen Cathy since – until today!

Now she was back. And if her track record was anything to go by, it wouldn't be long before she caused more trouble. Annie's last thought before sleep overtook her was for her son. He'd already been hurt once; she wasn't going to stand by and let it happen again.

CHAPTER TWO

'Rory!'

'Yeah!' Rory answered without stopping work. He shovelled another load of broken bricks into a half-filled skip. Then, when no answer came, he leaned on the wooden handle of the shovel and, wiping the sweat from his eyes, looked at his brother and said, 'Well, what's up?'

Shaun Flynn, his face caked with dust, said hesitantly, 'I was wondering . . . Well, I wanted to ask if you'd mind if I asked Josie out one night.' He nipped at his lower lip at the look that came over Rory's face. 'Only, if you'd rather I didn't . . .'

Rory turned his back, his strong arm scooping another pile of bricks on to the flat shovel, and said tersely, 'You do what you want, mate. It ain't got nothing to do with me what Josie does.'

Shaun's face lit up with relief. 'Thanks, Rory.' He stifled a nervous laugh. 'Mind you, she might turn me down, she don't go out with any old Tom, Dick or Harry. She's very fussy, is Josie, not like some I could mention . . .' His voice trailed off as he realised what he'd said. Then, in a clumsy attempt to make amends, he muttered, 'Sorry, Rory, I didn't mean anything by . . .'

Rory's head seemed to jerk on his shoulders before he replied tersely, 'Look, just leave it, eh, Shaun?' He glanced over his shoulder at his brother's anxious face and sighed. He loved his brother, he loved all his family, but Lord above, Shaun could try the patience of a saint sometimes. He was twenty-two years old, and nearly six feet tall, yet he talked and acted like a ten-year-old at times. Like now, for instance. He put Rory in mind of a puppy, always eager to please, always wanting to make people like him, but what irritated Rory most was the way Shaun looked up to him. Since the time he could crawl, Shaun would follow his eldest brother everywhere. Not that Rory had minded back then; in fact, he had been quite proud at the open hero-worship. But that had been when they were children. They were all grown men now, yet still Shaun seemed to need Rory's approval for everything he did. Not like Pat! Rory looked beyond Shaun to where his other brother was busily giving out orders to a group of workmen. Rory was both proud and envious that his brother was the gaffer. Proud because of the way Pat had worked to the elevated position he now held; envious because Rory didn't like to be second best at anything.

As if aware of his brother's scrutiny, Pat looked over and shouted good-naturedly, 'What you two doing? It ain't dinner time yet, so get your arses

21

moving if you want paying at the end of the week.'

Rory waved back.

'All right, guv, anything you say, guv. Lick your boots, guv?'

Pat grinned widely.

'Don't push your luck, you Irish git. And that goes for the rest of you lot.'

All the men on the building site resumed work with enthusiasm, glad they had a gaffer like Pat Flynn. Not that any of them would take liberties with the Irishman. Oh, no! He might like a laugh and a joke with his men, but if one of them were to step out of line he would come down on them like a ton of bricks.

'Eh, he's a laugh, ain't he, Rory?' Shaun was beside his brother, a wide grin on his homely face, and somehow this only served to annoy Rory more.

'Yeah, ain't he just. Maybe he should pack in his job and try an' get work on the stage as a comedian. Now, for Gawd's sake, get on with your work, instead of waffling on like an eejit.'

The Irish word came naturally to Rory's lips. The way the various accents of the family conflicted was a constant source of amusement to everyone who knew the Flynns. There were Paddy and Annie, who still spoke in the thick Irish brogue of their native land, despite having lived in England for over twenty-five years. Then there were their sons, with their cockney accents, punctuated by the occasional Irish word or expression picked up from their parents; and lastly there was the daughter, her refined speech the result of her convent education.

'Sorry, Rory.'

Shaun, knowing when to keep quiet, continued mixing cement, his eyes downcast. If it had been anyone else speaking to him like that he would have floored the man, but Rory was different; Rory was his brother, and as such could do no wrong in Shaun's eyes. At the same time he was wondering how long it would be before Rory found out Cathy was back. He and Pat had wanted to tell him, rather than run the risk of him finding out from someone else, but their mother had been adamant about keeping quiet until she'd had a chance to visit Cathy and find out how long she was planning to stay. After all, she'd reasoned with them, the woman might well just have come back for the weekend to visit her parents. Furthermore, she had added, what was the point of causing Rory more pain unless it was absolutely necessary? Remembering his mother's anxious face, Shaun felt a moment's guilt. He shouldn't have said anything about Josie, but tact had never been his strong suit. But the truth was, he had been in love with Josie for years. Even so, he told himself, he could have picked a better moment to bring the subject up.

Moreover, just as Shaun was thinking about his brother, Rory was doing likewise. As they worked side by side in silence, Rory thought guiltily, Damn! Why do I always have to go for him? It ain't his fault I was taken for a mug. It was just that hearing Josie's name had struck a painful chord; especially after yesterday's run-in with Barney Hobbs. And there was something else that had been nagging at him since yesterday. It was nothing he could put his finger on, just a feeling that his family seemed to be behaving strangely. Then again, he was probably imagining it. He hadn't been in the best of moods yesterday. Summoning up a cheerful countenance, he slapped Shaun on the back.

'Sorry, mate. Don't take no notice of me. I can be a miserable bugger at times. I don't know how you put up with me. I know Pat wouldn't.' He let out a false laugh. 'Bleeding hell! If I spoke to him like that I'd be flat on me back, and probably missing a couple of teeth into the bargain.'

Shaun smiled back, but there was a sadness in his eyes that Rory noticed immediately. Worst of all, he knew the reason behind his brother's pitying look, and that knowledge brought with it a surge of rage. With renewed vigour he shovelled another load into the skip, throwing himself into the back-breaking job in an attempt to work out his frustration.

The rest of the day passed uneventfully until they were on their way home. Pat had gone on ahead, eager to get cleaned up before the latest love in his life, Freda Harris, arrived for her weekly visit; and the prospect of sitting down at the same table with Pat's new lady friend seemed to Rory like a crappy end to a crappy day, for he couldn't stand the woman.

Rory wasn't aware that a silence had fallen between him and his brother until Shaun broke into his thoughts saying, 'D'yer think Pat's serious about Freda? Only I wouldn't fancy 'aving her as a sister-in-law, would you, Rory?'

Rory shot a quizzical look at his brother. It wasn't like Shaun to badmouth anyone. Then he realised that the man by his side was simply trying to make conversation. The tautness went out of Rory's limbs and he laughed.

'Bleeding 'ell, Shaun, don't say that. It makes me skin crawl just thinking about it.'

Shaun gave a watery smile, then his head drooped, his eyes fixed on the pavement. Avoiding Rory's eyes, he said softly, 'About Josie, Rory. I meant what I said. If you don't want me to . . . well you know, try me luck, then I won't.' He gave a self-deprecating laugh. 'She probably won't want ter go out with me anyway. I've been trying ter pluck up the courage to ask her out for ages, but I thought that maybe you'd get back together one day, so I kept quiet.'

Rory stared at Shaun in amazement. All these years he had seen his younger brother as soft, the sort of bloke who blended into the background, a man with a weak personality, always larking about like a schoolboy. Yet in a matter of seconds Shaun had revealed his true character. He must have gone through hell watching his big brother going out with Josie, and yet he'd never said a word. He had kept his feelings hidden, and faded into the background after Rory had walked out on Josie, just in case his beloved brother should change his mind and take up with her again.

The knowledge of Shaun's selflessness should have made Rory feel humble, but it didn't. Instead it made him uncomfortable, as if he had been put in the wrong. And for a moment, as he stared hard into Shaun's guileless face, he experienced a hatred for the happy-go-lucky man who, without knowing it, had delivered another blow to his already damaged ego. Yet he had the grace to feel something of a hypocrite

25

as he thrust out his hand and gripped Shaun's arm.

'Give over, yer soppy sod. Course I don't mind. Wouldn't be much use if I did, would it? Nah! You go for it, mate, and good luck to yer. I'll tell you this, though.' With his other hand he punched Shaun's chest. 'If she says yes, you look after her, 'cos she's one of the best, and I should know. G'wan now, get going before some other bugger gets his foot in the door.'

He gave him a push, and Shaun, laughing now, said, 'Oh, thanks, Rory. You don't know what a relief it is to finally get it off me chest. The worry of it was beginning ter put me off me food, an' yer know how much I love me grub.'

They both laughed, loud, hearty laughter.

'You're a bloody fool, always have been,' said Rory with a forced heartiness he knew he couldn't sustain for much longer. The idea of Shaun and Josie together had caused in him an ache he couldn't explain. After all, it was he who had finished with Josie, not the other way round. He needed to be on his own for a while, to think things through. With this in mind he said, 'Look, I think I'll pop into the pub for a quick pint, just the one, mind. Tell Mum I'll be home in plenty of time for me tea.'

Shaun said no more; he didn't have to. The look of gratitude and relief in his eyes conveyed more than any words could have done. With his hands dug deep in his jacket pockets he strode on towards home, whistling a tuneless song.

Rory walked slowly towards the pub, deep in thought. Well, that had been a turn-up for the book. Fancy Shaun wanting Josie. He still couldn't believe it. In one way, it was a relief, because if Josie was willing to go out with Shaun, then Rory would finally be able to shake off the feeling of guilt that had hounded him since he'd broken off the relationship.

He paused and blinked into the sun, his thoughts returning to his brother, bringing with them a feeling of resentment. A feeling brought about by the knowledge that he himself would be incapable of being so unselfish. There was no way he would stand aside and let some other fellow muscle in on a girl he fancied. He had wanted Josie once, and he had got her. He remembered the first time he had stopped looking on her as just a friend of the family, and seen her for the attractive woman she had grown into. It had been at a friend's birthday party. Up until that time he had never seen Josie in anything but drab skirts and blouses, clothes bought by her mother. But that night she had been wearing a red silk dress, and her hair, normally tied back from her face in a tight old-fashioned bun, had been falling in waves over her neck and shoulders. She had looked stunning, and he hadn't been the only man to notice the transformation. All of his friends had crowded round the bewildered young woman, who was incapable of handling the attention being paid to her. He had known in that moment he wanted her for his girl; and of course he had revelled in the open envy and admiration of the other men at seeing Josie snatched out from under their noses.

He'd found out later that she'd had to creep out of the house wearing the dress she had made in secret, knowing her mother would never let her be seen in such a garment. Unfortunately the old cow had been waiting up for her after the party. Looking back, it was hard to remember if Mrs Guntrip had been more shocked at witnessing her only child being brought home by one of the Flynn brothers, or seeing her dressed in the red silk dress. Josie had never worn it again, for that vicious old cow had ripped it to shreds in front of her sobbing daughter. There had been an unpleasant confrontation, culminating in Josie being forbidden to go out in the evenings for nearly a month. But Rory wasn't to be deterred so easily. In fact, if anything, the challenge of getting Josie had whetted his appetite; and he had got her.

It had been so easy, with no effort on his part, or coyness on hers. She wasn't like other girls he had known. He'd never seen Josie walking out with a friend, or on her own, like most girls of her age did on a Sunday afternoon, making the most of the weekend break from work. Of course there was a reason for that. Her mother! If ever he hated any human being, it was Mrs Guntrip. Right from the start she had tried to stick her oar in, playing on her bad health to keep Josie tied to her. She had attempted various ploys to split them up, including emotional and physical blackmail; but for once Josie had refused to be intimidated. Then her mother had come out in the open and said she didn't want her daughter to take up with what she termed a common Irishman. Rory never knew how he had stopped himself from telling her what everybody knew: that she didn't give a toss about what Josie wanted; it was more that she was afraid of losing her unpaid skivvy and nurse.

When Mrs Guntrip had suffered a mild heart

attack, it looked for once as if she wasn't shamming. Josie continued to work, as she had done since leaving school, at Joe Lyons' café, and when she was finished there, the rest of her day was taken up with running the house and looking after an invalid, for now Mrs Guntrip was completely bedridden in her upstairs room. How many hours had Rory spent in the Guntrips' kitchen, watching Josie, weary after a day of standing, running up and down the stairs to answer the tinkling of the bell kept close to her mother's hand? There had been many times when he had been sorely tempted to run up those stairs himself and ram the blasted bell down the old trout's throat.

If it had been anyone else but Josie he wouldn't have put up with it. He was used to going out in the evenings, to the pub, or sometimes the variety halls, depending who was on the bill. In short he loved life and the pleasures it afforded him, especially when he had a girl on his arm. But he was genuinely fond of Josie, and knew that if he stopped seeing her, she would have nobody else in her life but her mother – and he couldn't do that; not to Josie. To him Mrs Guntrip seemed like a witch. Every time he entered by the back door he was careful not to make any sound that might alert her to his presence, but she always knew when he was in the house. Perhaps, he had surmised, she had gauged it from Josie's eyes, for Josie had never been able to hide her love.

Recalling this now made him hot and ashamed. God! What must Josie have gone through when he had left her for Cathy? Look at what he himself had gone through since. Though to be fair, he reasoned with his conscience, he had never led Josie to believe there was any long-term future for them. The subject of marriage had never arisen, and she had never tried to push the issue.

The memory of Josie's goodness and kindness was now flooding back. If she had ever wanted to get her own back, by God she had got it. She'd had it in her power to openly gloat, to heap further humiliation on him, but Josie wasn't made that way. There wasn't an ounce of spite in her entire body; just like Shaun.

His step now was heavy and slow. His pace quickened, then he came to an abrupt halt. Ahead of him, her back to him, was Josie herself. There were others walking along the pavement, but he would have recognised her anywhere, even though her posture was now slumped, as if she was carrying the weight of the world on her shoulders. The sight saddened him, and quickly he turned left, taking a short cut through the rows of houses but in his effort to avoid Josie, he had forgotten that the short cut would lead him into Shore Road. His face set, he crossed over, passing the red-brick house that held so many memories for him; memories that were firmly in the past now.

As Rory entered the scullery, his mother came out of the kitchen.

'Hello, son,' she said quietly.

He returned the greeting, then walked over to the sink, scooping up water in his cupped hands, splashing it over his face and neck, as he did every evening before sitting down to dinner.

Annie stood behind her son, watching his every movement, her heart pounding with anxiety and love for her eldest son. Mixed with these emotions was anger, an anger so strong it momentarily frightened her. She had been brought up a Catholic, to love her neighbour and respect the sanctity of life; yet after her visit to Cathy Meadows, she had felt such hatred that for a brief moment the thought of murder had touched her soul. The feeling had been so overwhelming she'd had to slip into the church on her way home to beg God to forgive her for allowing the devil into her heart. Yet surely God would understand her lapse, for even St Patrick himself would have been hard pressed to keep his temper in check if he had been put in the same circumstances.

Her gaze still fixed on her son's back, Annie remembered her meeting with Cathy Meadows. She had been prepared to keep calm, to maintain a neighbourly interest in why Cathy had returned home, hoping to hear what she wanted to hear: that the woman who had broken her son's heart was only back for a short visit. But the moment Annie had seen that painted, smirking face, all the words she had so carefully rehearsed flew out of the window. She had never been one to mince her words, and she had told Cathy Meadows just what she thought of her, letting loose with both barrels and ending with a warning to leave Rory alone if she knew what was good for her. That brazen hussy had listened in silence, then she had laughed. Laughed right into Annie's face, telling the furious woman she would do as she pleased, and to keep her nose out of her business.

'What's up, Mum, yer look miles away.' Rory was staring at her, his head to one side, a lopsided smile on his lips.

Annie swallowed nervously. She wished now she had kept a civil tongue in her head when dealing with Cathy Meadows. Instead she had made matters worse, and all for nothing. She was still none the wiser as to why Cathy had come home, or for how long. So now she had to tell Rory the truth; and she was dreading it.

Her breathing was becoming rapid as she tried to find the right words. They were there, in her mind and on the tip of her tongue, but as hard as she tried, they wouldn't pass her lips.

'Hello, Rory.'

Jane came into the scullery, and Annie, her body slumping with relief at the reprieve, turned to her daughter.

'Take the plates in, will you, love?'

Jane looked first at Rory, who was drying his face with a towel, thus obscuring his vision. Which was just as well, else he would have seen the look that passed between his mother and sister. And Jane, realising that Rory didn't yet know, did her mother's bidding.

'Well, get a move on, lad, before the dinner gets cold. Oh, and by the way, Freda's here. Now I know ye don't like her – I don't much care for her meself – but she's Pat's choice, so we'll be having none of your sly comments tonight, d'ye understand?'

Rory grinned.

'Don't worry, Mum. Even if I do let something slip out, you don't have ter worry, 'cos she's too thick to understand anything that has more than four letters in a word.'

At any other time Annie would have laughed with

her son, but tonight her mind was elsewhere. She knew she must act as normal for now, but tonight she'd get Rory on his own and break the news as gently as she could.

Chatting as she would have done on any other day, she went through into the kitchen, her sweeping glance and quick shake of the head silently warning those seated at the table to hold their tongues.

Taking his chair beside Jane, Rory helped himself to the food laid out on the table. He was halfway through his meal when he happened to look up and found Freda staring at him. This in itself was unusual, for she disliked Rory as much as he did her. But what set alarm bells ringing was the satisfied smirk on her plump face, which told Rory that something was amusing her, and that something was obviously connected to him. The look in her eyes deepened and her smile grew wider.

'Let us in on the joke, Freda, 'cos something's tickling you.'

Everyone at the table held their breath, then Annie, jumping into the conversation to prevent Freda from goading Rory further, said, 'Did ye read the latest gossip about the King and that Lily Langtry? It was all over the *Daily Mirror* this morning. The auld Queen would be turning in her grave if she knew the shenanigans—'

But Freda wasn't to be put off so easily. Ignoring Annie, she addressed Rory, her tone haughty.

'Why, I don't know what yer mean, Rory. And anyway, if there was a joke, it'd be on you.' Her face suddenly hardened as she remembered all the insults the man opposite had levelled at her. 'You think you're so clever, don't yer? Always looking down yer nose at me. You're nothing but a jumped-up nobody, and—'

Rory, his nerves still frayed by the events of the last two days, snapped back, 'Oh, shut up, yer silly cow. If anyone's a jumped-up nobody it's you, so why don't yer just shut yer gob and leave the rest of us in peace.'

Pat slammed down his knife, his face suffused with anger, and was about to jump to Freda's defence when she stood up, her face tight.

'Well! I've never been so insulted in all me life.'

Rory looked her up and down, then said wryly, 'Well, sit yerself down, love, and let me 'ave another try.'

Pat got to his feet and would have launched himself at Rory if Paddy hadn't got between them.

'That's enough, the pair of yous. I'll not be having me own sons fighting in front of your mother. Now sit yourselves down and behave, else I'll throw ye both into the yard, and don't think I couldn't do it. I may be getting on, but I'm still capable of tanning your backsides, as big as ye are.'

Pat and Rory glared at each other before resuming their seats, and the incident would have ended there if Freda had kept quiet; but she was bursting to tell Rory that his old girlfriend was back, revelling in the thought of seeing him brought low. Arching her eyebrows, she simpered, 'Well, sorry, I'm sure. I didn't know I needed permission to speak me mind; especially as I'm gonna be part of the family soon.' She looked now at Pat, as did the rest of the family,

34

hoping Freda's remark wasn't what they all dreaded. Annie turned to Pat and spoke quietly.

'Is this true, lad?'

Pat, his cheeks flushed, his body wriggling uncomfortably, answered, 'Yeah, it is. Sorry, Mum, I was gonna tell yer.' He shot an angry look at Freda. 'Only I didn't expect Freda to spill the news like this.'

Ignoring the disappointment on the faces of everyone present, Freda again turned her attention to Rory, saying spitefully, 'Ain't yer got anything ter say, Rory? I mean, yer could at least offer me and Pat your congratulations.'

Rory returned her stare. He couldn't believe that Pat would get himself tied up with the blowsy, hard-faced bitch, let alone consider marrying her. He must be stark raving mad. Despite his father's warning, Rory couldn't hold his tongue. He glanced first at Pat, and saw his brother lower his eyes in embarrassment; then he slowly turned his head towards the triumphant Freda.

'Offer me congratulations for what? Should I be happy that me own brother's getting married to a fat old slag like you?'

The words had hardly left his lips before pandemonium broke out. This time Pat came at Rory, his hands clenched into fists.

'You take that back, Rory, right this minute. Or we can take it out in the yard.'

Everyone was speaking at once, but over the raised voices Freda shouted, 'You've got a bleeding cheek calling me an old slag. You weren't so particular when yer took up with Cathy Meadows, and what was she but a slag? At least I don't go round picking

35

up one bloke after another, depending on how much money they've got. And she dropped you quick enough, didn't she, when Barney Hobbs started flashing his wallet about. Then she goes off with some fat old man just so she could get her greedy hands on his money, poor old sod. But he couldn't have been that stupid, 'cos by all accounts he's washed his hands of her an' all. So she's come back home, looking for another mug to latch on to. If you're quick yer might get her back, that's if you've got a full pocket, 'cos she won't look at yer twice otherwise.'

Freda paused, her breath coming in short gasps, then she caught Rory's eyes and experienced a moment of fear, for he looked as if he could do murder.

The silence in the kitchen hung heavily, all eyes on Rory now.

Aware of the scrutiny, Rory, a slow, dull red creeping up from under his collar, flushed darker still on his face and neck. His body stiffened, then, without a word or glance to anyone, he left the kitchen and headed for his room – and no one attempted to stop him.

Once in the bedroom he shared with his brothers, Rory sank down on his bed. He didn't move, couldn't move; it was as if his body was frozen. Even his breathing appeared to have stopped. After what seemed to be an eternity he drew in a deep gulp of air as the reality of Freda's spiteful words sank in. Fierce anger mixed with pain and amazement flooded his body. So she was back. His clenched hands began beating his knees. He'd kill her! If he was to set eyes on her again he'd kill her. Lifting his head, he looked in the mirror hanging on the wall. It could have been a stranger staring back at him, for he didn't recognise the cold, hard-faced man in the mirror. Cursing under his breath, he got to his feet, his mind screaming out one question. How long was she back for? He had to know. There was an urgency in him now. Not wanting to face any of his family, he crept down the stairs, pulled open the back door and went out.

CHAPTER THREE

Josie Guntrip was coming down the stairs carrying her mother's empty tray when she heard the knock on the front door. Immediately her mother called out in a querulous voice, 'Who's that at the door, Josie?'

Biting back the words that hovered on her lips, she answered curtly, 'I won't know till I open it, will I?'

Laying the tray on the hall table, she opened the door, the tightness of her lips softening when she saw who her visitor was.

'Hello, Shaun,' she said warmly, holding the door wide for him to enter. 'This is a nice surprise. Come on into the kitchen, and I'll make some tea.'

'Josie! Josie! Who is it, girl?'

Shaun closed the door behind him, his eyes darting warily upwards towards the fretful voice.

'No one for you, Mum. Go back to sleep.'

Turning to Shaun, Josie shook her head, her eyebrows arched in exasperation.

'Don't take any notice of her, Shaun. Come on through.'

Again Shaun's eyes darted up at the ceiling, as if expecting Mrs Guntrip suddenly to appear and order him out of the house. This was only the second time he had come to this house, as Josie's mother hadn't encouraged visitors. Over the years the Guntrips' few friends had slowly drifted away. It was said around the street that the happiest day in George Guntrip's life was the day he had died, freeing him from the hell that had been his marriage. He had been lucky. But for Josie his death couldn't have come at a worse time, for her quiet, hen-pecked father had been her only source of comfort in the gloomy house she had been brought up in. George Guntrip's demise had dealt Josie a double blow, for it was at that time that Cathy Meadows had appeared on the scene. With both her father and Rory taken from her, Josie had been left with only her mother for companionship; and nobody, especially someone like Josie, deserved that fate.

Sitting in the kitchen, Shaun watched Josie's every move, his eyes filled with love and pity. And for the first time in his life he felt a stirring of anger directed at his older brother for bringing her to this low state. In all the years he had known her, Josie had always carried her full, rounded figure well, with her shoulders straight, and her head held high. Without realising it, Shaun was thinking the same as Rory had done earlier: that the once proud body looked as if the weight of the world was resting on it. His gaze flickered around the room, silently comparing it to the kitchen back home. His family had always revolved around the warm, cheery kitchen, where they ate, exchanged news and jokes and occasionally argued. Josie's kitchen seemed stark and drab in comparison. Everywhere he looked, from the walls to the linoleum, was all muddy browns and greys, with not even a vase of flowers to brighten the dismal room.

'Give you a penny for them, Shaun. You look miles away.' Josie pushed a mug of tea towards him and sat down opposite. Shaun looked across the table at the face he had loved for years and felt a jolt of compassion flood through him, for, like the room itself, Josie looked drab. In the short time since he had last been this close to her, she seemed to have aged, and the change in her shocked him to the core. She was only twenty-five, yet she looked like a woman in her forties.

'You look tired, Josie,' he said simply.

Josie blinked, then shrugged.

'Oh, I'm all right, Shaun. You've just caught me on a bad day, that's all.'

Shaun's hands tightened around the hot mug of tea.

'Seems to me like you've had a lot of bad days lately.' For a brief moment he stared into her soft brown eyes, eyes that had once lit up at the sight of Rory, but that were now dull and without hope. She looked, Shaun thought sadly, as if the life had been sucked out of her.

Josie was the first to lower her gaze. She hadn't realised before just how alike Shaun and Rory were, but then she'd never really looked at any other man, not since Rory had left. Suddenly uneasy, she was for once grateful when her mother began banging on the ceiling with the walking cane she now used solely to summon Josie to her bedside.

'I'm sorry, Shaun, I'll have to see what she wants. I thought I'd get a bit of peace when I conveniently lost her bell. I should have known she'd find some other way to get me running about like a blue-arsed fly.' She hesitated, then added, 'You're quite welcome to stay if you want.'

But Shaun wasn't as daft as people thought. Clumsily pushing back his chair, he took a long gulp of the hot tea.

'That's all right, Josie. I can see you've got your hands full. I'll leave you to it.'

They exchanged shy, uneasy smiles.

'I can let meself out the back if you like.'

Josie shook her head.

'No you won't. You'll leave the same way you came in – and no argument,' she added firmly as Shaun made to protest.

They were at the front door when Josie, her hand on the doorknob, said, 'You never did get round to telling me why you called. Not that you need a reason to drop by,' she added quickly. 'Only I just wondered . . .'

When Shaun dropped his gaze, a flicker of alarm rippled through Josie's body.

'There's nothing wrong at home, is there, Shaun? Your mum and dad are all right, ain't they?' When he began to shuffle from one foot to the other, her fear deepened. The last time – in fact the only time – Shaun had visited the house it had been to offer a shoulder to cry on after Rory had gone off with that . . . that hard-faced bitch.

She wasn't aware she was clutching Shaun's arm until he cried out, ''Ere, leave off, Josie. You're hurting me arm.'

At his words, Josie's fingers jumped as if they had come into contact with a hot iron. Her head lowered, she muttered, 'Sorry, Shaun.' She attempted a shaky laugh. 'Like I said before, you've caught me on a bad day.'

Rubbing his arm, Shaun ruefully pondered his next move. After that unpleasant scene at home, he had made his escape as soon as he could. It had taken a lot of courage on his part to come here, but he'd been so nervous and excited, he hadn't stopped to think; hadn't stopped to wonder if Josie knew Cathy Meadows was back. Yet how could she know? He and the rest of the family had only learned the news yesterday. Even Rory hadn't known until that loud-mouthed cow had shouted the news in his brother's face across the kitchen table. God! Rory was right about one thing. He, Shaun, was daft, soft in the head. Galloping round here like some sort of knight in shining armour to sweep Josie off her feet. Huh! He laughed inwardly. He couldn't ask her out, not now. Not until she knew her rival was back and, according to his mother, out to cause trouble. What if the two women were to meet by accident? If Cathy was preparing to stay, it would only be a matter of time before that happened. And while that bitch would relish such a meeting, poor Josie would suffer further humiliation. It was best if she heard the news from a friend, and from where he was standing that dubious honour had landed right in his lap. There was no easy way to break the news, so, taking a deep breath, he simply blurted it out.

'Cathy's back, Josie. I'm sorry, love. I . . . I thought the news might be better coming from a friend.'

As Shaun's words sank in, Josie's mind shut down as if in denial at what she'd heard.

'Bloody 'ell, Josie, don't look at me like that. Please, Josie! Say something, anything. Shout and scream, swear if it helps, only don't bottle it up inside . . .'

But Josie was no longer listening. She heard herself thanking Shaun for his thoughtfulness before closing the door on his anxious face. She didn't remember walking back to the kitchen, she didn't hear her mother's fractious calls; her mind was still reeling in a state of shock. Cathy Meadows was back!

Dropping down on the hard-backed chair that Shaun had recently vacated, Josie laid her arms on the table, dropped her head into their soft folds and let the tears rain unchecked down her cheeks. The only thing that had kept her going this past year was the hope that one day Rory would come back to her. How many times had that same hope stopped her from losing her mind, from going stark raving mad! And it would have been so easy to do, so easy to just let go and drift into a world where she would no longer have to bear the daily torment that was her life.

The banging on the ceiling became fainter and finally stopped. Josie lifted her head and stared upwards, visualising the frail, wasted body that was her mother, and she felt nothing but anger and resentment against the woman who had given her life. If only she could remember some moment in time when her mother had held her close, or kissed her good night – shown her any sign of affection at all – then Josie would have felt some pity for her, but the fact was that Elsie Guntrip was, and had always been, a cold, spiteful woman without a good word to say for anyone. Many a time Josie had wondered what had made her kind, good-natured father fall in love with such a woman. But then who knew what made people fall in love? She of all people should know it wasn't something anyone had control over; it just happened.

Tired and drained by the bout of crying that had racked her body, Josie fell asleep. When she awoke, some time later, she realised with a start that it had grown dark. Quickly getting to her feet, she lit the gas lamps on the wall and table, then stopped, a puzzled expression on her face. Still sleepy, she felt something was wrong, but couldn't put her finger on what it was. Then it came to her. The house was quiet; too quiet. Slowly raising her eyes, she stared at the ceiling, her heart beginning to thump wildly.

She took the lamp from the table and walked through to the hall, stopping to light the gas brackets on the landing wall. Her steps hesitant, she climbed the stairs, her mind churning out the words she had repeated over and over this past year: Please God! Let her be gone. She stopped and squeezed her eyes tight shut. It was an awful thing to wish someone dead, especially her own mother, but she couldn't help how she felt. For a long time now Josie had begun to fear she might even harm the bedridden woman herself, so worn out was she with the constant demands and cruel taunts hurled at her day and night.

Outside her mother's bedroom Josie paused, her

fingers on the wooden handle, her ears listening for some sound coming from the room, but the house was as still as an empty church. Gathering her courage, she turned the handle and entered the darkened room and knew at once, even without approaching the bed, that her prayer had been answered; her mother was dead – and she felt nothing but a sense of relief at the knowledge that she was at last free.

Holding the lamp in front of her, Josie walked slowly towards the bed. There, lying still, her eyes wide, her mouth slack, was Elsie Guntrip, looking even in death as if she had protested to the last.

Josie backed from the room, closed the door, then leaned against the wooden frame, her body suddenly trembling as the enormity of the situation sank in.

Her mother was dead. She was free. And Cathy Meadows was back!

Not trusting her legs to carry her downstairs, she went to her own room and lay down on the bed. She should fetch one of her neighbours, her mother would need laying out, but she was reluctant to move. She needed some time to herself before announcing her mother's death, because once the news was out, her neighbours would start pouring into the house, and she wasn't ready for that yet.

It was another hour before she moved, but she had used that time well.

Her initial reaction at hearing that Cathy Meadows was home had passed. She no longer felt sorry for herself. Everyone would expect her to fall apart, or stay hidden away once that slut started making her presence known, but they would be disappointed. Getting to her feet, Josie's body straightened, her head held high once more. Let the gossipmongers do their worst; they couldn't hurt her any more. Once the funeral was out of the way she would make her plans for the future. She was still young enough to start her life over; and by God, she was going to make the best of it. There was a smile on her lips now as she left the house to fetch Annie Flynn.

CHAPTER FOUR

'You all right, Rory? Only you've been a bit off with me lately. It ain't got nothing ter do with me seeing Josie, is it? 'Cos if it is, you ain't got anything ter worry about; more's the pity. She stills sees me like a mate.' Shaun shrugged, then grinned. 'Still, I don't mind too much, I'm happy just being with her.'

Rory looked sideways at his brother, his teeth clenched with irritation. He'd heard nothing but Josie this and Josie that for the past week. It didn't help matters that he hadn't yet seen Cathy. His pride wouldn't allow him to go cap in hand to her house. But every time he left for work, or on the journey home, he'd hoped and prayed he would run into her. This hope in turn created such a rage inside him that he truly feared what he might do if their paths were to cross. And if he hadn't enough to contend with, he had to endure Shaun's incessant ramblings.

Not trusting himself to speak, Rory smeared a liberal coating of cement on to the brick he was

47

holding, then slammed it on top of the steadily rising wall forming the side of the building he and Shaun were working on. But despite his brother's obvious foul mood, Shaun, working alongside him, happily continued the one-sided conversation.

'. . . and not only that, but she's chucked nearly all the furniture out. Well, not exactly chucked out. She's sold the lot ter the rag and bone man. Old 'Arry's well chuffed. 'E must think Christmas 'as come early, 'cos 'e's got some good pieces for next ter nothing. The neighbours can't believe the change that's come over Josie, but as Mum says, good for 'er. It's about time she stopped being a doormat. Honestly, Rory, you should see 'er now, yer wouldn't recognise 'er. She's—'

It was too much for Rory's frayed nerves. Throwing down his trowel he shouted, 'For fuck's sake, Shaun. Can't yer give yer tongue a rest? You ain't stopped rabbiting on about Josie all week. For the last time, I ain't bothered about you and Josie, but d'yer have ter give me a blow-by-blow account of every bleeding minute of every bleeding day?'

So engrossed was Rory in his own problems, he failed to notice the silence that had descended on the building site. He did, however, glance at Shaun, and the hurt etched on the normally happy face shamed Rory to the core of his being, for his brother looked as if he'd been kicked in the stomach. He swung his head from side to side, and each time his eyes met those of one of his workmates, he saw the look of disgust directed at him.

Then Pat was striding towards him. His eyes darting over his crew, he barked, 'I don't remember telling yer to stop work. Now get yerselves moving if yer want paying at the end of the week . . . Not you, mate.' He caught hold of Rory's arm. 'I want a word with yer, over here.' Without looking to see if Rory intended obeying his order, Pat strode towards his work hut, his face and body stiff with anger. Rory wasn't the kind of man to take orders lightly, but he followed Pat without a murmur, fully aware of the hostile eyes boring into his back.

'Close the door, Rory.' Pat was staring at his older brother, his face tight, his fists clenched at his sides.

'Look, Pat, I know I—'

Pat moved so quickly Rory didn't have time to defend himself as his younger brother's fist shot out, catching him squarely on the jaw.

'That's for Shaun, you bastard,' Pat said grimly as he watched Rory stagger backwards from the unexpected blow. Rory, no stranger to fist fights, was soon back on his feet, but he made no move to retaliate until Pat raised his arm again, saying, 'And this one's for Freda . . .' Before his fist could connect with Rory's face once more, Rory thrust out his arm, his hand grasping Pat's wrist.

'Oh no, Pat. I took the first punch 'cos I deserved it, but I'll be damned if I'm gonna stand 'ere and let you land another one on account of that spiteful old cow.'

The two men glared at each other, their breath coming in short, ragged gasps, neither of them willing to give ground; then Pat cursed loudly and turned his back on Rory.

'Go on, get out. I ain't gonna risk losing me job over a big-'eaded sod like you. You're bleeding lucky

Dad ain't working 'ere today, 'cos if 'e was, yer wouldn't be getting off so lightly. But I'll tell yer this; brother or no brother, you step outta line again and I'll sack yer and give your job to Dad. He might not be as strong as you, but 'e could still put in a full week's work given half the chance, instead of the odd day when we're behind schedule, or short-staffed. But if you ever hurt Shaun like that again, we'll take up where we left off, and I swear the fight won't be over till only one of us is left standing.'

He paused breathlessly before continuing.

'And one more thing before you go. You've got a bleeding nerve calling Freda spiteful. What d'yer call the way you treat Shaun?' Rory, already halfway out the door, stopped in his tracks, but he had no words to defend himself. And still Pat hadn't finished with him. 'The poor sod worships the ground you walk on, just like our Jane. But one of these days they're both gonna see you for the big-'eaded bastard you really are . . .'

Rory couldn't take any more. He left the hut, slamming the wooden door behind him with as much force as he could muster, but he couldn't stop Pat's words ringing in his ears.

His torment wasn't over yet. Walking back to the site he had been working on, he saw Bob Andrews busy at work at the spot where Shaun had been. He looked around and spotted Shaun, no laughter on his face now, working alongside Jim Wilson. Nipping his bottom lip, Rory set to work, but it was performed in a strained silence. Apart from one sideways glance from Bob, there was no friendly banter, no exchanging of the jokes that usually accompanied the daily grind of hard work. Not wanting to take the chance of being deliberately snubbed, Rory carried on without a word. It was the first time he had worked with this man, or any of the rest of the crew, without exchanging a word; their deafening silence leaving Rory in no doubt whose side they were on. And he didn't like it, didn't like it one bit.

The end of the day couldn't come too soon for Rory, and when it did he was in for another shock. Usually he and Shaun would wait in the hut for Pat, along with their dad on the days he was working. If Pat was busy with paperwork, the others would go off home without him. Rory had been rehearsing his apology to Shaun all afternoon, but he didn't get the opportunity to utter it. For, mingled with the building crew leaving the site, were Pat and Shaun, and the deliberate snub wasn't lost on Rory. Jamming his cap on, he pulled the rim down hard, partially hiding his face, hoping he could avoid his mother before seeing for himself how badly bruised he was. Rubbing the left side of his jaw, he winced ruefully. It wasn't the first time he and Pat had exchanged punches, but that had been back when they were boys. Even then Pat had possessed a powerful punch; and judging by the pain Rory was experiencing, his brother hadn't lost his touch. He had no doubt today's fracas would blow over given time. They'd fallen out before, all brothers did, though he had to admit that all the fights they'd had in the past had been childhood brawls, usually ending with a clout round the ear from their mother.

He walked on, careful to keep a decent distance

between himself and his brothers. And as he walked, his steps slowed hesitantly, and he started to wonder whether this particular fight was going to blow over as easily as they had done in the past. Suddenly he wasn't so sure of being forgiven; at least not for the foreseeable future. He knew he'd been a right bastard to Shaun, but was comforted by the knowledge that his younger brother wasn't one to hold a grudge. Pat, on the other hand . . .

With this in mind, he decided to take the long way home. On the way he stopped for a smoke, leaning against a wall beside an alley that backed on to the row of houses opposite his home. He lit up and took a long, satisfying drag of the cigarette, stretching out the time as long as he could before going home. Standing with one leg bent against the wall, his cap drawn over his eyes, he dropped the cigarette butt on the ground and sighed. There was no point in stalling any longer; he had to face the family sooner or later, so it was best to get it over and done with. Funnily enough, he was more frightened of facing his mother than his brothers. That silent acknowledgement brought a wry smile to his lips.

Stamping on what was left of the smouldering cigarette, Rory's gaze was caught by a pair of highly polished ladies' shoes, and without looking up he knew, knew without a shadow of doubt, that it was Cathy.

'Hello, Rory. Long time, no see. Aren't you pleased to see me?'

He couldn't move, couldn't breathe. It was as if he'd been turned to stone; as if time had stopped. He could feel his heart pounding against his chest, yet he remained mute. Desperately he tried to recapture the rage that had been tearing him apart since learning Cathy was back – the same anger he had vented on his loving, hero-worshipping younger brother. Instead he felt a ripple of excitement run through his body at having her so near to him. A heady aroma emanated from her, and somewhere at the back of his mind he realised that what he was smelling was perfume; a wonderful, expensive perfume. He knew it must be expensive for he had never smelt anything as fragrant before. It was certainly nothing like the lavender water his mother and Jane used for special occasions.

'What's up, Rory? Anyone would think you were frightened to look at me. You haven't gone soft while I've been away, have you, sweetheart?'

The mocking, throaty laugh brought him sharply out of his stupor, along with the hatred he had nurtured towards Cathy since she had thrown him over for Barney Hobbs, and her subsequent departure a year and a half ago. For he, like his mother, remembered the date vividly.

Slowly, very slowly, he moved his head, his eyes taking in the expensive blue outfit she was wearing – an outfit he would never be able to afford to buy her, or any other woman for that matter. Seconds passed until their eyes made contact, and it was that look in Cathy's eyes, a taunting, arrogant look, that broke his silence.

'You've got a nerve coming back here like nothing's happened. What's the matter, your fancy man chucked you out? At least that's what I've 'eard.' The words seemed to be forced out of him. 'Well, you're not welcome round 'ere, so if I was you I'd piss off again before I do something I regret.'

At the sound of his harsh words Cathy's confidence faltered, but only for a moment; she was a woman used to getting her own way, especially where men were concerned. Moving her hips in a provocative manner, she replied, 'You've got a high opinion of yourself. What makes you think I've come back to see you? As a matter of fact I'm here to see me mum and dad. And despite what you've heard, Jonathan hasn't chucked me out, and he isn't likely to either. If you must know, he's gone away on business. In fact he often goes away, he's an important man. I usually go with him, but I started to get bored. It's always the same. Dull meetings with stuffy businessmen, and dinner parties with their equally dull wives. So I thought I'd give it a miss this time and take the opportunity to visit my old home – and look up old friends.'

She moved nearer, her lips curving in the inviting smile she had always used when she'd wanted something from him. But this time, instead of inciting desire in Rory, it only served to fuel his building rage. Grabbing her roughly by the arm, he dragged her into the adjoining alley and pushed her against the wall.

'Leave it, Cathy. Those old tricks of yours are wasted on me. You do remember me, don't yer? I'm the mug that used to think yer smiles and yer body were reserved only fer me. Christ! I can't believe I fell for it all. Me only consolation is that Barney Hobbs got the same treatment.'

His breathing was laboured, his stomach churning

at being in such close proximity to the woman he had once loved – still loved and wanted. His mind mocked him for his pathetic show of indifference. Yes, he still wanted her, but by God, he wasn't going to be made a fool of again.

Cathy was watching him intently, her eyes knowing, her smile growing broader. It was dark in the narrow alley, creating a sense of intimacy. She reached out and touched Rory's hand, and the feel of her sent a jolt of pleasure and excitement coursing through his body; but still he resisted her. Without realising what he was doing, he shook off her warm hand and raised his arm high, the pain and humiliation he had endured suddenly reaching boiling point. But before the back of his hand could make contact with her face, he halted its movement, and there it hung in mid swing before dropping back uselessly by his side.

It was then that he looked at her properly in the dim light. Not at her face, but at the clothes she was dressed in. Even in the poor light he could tell the quality of the blue outfit she was wearing. His eyes travelled down once more to the leather shoes peeping out from the hem of the full skirt. He knew that such footwear would cost him more than a week's wages; and that simple piece of knowledge reminded him painfully of his inadequacies. If that wasn't bad enough, an image of Mrs Guntrip now rose before his eyes. He could almost hear her scathing remarks concerning his menial job; a job, she had added spitefully, that could be done by any imbecile. But Josie hadn't minded what job he did; she would still have loved him if he'd worked down the sewers.

'Go on, Rory. Give me a slap if it'll make you feel better. It's no more than I deserve. Go on, hit me.'

Cathy's voice broke into his thoughts. Shaking his head to clear the images of Josie and her dead mother from his mind, he now focused his eyes on Cathy's face. Because of the poor lighting in the alley he couldn't see her features clearly, but he didn't have to. Her face was ingrained on his brain. The dark blue eyes, the full, inviting lips, the contours of her body and the waist-length hair that had always reminded him of spun gold were vivid in his mind's eye.

They were no more than a few inches apart now, and Rory could feel the heat generating from Cathy's body, smell her perfume and recall the sensation of his lips on hers, and he knew he was lost. Yet still he struggled against the pull of her nearness, even though he knew he was fighting a losing battle.

'Why me? Why not Barney? After all, yer did dump me for him, didn't yer?'

Cathy relaxed. She had him, just as she'd known she would. She had a whole month before Jonathan returned from his business trip, and she meant to make the most of his absence. She had no intention of leaving the besotted man; she'd become too used to living the life of the rich to go back to being poor. But she missed the intense lovemaking she'd experienced with Rory. Barney Hobbs, for all his good looks, hadn't come anywhere near in that department. For the past year she'd had to endure the attentions of a pot-bellied, middle-aged man, and she yearned for the closeness of a firm, muscular male body next to hers. There had been no shortage of willing young men who would have been only too happy to oblige her, but she had resisted the temptation. Not out of loyalty to Jonathan, but for her own self-preservation. The circle she and Jonathan lived in was a small one, and she wasn't about to risk being caught with another man.

There was another reason she had come back home, a reason she wouldn't admit even to herself. She was still in love with Rory, inasmuch as a woman of her nature could love anybody, even though that love wasn't enough to make her throw her new life away. Now she was only a breath away from the man she had dreamed of this past year, and she found herself dropping her nonchalant demeanour. A demeanour she had adopted on the off chance Rory would reject her; if that had happened, at least she wouldn't have had to suffer the humiliation of being rebuffed.

Her voice soft now, she said, 'I've missed you, Rory. Barney Hobbs never meant anything to me. It's you I want, what I've always wanted. I know I treated you badly, and I'm truly sorry. But I've always wanted nice things. I was sick of living from hand to mouth, so I found a man who could give me what I wanted. I'm not proud of what I am, but I can't change my nature. Now it's up to you. If you really don't want to see me again, I promise I'll keep out of your way. You just say the word and I won't bother you again.'

Rory didn't speak, didn't move. Did he want her? God forgive him, he wanted her more than life itself. Yet could he take the chance of rejection again? his mind asked of him, and the answer was a resounding no. But had he the strength to reject the opportunity to be with her again, even if it was only for a short while? Again the answer was no.

With bated breath Cathy watched Rory's silent struggle. Up until this moment she hadn't realised just how much she wanted him. The seconds ticked by until, unable to bear the silence any longer, she said, 'Is it Josie? Or should I say old iron knickers. Have you gone back to her? If you have, then . . .'

Now Rory did move, and with a swiftness and anger that startled her.

'You leave Josie outta this, you bitch. She's worth a dozen of you.'

'Then what you doing still here with me, if that's how you feel? Go on, bugger off. I ain't ever begged for a man in me life. I ain't gonna start now.'

'You're right there, I will bugger off.' He uttered a harsh laugh. 'I can see the high life ain't improved your grammar. Yer better watch yer don't slip back ter your old way of talking in front of your posh friends. I don't think they'd be very impressed, do you?' He made to walk away. 'Go an' find yerself another mug. Perhaps Barney Hobbs will oblige you while you're here; he never was that fussy.'

Staring at Rory's back in disbelief, Cathy was struck dumb. She had been so sure he would take her back, even if only for a short time. Then she moved. Catching hold of his arm, she hissed, 'All right, I will. And while we're lying in bed, I'll give him your best wishes, shall I? I'm sure he'll be—'

A soft scream of pain spurted from her lips as Rory, with a twist of his wrist, pulled her hand from his arm and sent her reeling against the wall. He watched as she fought to stop herself from falling on to the cold ground and in an instant he had her in his arms, holding her close, muttering, 'Oh God! I'm sorry, Cathy. I'm sorry. I don't care what you've done. I tried, I tried so 'ard to 'ate yer, but I can't.' Like a man possessed he rained kisses over her face until she lifted her lips to his. And then they were swept away in a world of their own.

Rory's arms were crushing her body, but Cathy didn't care. There was something she had deliberately kept from him; and that something would remain a secret for as long as possible. For now she had him back. Nothing else mattered.

CHAPTER FIVE

As Annie Flynn approached the Guntrip house she paused, her face lighting up with pleasure at the sound of loud, hearty laughter coming from within. It was a sound that had never been heard while Elsie Guntrip was alive, apart from the early days, when Elsie was able to get out on her own. Then George Guntrip had used those precious times to bring some fun and humour into his little girl's life.

Annie was about to knock on the front door when she remembered Josie's words to her at the funeral. It had been the smallest turnout of any funeral Annie had attended; back in Ireland, especially, such an event would have whole streets turning out to pay their respects to the deceased. She had been thinking that very thought when Josie, her eyes dry, had hugged her and asked her to visit as often as possible, adding sadly that Annie had been more of a mother to her than her own had ever been. She had gone on to say that, as family, Annie need never knock at the front door, but should use the back door, and that invitation extended even to the times when Josie was out. For that eventuality she had given Annie a spare set of keys.

Annie was just about to walk round to the back when Ida Black came out into the street. Looking at Annie, the small, thin woman shut her door, then, arching her eyebrows, said snootily, 'I see you're going ter see Josie. It's getting to seem like a second home to you and yer family. Shaun's never off the doorstep, and now your Jane's getting just as bad. As fer Josie, pshaw!' The woman's eyebrows rose even further. 'If I hadn't seen it with me own eyes, I never would 'ave believed it. Nearly all of poor Elsie's furniture sold fer a few bob ter the rag an' bone man, and all her clothes bundled up and given ter the Sally Army. I mean ter say, she might 'ave had the decency to ask Elsie's friends if they'd 'ave liked ter 'ave some sort of memento to remember her by. Now she's got your Shaun redecorating the whole house. The next thing yer know she'll be getting 'erself all tarted up and walking the streets looking fer a man; that's if she hasn't got her claws into your Shaun yet. I'd do something about it before it goes too far if I was you.'

'Oh, would ye now?' Annie bridled, her blue eyes dark with anger. 'Well, Mrs Black, I think 'tis a wondrous sight to see Josie happy after what she's had to put with all these years. An' you've a nerve on you, talking about Elsie like she was your best friend. Sure an' ye never had a good word to say about the woman while she was alive, so don't go getting all sentimental now she's gone – may the

61

Lord have mercy on her soul.' Annie crossed herself involuntarily. 'And as for wanting something of hers to remember her by, huh! Go tell that one to the next flying pig you see. You're just plain jealous at seeing all those good pieces of furniture and clothes go without having the opportunity to get your greedy hands on some of them.'

Hitching up her ample breasts, Annie turned her back, afraid she'd say something else she might regret later. She knew better than anyone what she was like when her dander was up; and by God, that woman back there was lucky she was still standing after what she had said concerning Josie and her family.

She hadn't gone more than a few steps before Ida Black, her own temper roused, shouted after the retreating back, 'So, I've got a nerve, 'ave I?' She sniffed disdainfully. 'I wouldn't be a bit surprised ter find out some of those bits of furniture 'ave found their way ter yer 'ouse; an' as fer poor old Elsie making Josie's life a misery, I seem ter remember your precious Rory dumping her like a sack of old rubbish fer the first little tart that came along.'

Annie stopped abruptly, her short, plump figure rigid with anger, and Ida Black, already regretting her outburst, retreated backwards, not willing to take her eyes off the woman who was already turning to face her. The sheer rage in the steely blue eyes brought a shiver of fear down Ida Black's spine. She continued to walk backwards as Annie advanced on her.

'Now 'ang on, Annie, I didn't mean what I said . . . All right, all right, I'm sorry.' Her voice, rising now, was beginning to attract attention. 'Look, Annie, I've said I'm sorry—'

A scream burst from Ida's lips as Annie's heavy hand landed a stunning slap across her face. The skinny woman was sent reeling as doors began to open, and curious eyes focused on the scene taking place on their doorsteps. Within minutes the street was filled. One man, holding the remains of a pork chop between greasy fingers, remarked, 'Bleeding 'ell! Fancy picking a fight with Annie Flynn; I wouldn't wanna take 'er on. She's got 'ands on 'er bigger than a navvy,' before going back indoors.

Unaware of the growing audience, Annie moved forward menacingly.

'Talk about my family like that, would ye! 'Tis lucky for you I'm a God-fearing woman, so it is, else I'd skelp the skin off your mangy backside an'—'

'Mum, Mum, pack it in. You've got the whole street out.' Shaun had appeared and was trying to hold on to his enraged mother, a broad smile splitting his face in two. He knew only too well what the feel of his mother's hand was like; he'd been on the receiving end of it more than once, though to be fair to Annie, on those occasions he'd deserved it. 'Come on, Mum, come inside and calm down a bit.' His arms tightened around Annie's shoulders, every muscle in his body straining to keep a hold on her.

'Will ye let go of me, man. There's still a few home truths I've to say to that evil-minded bitch.'

The sound of a swear word coming from his mother's lips so startled Shaun that his grip on her slackened. In all of his twenty-two years he had never heard his mother swear; his father, yes, though only on rare occasions after he'd had a drink, and most certainly never in front of his wife.

Annie too was shocked. She abhorred swearing in any form, but accepted it from the mouths of men. But for a woman . . . she had acted like some common fishwife, and the knowledge brought a feeling of shame on to her bowed shoulders.

'All right, son. I've had me say, but I'll not be apologising for me actions. Now let go of me, ye great gormless eejit.'

Shaun released his hold cautiously. Then Josie and Jane were by his side, surrounding Annie in a show of unity and friendship. With the two girls on one side and Shaun on the other, Annie let herself be led into Josie's house. Shaun entered first, stepping aside to let the women in. Josie was the last to enter, but instead of shutting the door on the curious faces, she faced her neighbours defiantly.

'I know there's a lot of you that think I should be dressed in black and mourning me mother; and for the life of me I can't understand why. You all knew me mother and the way she treated me. You also know she never loved me, so why should I mourn a woman who treated me like dirt? Well, now I'm free, and I'm gonna make up for all the time she stole from me. I've known all of you since I could walk, and if you're real friends, then you'll always be welcome in my house. Those of you who think I'm a cold-hearted woman because I refuse to be a hypocrite, well then, you're no friends of mine.'

A few of the women looked away from Josie's gaze, but the majority of the neighbours applauded her bravery in not being coerced into playing the role that was expected of her.

One woman across the street shouted out, 'You tell 'em, Josie love.'

Josie smiled broadly.

'Thanks, Mrs Truman, I intend to.'

As she went to close the door, she looked at Ida Black still sprawled on the pavement, a handkerchief held to her bleeding mouth. The woman was looking round for some kind of sympathy vote, but none seemed forthcoming. Josie stared hard at her before addressing the assembled neighbours.

'Can one of you help Ida up? I'd do it meself, but I've gotta get meself tarted up and go looking for a man.' She gazed down at the thin figure. 'That is what you think of me, ain't it?' Before the woman could answer, Josie added calmly, 'Oh, one more thing, Mrs Black. If in the future you 'appen to pass my 'ouse . . . Well, let's just say, I'd appreciate it.' With that parting shot Josie took one last look at the rumpled woman and closed the door.

Outside Ida Black waited for some assistance, along with a sympathetic ear to listen to her grievances. Feeling braver now that Annie was safely indoors, she looked around, her face falling as one by one the doors closed, leaving her alone, feeling betrayed and somewhat foolish. Getting to her feet, she forgot her shopping trip and returned to the safety of her home.

'Here you are, Annie. Get that down your throat, it'll calm your nerves.'

Josie put a small glass of brandy in front of Annie. Annie looked at it in amazement.

'Begod! If your mother wasn't already dead, the

shock of seeing alcohol in the house would've killed her for sure.'

Josie slid on to the chair opposite Annie, with Shaun and Jane either side of her, and felt a wave of affection flow over her. If only she'd been born into a family like the Flynns, how different her life might have turned out.

'Actually, Annie, I found it tucked away at the back of the bedroom closet. Me dad must have hidden it there, poor old sod!' Josie said wistfully. Then she brightened. 'Let's have a toast to me dad.' Holding up her glass she said, 'Cheers, Dad! The drinks are on you.'

'Hear, hear!' Shaun responded. Picking up his own glass, he took a long gulp of the brandy, with his mother following his example. Jane had to make do with a cup of tea.

The brandy slid down Annie's throat like warm silk. Taking another, smaller gulp, she held on to the glass and looked around the kitchen, her jaw dropping at the changes that had been made. She hadn't noticed at first; her mind had been too busy dwelling on Ida Black's vicious words. Now she took another look, not knowing if she liked what Josie, or rather Shaun, had done.

All the walls had been stripped of their dull brown paper and painted white. Gone were the old sepia photos and depressing pictures, leaving the walls completely bare. Then Annie raised her eyes and blinked, for the ceiling had been painted a pale blue. She'd never seen anything like it in her life.

The three young people around the table exchanged glances, but it was Jane that spoke.

'It does look a bit bare at the moment, Mum. But Josie's got a lot of ideas to make it look like a proper kitchen, haven't you, Josie?'

Josie took hold of Jane's slim fingers and smiled.

'Thanks for the vote of confidence, Jane, but I haven't a clue what I'm gonna do next. There's still a lot to do. I'm just gonna make up plans as I go along. Now then, I've got a lot of things to sort out, mostly Dad's stuff. You know, his medals and things he valued.' She released Jane's hand and stood up. 'I'm really grateful for all your help, but I'm afraid I'm gonna have to chuck you out now. I've been putting off going through Dad's things, but it needs to be done, and it's something I have to do on me own.'

Draining the last of her brandy, Annie stood up, then staggered and giggled. Jane and Shaun looked at their mother and laughed.

'Blooming 'ell, Mum. You've only 'ad the one drink, and yer look pi— I mean drunk,' Shaun amended hastily. 'We'd best get yer home ter bed, but try and keep on yer feet, will yer? We don't want people thinking you make a regular 'abit of drinking in the middle of the day.'

His words hit Annie like a bucket of cold water. After that business with Ida Black, the last thing she wanted was to add any more fuel to that vicious woman's tongue. Straightening up, she said firmly, 'Drunk, ye say? I'll give ye drunk, our Shaun. Out of the way with ye, I can walk without your help, so I can.' Then her mind conjured up a picture of Ida Black's skinny carcass sprawled on the pavement, and she started giggling again.

'We'd better go, Josie.' Shaun looked at her, his

face and hands smeared with paint. 'You know where to find me if yer need anything.'

'Thanks, Shaun, but I warn you, I'll probably take you up on that offer. Like I said, there's still a lot to be done. And thank Pat for me, will you, for letting you have the time off to help me.'

Shaun lifted his shoulders.

'Yeah, I will. We only work mornings on a Saturday anyway, and me dad stood in for me. So it worked out fine all round.'

When they had gone, Josie returned to the kitchen and sat down, the smile no longer on her face. She had thoroughly enjoyed the morning spent with Shaun and Jane; oh, and she mustn't forget Annie. A wry smile touched her lips. Dear Annie. What would she have done without her and the Flynn family all these years? Even if Rory had never existed, she would still have blessed her good fortune at having such staunch friends. But Rory did exist, and no matter how she tried, she couldn't get him out of her mind.

A frown creased her forehead as she recalled Ida Black's spiteful words concerning Shaun. She was very fond of Shaun, always had been. It would be hard not to like the amiable young man. But she would never feel for him what she felt for Rory; even though, deep down, she knew Shaun was a far better man than Rory could ever be. Since the affair with Cathy Meadows, Josie had said nothing against Rory, and when Cathy had disappeared Josie had waited and prayed that he would come back to her. All that time there she had been, like the big fool she was, hoping against hope that one day Rory would knock at her front door. Every day she had prayed, mostly even without being aware of it, that he would seek her out and ask if they could take up where they had left off; but that day had never come, and now that Cathy had returned, she must try to accept that he was never coming back to her. Such was her love for him, it saddened her that almost everyone, including his own family, had offered no sympathy for him when Cathy had dropped him for someone with more money. Now that same woman was back, and although no one knew for sure if Rory was seeing her, their condemnation of his actions was well known.

Aware that she was in danger of slipping into a maudlin state, she rose from the table and, with a deep breath, ventured upstairs to go through her beloved father's meagre possessions. Not for him the rag and bone man. Oh no! He deserved better than that. Her mother had given his clothes to the Salvation Army only two days after his death, before Josie could stop her. She would have sold his medals and gold hunter watch too if she'd been able to get her hands on them. But Josie had been one step ahead of her mother on that occasion. She had taken the old biscuit tin her father had kept his possessions in and hidden it at the top of her wardrobe. Her mother had been furious, but for once Josie had stood her ground. No matter how much Elsie had shouted and threatened, her normally pliable daughter had remained steadfastly silent. For two weeks Josie had to keep moving the box from one hiding place to another, for fear her mother would find it. Then, just as she was about to ask Annie if she would keep the box at her house, Elsie had fallen ill and taken to her bed. After that, Josie could have looked through her father's tin at any time, but she hadn't been able to face delving into the past, afraid that the distant memories would only serve to upset her fragile state.

Now, as she looked at the treasured possessions her father had left, Josie felt a sudden rush of emotion. There was the hunter watch and the three medals he had won during the Boer War, together with four faded photographs of him with his parents; the grandparents who had died shortly after her birth. There was also a framed photograph of herself taken the week before she had started school. She could still remember the row that had ensued, with her mother going on and on at her father for wasting money. Josie had been so proud of her dad that day, because instead of giving in like he normally did, he had gone straight back out and had it framed. Tears misted her eyes at the memory. He hadn't dared leave it around the house, knowing that his wife, if she got her hands on it, would destroy it out of spite. So he had kept it in his tin box, and every now and then they would look at it together when they had the house to themselves. Hugging the frame to her chest she shed a few tears for her dead father.

There was one other thing her father had kept in his box that puzzled Josie: the wedding photograph of himself and her mother; this too was framed. Josie looked at it more closely, shaking her head in puzzlement. Taking it over to the window for a better look, she stared down at her parents. Even that far back Elsie looked as if she'd just trodden in something unpleasant. A small laugh escaped her lips as she recalled one of Rory's numerous comments about her mother. Josie had just come down the stairs for the fourth time that particular evening, and Rory had said sarcastically, 'That bleeding woman's the type whose nose would be put out at a funeral, just 'cos she's not the centre of attention.'

She was about to put the photo back in the box but paused. For whatever reason, her father had held on to it. Maybe it had reminded him of happier times. He must have loved her mother once. Who was she to question his motives in keeping his wedding photograph?

At the bottom of the well-worn tin were some loose documents pertaining to the Boer War; a bank book, which, judging by its condition, had been in the tin for a good many years; and a small bundle of old letters, written by friends who had fought alongside her dad. Josie could vaguely remember several men dressed in khaki uniforms visiting the house, but her mum had soon put a stop to that. Instead of greeting them as war heroes, like a normal person would, Elsie Guntrip had deliberately made them feel uncomfortable, just because she couldn't bear to see her husband happy. She would stay in the room, knitting or reading, her hostile manner making it quite clear that the men weren't welcome in her house. After a while her dad's friends had started to drift away, until finally they had stopped coming. That was probably why her dad had kept the letters, few as they were. She knew they had given him comfort, and reminded him that he had once had such good friends. Josie put them to one side. She would find a safe place for them later.

For now she had something more important to do.

Holding both frames to her chest, she went back downstairs and placed them on the mantelpiece in the parlour, then stepped back to see the effect.

'There you are, Dad,' she said, smiling. 'Your favourite photographs are on show at last.'

'Please, Mum, let me go on my own. I'm not a child any more. I'm perfectly capable of running a simple errand.'

Jane was sitting by Annie's bedside, holding a cold flannel to her mother's head.

'Go on, Mum. Mrs Collins will be waiting for the dress. You promised you'd bring it around today. She was expecting you over an hour ago.'

Annie groaned. That blasted brandy. She never had been able to hold her drink. The annoying thing was that she had only stopped by Josie's on the way to deliver a dress to one of her customers; and to see if Jane fancied going for a walk with her. But after that altercation with Ida Black she'd felt in need of the inviting brandy. Perhaps if she'd sipped at it slowly, instead of gulping it down like it was water, she wouldn't be paying the price now, but that was beside the point. She had been making clothes from home for years now. It wasn't what anyone could call a business, far from it. She could go months at a time between orders, so she couldn't afford to lose custom, as small as it was.

Gingerly opening her eyes, she winced and nodded carefully.

'All right, all right, child, don't be going on at me. Take the dress, just take it and leave me to die in peace.'

Before she could finish speaking, Jane was off the bed and out of the door in case her mother suddenly changed her mind, or her dad and older brothers arrived home from work. Shaun was in the scullery scrubbing the paint off his face and hands, so the coast was clear.

Apart from meeting her brothers on Sunday, Jane was never allowed out on her own. And although she knew that her almost captive existence was due solely to her family's love for her, nevertheless she had begun to resent their smothering attention. With the wrapped parcel under her arm, she slipped out of the back door and headed towards her destination.

Fifteen minutes later, Jane was walking happily across Victoria Park. It was a lovely warm summer day, and if it hadn't been for the birthmark she would have taken off the wide-brimmed straw hat tied with equally wide ribbons that formed a bow under her chin, and lifted her face to the sun. Normally this notion would have depressed her, but not today. For today she was on her own, with no mother or watchful brother by her side, and it was giving her the same feeling of euphoria the brandy had given her mother, though without the painful hangover. Almost skipping now, she hummed cheerfully on her way across the park.

Mrs Collins, one of her mother's regular customers, showed her surprise at seeing Jane standing on her doorstep unaccompanied. She tried to engage the girl

73

in conversation, hoping there might be a bit of gossip as to why she had been allowed out on her own, but Jane, smiling sweetly, expertly avoided the obvious curiosity.

With the dress delivered and the five shillings owed to her mother tucked safely in her purse, Jane strolled aimlessly back across the park, enjoying her freedom and making it last as long as possible. She was walking past the duck pond when, out of the corner of her eye, she glimpsed Rory, and for once she wasn't pleased to see him. She had been enjoying her walk so much; now Rory would probably drag her home. Her step slowed, then she stopped completely. Her eyes wide with shock, she watched in disbelief as her adored brother walked quickly towards the pagoda, where Cathy Meadows was sitting elegantly on a green wrought-iron chair, obviously waiting for someone.

Jane stepped behind a tree, hardly daring to breathe, her mind begging over and over, 'Oh, please, Rory, don't . . . Please, don't.' But she knew her silent appeal was useless. All she wanted to do now was to slip quietly away, but first she had to make sure; she owed Rory that much. Peeping around the huge trunk, she watched in despair as Rory pulled Cathy into his arms. She heard the woman's deep, throaty laugh, then they were walking away, further into the park, heading for the spot that was known to be frequented by courting couples.

Tears stung at Jane's eyes. The day had started out so well. First those few hours at Josie's house, and then the unexpected pleasure of being out on her own. Now her day was ruined. She walked slowly on, all the joy in her wiped away. All she could say on the way home was, 'Oh, Rory, how could you?' These words were soon followed by 'Poor Josie, poor, poor Josie.'

CHAPTER SIX

'Am I gonna see you tonight, Barney? 'Cos to be honest, I'm getting a bit fed up with being mucked about. One minute you're all over me, and the next you act as if I don't exist . . . Are you listening to me, Barney?'

'What?' Barney remarked absently, his mind clearly elsewhere.

This fact wasn't lost on the girl holding his arm. Pulling away from him, she said petulantly, 'You ain't 'eard a word I've said, 'ave yer? Well, that does it, Barney Hobbs, we're finished. So don't bother trying ter see me again . . . D'yer 'ear me? Oh, sod you, I'm going. But don't think I don't know what's going on. It's that Meadows bitch, ain't it? Ever since she came back you've been walking about like you've swallowed a bleeding wasp. Ain't yer got any pride? If she wanted to see yer, she'd 'ave got in touch with you, wouldn't she, instead of running back to Rory Flynn. So, why don't yer take the 'int? She don't want yer.'

Her words finally penetrated Barney's distracted mind. With lightning speed he grabbed the girl's throat, cutting off the flow of spiteful words.

'You shut yer gob before I shut it for you.' His face, livid with anger, hovered over the now thoroughly frightened girl. Then, with a gesture of contempt, he released his hold and threw her from him, snarling, 'Now piss off, you slag. Go on, get going.'

Clutching her throat, the girl staggered back, her eyes fastened on the enraged man until she felt safe enough to turn her back on him and run away.

Barney watched her go, his eyes blazing with fury. Yet he was honest enough to admit that the powerful emotion he was experiencing was directed at himself. It was just unfortunate that . . . His forehead screwed in puzzlement as he tried to recall the girl's name, but the memory eluded him. Oh, what the hell. She was only another little tart in a line of dozens just like her. But she had spoken the truth, thrown it in his face, and knowing she was right had only fuelled his anger. No man worth his salt liked being made a fool of, especially a man like him – a man who was used to getting his own way.

For as far back as Barney could remember, his family had never been short of money, which was a rare occurrence in the East End; unless of course the money had been made through crime. But Will Hobbs was no criminal. He had worked all his life to better himself, starting with a small stall down Roman Road market, and, over the years, building up a profitable business, which included three shops in prime locations in the East End. Another man might have let his success go to his head, but not

Will Hobbs. As he had often told his late wife, he was born and bred in the East End, and no matter how much money he had, he would never leave his roots. His only concession had been to buy a larger house to keep his wife happy. Barney had been their only child, and when he had reached the age of eighteen, Will had taken him into the business. To be fair to Barney, for all his faults, he had never been afraid of hard work. Like his father before him, he had done his fair share to help make the small business prosper; and it had.

The Hobbs family were known for being comfortably off, but whereas Will had remained true to his origins, Barney, like his mother, had always thought himself a cut above his neighbours. To all intents and purposes he seemed to have it made. For not only was he a partner in his father's business, he had also been endowed with good looks, and an easy charm that radiated from him whenever he was in the company of the opposite sex. So it was no wonder that the girls had flocked around him since he first went into long trousers. But he hadn't been the only boy who had been popular with the girls. Barney paused in his reminiscences, his face taking on a fierce scowl, his gaze fixed on the narrow pathway in front of him. He had come to the park for the same purpose as all couples did on a weekend afternoon, but his ardour had soon been dashed at the sight of Cathy and Rory Flynn wrapped around each other, totally caught up in a world of their own.

A couple pushed past him, laughing happily.

'Sorry, mate.' The young man grinned at Barney, a smile that disappeared at the look on the other man's face. It was a look that said this man wasn't to be messed with. The young man hurried on, anxious not to get involved in any trouble.

Barney watched them go, his fists clenched tightly by his sides. There was nothing he would have liked better than to start a fight; but he knew that would achieve nothing. His problem was with Rory, not some passing stranger.

Leaning against an oak tree, he let his mind run wild. He had first clashed with Rory Flynn back in their school days. Even at an early age the two boys had taken an instant dislike to each other; and that feeling hadn't abated over the years. It had always galled Barney that the red-haired Irishman could attract girls by his personality alone, without any of the trappings that Barney had. But their feud had been reasonably quiet, confined to playground skirmishes, both of them giving as good as the other until the teacher pulled them apart. A smile touched Barney's lips as he remembered those long-ago days. For not only had the two boys received the cane for fighting, they had also been given a note to inform their respective parents of their troublemaking. The dreaded notes had resulted in both boys getting a good hiding from their fathers for getting into trouble at school in the first place. Those incidents had occurred on a regular basis during their formative years.

After they had left school their paths had often crossed, which was understandable as they both lived in the same area of the East End. When they did meet up they invariably ended up fighting, and if anyone had asked why, neither boy could have given a reason; it was almost as if they continued to fight out of habit.

As the years passed and they grew into adulthood, they had graduated to verbal abuse rather than physical, again out of habit. It was as if they thought it was expected of them. The one thing neither of them would ever have admitted, even to themselves, was the grudging respect they held for each other.

In recent years they had simply ignored each other whenever their paths crossed; until Cathy Meadows appeared on the scene.

From the time the Meadowses had moved into a modest terraced house in Shore Road with their seventeen-year-old daughter, all the eligible men within a two-mile radius had tried their luck with the beautiful, golden-haired girl with her provocative figure and sensual, come-hither eyes. But out of all the eager would-be suitors, Cathy had turned her attention to Barney Hobbs and Rory Flynn. She had toyed with both men until finally settling for Rory, and by doing so had flung them back to their childhood days of resentment and bitter competition.

Cathy had loved the power she held over the two men, a power she had recognised from the time she had taken her first step. Her earliest memories were of being pampered by her uncles and her father, all of them forever telling her how beautiful she was. She had quickly learned how to get what she wanted from her adoring male relatives. A sad look, a flutter of innocent eyes would result in her getting whatever she wanted; it was an act she had mastered to perfection over the years. Barney had recognised the kind of girl she was straight away; he had met many just like her over the years. But Cathy had had that something extra. It was nothing he could put his finger on, it was just there; that special something that attracted men to her like moths to a flame.

Barney's eyes focused on the narrow path that Cathy and Rory would have taken earlier, his face a mask of stone. She had used both him and Rory, finally dumping them both for a man old enough to be her father. His only consolation at the time was that she had humiliated Rory just as much as she had him.

He had learned of her return before Rory knew she was back, and had fully expected her to seek him out, especially as he now had a good deal more money than the last time they had been together. But his hopes had been quickly squashed. When they had met up on that Sunday afternoon, she had smiled at him pleasantly, then walked on, cutting him dead. It was bad enough being made a fool of, but to have his humiliation witnessed by his friends was more than Barney could stomach. Then he had spotted Jane standing on the corner as she did every Sunday, waiting for her brothers, and the sight of the red hair, so similar to her brother's, had triggered a wave of resentment towards the entire Flynn family.

He had only meant to tease her, to give her a bit of a fright, but then he had seen Cathy watching them from across the road; directly opposite the pub the Flynn brothers frequented every Sunday. It was then that it had crossed Barney's mind that she must be waiting for Rory, and something inside him had snapped and he had taken his aggression out on the vulnerable Jane Flynn, an act for which he and his friends had suffered dearly. But Barney had barely felt the blows rained down on him, so preoccupied had he been with thoughts of Cathy. She should have come to him, but instead she had sought out that ignorant Irish labourer, a man who would have to work a whole year to earn what Barney made in a month.

Another couple brushed past him, their arms entwined, their faces alight with happiness, and Barney had to fight down the urge to pull them apart and smash the male stranger's face to a pulp. His fists clenched and unclenched, his mind telling him not to be such a fool. If he didn't keep a tight rein on his temper he would find himself behind bars, and Rory Flynn would love that. Yet he needed to vent his spleen on someone before he did something stupid. He could of course take the same path as Rory and release his burning anger on the man he held responsible for his present state of mind. But as he knew to his cost, Rory wasn't a man to be easily taken on.

Barney shook his head in frustration. He wasn't afraid of tackling Rory; he never had been. But in all their years of feuding, neither of them had ever come out the victor, due to the intervention of others. Just like their last encounter. If Rory's brothers hadn't pulled him away, they would have continued the fight until there was only one man left standing. With this in mind, Barney decided not to tackle Rory, especially in front of Cathy. For if Rory was to get the better of him, he knew he would never get over the humiliation. It would eat away at his insides like a cancerous growth until it finally destroyed him.

He felt his breath coming faster, and his heart racing, and he knew he had to put some distance between him and the couple before he lost control of his emotions. With a low growl of anger he turned on his heel and walked away, but he couldn't stop the mental images of Cathy with that Irish bastard's hands all over her willing body, just where his own had been in the past. He could almost feel her soft, silky skin beneath his fingertips. Cursing violently, he stormed away from the well-trodden lovers' path. He needed a drink, and not just one, but as many as it took to blot out the graphic images that were tearing his insides apart. He also knew that until he managed to best his lifelong adversary, he would never be able to rest.

He was trying to form some kind of plan when he spotted Jane, and judging by her downcast head and slow tread it didn't take a genius to work out that he wasn't the only one who had seen the couple enter the woods. He stopped in his tracks, a slow smile tugging at his lips. Well, well, well! Now if that wasn't some kind of divine intervention, then he didn't know what was. He might not be able to break Rory with his fists, but there was one way he could bring him to his knees. If there was one thing Barney was certain about, it was the love and strong bond that existed between Rory and his scarred sister. His smile widened. What was that old saying? There was more than one way to skin a cat.

He watched Jane until she disappeared from view. Feeling much calmer now, Barney ambled on, a satisfied smirk spread across his face.

* * *

Annie awoke with a start at the sound of the front door banging, followed by the loud voices of her men back home from work, expecting their dinner ready on the table once they'd had a quick sluice under the cold tap in the scullery. And here she was, lying on the bed, with not even a potato peeled. Squinting at the bedside clock, she saw with dismay that it was almost three o'clock. Lord help her! She'd been asleep for nearly two hours. She wished now she had prepared dinner before leaving the house; it was what she normally did when she had to go out to make a delivery to one of her customers. But she hadn't anticipated running into that old cow Ida Black. Neither had she meant to stay so long at Josie's, but what with her encounter with Ida preying on her mind, and the brandy she had downed like water, the time had just flown by.

She jumped up quickly, then uttered a soft groan as a sharp pain shot across her forehead. Down below she could hear Shaun's voice, then a roar of laughter from Pat and Paddy. The next thing she heard was loud footsteps running up the stairs, then the bedroom door was flung wide and her husband stood framed in the doorway, a wide grin plastered across his grimy face.

'Begod! If I hadn't seen it with me own eyes I wouldn't have believed it. Me own wife drunk in the middle of the day. Why, I'll not be able to hold me head high when the news gets out me wife's a drunkard. And what if Father Murphy hears about your lapse to the demon drink! Not to mention fighting in the street like a common fishwife. Well, one thing's for sure. Come tomorrow, me and Jane will be sitting in a pew as far away from ye as possible. That's if Father Murphy lets ye through the church doors at all. Ye'd best be getting yourself down to confession, though if ye do, we won't be expecting ye back till supper time, not with the penance ye'll be getting. And while you're there, say a couple of Hail Marys for me.'

Paddy threw back his head and roared with fresh laughter, and the noise caused Annie's eyes to screw up in pain.

'Ah, don't, Paddy. I feel bad enough as it is. There's no dinner ready for ye or the lads, and after the lot of yous working since eight this morning. I'm a disgrace, so I am. But I swear on me mother's eyes, God rest her soul, I only had the one drink, Paddy, that's all, just the one.'

Paddy's face creased into an affectionate smile and he shook his head in mirth. His Annie had never been one to hold her drink. She could get drunk just breathing in the fumes, Lord love her.

'Help me up, Paddy. I've the dinner to get ready . . .'

'Ye'll do no such thing, woman. Shaun met us on the way home and told us what happened. I've sent him and Pat down to the chippie. They shouldn't be long. Ye'll soon feel better once ye've some food inside you. Here, take me arm, we don't want ye falling down the stairs, now do we?'

A mischievous smile tugged at Annie's mouth.

'Sure, and I can remember a time when ye could carry me down the stairs, Paddy Flynn. Though if memory serves me well, ye were always more willing to carry me up them.' She gave a dramatic sigh. 'Still, it comes to all of us sooner or later. The truth is, ye're an old man now. Your days of carrying me are well over.'

Paddy looked at his wife with love in his eyes, together with a glimpse of merriment.

'Old man, me eye. I'm in the prime of me life, woman. I could still carry ye . . . if ye hadn't doubled in size over the years.' He ducked as a pillow came flying at him, and chuckled. 'Begod! There was a time when ye could throw the nearest thing to hand and always find its mark, and I've the scars to prove it.'

Annie got unsteadily to her feet, her face wreathed in smiles.

'Aye, ye're right enough there, Paddy. But don't go getting all smug on me. Me aim's just as good as it was back in the days when we were first wed. Lord knows I've had plenty of practice over the years. It's the drink that spoiled me aim, not me age, and don't ye forget it.'

Taking the plump body in his arms, he said softly, 'I'm not a complete eejit, me darlin', and I deserved every one of those scars. And d'ye know something else?' He stepped back from her and smiled gently. 'I'd not swap a single one, 'cos every one of them has its own special memory.'

Annie moved her head back and looked up at her husband.

'Ah, away with you, ye daft divil.' She waved a hand in his face, then stopped and sniffed his breath. 'Why, ye crafty old beggar. 'Tis not only me that's had a drink the day, is it?'

Paddy took her arm and walked her to the door.

'Well, I couldn't help it, me darlin'. Like I said, Shaun met us on the way home, and said we might as well stop for a drink 'cos there wasn't any chance of dinner. I said to the lads, no, I'll not be having a drink the day, 'cos I want to get back home to me darlin' wife in her hour of need, but they dragged me in with them anyway.' He shrugged his shoulders, a sheepish look coming over his face. 'Shaun said ye'd be best left to sleep it off, and Pat agreed with him. Now what was I to do? Like I said, I'm still in me prime, but Lord above, woman, I'm no match for two strapping lads, now am I?'

Annie stared into the eyes of the man she still adored after twenty-seven years of marriage, saw the twinkle in his eyes and leaned her head against her chest.

'Ye're right enough there, Paddy. But, by, ye must have put up a dreadful struggle to stop them forcing ye into the pub.'

They both began to chuckle, and were still laughing as they came down the stairs, just as Shaun and Pat walked through the door accompanied by Jane.

'Look who we bumped into on the way home,' beamed Shaun, ushering an unusually subdued Jane into the house, a fact that wasn't lost on Annie. Hungover or not, Annie knew her children, and the false smile Jane quickly pasted onto her face didn't fool her mother for a moment. Her heart sank. Obviously someone had made fun of her daughter and it was all her fault for getting drunk in the first place. If she hadn't, Jane wouldn't have had to go out alone, and whatever had happened would have been prevented. Suddenly Annie was stone-cold sober. Even though she knew Jane had wanted desperately to go out on her own, it didn't help to allay her guilt. She wouldn't say anything now, but later on she would get Jane on her own and find out exactly what, or who, had caused her daughter's distress.

All bustle now, she shouted orders left, right and centre, and within five minutes the table was set with plates and cutlery laid out on the snow-white tablecloth, even though her family would have been quite happy to eat their meal straight out of the greasy bags. But Annie liked to lay a meal out properly, even when she hadn't cooked it herself.

It was only when they were all seated and Paddy had said grace that Pat said, 'Hang on. Shouldn't we wake Rory? He must have had enough sleep by now. I sent him home over two hours ago. It's lucky we're ahead on schedule, else I'd've been two men down. It's a good job Dad's still young enough to do a day's work, otherwise Josie would have had to find someone else to help her with her decorating.' He ended his words with a smile, then jumped as Jane, who was sitting beside him, dropped her knife and fork, the sound of the metal cutlery hitting the linoleum with a loud clatter.

'Oh, I'm sorry,' she stuttered nervously as she bent to pick up the cutlery. Forcing a laugh, she added, 'I'm all fingers and thumbs today. I don't know what's the matter with me. It must be the excitement of being out on my own for a change.'

All the men smiled at Jane with affection, but not Annie. If she'd thought something had happened on

Jane's short journey she had no doubts now. Her eyes swept around the table, and she shook her head imperceptibly, wondering at the stupidity of men. None of them had a clue when it came to women. What was glaringly obvious to Annie was completely lost on the male members of her family. Then her head shot up and round to face Pat.

'What d'ye mean, wake Rory? He's not home; at least not to my knowledge. And why in heaven's sake did ye send him home early in the first place?' Her eyes on Pat, she waited for an answer.

Pat shrugged.

'Like I said, Mum, we're well ahead of schedule, so when Rory asked if he could go early 'cos he hadn't had a lot of sleep last night I let him go. He's probably upstairs right now, dead to the world. But if it makes you feel better, I'll go up and check.' Pushing back his chair, he stood up. 'If he ain't, I'll go straight to the police and demand they get up a search party.' Pat laid his hands on the table, grinning. 'Or we could just share his dinner between us and let him get his own when he turns up.'

He had no sooner uttered the words than Rory strolled through the door, looking relaxed and happy. Pat stared at him, all signs of humour wiped from his face. Then, resuming his seat, he said grimly, 'You seem to 'ave perked up since I last saw you. In future if you want some time off, just ask instead of lying. Just 'cos I'm your brother don't mean you can take the piss—'

His words were cut off as Paddy slammed his knife down on the table.

'We'll have none of that language in this house,

Pat. Ye know well enough not to swear in front of your mother or our Jane. I don't want to be having to tell ye again. Now, all of yous, sit down and have your dinner, and we'll be having no more ructions, d'ye understand?' His eyes swept over his sons. 'If you've any quarrels between yous, ye can sort it out in the yard.'

Both Pat and Rory dropped their gaze, each muttering, 'Sorry, Dad' before tucking into their dinner.

Minutes passed before conversation started up again, the awkward moment easing quickly. Addressing Pat, Rory said quietly, 'I did come home for a kip, Pat, but I couldn't sleep so I went for a walk. Sorry, it won't 'appen again.'

As Pat lifted his eyes, Rory couldn't meet his brother's gaze and quickly turned his attention to his food. Mollified, Pat nodded.

'Too right it won't, mate,' but the words were said with clipped humour, which only added to Rory's guilt.

Putting a good-sized portion of cod and chips into his mouth, Rory chewed quickly then looked across the table at Jane and said fondly, 'All right, love?'

Annie, who had been watching her family carefully, saw a startled look enter Jane's eyes. Usually even one word from Rory would light up her daughter's face, but not today. Instead she dropped her gaze, mumbling, 'I'm fine, thank you, Rory.'

Now Annie's gaze shifted to Rory, and she saw the genuine surprise etched on his face.

''Ere, what's up, Jane? Has someone upset yer? 'Cos if they have, you just tell me and I'll soon sort 'em out.'

'You'll do no such thing, Rory.' Annie's sharp voice cut Rory's words off. 'If Jane says she's all right, then she's all right. Now get on with your dinner, I've had enough upsets for one day.'

An uncomfortable silence once again settled on the people present, and they were all relieved when the meal was finished and they could get up from the table.

Leaving the men to their own devices, Jane carefully stacked the plates, her mind whirling. She had to gather her wits before facing her mother. She'd had plenty of time to think since seeing Rory and Cathy in the park, and the more she reflected, the more she convinced herself that if anyone was to blame it was Cathy Meadows. A woman like that knew how to manipulate men, and as much as Jane hated to admit, even to herself, that Rory was different, when it came right down to it he was still a normal man, and therefore just as susceptible to the attraction of women like Cathy.

But her brother was no fool. Perhaps he was simply toying with Cathy to get his own back for the way she had treated him. Jane's eyes lit up. Of course, that must be the reason. It wasn't a very nice thing to do, but she couldn't blame Rory if that was the case. Cathy Meadows deserved everything she got. Oh, why hadn't Jane realised earlier what Rory was up to? It all made sense now, because there was no way her brother would let himself be used again. He was much too smart to fall for the same trick twice. Feeling as if a great weight had been lifted from her shoulders, Jane carried the crockery into the scullery, where her mother was standing by the sink waiting for her.

'Well!'

The one word spoke volumes, and Jane sent up silent thanks that she'd been given time to compose herself. If her mother had got her on her own earlier, she knew she wouldn't have been able to lie. If that had happened . . . A shudder rippled through Jane at the very thought of her mother's reaction if she had told her what she'd seen.

'I'm waiting, Jane. And don't even bother trying to lie to me. Something happened today, and ye'll not be leaving this room till ye tell me the truth.'

Jane knew her mother meant what she said and quickly came up with an excuse for her behaviour at the dinner table. Not able to quite meet her mother's steely gaze, she lowered her head and said, 'It was nothing really, Mum. Just some men in the park. They stopped me on my way back home and started making fun of my face. They'd been drinking, and they frightened me, but a policeman came along and they walked off.' Jane kept her head down, amazed at the ease with which the lies were rolling off her tongue. 'I know I shouldn't have been so upset, but it really scared me. And I didn't want to tell you, because I knew you'd think it was your fault. Then, when Rory asked if I was all right, I got myself into a state. You know what he's like, Mum. He'd have gone mad, and it wouldn't have done any good.' She lifted her gaze to meet Annie's, and saw the relief in her mother's eyes. 'I'm sorry I worried you, Mum. You won't say anything to Rory, will you?'

Annie took the greasy plates from Jane, her face averted.

'Now, what sort of an eejit d'ye take me for? Of course I won't. But if ye ever see those men again when we're out, ye tell me, and by God, they'll rue the day they ever clapped eyes on ye. Now, get yourself away upstairs and rest. I'll see to the washing-up. G'wan now, do as I say.'

Kissing Annie's cheek, Jane didn't offer any argument. She'd never lied to her mother before and was beginning to experience guilt. She almost ran from the room, afraid her conscience would get the better of her, and in doing so cause her to spill the real truth.

Left alone, Annie slumped in relief. Thank God her suspicions had been proved wrong. When Rory had come through the door after Pat had just been telling them he had let Rory come home early for a sleep, she had immediately thought the worst. Her fears had been given further substance by Jane's reaction to her favourite brother, thinking her daughter must have seen Rory with the Meadows girl, but thankfully the reason for Jane's nervousness had now been cleared up. Yet for a while back there Annie had been almost certain . . .

She shook her head, her rough hands immersed in soapy water as she scrubbed the greasy plates. She should have known that her Rory had more sense, not to mention pride, than to get mixed up with that common trollop again.

The rest of the evening was uneventful, but later, when everyone had gone to bed, neither Annie nor Jane could get to sleep, and in each case for the same reason. For no matter how hard they tried, neither woman could shake off the unvoiced but nagging thought that she was fooling herself regarding what Rory was doing in his spare time.

And they both also knew that neither of them would know a moment's real peace until Cathy Meadows returned to her fancy man.

CHAPTER SEVEN

''Ere, watch what you're doing your end, yer clumsy git. You nearly dropped the bloody thing on me foot.'

'Stop moaning, you miserable bugger, and put your back into it, otherwise we'll be here till midnight.'

'All right, all right,' Pat snapped back. 'I didn't know it was gonna be so heavy. The bleeding thing weighs a ton.'

Josie watched from below as Pat and Shaun struggled to ease the upended double bed out of her parents' room. The mattress had been removed and was propped up against the landing wall, alongside the door, which had been taken off its hinges. But no matter which way the two men attempted to manoeuvre the cumbersome bed through the doorway, it remained stuck tight.

'It's not going to budge, is it?' Josie called up the stairs, her voice betraying her disappointment, for as long as the bed remained in the house, she would never be able to rid herself of her mother's presence, or the painful memories it evoked. 'Look, thanks for trying, both of you, I'm really grateful, but I don't want to take liberties. If you could just push it back to where it was . . .'

'Give over, Josie, we're not giving up that easily.' Pat was breathing heavily from the exertion of the last half an hour. 'If it was possible to get it in the room, then it stands to reason there must be a way to get it out. All we've gotta do is find out how.' Wiping the sweat from his face with his shirtsleeve, he looked first at Shaun, then at Josie. 'We could chop the legs off, but it seems a shame to ruin a good bed. I mean, look at the workmanship.' He ran a hand over the thick carved legs, his face showing his admiration for the craftsman who had built the bed. 'And besides, I don't like to be defeated.'

Josie stared at the two men, her eyes filled with a silent plea.

'I honestly don't care what you do. If that's the only way to get rid of it, then that's the way it'll have to be. I just want it out of the house.' A shiver ran down her spine. 'I haven't had a proper night's sleep since the funeral. It's like me mum's still in the house, haunting me.' She smiled wanly. 'I know I'm being silly, but I can't help how I feel.'

'Well, if you're sure, Josie,' Shaun said. 'Though like Pat says, it seems a shame.' He looked at his brother. 'Let's give it one last try, eh, Pat?'

Aware of the passing time and the knowledge that he had to be round Freda's house by eight, Pat nodded his head.

'All right, bruv,' he said good-naturedly. 'One last

try, then I'll have ter be off. I don't wanna keep Freda waiting, 'specially on a Friday night. An' I've still gotta get ready.'

Immediately Josie was all contrition.

'Oh, I'm sorry, Pat, I didn't think. Look, you get off. I don't suppose one more night will make much difference.'

Shaun shot Pat a withering look.

'And another few minutes won't make much difference either.'

Josie gave a nervous laugh.

'It's a shame you can't just unscrew the legs . . . What?' she asked, seeing the startled look on both men's faces.

Shaun slapped his forehead. His eyes met those of his brother and he saw the same thought mirrored there.

'Nah!' Pat said. 'We would've noticed, wouldn't we?'

'Well, there's only one way to find out, ain't there? Though we're gonna be a laughing stock if anyone finds out we've been struggling all this time to get this monstrosity through the door, when all we had to do was take the bleeding legs off.'

Much to the sheepish amusement of the brothers, Josie's careless remark proved accurate, and with a good deal of banter, mainly to cover up their embarrassment, they set to work.

Fifteen minutes later, the carved legs and mattress were deposited out in the back yard, ready to be picked up by the rag and bone man in the morning. With most of the hard work behind them, Pat, his mind on Freda and the frosty reception that would greet him, absentmindedly lifted his end of the bed over the banisters and pushed before Shaun was ready. Realising too late what he had done, Pat frantically tried to pull it back, but the wooden base, all that was left of the bed, was too heavy to hold on to.

'Look out!' he shouted, panic-stricken, as it careered out of control.

Shaun, who had been climbing the stairs, saw the danger and turned, leaping down the stairs, his only thought being for Josie, who was standing at the foot of the stairs, rooted to the spot. With no regard for his own safety, he dived towards her. His arms enveloping her, they fell, then rolled over out of harm's way.

Pat was stunned. He could do nothing more than watch helplessly as the wooden base bounced off the wall and hit the stairs. The noise was deafening as what was left of the bed landed with a sickening thud only inches from Shaun, who was still shielding Josie's body with his own.

The silence that followed was almost as deafening. Then suddenly Shaun was on his feet, his face suffused with fury.

'You stupid bleeding bastard. Yer could've killed us. What the hell was yer thinking about? Worrying about getting an earful from that fat slag for being late, was yer?'

As if he hadn't heard Shaun's words, Pat vaulted over the wooden base, his face ashen at the thought of what might have happened.

'Gawd! I'm so sorry, it was all my fault. You two all right?'

Still seething at his brother's gross carelessness, Shaun snapped back, 'Yeah, we're all right. No thanks to you, yer—'

Badly shaken, Josie stepped between the two men.

'Leave it, both of you. Me nerves are all shot to pieces. The last thing I need is you two fighting.'

Her voice, breathless with delayed shock, quickly brought the impending fight to an abrupt end.

'Sorry, Josie,' Pat muttered, unable to meet the eyes of the woman he had almost injured, maybe even killed, through his own stupidity.

Shaun, rubbing the back of his neck nervously, said quietly, 'Yeah, me too, Josie.'

An uneasy silence hung in the air until Pat, his face flushed, said apologetically, 'I'll make up the money 'Arry will knock off for the damage, Josie. It's the least I can do.' He squatted down and looked at the battered bed. Shaking his head, he noted the deep dents and splintered wood and added, 'It's lucky you've got thick carpet on the stairs. That cushioned most of the fall. If they'd been covered in lino, the whole lot would probably have smashed to pieces. But like I said, I'll pay for the damage.'

Looking at his face, Josie took pity on the hapless man.

'Oh, don't be daft. It was an accident . . . It's not like you did it on purpose, and after all, you were only trying to help me. Look, let's all have a sit-down and a drink. I know I could do with a cuppa.'

Now that the incident had passed without harm, Pat said awkwardly, 'Thanks, Josie, but I'd rather get this out to the yard and get off home . . . if yer don't mind?' he added almost humbly.

99

'No, course I don't mind, you silly sod.' Josie, feeling calmer now, added, 'You get off home. I've kept you here too long already.'

Sensing a chance to be alone with Josie, and stay on friendly terms with his brother, Shaun said quickly, 'Josie's right, Pat. You get off. I can manage on me own from here. After all, I ain't got any plans for tonight.'

A look of relief crossed Pat's face, and he swiftly took his leave, with Josie's words of thanks following him.

She had barely closed the door behind him when there came a knock. Thinking Pat had forgotten something, Josie pulled it open again, her face falling at the sight of Ida Black on her doorstep.

'Sorry ter bother yer, Josie love, but I couldn't 'elp hearing the racket from next door, an' I was wondering if yer was all right.' Ida's bird-like eyes drifted over Josie's shoulder to Shaun and the badly dented piece of furniture lying in the hallway. 'Oh dear, what's 'appened, love?'

Taken by surprise, Josie stood still, only moving when Ida attempted to get her foot over the threshold.

'Hang on, Mrs Black. Where d'yer think you're going?' She moved quickly, barring her neighbour from entering, and also to block the nosy woman's view.

'I'm only being neighbourly, love. I mean, what with you being on yer own now.'

Josie's mouth tightened.

'Thanks for your concern, Mrs Black, but I'm all right, so you can go back home.'

Undeterred, Ida Black tried another tack.

'That ain't part of yer mother's old bed, is it, Josie love? Gawd love us, they've made a right old mess of that, ain't they?' This time her voice was tinged with anxiety, but Josie, after a long day's work and the events of the past hour, was too tired to notice.

'Look, I don't mean to be rude, though I'm sure I could be if I tried,' she snapped. 'But I've been on me feet all day, and I don't have time to stand here talking to you.'

As if she hadn't heard, Ida, her foot still resting on the doorstep, seemed determined to enter the house.

'I've been meaning ter call. But after that—' Conscious of Shaun's presence, Ida pulled back the words hovering on her lips. She didn't fancy another run-in with Annie Flynn. Choosing her words carefully, she continued, 'What I mean ter say is, I'm sorry about upsetting Annie, I didn't mean any harm, honest.'

'Yeah! I'm sure you are, Mrs Black. But like I said, I'm not in the mood for a chat . . .'

To her amazement, Josie felt herself being pushed aside, and by a skinny middle-aged woman at that. Then her neighbour was in the hall, her eyes fixed on the heavy wooden base. Looking at Shaun, Josie shook her head in bewilderment.

Shaun, taking in the uninvited woman's presence, said sharply, 'You heard Josie, Mrs Black. You ain't wanted 'ere, so clear out before me mum comes over.'

At the mention of the dreaded Annie, Ida faltered, then seemed to regain her courage.

'All right, I get the message. Like I said before, I was only being neighbourly, but I'd like a word with yer, Josie . . . On your own, if yer don't mind.'

Her head spinning, Josie screwed up her face, wondering what on earth this woman, whom she'd never liked, could possibly want to talk about. Turning to Shaun, she shook her head as if asking for help.

Quick on the uptake, Shaun came and stood beside Josie, his arm going around her shoulders protectively. To his delight, Josie didn't pull away. Instead she leaned against him. His chest swelling, he tightened his hold, his gaze meeting that of the clearly agitated woman.

'Josie's asked you ter go, Mrs Black, so sling yer 'ook. 'Cos if yer ain't outta 'ere by the time I count to ten, I'll chuck you out.'

Ida looked into the steely blue eyes and swallowed nervously. She had imagined Shaun to be easily intimidated; now she was beginning to see she had underestimated the youngest of the Flynn men.

With a strength born of desperation, Ida stood her ground. Avoiding Shaun's gaze, she turned her eyes towards Josie, licked her lips and blurted out, 'All right then, I'll say me piece.' Her voice quavering, she thrust her chin out, saying, 'I thought better of you, Josie, but I can see I was wrong. Elsie said I could 'ave that bed, seeing as I was the only one who ever bothered to visit her; despite what other people say.' Her eyes darted to Shaun, then back to Josie. 'You must know that, Josie, it was all written down, legal like, in her will. She—'

Before Ida could finish, Josie's feet seemed to leave the air.

'Will! What will? My mum never made a will, she had nothing to leave. As for the bed, well, you're too

102

late. I've already sold it. Harry's coming with his sons to pick it up tomorrow. If it means that much to you, you can buy it off him. Now piss off before I really lose me temper.' Josie glared at the irate woman, her entire body shaking with anger. She felt Shaun's arm pull her close, and for a moment was grateful for his strength; then she remembered Ida's previous taunts concerning Shaun and gently pulled away. Whatever happened, she mustn't give Shaun any false hopes regarding their relationship. He was too kind, too good to be taken advantage of.

Grabbing Ida's arm, Josie marched her to the door, literally throwing the woman out on the street. Then she slammed the door and leaned against it, her body heaving. She couldn't cope with this, she just couldn't. All she wanted right now was some peace.

But Ida Black wasn't giving up so easily. Pushing open the letterbox, she cried, 'You ain't getting away with this, Josie Guntrip. That bed belongs ter me an'—'

She yelped in pain as Josie slammed the metal letterbox in her face. A blissful silence followed, then Shaun led Josie gently towards the kitchen.

'Here yer go, love. You sit yerself down while I make us some tea, and don't yer worry about that old trout. I'll make sure she doesn't give yer any more aggravation.'

Josie groaned silently. That was just what she didn't want. She was quite capable of dealing with Ida Black; she was just feeling a bit vulnerable at the moment.

'Thanks, Shaun, but I can manage, honestly.' She smiled up at the concerned face, and for a brief moment wished she could love Shaun instead of Rory, but she knew, deep down, that that would never happen, as much as she'd like it to. 'I'm really grateful for all your help, Shaun, but I'd like to be on me own for a while.'

Shaun's face fell, causing Josie to lower her eyes. She felt rather than saw him move away.

'Okay, love, I understand. I'll just get that base out into the yard then I'll be off. You know where to find me if yer want anything.'

Keeping her head bowed, Josie said softly, 'I know, Shaun, thanks.' Then, realising he would need help in moving the base, she started to rise. 'Hang on, Shaun, I'll give you a hand shifting it.'

'No you won't.' Shaun, his hand on her shoulder, gently pushed her back on the chair. 'Like I said to Pat, I can manage on me own.' He winked, a cheeky smile on his lips. 'If I ain't as strong as I think I am, I'll give yer a shout.'

While she waited for Shaun to drag the battered piece of furniture through the kitchen to dump it alongside the rest of the bed, Josie set about making a pot of tea. A few minutes passed without a sound, causing her face to pucker up in bewilderment. Wondering what he was up to, she left the tea to brew and was about to go and see what was happening when Shaun's loud, excited voice made her jump.

'Josie, come 'ere, quickly.'

The urgency in his voice brought Josie running into the hall.

'What? What is it?'

'Look, Josie.' Shaun was on his knees beside the

wooden base. 'I thought that old bag was up ter something. She seemed too keen ter get in the house, an' she was so worried about the bed . . . well, this bit of it anyway. She wouldn't 'ave been that brave if she wasn't desperate ter see what was going on, and that made me suspicious, so I thought I'd 'ave a look – and I was right.' His face alight with excitement, he cried, 'Look, Josie, look!' He grabbed her hand and pulled her down beside him. And there it was. The reason why Ida Black had overcome her usual cowardliness in her desperate attempt to take possession of the bed.

Built into the base was a drawer, and in that drawer nestled a number of small chamois bags and a flat wooden box. As if in a dream, Josie lifted out the bags first, nine in all, and then the box. Still kneeling, she pulled the string of one of the bags and gently tipped the contents on to the floor.

The sovereigns made no sound as they tumbled out, for they had been carefully wrapped in old newspaper to stop them from rattling. Josie didn't count them. Instead she opened another bag, and another, until they lay in a pile on the carpet. Then she opened the box, and what was in there brought a gasp of surprise from Shaun, for there were six thick wads of five-pound notes, but still Josie made no sound. And it was this fact that finally penetrated Shaun's excited mind.

'Josie?' he said tentatively. 'Josie, you all right, love? Shall I fetch me mum?'

Dumbly Josie nodded, and Shaun, feeling the first pangs of concern for her state of mind, quickly got to his feet. 'I won't be long, Josie. You just stay there, and don't open the door till me mum comes, all right? . . . Oh, shit!' He clapped his hand hard against his forehead. 'I forgot. Mum's gone ter see one of her customers, but she shouldn't be long.' He hesitated, unsure if he should stay or go and find Annie, then he glanced at Josie, and his mind was made up for him. Like most men, Shaun was ill equipped to handle an emotional situation. Such matters were best left to women. Clearing his throat, he mumbled, 'I'll be as quick as I can, love, okay?'

Again Josie nodded. It was as if she had been deprived of speech.

Taking one last look at the silent figure kneeling by the pile of money, Shaun raced from the house in search of his mother.

Josie sat at the kitchen table staring down at the pile of coins and notes, still unable to believe her eyes. She had never seen so much money in all her life. And it was only by a quirk of fate that she had found it at all. But instead of feeling happy, Josie was trying hard to bite down on the rage that was threatening to engulf her.

If she hadn't hated her mother in life, she certainly did now.

As far back as she could remember, money had always been tight, a situation her mother had blamed on her husband for not being capable of getting a better job which would enable them to live a more comfortable life. Even when Josie had started to bring home a wage, Elsie Guntrip had continued to complain, never missing an opportunity to point out to her husband and daughter how much it cost to feed and clothe them all. She had also never tired of telling them how lucky they were to be living in a house that was fully paid for, unlike their neighbours. In fact, theirs was the only house in the entire neighbourhood that was bought and paid for, thanks to Elsie's late grandmother.

Elsie had heard all about her grandmother at an early age at her mother's knee. According to Elsie, her grandparents had been comfortably off, due to shrewd investments, which was why they had been able to afford to buy their house outright. From what Josie and her father had gleaned, they hadn't been short of a bob or two, and on their deaths, the house and money had gone to their only child, Elsie's mother, who in turn had willed all her possessions to her only daughter. Yet when George Guntrip had dared to ask how they could be so poor when they didn't have rent to pay, Elsie would become defensive, deliberately starting an argument with her husband, who was no match for his sharp-tongued wife.

Josie's eyes hardened as she recalled her dad coming home from working a fourteen-hour day to be met by a cold kitchen and a chunk of bread and cheese, usually his only meal of the day, while his wife sat on her backside beside a roaring fire. Tears pricked her eyes as she remembered her father's worn expression as he ate his meagre meal. Yet as tired as he was, he'd always found time to play with his daughter, knowing that the only signs of affection his child knew came from him. If it had been left to Elsie Guntrip, Josie would never have known the comfort or joy of an affectionate cuddle, or even the most basic parental caring, like being tucked into bed, or a good-night kiss. Looking back, Josie knew that her father had only remained in his loveless marriage because he wouldn't leave his beloved child in the hands of the cold woman he had married.

But Elsie hadn't been as clever as she'd imagined.

Josie looked towards the mantelpiece and smiled grimly. Somehow her father had managed to put a bit of money by each week, as the photo of Josie as a young child proved. How her mother had ranted and raved at her husband, furious that he'd had the money to spare for what she termed trivial items. But what had really stuck in her craw was knowing her meek husband wasn't as pliable as she'd imagined. No matter how hard she'd tried, she'd never found out how he had been able to pay for a professional photograph of their only child.

Turning her attention to the bank book she had found in her father's box, Josie studied the savings account George Guntrip had opened for his daughter. The regular payments, low as they were, amounted to just over two hundred pounds. The first entry, for five shillings, had been made on Josie's second birthday, and somehow her father had managed to deposit a little each week. There were gaps in the entries, and Josie could only surmise that on those dates, for whatever reason, her dad hadn't been able to put anything aside. As her misty eyes roamed down the faded columns, she shook her head in bewilderment, seeing how the entries for a few pence one week, threepence or sixpence another, had mounted up over the years. And during all that time her dad had gone without the basic pleasures of life, such as an ounce of tobacco, or a pint of beer at the weekend with his friends.

Josie licked away a salty tear from her lip but made no effort to stop the rest of them from falling. If only she'd known about the money. She could have used it to ease her dad's life. Maybe they could even have gone away, just the two of them, on a little holiday somewhere in the country, maybe. He would have liked that. Her only consolation was knowing that she had been at his side when he died.

Josie remembered his death vividly. He had been asleep on and off for days, and during that time she had hardly left his side. The last face he had seen was the one he'd loved the most. He had smiled before closing his eyes for the last time.

The house without his presence soon became unbearable, and Josie had been wondering if she was brave enough to leave home when her mother had been taken ill again. It was as if Elsie had sensed her daughter was on the point of rebellion, and was frightened of being left on her own. But unlike her past mysterious illnesses, this time she hadn't been faking, and Josie's secret plan had been scuppered.

There had been many times when Josie had thought of ending it all, because, as she'd tell herself, she didn't have a life anyway; she was just existing from one day to the next. With both Rory and her dad gone, she'd seen no reason for carrying on. But the self-preservation instinct is always strong, so Josie had hung on, just taking things day by day. If it hadn't been for the Flynns' friendship, she would have had no one.

Thinking of the Flynns, Josie's head shot up

quickly. Annie would be over soon. Josie stared down again at the pile of money. The money her mother had been lying on for years. If she hadn't asked Shaun and Pat to help get rid of the heavy double bed, she would never have found the hidden stash.

A sudden noise in the back yard galvanised her into action. If it was Ida again, and she clapped eyes on the money . . . Well! It didn't bear thinking about. Quickly now, she put all the sovereigns and notes into the drawer beneath the sink, then picked up the scraps of old newspaper the coins had been wrapped in and threw them in the kitchen bin.

Her ears pricked for any further sound from the back yard, she sat back and waited for Annie Flynn to arrive.

CHAPTER EIGHT

'Holy Mary, Mother of God!' Annie breathed in stunned amazement; and yet some part of her wasn't surprised. It was just what she would have expected from that bitter old woman. She had always known Elsie Guntrip to be a cold-hearted devil. It was just like her to sit on a pile of money while her family went without the basic luxuries of life. Well! She smiled grimly. A lot of good it would do her now. And if there was any justice in the world, the money would change Josie's life for the better; for she couldn't think of anyone who deserved a bit of good fortune more than the young woman Annie was proud to call a friend. She looked again at the pile of coins and notes heaped on the table and felt a warm feeling of contentment wash over her. And a fortune it was too, in every sense of the word. Raising her eyes upwards, she grinned. If Elsie was looking down on them, and that was debatable, she'd be squirming like a fish on a hook.

'Have you counted it all, Josie?'

Josie smiled widely. In the forty minutes she had waited for Annie to turn up, her former state of shock had given way to pure joy.

'Oh yes, Annie, I certainly have. All in all it comes to a grand total of six hundred and seventy-eight pounds, twelve shillings and sixpence. Plus I've also got the money Dad put by for me.'

'What will you do with it, Josie?' Jane was hovering behind her mother, her face stretched in a grin of genuine happiness for Josie.

'I don't really know yet, Jane. It's gonna take some getting used to – having money, I mean. I still can't believe it meself. Of course I'll put it in the bank first thing Monday morning. I'm not gonna just sit on it, or rather lie on it, like me mum did. I'd never have a good night's sleep thinking of all that money in the house. But I've still got to decide what to do with it in the long run. I suppose the bank manager will have some advice to give me, but I'd like to have a plan of me own to fall back on.' Looking to Annie she said, 'What would you do in my place, Annie?'

Taken by surprise, Annie twitched, then scratched her neck absently.

'Jasus, child, what a question. It's not something I've ever thought of; being rich, I mean.' Looking to her daughter she asked, 'How about you, Jane? D'ye have any ideas for Josie?'

Now it was Jane's turn to be taken by surprise – but not for long. Pulling up a chair, she sat down and said excitedly, 'I don't know what I'd do in the long run, but I do know what I'd do while I was making up my mind.' She looked from her mother

112

to Josie before adding, 'I'd go on a spending spree and buy myself everything I'd ever wanted but couldn't afford, that's what I'd do.'

Josie and Annie stared at Jane, feeling themselves being caught up in the young girl's excitement and enthusiasm.

'She's right, Josie,' Annie grinned. 'Sure and ye deserve a treat. And if ye don't mind me saying so, you could be doing with some new clothes. When was the last time ye bought anything for yourself?'

'I can't remember, Annie, I honestly can't.' Josie shook her head slowly. 'I've always made me own clothes. It was either that or the jumble stall, and I never did fancy wearing clothes other people had chucked out. I mean, you don't know who wore them last, do you?'

'Now don't you go turning your nose up at buying clothes second hand, love.' Annie waved a finger under Josie's nose. 'There's many a bargain I've had at Paddy's Market.'

'Mum!' Jane laughed. 'Josie doesn't have to shop at Paddy's Market. That's the whole point. She can shop anywhere she likes now.'

Josie stared hard into Jane's excited face and felt a pang of compassion for her young friend. If money could remove the ugly birthmark, she would gladly give up every penny she now had. But there was something she could do.

'Are you doing anything tomorrow, Annie? 'Cos if you're not, I'm taking you both shopping; and no arguments.' Josie beamed at the two women who were the closest to family she would ever know.

'Oh, now, love, hold your horses a minute. Don't

113

ye be letting the money go to your head . . .' Annie said, a note of embarrassment in her voice, uncomfortable at the idea of having Josie spend money on her.

But Jane had no such scruples. Her face alive with excitement, she jumped to her feet crying, 'Oh, don't be such a spoilsport, Mum. It's no fun shopping on your own, and besides . . .' She smiled at Josie, slipping her arm through her friend's. 'Someone has to go with Josie, if only to make sure she enjoys herself.'

The genuine warmth that was emanating from the young girl transferred itself to Josie, and she felt a jolt of happiness envelop her entire body. It was a good feeling, and one she hadn't experienced for a long time; not since . . .

Josie forced her mind to focus on the present; she had spent far too long dwelling on the past. She would put all thoughts of Rory firmly behind her – yet why did the memories still hurt so much?

Gripping Jane's hand, Josie held it tightly.

'Well, Annie?'

Annie looked up at the two young women and shook her head. Getting to her feet, she said, 'All right, all right. I give in. But I'll have to be away back over the road. The men will be wondering what's going on—' She stopped abruptly, her words faltering. 'What I mean is, they'll not be being nosy, but they'll be bound to be—'

Josie reached out with her free hand and clutched Annie's plump fingers warmly.

'I know what you mean, Annie. Of course they'll be wondering what's going on, they wouldn't be

114

human if they didn't. Besides, if it wasn't for Shaun and Pat, I would never have found the money. In fact, if I hadn't had your friendship all these years, I might not be standing here today. 'Cos there's been times I've wondered if it was worth going on . . .' Josie heard her voice crack with emotion and lowered her head. She was going to cry. She'd promised herself she wouldn't; she'd been determined she would shed no more tears, for she'd had enough of them to last a lifetime. But her mind clearly had other ideas. Then she was being held tight, and she gave herself up to the flood of tears that had been building up since the discovery of the money, made all the more bitter by the brutal revelation that her own mother must have really loathed her.

Minutes later, Annie pulled herself away and, with tears rolling down her cheeks, and a trembling smile on her lips, said, 'Would ye look at the three of us. Begod! You'd think someone had just died.' Raising her eyes to the ceiling, she added, 'If you're up there, Elsie, I hope ye can hear me, ye miserable auld divil.'

Then the three of them were laughing and wiping the tears from their blotched faces.

'I'll be away home, Josie, but you get that table clear. Ye don't want Ida Black to be knowing your business. And I wouldn't put it past the auld beggar to come sniffing around on some excuse.'

Josie gave a nervous start at the mention of her neighbour's name.

'Blooming 'ell! That's all I'd need, isn't it? If I wanted me business known to all and sundry, I'd be better off writing to the papers than have Ida find out about the money.'

Moving quickly, she once again cleared the table, putting the money back under the kitchen sink, hopefully safe from prying eyes. Then she paused. Opening the drawer again, she took out six five-pound notes and twenty sovereigns.

'It's no good going shopping without money, is it?' she said happily as she closed the drawer.

Annie's jaw dropped in amazement.

'Jasus, love. When ye said we were going shopping, I thought ye meant to buy from the shops, not buy one of your own.'

'And why not, Mum?' Jane cut into the conversation, her voice merry. 'Josie could buy herself a shop if she wanted to, couldn't you, Josie? Then you wouldn't have to stand on your feet all day making more money for Mister Joe Lyons.'

The words were spoken casually, but they struck a chord in Josie's mind.

As Annie and Jane made to leave, Josie said, 'Actually, Jane, would you mind if your mum stayed here for a while? There's something I need advice on . . . You're not offended, are you?' she asked guiltily.

But Jane merely grinned.

'Of course I'm not offended. Besides, it gives me the chance to break the news to my dad and the rest of them. Pat's gone round to Freda's, but Shaun and Rory are still home. They'll be so pleased for you.' Jane stopped as she heard the words tumbling from her lips; now it was her turn to feel guilty. 'That's if you don't mind them knowing your business.'

'Don't be daft.' Josie looked at Annie. 'I've no secrets from me family.'

Annie returned the look, saying slowly, 'That's

nice of ye to say so, love. And ye can be sure they'll not be opening their mouths outside the house. Ye have me word on that. Though I can't speak for Freda. She's a gob on her the size of the Blackwall Tunnel. Mind you, ye'll suddenly find ye've a new friend, 'cos that one would sell her own mother for a packet of Woodbines.'

As soon as Jane had left, still laughing, Annie, her face thoughtful, said, 'All right, Josie. Let's be having it. There's something worrying ye, else ye'd not have asked me to stay.'

Sitting across the table, Josie met Annie's shrewd gaze.

'It's about Ida, Annie. She knows about the money. Oh, maybe not how much, but she knows there was some. Why else would she have been so desperate to get the bed? She said me mum left it to her in her will, but I don't know anything about a will.' Josie lifted her shoulders listlessly. 'Then again, I'd've been the last person she'd have told.' She attempted a watery smile, and Annie's heart went out to her.

For the life of her, Annie couldn't understand Elsie's unfeeling behaviour to her only child. Being a mother herself, Annie knew only too well the trials and tribulations of raising a family. Many a time she'd been driven to distraction by one or another of them, especially when they were younger and she'd had them under her feet all day. But for all the smacked backsides she'd meted out, and there had been many, her children had been compensated tenfold by an affectionate kiss and cuddle from their mother at bedtime.

Afraid she would start bawling again, Annie said

117

quickly, 'Now then, we'll be having no more tears or sad faces. I don't know why your mother was the way she was, but ye mustn't blame yourself. She could have given birth to the Lord himself, and still found fault. She was lucky to have a daughter like you, love. Ye could have walked out and left her to fend for herself, an' there's many who would have done, believe me.' Her head bobbed up and down vigorously. 'She made your life hell when she was alive, and I'll not stand by and see ye haunted by guilt, 'cos ye've nothing to be guilty about. Besides . . .' she gave a hiccup of a laugh, 'that's the prerogative of us Catholics.'

Josie stared into Annie's twinkling blue eyes and felt the corners of her mouth turn up in a grin.

'Oh, Annie,' she laughed. 'What would I do without you?'

'You'd do just fine, love,' Annie said brightly. 'An' ye know why? 'Cos ye've a strong character. If ye hadn't, ye'd never have been able to put up with your mother all these years.'

'Thanks, Annie. I needed to hear that.'

Patting Josie's hand, Annie said briskly, 'And now ye have, so ye can put the past behind ye. Now then, that just leaves Ida to deal with. Ye say she's certain Elsie left a will? Well, to my mind something must have put the thought into her head, 'cos she hasn't the brains to think up something like that by herself. Come to think of it, I saw Ida coming in here a few times, while ye was out at work. I never thought anything of it at the time. But now . . . Well, let's face it, who else would have time for either of them?'

Annie's forehead creased in thought as she tried

to determine what to do concerning Ida Black. For until the business of this so-called will was sorted, Josie would always live in fear of having the money taken away from her. Because if there was a will, Annie would bet her life that it wouldn't benefit Josie. Then she jumped as Josie, as if reading her mind, said timidly, 'What if there is a will, Annie? What if I spend that money and one day it turns up! I know I've seemed happy about my good luck, and I am, but inside I'm scared. Scared it'll be taken away, an' I'll be left with nothing again.'

Annie stood up abruptly, her face set in hard lines.

'Then there's only one way to find out, and that's to get Ida in here and hear what she has to say for herself.'

Before Josie could protest, Annie was out in the yard calling for Ida to come over. To Josie's dismay her neighbour appeared, and that act alone spoke volumes. For if she didn't think she was wholly in the right, there was no way Ida Black would face Annie's wrath.

Josie's heart began to race as Ida, her expression fearful, came into the kitchen with Annie behind her. Without any preamble, Annie said curtly, 'Now then, Ida, what's all this about a will? Or were ye just making it up to get your greedy hands on Elsie's bed? 'Cos a bed like that's worth a few bob. So, let's be having the truth.'

Josie looked from Ida's fear-filled face to Annie's grim one, and for a moment she felt sorry for her neighbour – but not so Annie Flynn.

'Well?' Annie barked. 'We haven't all night.'

At the tone of Annie's voice, Ida crumbled. Her

mouth quivering, she said, 'I wasn't lying, honest I wasn't.' Frighteningly aware of Annie's presence, the words spilled from her lips. 'I was visiting one day while you was at work, Josie, an' your mum asked me to witness her will. I . . . I didn't see what was in it, like, 'cos it was all folded up except for the bottom bit where I signed. She . . . I mean, your mum, she said she'd leave me her bed . . . That's the truth, Josie, honest.'

Josie looked hard into the pinched face, trying to gauge if Ida was indeed telling the truth, but she could see no evidence that the woman was lying.

Annie, on the other hand, was older and wiser, and not so easily taken in.

'D'ye think we were born yesterday, Ida? There must have been something about that bed that made ye so desperate to get your hands on it: and ye'll not be leaving this house till we hear the truth.'

Faced with the formidable woman, Ida's last vestige of courage collapsed. Licking her dry lips, she said in a tear-filled voice, 'All right, I'll come clean . . . Can I sit down, Josie?' she appealed to the younger woman. This time Josie didn't look to Annie for guidance.

'Of course you can, Ida,' she said kindly, thinking that the woman had already suffered enough from Annie's harsh demeanour. Though she was perfectly prepared to change tack if she thought Ida was concealing the real truth of the matter in hand.

Sitting herself down, Ida placed her elbows on the table, and tried to concentrate on Josie's face while ignoring Annie, who had sat down beside her. She took a deep breath and began to talk.

'It all started on Christmas Eve. I was out in the yard bringing me washing in when your mum pulled up her window and asked me in. I was glad of the invitation, 'cos I didn't 'ave anything better ter do. I was feeling a bit low, what with it being Christmas an' 'aving no family ter share it with, so I let meself in the back door an'—'

An angry grunt from Annie interrupted Ida's flow of words.

'Jasus, woman, we don't want to be hearing your life story. Just get to the point.'

'Annie,' Josie said reproachfully, 'let Ida tell it in her own words.'

Annie fell silent, but not before she had cast a malevolent look at the skinny woman sitting next to her.

'Go on, Ida,' Josie said, trying to inject some warmth into her tone.

Swallowing hard, Ida continued.

'Like I said, I let meself in an' went up ter see yer mum. We 'ad a nice chat, Elsie asked me ter make some tea, an' I ended up staying fer nearly two hours. I would've stayed longer, but Elsie wanted me outta the 'ouse before you got 'ome from work. Anyhow, I started coming in ter keep yer mum company while you was working. Then one day I fancied some fish an' chips an' I popped in ter see if your mum wanted some. She didn't 'ear me coming up the stairs, an' when I looked in she was kneeling on the floor. At first I thought she'd fallen outta bed, so I ran in ter 'elp, but when she saw me she started shouting something awful. Well, I couldn't understand it. Then I saw the money . . .'

Ida stopped for breath, then carried on, reluctantly now.

'There was a bundle of fivers on the floor. She must've been counting it before I came in. I only caught a glimpse of it though, 'cos, quick as lightning, she turned 'er back on me. I 'eard a sound like a drawer closing then she pulled the sheets and quilt over the mattress and got back into bed. I didn't know what ter do at first, it was a bit awkward like, but yer mum apologised fer shouting, then acted like nothing 'ad 'appened. I went an' got the fish an' chips, and that was the end of it at the time. But she must 'ave got scared that I might tell someone what I saw, 'cos a couple of weeks later she asked me ter sign her will, and said she'd left me her bed, fer being a good neighbour an' friend.'

Ida paused again, and Annie began fidgeting beside her. Ida knew only too well what Annie thought of her, and that knowledge brought with it a flash of bravado. Pulling her chair sideways so her back was to her old adversary, she said, 'I know what some people think of me, your mum and present company included, but I ain't daft. When I was a kid my auntie 'ad a box bed. She kept all 'er money in there, said she didn't trust banks. She showed me once. There was a sort of panel built into the bottom half of the bed, an' that's where she kept 'er life savings. That was over fifty years ago, but I never forgot it. After that it didn't take a genius to figure out that your mum's offer of the bed was ter keep me mouth shut. Oh, I knew whatever money was in it would be long gone before I got me 'ands on the bed. But I couldn't 'elp but 'ope there might be a few quid left in it: yer know, money your mum didn't get the chance to move before she died.' Her voice trailed off sadly.

'Anyway, that's the God's honest truth. If you don't 'ave it, then I ain't got a clue where that money is now. The only thing I do know is that I'm never gonna see a penny of it.' Her voice was weary now, as was her thin body. 'There's nothing more I can tell yer, so if yer don't mind, I'll get back ter me own 'ouse.' She rose unsteadily to her feet and, without another word, left the house.

'Well!' Annie was the first to speak. 'I thought she knew more than she was letting on. Mind you, if she hadn't made such a fuss over that blasted bed, Shaun wouldn't have taken a closer look, and the whole lot would have ended up in Harry's scrapyard.'

Josie nodded in agreement.

'And if Pat hadn't dropped it, the spring that kept that drawer in place wouldn't have broken, and that money would never have been found, unless someone knew where to look. You know, Annie, that bed first belonged to me great-grandmother. She had it made 'specially for her when me great-grandad died. It must have been her idea to have that secret drawer built into the base. Me mum loved telling me dad about how her side of the family had money, but whenever he asked where it'd all gone, Mum used to fly into one of her rages, so in the end he stopped asking. Though he often said to me he wouldn't be surprised if Mum had a secret bank account some-where. But he never suspected he'd been lying on hundreds of pounds for years. He might have been mild-tempered, but he'd never have stood for that.'

Josie looked at Annie and asked in bewilderment, 'Why, Annie, why? Me mum always liked nice things. That was the main cause of me parents fighting, 'cos she never missed an opportunity to tell him how she'd married beneath her, and how she'd had to go without the luxuries she'd had before marrying him. I don't understand, Annie. I know she'd have resented sharing the money with me and Dad, but by hiding it she had to go without as well. It just doesn't make sense. I'd've thought she'd have liked nothing better than to show off to the neighbours, making sure they knew she was better than them. You know what a snob she was.'

Annie sighed heavily.

'I've lived a long time, love, an' seen things that made no sense. Sometimes we have to accept there is no reason for why people are the way they are: they just are. I've known many a soul to hoard every penny they owned, and go hungry rather than spend any of it. I've never understood it. After all, they can't take it with them, can they? And at the end of the day, people like your mum end up cutting off their nose to spite their face.'

Seeing Josie's expression, and fearing she was about to fall back into her maudlin mood, Annie rose briskly to her feet and said brightly, 'Well now, that's Ida sorted, an' I don't know about you, Josie, but I'm ready for me bed.'

Josie smiled gratefully.

'Me too, Annie. And thanks, I couldn't have coped without you.'

Wagging her finger in mock anger, Annie said, 'We'll be having no more of that nonsense. I told ye before, ye're stronger than ye think. Now I'll get meself off before Paddy starts a search party. No, you stay where ye are,' she added as Josie made to stand up. 'I'll show meself out, I know the way. You get a good night's sleep, love. After all, we've a long day ahead of us tomorrow, 'specially with Jane tagging along. She'll have us in and out of the shops more times than a baby needs its nappy changing.'

She glanced at the clock on the mantelpiece and was shocked to see it was nearly ten thirty. She deliberately ignored the wedding photograph next to the clock. Josie must have wanted it on show for the sake of her father; she certainly couldn't have wanted it there to remind her of Elsie.

'Jasus! Will ye look at the time,' she cried. 'It's just flown by.' Hurrying now, she was moving towards the hall when a sudden thought stopped her. Turning round, she said, 'Will ye be all right on your own, Josie? I mean, what with all that money in the house. I could come back an' stay the night, if ye want me to.'

Josie's face registered her surprise.

'I never thought of that,' she said, then shrugged. 'If it's been here for the last twenty years or longer, then I don't suppose another couple of nights will matter. Though I will take it up to bed with me.' She smiled tiredly. 'Just to be on the safe side,' she added.

Worried now, Annie replied, 'Are ye sure, love? Now I think of it, I don't like leaving ye on your own.'

'I'll be fine, Annie. I've got good strong bolts and locks on the doors. Mum got me dad to fit them. He did tell me he thought it strange she was so adamant about making the house secure; now I know why.'

'Well, if you're sure, Josie.'

'I'm sure, Annie. Now get yourself off home. I'll see you in the morning.'

'Good night, love.'

'Good night, Annie.'

Annie yawned loudly as she crossed the hall. Stopping for a moment to adjust her shawl, she looked at the ordinary piece of furniture, and marvelled at the fortune it had been protecting for years. Her inquisitive nature overcame her, and she bent down to look at the broken drawer. Pulling it out further, she spotted what seemed to be a folded piece of paper. She picked it up, intrigued and suddenly fearful.

'Annie? You all right?' Josie shouted from the kitchen.

Quickly now, Annie put the paper in her pocket.

'Just being nosy, love. It's not every day ye see a treasure chest, 'cos that's what this bed is. Good night again, Josie.'

Her heart pounding, Annie headed for home, the paper seeming to burn through her pocket. Because if it was what she thought it was, it would be up to her to decide Josie's fate, and she feared the burden she might have brought upon herself would be too hard for her to handle alone.

CHAPTER NINE

It was only ten thirty and already Annie's feet were killing her. She was also tired and thirsty. Tired because she'd hardly had a wink of sleep worrying about the paper she had found. She'd wanted to confide in Paddy, but realised it would be unfair to drag her husband into something that might well have legal repercussions. As yet she hadn't read it. She'd tried to, but her courage had failed her. For all she knew, it might just be a letter from an old friend. But as desperate as she was to believe it, that notion was too implausible even for her to swallow.

'You all right, Annie? You look worn out. Would you like to sit down for a minute?' Josie looked with concern at the middle-aged woman. Annie's face was flushed and sweating, though it wasn't that that Josie was worried about. It was a hot day, and they were all feeling the heat. But Annie had seemed preoccupied all morning, her normal cheery character noticeably absent.

'Mum!' Jane looked at her mother guiltily. She'd been having such a good time she had neglected to keep an eye on her mother. Jane knew Annie couldn't take too much heat, it made her ill; it always had.

Flustered by the fuss being made of her, Annie firmly pushed her worries about the letter to the back of her mind, summoned up a smile and said, 'Course I'm all right. I'm not in me dotage yet. It'll be a while before I'm pushing up the daisies.'

Josie and Jane exchanged amused glances. Then Jane laughed.

'Mum, you've been saying that for years.' She turned to Josie. 'Every time one of us worries about her she comes out with that old saying. Then my dad says she's as tough as old boots, and they'd have to put her down, because that's the only way she'll leave this mortal coil.'

Not wanting Annie to feel she was spoiling the day, Josie blew out her cheeks, saying, 'Well, I don't know about you two, but I'm sweating. How about getting some ice cream before we carry on?'

Annie inwardly breathed a sigh of relief. She'd be fine after a bit of a rest and something cold to cool her down.

Left alone on an ornate iron bench outside a posh jeweller's in the middle of Oxford Street while Jane and Josie went in search of an ice-cream vendor, Annie looked around her surroundings feeling totally out of place. Why they couldn't have gone to one of the markets at home she didn't know. If she'd known Josie was planning on taking them to the West End, she would have tried to get out of going. But Josie, bless her, had thought she was treating them by taking them up West. She and Jane had been so excited when they had boarded the tram, Annie hadn't had the heart to pour cold water on her young friend's plan. Though she had to admit, albeit grudgingly, that although the journey had taken well over an hour, the ride on top of the tram had been a thoroughly enjoyable experience.

Letting her eyes wander, she took in the well-groomed women in their fancy gowns, twirling dainty parasols to ward off the sun, even though they were wearing what Annie surmised to be the latest fashion in hats. Then there were the men, dressed in their smart three-piece pinstripe suits and bowler hats, striding along the pavements, full of their own importance. Annie stifled a giggle thinking of what her lads would say if they were here with her now. For all these busy, harassed-looking men reminded Annie of a flock of penguins.

And the noise! She was used to pushing her way through the various markets in the East End, but this place was like being landed in bedlam. She didn't mind the crowded streets; it was the never-ending flow of traffic she couldn't get used to. The roads were packed solid with trams, horse-drawn buses, hackney cabs and private carriages. And that wasn't counting the delivery vans on their daily journeys to the numerous shops and restaurants.

Feeling self-conscious in her plain attire of old white blouse and black skirt that had seen better days, Annie looked over the road in the direction Josie and Jane had gone. When she spotted them her face lit up with relief, then changed to worry as she watched them trying to negotiate a safe passage through the heavy traffic, while holding on to their ice-cream cornets. When they finally stepped on to the pavement Annie breathed a sigh of relief.

At that moment she felt something drop on to her skirt and looked down. To her horror she saw three shiny pennies lying in her lap. Then a posh voice said haughtily, 'Buy yourself a decent meal, woman. Though I suppose it will go straight into the nearest public house.'

Annie jumped up as if she'd been stung, her face the colour of beetroot.

'Ye cheeky . . .' Words momentarily failed her, but not for long. Outraged at what she perceived to be an insult, she picked up the coins and thrust them against the startled man's chest with such force he staggered back. Her arms akimbo, Annie yelled angrily, 'Just 'cos I'm not dressed up like a dummy doesn't make me a beggar. Now g'wan. Be off with ye, afore I really lose me temper.'

The woman with him raised her eyes disdainfully, twirled her parasol and said, 'Come away, Frederick. There's no use arguing with people like these; especially the Irish. Though I've never known one to turn down a free drink before.'

A red mist fell over Annie's eyes, her Irish temperament reaching boiling point. Then she heard Jane's voice, high-pitched with anxiety, and her temper abated.

'Mum! Mum. Come away, please.'

Patting Jane's arm, Annie said with a calm she was far from feeling, 'It's all right, love, don't fret yourself.' But her tone didn't coincide with the fiery, burning anger reflected in her eyes.

The couple backed away.

'If you are related to this . . . this woman, I suggest you take her home before I call a policeman. In fact—'

Josie swung round on the man.

'Listen, mister, and you, lady.' She glared at the couple. 'If I was you, I'd sling me 'ook while you can. 'Cos you're in so much danger here, an' you don't even know it.'

A small crowd was gathering, and Jane, mortified at the attention they were attracting, leaned against her mother, begging, 'Let's go, Mum, please.'

'It's all right, Jane, we're going.' Josie, her voice strong, cast a scathing glare over the curious bystanders. 'Well! Seen enough, have you?'

The small crowd fell back, but only to what they deemed a safe distance from the three women.

Annie felt the trembling body of her daughter and experienced a jolt of remorse. Why couldn't she have kept her blasted temper? Now, because of her, she had ruined the day for Jane and Josie. Her head drooped.

'I'm sorry, love, and you, Josie. I've ruined your day, so I have. Ye should have left me back where I belong, not brought up here with the toffs. I've disgraced meself and yous into the bargain. You two go on without me, before I show ye up again.'

'Don't be daft,' Josie said, her voice strong and forceful. 'We're not gonna let a pair of toffee-nosed sods spoil our day.' She stared hard at Annie. 'I've waited a long, long time for a day like this. If it wasn't for you I'd never have gotten the nerve to start my life over. There's not many people who get a second chance, but you gave that to me, and I'm not going anywhere without you by my side.'

Annie returned Josie's gaze and nodded. Lifting her chin proudly, she replied, 'You're right, love. It's your day, and I'll not be spoiling it again.' Grabbing Jane's hand, she turned to the remaining onlookers and said brusquely, 'Well! What are you lot gawping at? Haven't ye any homes to go to?'

Those waiting in the hope of further entertainment quickly dispersed, leaving a wide berth for the three women to pass through. They had hardly gone more than a few steps when Annie, a perplexed look on her face, said, 'Where's me ice cream?'

It was the perfect thing to say to relieve the tension. And it worked. Josie and Jane burst out laughing at Annie's audacity.

'Oh, Mum, you are the limit. Josie and me risked life and limb to get you your ice cream, and then we had to drop the lot to stop you getting arrested for creating a public disturbance.'

Linking arms, they proceeded on their way. And while they joked, each of the women was thinking different thoughts.

Jane was still shaken by what could have turned into a very unpleasant scene, Annie was cursing herself for letting her Irish temper get the better of her again, and Josie was inwardly seething at the way her dearest friend had been treated like a common beggar just because of the way she was dressed.

Josie's back straightened, her chin jutting out determinedly. By the end of the day they would all be dressed well enough to get into Buckingham Palace itself if they had a mind to.

The next hour was spent going in and out of shops without buying a single item, and Annie was finding it very hard to bite back words of complaint for Josie and Jane's sake. It was the least she could do after the earlier fracas, minor as it was. Josie too was getting impatient, but with herself for dithering and wasting the best half of the morning. When she had left home she had been determined to buy herself, Annie and Jane new outfits and bugger what the neighbours thought when they saw them dressed up to the nines. Ida Black would know at once that Josie had found Elsie's money, but without the elusive so-called will, she could do nothing.

Still Josie hesitated. She glanced at the women either side of her. Jane's earlier enthusiasm was fading fast, and Annie looked as if she was ready to drop, and again Josie cursed herself for a fool. But after a lifetime of watching every penny, of making her clothes from remnants bought down the markets, it was extremely hard for her to start throwing money around. She wished now she had come alone, for if she had she'd have had no compunction in turning and going back home empty-handed. That option was now closed. Furious with herself for being so weak, she said, 'I'm sorry I've been mucking both of you about. It's just that . . . Well, I still can't believe I've got money to spend. But I promised you both a new outfit, and one for meself. So the next shop we come to, I'm going in and not coming out again until we've all bought something.'

Jane immediately brightened, but Annie knew how Josie was feeling.

'Listen, love. Ye don't have to be worrying about

us. There's always another day, and maybe we'd be more comfortable shopping in our own back yard.'

A lump was forming in Josie's throat. She had let her friends down. Not intentionally, but that was what she had done nevertheless. Annie had been right in one respect. One of the reasons they hadn't lingered long in any of the impressive shops was because all three of them had stuck out like sore thumbs. In Selfridges they had even been followed round the various departments by the store detective, not only because they looked out of place, but because their nervousness at being surrounded by such expensive items of clothing must have made them appear suspicious. What they needed was a small shop, one that sold clothes of good quality without being too ostentatious. More importantly, somewhere they would be made welcome.

'Here, Josie. Will ye look at this dress. By, you'd look grand in that, love.'

Shaken from her reverie, Josie started.

'Sorry, Annie, what did you say?'

Grabbing her by the arm, Annie turned Josie towards the display window of a small but elegant shop. Josie's eyes widened. It was uncanny. She had been thinking about just such a shop, and here they were now standing right outside it.

'I said look,' Annie repeated in exasperation. 'It could have been made for ye. It puts me in mind of that dress ye made for that party. You know the one I mean. The one our Rory—' Annie sucked in her cheeks as she realised what she'd said.

'You needn't worry, Annie. I'm not gonna faint away every time I hear his name mentioned.'

Josie was staring at the dark red dress displayed on a mannequin in the shop window, her eyes lighting up with excitement. It was everything she had dreamed of owning one day. And despite Annie's kind words, it was nothing like the cheap outfit she'd made for herself. The only comparison was the colour, and even that was different. For the dress in the window was of a deep red, as opposed to the bright red silk she had so painstakingly stitched. The sleeves were long, tapering into wide silk-braided cuffs. The bodice had a wide white frill inserted at the neck, which ran into a V shape in the middle of the bust. The dress tapered in at the braided waist, flowing into a full skirt with a discreet bustle that added an elegant touch to the garment.

Unlike the famous stores, this window display was sparse, containing only the dress, a three-quarter matching coat, hat, gloves and shoes. There were no price tags on any of the articles, which in itself should have brought back Josie's misgivings, but it didn't. This was the kind of thing she had been looking for, the kind of clothes she had dreamed of for years. But would they fit her? Her doubting eyes lifted to look over the curtain that was hanging from a shiny brass rail, and she could see the shop was empty. Her previous reluctance to buy anything had been partly because she was afraid of facing the smartly dressed assistants. But this shop was tiny by comparison, small but good class. That much was evident from the window display. Too good for the likes of her. All she had wanted was something a bit out of the ordinary, something different from the store-type clothing. Oh, but that was a lovely outfit; yet where would she have the chance to wear it?

Before she could lose her nerve again, she pushed open the door and stepped on to a thick pile carpet with Annie and Jane following her. A bell tinkled over the doorway and immediately a smartly dressed woman emerged from a side room. All three women held their breath, expecting the same snooty reception they had been subjected to all morning; instead, the woman smiled warmly.

'Good afternoon, ladies. How may I help you?'

The tension ebbed from their bodies, though they remained wary. Licking her dry lips, Josie said tentatively, 'That . . . that outfit, the one in the window. Could you tell me how much it is, please?'

The tall, slim woman, whom Josie surmised to be in her late fifties, smiled graciously.

'Would that be for you, madam?'

Josie swallowed nervously.

'Yeah . . . I mean, yes, it's for me . . . If it fits. And I'd also like to buy my friends new outfits as well.'

Edna Walker let her eyes roam over the three women. They didn't look as if they could afford her prices, but one never knew in this business. She also noted their apprehension and quickly set about putting them at their ease.

'Please, ladies, will you follow me to the changing rooms? We will be more comfortable there.'

Like children obeying their teacher, they did as the elegant woman asked, following her towards a thick velvet curtain. Pulling it aside, she beckoned them forward.

Sticking close together, the women entered, and

as one gaped at the opulence of the room.

'Come, sit down and make yourselves comfortable.' Edna gestured towards four plush armchairs.

Definitely uncomfortable now, Josie stuttered, 'I'm . . . I'm sorry. I'm afraid we'd be wasting your time.'

The proprietor leaned her head to one side as she studied the three women. Part of her successful business acumen was her ability to empathise with human nature. Before her she saw not just three women of various ages, but three unique individuals.

The youngest of the trio, though as apprehensive as her companions, still radiated an air of excitement. Edna had noticed the scarred face, even under the large hat she guessed had been made especially for her. What a shame; particularly for one so young and pretty. She turned her attention to the eldest of the group, and had to suppress a smile, for the poor woman was practically squirming with embarrassment, most likely wishing she was anywhere but here in what to her must seem like another world. Finally she let her glance linger on the third woman, who was dressed in a drab, shapeless outfit that screamed of being hand-made, and, unfortunately, not very well. Yet Edna was able to see beyond the women's outward appearance, visualising instead how they would look when they left her establishment. Providing, of course, they could afford her prices.

'Please, ladies, sit down. I ask only that you let me show you some of my designs. You can try them on, as many as take your interest. I normally close at one on Saturday, but I think I can make an exception today. One of the advantages of owning one's business is being able to close when one desires. So, ladies, what do you say? Will you stay and see what I have to offer? No other customers will disturb us. If you decide to purchase some of my designs, I will, of course, be delighted. If you don't . . .' She raised her shoulders and smiled. 'Well then, we shall hopefully have had an afternoon of fun.' She looked at the women, trying to gauge their feelings, and sensed rather than saw the slight relaxation in their bodies.

Josie's face intrigued her the most, in terms of the purity and pain etched upon it. Edna Walker had lost her husband and three sons in the Boer War; she knew only too well what pain was like. This woman had been hurt, and hurt badly. Not physically, but mentally. And Edna guessed that that hurt had been inflicted by a man; it usually was. Suddenly she felt a need to help her, to take the pain from the kind face. She had no intention of making her pocket suffer through sentimentality, but there was something about this woman. It felt to Edna as if she had been handed a challenge.

She studied Josie's face and saw the high cheek bones, the smooth line of her jaw and the full lips, and experienced a sudden urge to transform the badly dressed, shy and awkward woman into a confident, attractive one. Hopefully, when she left her shop, she would look like a new woman. But first things first, Edna cautioned herself. The costume had yet to be tried on to ensure it was the right size.

Locking the door and turning the sign to 'Closed', Edna stepped up into the display window. Handling the clothes as if they were precious items, she held them out to Josie, and saw the excitement mixed with trepidation on the woman's face. She could almost feel the tumultuous emotions racking Josie's body and mind.

'Now, madam, if you would care to step into one of the cubicles to ascertain if the outfit is suitable, I will endeavour to help your friends.'

Edna turned to Annie and Jane.

'Now then, ladies, will you follow me.'

The dignified woman crossed to a full-length wardrobe and slid the door open. Beckoning to the silent figures, she hid a smile at their obvious discomfort. She would soon put them at their ease. In her thirty years of running the shop, Edna had never before encountered people such as these, at least not in the past twenty years. She had become used to catering for the upper class, and with the exception of a few, most of her clientele still treated Edna as if they were superior to her. Now these three women, devoid of airs and graces, had walked into her shop, and brought with them a breath of fresh air. Edna had warmed to them straight away.

'I would very much like to dress you, madam.' Her eyes were on Annie. 'Let me see now . . .' Expertly she assessed Annie's body. 'I would hazard a guess at your size, madam. You fit a forty hip; am I correct in my assumption?'

Annie could feel her face flush, and chastised herself for an old fool. What was she afraid of anyway? More to the point, when would she get another chance to be fussed over in a swanky shop like this? Besides, this woman had been kindness itself since they had first walked through the door.

Annie relaxed.

'I've been making me own clothes for donkey's years, and using the same auld pattern; but aye, you're probably right.' Her confidence returning, she stepped nearer the cupboard. She had willed herself to remain polite but aloof; that was until she saw the rows of clothes hanging on a gold-plated rail. Beside her Jane gasped audibly, for she too had never seen such grand clothes as these – not even in all the posh, well-known stores in Oxford Street.

Edna saw their open appreciation and felt a warm glow of pride. She searched through the rows of clothes, her hand resting on a silver-grey costume. It was a plain outfit, but the cut of the design and the feel of the cloth screamed quality.

'I think this will fit you, madam. Unless you don't like it. There are many outfits I can show you. I can also assure you that every garment you see is my own original design. So when you wear it for a party, or social occasion, you won't have to worry that another woman will turn up in the same costume.'

Annie let out a gusty laugh.

'I don't think there's any chance of that, love, not where we live.' Then her mood changed. Taking the soft material, she ran her hands over the smooth silk, her eyes wistful. She had never been a woman to covet expensive clothes. Raised in Ireland, one of eight children, living from hand to mouth, she had been grateful for any item of clothing. It had been the same when she married and started a family. Her top priority, like her mother before her, had been to make sure her children were fed and warm. Their clothes had either been bought from Paddy's Market, or she had made them herself. So the notion of one day wearing fine clothes had never even entered her mind.

Now, looking at the outfit draped over her arms, Annie felt a sudden urge to cry. She again felt the soft fabric, then she too was in a cubicle. For five long, agonising minutes she stood still, holding the material as if it would break if handled too roughly. Then she was pulling off her old clothes with indecent haste.

Slightly nervous at being left on her own, Jane gulped loudly as the posh lady said, 'Well now, miss. Have you seen anything that has caught your eye?'

There was so much genuine warmth in the woman's voice that Jane responded happily, 'Oh, yes, lady.' She let her fingers lovingly caress the rows of gowns. 'Everything. Just about everything in your beautiful shop.'

She let out a joyous laugh, and the sound brought a feeling of awe and admiration to Edna's heart for this girl who couldn't be much more than fifteen and was afflicted with such a terrible blight on her beautiful face.

'May I try on this one, please?' Jane was holding a sky-blue linen dress up against her slim figure.

'But of course, my dear, of course.'

Edna led the excited girl to the only empty cubicle left. As she had done with Josie and Annie, she pulled the curtain across to afford privacy, even though the shop was closed. Then she stood back and waited, and was surprised to find her stomach churning with pleasurable excitement. She hadn't felt this way for years.

After several minutes the end curtain was pulled back and Edna found she was holding her breath, then Josie stepped out and Edna exhaled.

'Does . . . does it look all right?' Josie asked hesitantly.

Edna's hands were folded across her flat stomach as she surveyed the woman before her. The transformation was extraordinary. The red dress fitted as if it had been made for her, except for the length. It was a little short, just covering Josie's ankles, revealing the soft red leather shoes beneath.

'You look magnificent, madam. It only needs lengthening a bit, but that can soon be remedied.'

Josie looked down.

'Actually, I prefer it like this. It would be a shame to drag the skirt along the street. It would be filthy before I got home. Besides . . .' She smiled shyly. 'What's the point of wearing these lovely shoes if they're gonna be covered up? The only thing I'm worried about is that I've lost quite a lot of weight lately. Now I'm feeling better I'm bound to put it back on again,' she said, adding almost apologetically, 'I do like me food.'

'Well then, madam, perhaps this outfit will harden your resolve to keep slim.'

They fell silent, and for a few minutes it seemed as if they were the only two in the room. Then the moment was shattered by Annie's booming voice.

'Will someone help me with these confounded fastenings. Jasus, but a body could tie themselves in knots trying to keep their modesty.'

Annie came trailing out of the cubicle, her hands behind her back, fiddling with the hooks that bound the dress together.

Edna sprang forward.

'Here, madam, let me help. It is quite easy once one gets the hang of it.'

Annie grunted.

'If ye say so, but I don't have the time to waste—'

She lifted her head and stopped, her jaw dropping at the sight of Josie.

'Holy Mary! Begod, Josie, sure an' ye look like a princess.'

Josie blushed, her head swinging from side to side. She wasn't used to compliments.

'Don't ye be shaking your head at me, Josie Guntrip. Ye look gorgeous, doesn't she?' Annie turned to Edna. 'Will ye tell her, woman?'

Before Edna could confirm Annie's remark, she heard the swish of a curtain, then Jane was staring at Josie, her expression mirroring that of her mother.

'Ooh, Josie,' she breathed quietly in admiration.

A sudden clapping of hands brought their attention back to the proprietor.

'Now, now, ladies. We still have work to do. If you will permit me?'

She looked to Josie. A little bewildered, Josie followed the prim, kindly woman to the saloon, and let herself be seated in a blue velvet chair. She gazed at her reflection in the gilt-edged mirror. She hardly recognised herself. Then she felt gentle hands undo her French pleat, allowing her hair to fall in soft curls framing her face. But Edna hadn't finished yet. Her steps light, she pulled open a drawer and took out an embroidered box. Taking out a sparkling jet necklace, she placed it around Josie's neck. Then she fastened a pair of matching earrings to Josie's lobes and stood back for a better look.

143

There was a silence in the air that was almost palpable.

Josie stared back at her reflection in wonderment and felt tears prick the back of her eyes – and hers weren't the only eyes in the room that were moist.

Edna busied herself fastening the back of Annie's dress. It wouldn't do to show emotion in front of customers.

'You will need a corset, madam,' she was saying to Annie. 'It will give the costume a better fit. I can also attach a bustle, if you like.'

Standing in front of a full-length mirror, Annie stared at her reflection, hardly recognising herself. She gave a short laugh to cover her embarrassment.

'Me backside's big enough, thanks very much, and I've never worn a corset in all me life.'

With the dress fastened, Annie could see the rolls of fat around her stomach and waist, her excess weight emphasised by the cut of the expensive cloth, and felt a wave of shame. There was a time when she'd had a beautiful figure. Then the children had started to arrive, and with each birth she had put on a little more weight. It had been a gradual process and Paddy had never complained. Oh, he'd teased her from time to time about her expanding figure, but his words had always been spoken with love.

'If you would like to try on another outfit, madam, I have a selection in larger sizes.' Edna was watching Annie with concern, as if she could read the older woman's thoughts.

Annie looked again at her reflection. It was a lovely costume. From the moment she had seen it, she had set her heart on having it.

'No thanks. This one will do just fine. But you're right about me needing a corset. You'd best be getting me the strongest one you've got, 'cos it's going to have its work cut out to make this body look presentable.'

CHAPTER TEN

The women had entered the shop just after twelve. It was now two o'clock, and they were still there, sitting in their new finery, drinking tea from bone china cups and generally getting on like a house on fire. Josie had parted with almost thirty pounds as if they were shillings, and she didn't begrudge a penny of it.

In the past two hours all formality had been dropped. Every one of the women had had a hugely enjoyable time, and, if asked about their day, each would have given a different version.

Annie had experienced her first day up the West End; and her last, for all she'd enjoyed it. She had come up here for Josie's sake, but even though the owner of this place had been kind, the East End markets were where she belonged. But she would always remember this day, and she had a new outfit to remind her. She couldn't wait to show it off to Paddy and the lads, though where she would get the chance to wear it she didn't know. Unless Pat married that loose piece. It would almost be worth having Freda for a daughter-in-law if it gave her the chance to show off her new look. She shuddered at the thought.

Jane, on the other hand, couldn't wait to show off her new blue dress, and the soft lemon blouse and skirt Josie had so kindly bought for her. But the clothes weren't the only new things Jane had acquired; for Edna Walker had kindly shown the young girl how to apply make-up. Annie hadn't been too pleased about that, as she considered any woman wearing make-up to be either an actress or a woman of loose morals. But even she had grudgingly admitted that the expert application of foundation did wonders in toning down Jane's birthmark, giving her daughter some much-needed confidence.

But it was Josie's day, and what a day it had been. And it wasn't over yet.

When it was time to leave, both Josie and Annie prepared to change back into their everyday clothes, but Edna Walker wouldn't hear of it. Before they could protest, she had their old clothes packed neatly away in expensive-looking carrier bags and was shooing them out of the shop, a wide smile on her face.

Closing the door, Edna went to the window to watch the three women walk away. When they had disappeared from view, she dropped the curtain. Still smiling, she began to tidy up before leaving for home.

When the door closed behind them, Jane, with the

exuberance of youth, almost skipped away from the shop, eager to show off her new appearance. Josie and Annie, on the other hand, stayed rooted to the spot, feeling exposed and uncomfortable. Then Josie felt a warm, rough hand grasp hers and gained a modicum of comfort from the gesture.

Like children pushed out into the world for the first time, they walked slowly behind Jane, their steps quickening as they realised that, instead of looking out of place, they now blended in with the affluent pedestrians.

Becoming braver with each step, they began to relax, their postures straightening, their heads held high. Gentlemen raised their hats as they passed, and Annie couldn't help but hope she would run into that snooty pair who had treated her like dirt. But what really lifted their spirits was when they walked past a group of workmen, and elicited loud, appreciative whistles; plus a few colourful comments that made Josie blush.

As they continued their journey, Josie attracted many admiring glances. She cut a splendid figure in the dark red costume and matching silk hat. She hadn't been sure about the hat at first. It was small and elegant, with a wisp of lace adorning the edge, and complemented the outfit perfectly.

With the sun picking out the flecks of gold in her shiny brown hair, she presented a splendid sight.

A sudden rumbling in her stomach reminded Jane that none of them had eaten since breakfast.

'I don't know about you two, but I'm starving. Let's find a restaurant. There must be dozens of them up here.'

'You're being very generous with Josie's money, aren't ye, love?' Annie remonstrated with her daughter.

'It's all right, Annie. I was thinking the same meself. I wouldn't have gone into one of those places before. But now . . .' She grinned. 'If I say so meself, we've scrubbed up well. We're as good as any of this lot. Besides, I'm sweating in this lot. I wish I'd asked Mrs Walker to put the coat in with me old clothes now. So let's find a restaurant before we pass out or lose our nerve; or both.'

Annie nodded in agreement, the sweat pouring from her.

'You're right enough there, love. Though I'm not sure if I'll be able to sit down in this blasted corset. I feel like a trussed-up turkey waiting to go into the oven.'

She stopped for a rest and caught sight of herself in the window of a bakery, and suddenly she forgot her discomfort. Even though she knew she looked grand, she still wasn't entirely happy with the grey hat that accompanied her new look. To her mind it looked like a dead pigeon perched on her head, and she said as much to Josie and Jane. Her comment brought forth gales of laughter from the younger women, which in turn attracted attention from passers-by.

The women walked on, still laughing. They hadn't gone more than a few steps before stopping outside a swish-looking restaurant.

'This one looks all right . . . doesn't it?' Josie asked tentatively.

Annie pressed her nose against the patterned glass,

149

trying to see inside, though with no success. Instead she turned her attention to the menu displayed outside.

'Jasus! Would ye look at these prices. It's downright robbery . . .'

'Annie!' Josie laughed. 'I doubt any of us will be coming back up here in a hurry, so let's round off the day with a nice meal.'

Before Annie could protest further, Josie, taking a deep breath to steady her nerves, had opened the glass-panelled door and ushered Jane and Annie inside.

They were greeted by a waiter impeccably dressed in a starched white shirt, black waistcoat and pinstriped trousers with a front pleat so sharp they looked as if they could cut paper.

'Good afternoon, ladies. If you would care to follow me, I'll lead you to your table; unless of course you've made a reservation.'

Flustered, Annie turned to Josie for guidance, but Josie's attention was elsewhere. Following her friend's gaze, Annie jumped as her own eyes came to rest on a couple sitting far back in the corner, their hands entwined, their heads close together in intimate conversation. The man said something then laughed. Picking up his glass, Rory idly glanced towards the door and almost jumped out of his chair at the sight of his mother, sister and Josie framed in the doorway.

CHAPTER ELEVEN

Rory looked into his wallet for the umpteenth time, his stomach churning as he realised how quickly his savings were dwindling. If he continued spending at this rate, he would be broke within a month; if not sooner. He had been giving his mother a bit extra along with his housekeeping every week since he'd first started work. Since Cathy had come back he had stopped this practice. He had been prepared for an inquisition from his mother, and that first week had braced himself for a ear-bashing. But Annie had just looked at the money, then up at him, before turning her back on him. And that had scared him far more than his mother's temper ever could.

For weeks he had been expecting some comment about where he was disappearing off to for hours on end, because before Cathy had come home he had spent all his free time with his brothers. He knew, without a shadow of a doubt, that his entire family must be aware of his renewed relationship with

Cathy, yet so far no one had said a word – not even that mouthy tart Pat had hitched up with.

A rush of guilt and shame engulfed him as he recalled the day he had asked his mother for his bank book. In all the years he'd been saving, he had never before taken the book from his mother. He'd frequently asked to look at it, to see how much he had saved, but had been happy to leave it with his mother. He had liked the idea of having money behind him. It made him feel secure; made him feel important. Now, after nearly ten years of saving, he had blown most of it in a matter of weeks. What would happen when it was all gone? Would Cathy still want him then?

A wave of panic swept over him, and he felt beads of perspiration break out on his forehead. She was due to leave tomorrow. Back to that fat, rich bastard in Knightsbridge! His mouth tightened into grim lines. He hated the thought of her being mauled by any man; he hated her leaving; but as much as he loathed the idea, he had to admit that her going would give him some much-needed breathing space. If he was to keep her then he had to find some way to make more money. Yet even as his mind worked furiously, Rory knew he would never be able to find the sort of money to hang on to a woman like Cathy. Worse still, he loathed himself for trying to buy her love. If it was some other man in his place, Rory would look on that man with scorn, mocking him for being gutless.

His hands balled into fists at his sides. It was ironic in a perverse kind of way. He had left Josie to be with Cathy. Now, in a twist of fate, Josie had come into the kind of money he needed to keep Cathy with him. Although he knew that even if he had the sort of sum Josie had inherited, it still wouldn't be enough. Cathy was used to having unlimited funds at her disposal. So even if he'd had Josie's good fortune, sooner or later the money would run out; and Cathy along with it.

He squirmed inside as he remembered how hurt Josie had been when he'd left. Now she was out with his mother and sister, treating them to new outfits, and not out of any spiteful intention to rub his nose in it, but because she felt a genuine warmth for his family; even after what he had done.

Pulling himself together, he took one last look in his wallet before setting off to meet Cathy.

She was waiting for him at their usual spot, on a bench in Victoria Park. He watched her for a while, hoping his feelings for her would diminish, but the sight of her only strengthened his love and resolve to make her his wife.

But how? In God's name, how?

Cathy turned, her face lighting up at the sight of him, and Rory's heart flipped over.

'Hello, darling.' She reached up to kiss his cheek.

'Hello, yourself,' he replied, his eyes devouring her.

Linking arms, they walked out of the wrought-iron gates to wait for a tram. Rory, although carefree and cheerful on the outside, was inwardly praying they wouldn't bump into anyone they knew. That fear was the reason they always spent their time up West; that and the fact that there were better restaurants and shops. No wonder Rory was fast running out of

153

money. Cathy had become used to the good life. It was a life he couldn't afford.

'So, where are you taking me today?' Cathy asked impishly.

Rory stared down into that lovely face and his heart skipped a beat. He couldn't let her go; no matter what the cost. And he would use any means in his power to keep the woman he loved more than life itself.

'How about a meal, and maybe go to the theatre afterwards – if I've any money left?'

He smiled, but Cathy was quick to note the anxiety in his eyes. Yet instead of offering words of reassurance, she smiled back at him.

'That sounds wonderful, just the sort of day I like most.'

They strolled arm in arm towards the nearest tram stop, talking and laughing, yet beneath their carefree appearance neither of them could relax properly until they were safely away from the East End. For Rory wasn't the only one who was afraid of being spotted. Cathy was fully aware of the feelings of her former neighbours. Any one of them would be delighted to inform Jonathan of her activities during his absence. And she couldn't risk that happening. Despite her genuine feelings for Rory, she had become used to the high life, and wasn't about to go back to being poor.

They got off the tram in Oxford Street and spent an hour walking around the shops while Cathy did a bit of window-shopping; which was all she could do, considering Rory's finances.

'Ooh, look, Rory. Isn't that hat lovely?' She was admiring a large floppy hat adorned with feathers.

'Yeah, and so is the price,' Rory answered quickly, adding, 'I'll bet there'll be a few dozen pigeons feeling the cold tonight.'

Cathy giggled.

'Oh, Rory, you do make me laugh.'

'I'm glad of that, darlin'. Now, I don't know about you, but me stomach thinks me throat's been cut. Let's find somewhere to eat before I pass out from starvation.'

'You must have been reading my mind. That's just what I was thinking.'

Minutes later they were entering a smart restaurant and being welcomed warmly by the maître d'.

'Good afternoon, sir, madam.' He led them towards a table, pulling out the chair for Cathy, and when they were both seated asked politely, 'May I suggest the salmon, sir?' He deferred to Rory, handing him a large, gold-trimmed menu.

The respectful tone of his voice gave Rory a sense of importance. It was a heady experience, and one that made him realise why money was so important to Cathy.

'Yes, that will be fine, thank you.' He spoke in what he hoped was a reasonably educated voice. 'And we'll go straight to the main course, please.'

'Of course. And the wine menu, sir?'

'A bottle of the house white, please,' Rory said quickly, before Cathy could speak.

'Very good, sir.' The waiter bowed to Cathy.

'You were quick off the mark, weren't you?' Cathy said, clearly annoyed. 'I wouldn't have asked for an expensive wine, if that's what you were worried about.'

Careful to keep his voice lowered, Rory leaned forward.

'Don't be daft. I didn't think any such thing. You—'

'I'm going to the rest room. I'll have plenty of time of freshen up, seeing as we're not even having starters.'

'Cathy . . .' Rory reached out for her wrist, then winced as she pulled away from him.

He watched her walk elegantly away, her curvy figure and golden hair attracting the attention of every man present, including the waiters. His lips tight, he felt a gnawing ache in the pit of his stomach, coupled with a wave of despair. Cathy could have any man she wanted. What chance did he have?

Tomorrow she would be gone, back to her posh house in Knightsbridge and the man who owned it – and her!

'Sorry, darling.' Cathy was back, sooner than he'd expected. Reaching across the table, she said softly, 'I'm a bit on edge, you know, what with having to go back home tomorrow.'

Rory tightened his fingers around the slim hand.

'Then don't go,' he said urgently. 'Stay here with me. I can look after you. Oh, not like the other fellow, but—'

The soft hand withdrew, and with it Rory's hopes.

'Don't start that again, Rory. You promised you wouldn't pressure me. I'm going back tomorrow afternoon, and that's the end of it. If you can't handle it, then you'll never see me again.'

A chill had entered her voice, silently warning Rory to back off. But Rory wasn't to be deterred so easily. He had too strong a character to give up without a fight; even when he knew it was hopeless.

But he had forgotten that Cathy too possessed that same trait. Before he could say anything further, she said, 'I mean it, Rory. If you leave things the way they are, we can still keep seeing each other. Jonathan's always going away on business trips. He doesn't mind me staying behind, providing I'm there when he gets back. We have an unspoken agreement. I don't ask him what he does when he's away, and he doesn't ask me.' She gave a slight movement of her shoulders. 'I know it wouldn't suit everyone, but it works for us. We can all be happy without anyone getting hurt. But if you have a problem with that arrangement, then it's best if you say so now. It's up to you. Then we'll know exactly where we stand. I've been honest with you, you can't say I haven't. I've been poor and I don't like it; what's more, I'm never going to be poor again, not if I can help it. So, like I said, it's up to you now.'

Rory stared hard into her brilliant green eyes, eyes that were filled with determination; and he knew she meant every word she'd said.

A discreet cough saved him from replying, giving him a bit of breathing space. Not that he needed it. Though his mind screamed at him to gather what was left of his pride and walk away from the woman who dominated his every waking moment, he remained silent until their meal arrived, moving back in his chair to allow the waiter room to place the beautifully presented salmon dish in front of him.

'Enjoy your meal, sir, madam.' The waiter gave a slight bow, and the respectful gesture, coupled with a desperate need to impress Cathy, made Rory reck-less.

'Hang on a minute,' he said, as the waiter was about to uncork the wine. 'I've changed me mind. Take that away and bring a bottle of champagne.'

The moment the words left his mouth Rory could have bitten his tongue off. He'd be lucky if he had ten bob left in his wallet after paying for this lot. So much for the theatre. Then he glanced across the table and saw the love and pride reflected in Cathy's eyes, and suddenly he didn't care about the money. His self-esteem was further boosted by the almost servile attitude of the waiter.

'Very good, sir.' Again he gave a slight movement of his head in deference to Rory.

'You didn't have to do that, darling.' Cathy, her eyes shining, smiled warmly. 'I know you can't really afford it, and that's what makes it all the more appre-ciated.'

Rory winked.

'You don't get this sort of service in the pie an' mash shop, do yer?'

They had finished their meal and were on their last glass of champagne when Rory, his gaze idly taking in his sumptuous surroundings, saw three women entering the restaurant. As he cast an eye over the well-dressed trio, he lifted his glass to his lips. Then his neck seemed to jerk back on his shoul-ders as he took another look, not believing his eyes. As the sparkling liquid slid down his throat, he gulped, then coughed, causing the champagne to spurt from his mouth and dribble down his chin in an undignified manner. Heads turned as Rory continued to cough loudly, and Cathy, embarrassed and angered by the undignified spectacle, leaned forward.

'Pack it in, Rory,' she hissed. 'Everyone's looking at us. You're embarrassing me.'

Still spluttering and coughing, Rory managed to croak, 'Me mum's here. And Josie and Jane . . . Look, over by the door.'

Cathy, growing angrier by the minute snapped, 'Don't be stupid. What would your mum be doing in a place like this, or the other two for that matter?'

She glanced dismissively over to the door, then blinked and looked again, and her jaw dropped as she realised Rory hadn't been joking. Her practised gaze roamed over the three women, recognising the quality of their clothing, the designs embodying the height of fashion and, like Rory, she could hardly believe her eyes.

But it was them all right. Even with their expensive finery, there was no mistaking the stout, formidable Annie Flynn, nor the scarred face of her daughter. Cathy's eyes narrowed. Someone had applied make-up in an attempt to soften the effect of the birthmark, and although it was still markedly evident, Cathy grudgingly had to admit that it was no longer so glaringly obvious. Then she glanced sharply at Rory and saw that his eyes were fixed on Josie, and she felt a surge of anger and jealousy.

Rory couldn't take his eyes off Josie. She looked stunning. Gone was the dowdy girl he had known since childhood. In her place stood a tall, elegant woman dressed in a deep red outfit, with long jet earrings dangling from her ear lobes, and a matching necklace adorning her smooth, creamy throat. The overall effect was breathtaking. But it was Josie's hair, falling around her shoulders in soft chestnut curls, that turned his mind back to that party long ago, when he had first realised what an attractive young woman she was. He also remembered her face as men who previously hadn't given her the time of day thronged around her. She had looked lovely then, her pretty features enhanced by her genuine fright and vulnerability at finding herself the centre of attention.

He squirmed on his chair as his eyes met Josie's. But the Josie returning his stare was no longer the shy, timid young girl, but a confident woman, at ease with herself and her environment, as if dining out in a place such as this was an everyday occurrence.

Rory would have been surprised if he could have seen beneath the confident façade. For inside, Josie was feeling exactly the same as she had on that evening that now seemed like a lifetime ago.

'Holy Mary! Begod! I'll skelp the head off his shoulders when I get him home, so I will, the sly beggar.' Annie bristled at the scene, her worst fears finally realised. For a moment she forgot where she was and started forward, only to feel her arm held fast.

'It's all right, Annie.' Josie was staring over her head, her face composed. 'I've been looking forward to a nice meal to round off the day. I'm not about to turn tail and run now. Besides . . .' she added bravely, trying to smile, 'we're all hungry, and we'd look a bit out of place in the chippie.'

Annie stood still, then stared down at herself and the silver-grey costume that clung to her ample figure as if it had been made for her. Drawing herself up, she thrust her chin out proudly and, addressing herself to the curious maître d', whose eyes lingered briefly on Josie, said, 'We'll be wanting one of your tables, lad. And look lively, we've not had a bite to eat since breakfast.'

'Certainly, madam.' He clicked his fingers at one of the ever-hovering waiters. 'Show these ladies to table twelve,' he commanded, thankful there was a vacancy due to an earlier cancellation. Somehow he didn't think this woman would have taken kindly to being shown the door.

Following the smartly dressed waiter, the three women walked slowly to the centre of the restaurant. To get to their table they had to pass Rory and Cathy. Josie and Jane completely ignored them, but Annie, being the woman she was, couldn't resist commenting.

'By, but I thought a place like this was supposed to be particular who they let in. It looks like I was wrong.'

Rory's head was bowed, showing the brick-red of his neck. But Cathy glared at the retreating backs of the three woman, her face stony.

Rory was already fumbling for his wallet.

'Drink up, we're leaving,' he said abruptly.

'No we bleeding ain't.' Cathy spoke through clenched teeth. 'I'm not having those three cows chasing me outta here like I was a piece of dirt.' In her angry state, she had reverted to her cockney mode of speaking. 'And another thing, how come they're all dressed up like they was royalty? Where'd they get the money from, eh?'

Ignoring her petulant voice, Rory beckoned the waiter over and asked for the bill.

He too still couldn't believe the transformation of all three of them, especially his mother. She looked every inch the lady – until she opened her mouth. Still, knowing his mum, it could have been a lot worse.

'What you laughing at?'

Rory, looking through his wallet, glanced up at Cathy in surprise.

'I didn't know I was,' he answered curtly. 'And don't talk about me mum and Jane like that, all right?'

Cathy curled her top lip and sneered, 'What! No mention of yer old girlfriend? Good old Josie the doormat.'

Rory was growing increasingly fraught. He had planned to make the most of this day, not knowing when he would see Cathy again. Instead everything had gone wrong. His instincts and every moral fibre in his body urged him to defend Josie, but he couldn't risk alienating Cathy any further. Hating himself, he spoke, his voice low.

'If yer must know, Josie inherited some money after her mum died; happy now?'

'No I ain't. And d'yer know why? 'Cos it's a bleeding waste, that's why. What's an old frump like Josie Guntrip gonna do with it? She wouldn't know what a good time was if it jumped up and slapped her in the face. She'll probably just put it in the bank and sit at home for the rest of her life letting the interest on it mount up, then leave it all to some . . . some cats' home.' She paused, her breath rapid, her entire being consumed with envy. 'Just how much did her mum leave her anyway?'

Feeling like a child caught stealing from his mother's purse, Rory went on the defensive.

'I don't know, and I didn't ask,' he lied. He was already in enough trouble with his mother without going back on his word to keep secret the amount of money Josie had come into. 'It ain't none of my business . . . or yours, for that matter. Now drink up or I'll go without you.' His words sounded hollow, even to his own ears, but Cathy didn't even hear him.

Finishing off the last of the champagne, she pushed back her chair, saying spitefully, 'Well, rich or poor, it won't make no difference to Josie. I mean to say, just look at her. It'll take more than some fancy clothes ter make that ugly cow look—'

'She looks all right ter me,' Rory snapped back angrily. 'In fact I think she looks bleeding beautiful. And judging by the rest of the men here, I ain't the only one ter think so.'

Her eyes blazing with fury, Cathy stood up.

'Well, don't let me stop yer. You go and see if she'll take yer back. I don't expect she'll get many other offers, unless it's for her money. Go on then. She'll probably throw herself round your neck in gratitude.'

Storming from the restaurant, heads turned as Cathy swept past them. Scenes at Café Rouge were almost unheard of, which made this unexpected incident vastly entertaining. Rory felt as if every eye in the room was on him. In particular, a pair of Irish eyes. He could almost feel the heat burning a hole in the back of his neck. Damn! What a day it had been. He had been determined to make this last day of Cathy's visit special. Instead it had turned into a complete balls-up. And he still had to face his mother's wrath when he got home.

Maybe if he hurried he could catch up with Cathy and salvage what was left of the day. She was probably waiting for him outside. She would make him suffer further, but he didn't care as long as they made up. Cheered by the thought, he picked up his wallet again and glanced down at the piece of paper lying on a small silver platter; then he took another look and swallowed hard. His stomach lurched and a wave of panic set in as he realised he hadn't enough money to pay the bill.

Outwardly calm, Rory fingered the five-pound note in his wallet, hoping against hope he might have another tucked behind it. He had imagined five pounds would be ample to pay for a meal, even in a place such as this. And it would have been if he hadn't tried to play the big man and order that blasted champagne. That alone had cost four pounds. Rory didn't even like the stuff. He preferred a pint of Guinness any day of the week. Right at this moment he wished the ground would open up and swallow him. His embarrassment was heightened by the presence of his fellow diners, who had just witnessed Cathy's angry departure. But the ultimate humiliation, in his eyes, was the knowledge that Josie, the woman he had dumped, was watching his discomfort. He fingered the note again, his panic mounting. Even with the two sovereigns in his pocket, he still didn't have enough to pay the bill.

'Is anything wrong, sir?' The waiter was standing patiently, the look on his face clearly showing that he had witnessed this scene countless times before. But on most occasions it was regular patrons who found themselves unable to pay their bill, and under those circumstances the establishment was only too pleased to add any shortfall to a patron's account. This man, however, was a stranger, and a common one at that, despite his attempt at adopting a refined tone.

Sitting only a few tables away, Josie could see at once the dilemma Rory was in, and her heart went out to him. She should have revelled in his predicament, but she couldn't derive any pleasure from watching his silent suffering.

'I'm just going to the rest room. You order for me, Annie. I'm not fussy what I eat. I won't be long.'

Annie had her nose in the large gold-edged menu, her eyes stretched wide.

'Will ye look at these prices, Josie. Jasus! Two bob for a bowl of soup, it's daylight robbery . . .'

'Don't worry about the prices, Annie. It's my treat, so make the most of it, 'cos I won't be taking you here again,' Josie replied absently.

Weaving around the tables, she came to a stop beside Rory. Tapping the waiter on his arm, she asked, 'Excuse me. Could you tell me where the ladies' room is, please?'

Rory winced as he heard her voice. So she had come to gloat after all. Well, he couldn't blame her.

'Of course, madam. It's to your right, just around

the corner. You can't miss it, it's well signposted.'

'Thank you. Lord, it's hot, isn't it?' Josie had her bag open as she searched for a handkerchief. She had positioned herself in front of the waiter with her back to Rory. Wiping her forehead, she smiled. 'Still, mustn't complain, must we? It'll probably be pouring with rain tomorrow. Thank you.'

She turned and bumped against Rory's side. 'Oh, I'm sorry,' she apologised, her hand going to his arm to steady herself.

Rory's eyes narrowed in bewilderment, then he jumped as he felt something being pressed into his hand; then she was gone. His heart racing, he looked down at the five-pound note crumpled in his fist and experienced a deep wave of relief.

Although his heart was still thumping against his ribs, his face betrayed none of his emotions as he casually threw the two five-pound notes on to the silver platter.

By the time the waiter returned with Rory's change, Josie was back at her table, her eyes studiously fixed on the menu.

Leaving a half-crown tip for the waiter, Rory left the restaurant expecting Cathy to be waiting for him outside. But there was no sign of her. And much to his surprise, he wasn't as disappointed as he'd imagined he would be. Instead his mind was on Josie. There weren't many women who, given the circumstances, would have helped him out of his predicament. But Josie had always been possessed of a kind nature.

He walked on in search of Cathy, but it was Josie's face that kept floating in front of his mind. First thing tomorrow morning he would go round and pay her back the money that had saved him from the utmost humiliation. It would be an awkward situation for both of them, but knowing Josie, she would make his visit as comfortable and cordial as was humanly possible.

Then he spotted Cathy ahead of him, and all other thoughts were swept from his mind.

CHAPTER TWELVE

'By, Josie love. It's been a grand day, so it has. I'll not be needing any rocking tonight. I could drop off to sleep right now, I'm that tired.'

'I know how you feel, Annie. I can hardly keep me eyes open,' Josie replied.

They were in Josie's kitchen, reliving the events of the day, and had been for the past hour. Then Jane spoke, her voice filled with joyous laughter.

'Well, I won't be able to sleep a wink tonight. I'm too excited to go to bed yet. Anyway, it's only just gone eight.' Her eyes twinkling, she added, 'Still, I suppose when I get to your age, I'll be the same as you two.'

Pushing her chair back, Jane stood up.

'Do you mind if I go home, Josie? I want to show off my new dress to Dad.'

'Of course I don't mind,' Josie replied, smiling. If the truth be told, she couldn't wait to be on her own. Seeing Rory with that trollop had hurt her more than she had imagined it would. It had taken every ounce of self-control she possessed to stop herself from breaking down in tears. That emotion had passed now, but the hurt still remained.

'I'll see you tomorrow, Josie,' Jane said from the doorway. 'Oh, and don't forget what I said about you setting up your own shop, will you? At least think about it, promise?'

Josie looked at the earnest face and nodded.

'I will. Think about it, I mean. But not tonight, eh?'

'All right. See you in a minute, Mum. Don't be too long, will you? Dad's probably dying to see you, and I want to be there to see his face when he claps eyes on you.'

Then, like a dog let out of its kennel, she was gone.

'Whew!' Josie slumped in her chair. 'She makes me tired just watching her. What I'd give to be young again.'

Annie shot her an angry glance.

'What are ye talking about, girl? Why, anyone would think ye was my age to hear ye talk. Ye're just tired is all. A good night's sleep and ye'll be as right as rain come morning. Speaking of which, I'd best be getting meself off home. I just hope Paddy doesn't want to take me to the pub the night. By the time I get this lot off, the pub will be closed. Lord only knows how I'm going to get out of this corset contraption. Paddy will have a field day when he sees it. Still, I mustn't stay here talking. You'll be wanting to have some time to yourself, I'm sure.'

'Well, I am tired, Annie. It's not every day I get to go up West and spend money without worrying about every penny.'

Since leaving the restaurant, Rory's name hadn't been mentioned, and Josie was grateful for Annie and Jane's consideration for her feelings. But there was one thing that had been playing on Josie's mind concerning Annie, and now they were alone she broached the subject.

'Earlier on, you seemed to have something on your mind. And before you say it was the heat, just remember who you're talking too. Something was worrying you, and whatever it is, I'd like to help if I can.'

When she saw the look of awkwardness on her friend's face, Josie jumped to the wrong conclusion. Biting on her lower lip, she picked her words carefully.

'Look, Annie, if you're short of money, I'd be only too pleased to—'

Startled, Annie stared at Josie in amazement.

'Good God, love. Whatever put that thought into your mind? How can I be short of money with four men bringing in a wage every week?'

Seeing Josie wasn't convinced, Annie thought furiously of an excuse to explain her earlier absent behaviour. Then it came to her.

'All right, Josie. I'll not lie to ye. I'm worried sick that our Pat'll take it into his head to get married in a Protestant church. That loose piece he's taken up with would make him do it just to spite me and Paddy. And ye know how I feel about me religion. If Pat doesn't get married in a Catholic church then in the eyes of God and the Church he'll not be married at all. And it'd break me heart if that happened.'

'Oh, Annie,' Josie said, her heart going out to her

friend. 'I'm sure Pat would never do that. He knows how much it would hurt you and Paddy. He's a good man and a kind one. But if you're that worried, why don't you have a word with him? At least then it'd put your mind at rest. Besides, he thinks the world of you. There's no way he'd put Freda's feelings before yours.'

Annie smiled wryly.

'That's where you're wrong, Josie love. When a man gets married, his mother has to accept she's going to take second place to his wife; and that's the way it should be. No man worth his salt would stay tied to his mother's apron strings once he's wed. There's nothing I can do, so I'll not be worrying meself until the time comes. Maybe if we're lucky Pat'll come to his senses and give her the push.' She heaved herself to her feet, puffing heavily. 'Jasus, but I'll be glad to get back into me own clothes, I can hardly breathe in this contraption. I hope Paddy doesn't want to take me down the pub—' She stopped in mid sentence and grinned. 'I've already said that, haven't I? Lord help me. It's a sure sign of old age when a body starts repeating themselves . . . And what is it that's making ye laugh, Josie Guntrip? Is it the mickey you're taking out of an auld woman?'

Trying to keep a straight face, Josie replied, 'I wouldn't dare, Annie. It sounds to me as if it's you that wants to go to the pub to show off your new clothes, only yer don't want to admit it. You'll be going to the pub tonight, and you know it. I feel sorry for poor Paddy, 'cos he'll be getting an earful all night for dragging you out. And you'll be having the time of your life seeing all the other women green with envy. I'm right, ain't I?'

Annie bridled, her mouth opening and closing without uttering a word. Then she let out a loud raucous laugh.

'Aye, you're right enough. By, but I'm going to have the time of me life tonight. I can't wait to see the looks on them old biddies' faces when they see me. I just hope I can last the night without passing out.'

Josie walked Annie to the door. As she stepped out into the street behind Annie, she saw next door's curtains twitching and grinned smugly.

'I wish I could be a fly on the wall in that house. Old Ida must be having a fit. Still, she can make as much noise as she wants, it won't do her any good . . . Annie! What's wrong, you've gone as white as a sheet,' Josie cried in alarm as Annie staggered back against her. 'Look, come back in. I'll help you outta that corset. There's no point in looking good if it's gonna make you ill.'

Josie's worried voice brought Annie back to her senses. She'd forgotten all about that blasted letter until Ida's presence had brought all her fears flooding back.

Forcing herself to remain calm, she said, 'Don't fret yerself, love, I'm fine. And me corset's staying on. I've managed to put up with it this long, I can last another hour or so. Besides, I'll want to be looking me best when Paddy drags me down the pub, won't I?'

Josie relaxed, relieved that her dearest friend was all right.

'Why don't ye come with us, Josie? Sure an' I won't

feel so out of place if you're with me. Aw, c'mon, love, it'll do ye good to get out for a while.'

Taken aback by Annie's offer, Josie stuttered, 'Oh, no, Annie. Thanks for asking, but . . . but . . . like I said, I'm tired. Anyway, it wasn't five minutes ago you was saying how you could hardly keep your eyes open.'

Annie flapped her hand in Josie's face.

'Oh, that was before. I feel much better now.' She put her head to one side, saying, 'C'mon, love, say ye'll come. I could do with some moral support. I'll send Shaun over for ye in about fifteen minutes.'

Before she knew what she was saying, Josie found herself agreeing to go to the pub, yet even before she had closed the door she was already regretting her decision.

Knowing there was no way she could get out of her promise, she made a strong pot of tea, hoping the brew would help revive her flagging body. After her third cup, she sat back and waited for Shaun to arrive.

Josie hummed to herself as she got into bed. Settling down under the sheets, she thought back over the day. And an extraordinary day it had been. She was glad she had decided to go to the pub, although her heart had been hammering so hard when they first entered the Rose and Crown that she had thought everyone would hear it. She smiled happily as she recalled the looks she and Annie had received, and also the proud faces of Paddy and Shaun as they had lapped up the compliments from all the regulars.

There had been many probing questions as the customers had tried to find out where the money for their expensive clothes had come from, but Annie had skilfully sidetracked them all. On the way home, giggly from two brandies, she had nudged Josie, saying in a slurred voice, 'Let them wonder all they like. We could always say we've taken up a new pro . . . profession. What d'ye say, Josie? How d'ye think we . . . we'd do as women of the night?'

Josie had been mortified, but Paddy and Shaun had roared with laughter. Her smile faltered a little as she recalled the look of disappointment on Shaun's face when she'd declined his offer to walk her to her door. Turning her thoughts to more pleasant matters, she remembered what Jane had said about starting her own business. At first Josie had dismissed the idea, but the seed had been planted, and had been germinating at the back of her mind all day. Now, alone in her bed, the idea didn't seem so impossible. And the more she thought about it, the more excited she became.

Suddenly she was wide awake. Knowing she wouldn't be able to sleep, she got out of bed and padded down to the kitchen. With a mug of hot chocolate in her hand, she sipped at it slowly, her mind whirling at the enormity of what she was proposing to do. She would have to look into it properly, of course, and for that she would need legal advice. When she went to the bank on Monday morning she would see the manager and ask him what he thought of her idea. Even if he wasn't in a position to advise her, then he would surely know someone who could. After all, she wasn't planning to attempt the impossible. All she wanted was a small shop she could call her own. And what better business to start with than a tea shop? After all, her years working in Joe Lyons would come in very handy.

Her hand started to tremble, spilling a few drops of chocolate on her nightdress. Suddenly she wasn't so sure she was doing the right thing. Perhaps it would be better if she slept on it.

An hour later, just as she was drifting off to sleep, she sat bolt upright. Staring into the darkness of the room she said aloud, 'Sod it, I'm gonna go for it. Maybe the bank manager will tell me I'll be wasting me time and money, but if I don't ask then I'll never know.' Satisfied she had made the right decision, she lay back down and in minutes was fast asleep.

'Are ye coming back to bed, darlin'? It's after twelve.'

Paddy yawned as he looked tiredly at his wife sitting in her favourite armchair by the fireplace. He had put her to bed over two hours ago. She hadn't stirred an inch while he and Jane had valiantly struggled to get the rigid corset from her body, trying hard to keep their laughter down. As usual after having a few pints of beer, Paddy's bladder had woken him. Annie had still been asleep when he left to visit the toilet in the back yard. He hadn't been gone for more than a few minutes, yet when he returned there she was sitting silently in her chair, gazing into the empty grate.

'Annie love, did ye hear me?'

Annie stirred then turned to face her husband.

'Sorry, Paddy, what did ye say? I was miles away.'

'I said are ye coming back to bed? And what are ye doing down here at this time of night? Is something troubling ye?'

'No, I'm fine. You get back to bed, I'll be up shortly. I only came down for a cup of water. G'wan now, be off with ye.'

Paddy shrugged, then went back upstairs to his bed.

Left alone, Annie took the crumpled letter from her dressing gown pocket and, getting up, peered at it in the dim light of the mantle lamp. Turning the light up, she read it again, still not believing the words written on the plain piece of paper: 'This is my last will and testament. I, Elsie Guntrip, being of sound mind and body, do leave my savings, hidden in the base of my bed, and any money received from the sale of my house to Battersea Dogs' Home.' Directly under these words Elsie had signed her name, and at the bottom of the paper was Ida Black's scrawled signature.

Annie sat down, shaking her head in bewilderment. She had always know Elsie Guntrip to be a mean, spiteful woman. But for the love of God, what kind of woman would do such a thing to her own daughter? It was bad enough she had wanted to deny Josie her savings, but to leave her homeless as well defied belief. Annie's tired mind tried to decide what to do with her find. She was in a difficult position. Only she knew of the will, and it was up to her what she did with it. She had always been an honest and God-fearing woman, and she knew it was her duty to hand the will over to some kind of authority. Yet if she did, Josie would be left with nothing. Not even a roof over her head.

She heard the bed creak upstairs as Paddy turned over in his sleep. Then she saw Josie's face, alight with happiness and optimism for the future, and knew she couldn't take those hopes away from the woman who was as dear to her as her own child.

Her mind made up, Annie got to her feet once again. Twisting the page into a thin taper, she took the glass off the lamp and held the paper to the dwindling flame. It caught alight immediately and Annie watched dispassionately as it turned black around the edge as the fire snaked slowly upwards. When she could stand the heat no longer, Annie threw it into the empty grate and watched it burn. Once she was sure it was completely destroyed, she turned away and walked up the stairs, her feet heavy.

What she had done was wrong, but she was willing to live with that guilt.

She climbed into bed beside Paddy and cuddled up by his side. But though she was now desperately tired, sleep eluded her. She knew there would be many nights like this. She also knew she would cope. And every time she felt any sign of guilt, she would look at Josie and know she had done the right thing. Not in the eyes of the law; but surely in the eyes of God. And the Almighty's blessing was more important to her than any court.

CHAPTER THIRTEEN

Josie lay in bed waiting for the dawn to break, just as she had done every day for the past week. Rolling her head towards the window, she lay still, her eyes heavy and dry from lack of sleep.

This was the first day of the rest of her life, and her heart was pounding and she had butterflies in her stomach. She was scared and yet more excited than she'd ever been. At last she was going to have the chance to prove to herself that she was capable of making something of her life.

Throwing back the quilt, she shivered and reached for the dressing gown at the foot of the bed.

Padding down to the kitchen, she made a pot of tea and drank it from a mug while looking out of the kitchen window, watching the sun's thin rays trying to break though the grey clouds on this cold, dismal October morning. She debated about lighting the fire then decided against it. It wasn't worth the bother, seeing as she would be leaving the house in another hour and wouldn't be back until early evening; providing everything went well, she added silently. She drank the last of her tea, wondering if she should eat something. She had a busy day ahead of her, and if all went well she doubted she'd have time to eat. Then her stomach lurched nervously and she decided not to chance it. The way she was feeling she wasn't sure she would be able to keep anything down.

Rinsing the mug in the sink, she glanced at the clock and saw it was getting on for seven thirty. She quickened her movements. As she washed and dressed, she thought back over the last four months, hardly able to believe that finally, after numerous meetings with the bank manager and estate agents to locate premises within her price range – not to mention the sleepless nights and anxious, fraught days when she'd questioned her own actions – the day she had been both longing for and dreading was finally here.

Then, for some reason, her thoughts went back to the day they had seen Rory and Cathy Meadows in the restaurant, and the help she had given to a desperate Rory. At eight o'clock the following morning he had been on her doorstep, his face red, his expression sheepish as he had given her back the five pounds and thanked her profusely for her kindness in helping him out of a difficult situation. Josie hadn't asked him in, nor had he shown any desire to do so.

Her hand stopped in mid air, her fingers curled around her hairbrush at the memory. She could still clearly see his face as he'd tried to avoid her gaze. Her fingers tightened as she began brushing her hair with renewed vigour. Damn him! Of all the things to remember on an important day such as this! It was uncanny how Rory could still creep into her mind.

She had just pinned her hair into a French pleat when the sound of the knocker resounded through the house. Josie smiled with relief. She had hoped Jane and Annie would come early, for mother and daughter were as excited and anxious as she was. Smiling broadly, she opened the door and was nearly knocked off her feet as Jane flung herself at her, her arms encircling Josie's waist.

'Here, go easy, love,' Josie laughed. 'I wanna be in one piece when we open the shop . . . Or should I say tea rooms?'

'Will ye calm down, Jane,' Annie admonished her daughter, but there was no censure in her voice, for she too was experiencing an overwhelming anxiety. She knew just how important Josie's new venture was to her.

'Oh, sorry, Josie. I can't help it, I'm so excited I could just burst.'

'Well, don't get too excited, mate. If it all goes well you're gonna be needing all your energy just to stay on your feet.'

'Well! Are we going to stand around talking all morning? We've a shop to open, don't forget. And I've still all the ingredients to mix. There must be ten or more mixtures to prepare, and that's afore I even start cooking. I want everything to be fresh. We can't be serving stale cakes on our first day, else we'll be out of business afore we get started.'

Josie looked at Annie. She was wrapped up in her winter coat, a black shawl covering her head and most of her face, and Josie's heart went out to her. For there was no mistaking the fear and anxiety in the older woman's eyes.

'Yeah, you're right, Annie. I suppose I'm just nervous, but I can't put it off any longer.' Taking a deep breath, she said, 'All right, enough stalling. I'll just get me coat on, then we'll get going before me nerves get the better of me.'

It was a good twenty minutes by foot to the market. They could have taken the tram, but they were all too buoyed up to stand around waiting. The stalls were already out and doing a brisk business when they arrived, but most of the shops, with the exception of the bakery, wouldn't open their doors until nine. It was now just after eight o'clock. Thinking they wouldn't get much business until any customers had completed their shopping, Josie had decided to open the tea shop at ten. She would see how it went today before putting an hours of business sign in the window.

'Well! This is it,' Josie said, unable to hide the anxiety in her voice. Taking the keys from her handbag, she opened the door.

Annie made straight for the kitchen, anxious to start preparing the ingredients for the various cakes they were planning to sell. She was a good cook, but her forte was mainly plain, nourishing food. For the last few weeks she had been trying out recipes from Mrs Beeton's cookery book; a birthday present from the boys many years ago. At the time she couldn't imagine ever having any use for it. Now she blessed her sons' gift. It had turned from an unwanted present to a godsend. To her surprise she had thoroughly enjoyed baking the small fancy cakes. It had made a welcome change from the standard fare she was used to cooking. She had tried them out on her menfolk and endured their teasing as they had scoffed them down with relish. Unfortunately the Flynn men would eat anything set in front of them, as long as it wasn't still moving, so Annie couldn't rely on their compliments.

At least she was familiar with the kitchen. She should be; she'd been here enough times over the past few weeks. And she had to admit it was more than adequate in respect of space, plenty of cupboards and utensils – plus a brand new oven that was twice as large as the one she had at home.

Rolling up her sleeves, she got to work. She'd know soon enough if her newly acquired talents were up to scratch. She sent up a silent prayer as she set out the ingredients. Josie had put nearly all of her money into this venture, God help her, along with faith in herself, Annie and Jane. And they wouldn't let her down!

With Annie busy in the kitchen, Josie and Jane began setting out the main room. The next hour was spent covering the fifteen circular tables with red-and-white-checked tablecloths. Then the cups, saucers and plates were laid at each place, with the cups turned upside down in the saucers – a tip Josie had picked up at the expensive restaurant they had visited that one and only time. The finishing touch was a silver-plated sugar bowl as a centrepiece.

Josie stepped back, looking at the overall effect, her eyes critical. The tables still looked bare, and she voiced her opinion to Jane.

'I know, I was just thinking the same.' Jane nodded. 'If this was a proper restaurant, we could lay out some cutlery, but no one's going to need knives and forks to eat cakes, are they?'

Josie grinned.

'No, you're right. They won't need proper knives and forks, but they might like a spoon and maybe a cake fork, you know, one of those little posh ones.'

Without waiting for Jane's answer, Josie rushed into the kitchen and, ignoring Annie's protests, rummaged through the numerous drawers until she found the cutlery she was looking for.

'There! That looks better, doesn't it?' She stood back, surveying the tables once more. This time she was satisfied with what she saw.

Josie looked at the clock on the wall. It was now nine thirty. The smell of baking was wafting through the tea room, the tables were set; all they needed now were the customers.

'Is there anything else you want me to do, Josie?' Jane asked.

Josie looked around the room and shook her head.

'No thanks, love.' Then she smiled. 'Unless you wanna go out and drag people in off the street.'

Jane's eyes widened.

'Oh no, Josie. I don't think—'

'Give over, you silly cow. I was only joking. Here, have a sit-down while I go and see how your mum's getting on.'

Pushing open the kitchen door, Josie stopped and sniffed the air.

'Hmm, that smells gorgeous, Annie. Let's have one, eh? I ain't had nothing to eat since last night.

I'm starving.' Josie looked happily at the rows of cakes and buns laid out neatly on baking trays.

Annie, her face flushed from the heat of the oven, grunted.

'All right, love. Just the one though,' she admonished as Josie took a large bite out of an iced bun, her hand reaching out for another one.

'Sorry, Annie,' Josie mumbled, her mouth full of the warm dough. 'I didn't realise I was so hungry. These are lovely. If this lot don't pull the punters in, then nothing will.'

Annie preened at the compliment, though she wouldn't show it. Instead she slapped Josie's hand as it hovered over another cake.

'Begod! Sure an' we won't have anything to sell if ye keep on eating all me hard work.' Wiping her hands down an apron covered with flour, she asked, 'D'ye think I've made enough, love? Only ye did say if we got busy ye'd be wanting me to help out in the shop.'

'Yeah, I know I did. But we've got to get today over with first, see how we go. Mind you, it was a bit of luck me getting this shop. For one thing people have to pass this way to get to and from the tram stop, and with the bakery at the other end, we don't have to worry about competing with them, 'cos there's nothing more mouth-watering than the smell of fresh bread.'

Her face became solemn as doubts set in again. She was sure that once people had sampled Annie's cooking and had the luxury of sitting down in a friendly, clean atmosphere, they would not only come back, but recommend the tea shop to their friends. Josie had taken into account the fact that the kind of women she was hoping to attract were not in the habit of dining out; they simply couldn't afford it. So she had cut her prices as low as she could. Of course she had to make a profit, but she could do that without charging exorbitant prices for a cup of tea and a cake. Her journey into the West End had shown her how much could be made out of a shop such as hers. But those places were frequented by people who weren't short of a few bob. She had briefly toyed with the idea of setting up in the West End, but had rejected the idea. Here was where she belonged – and Annie and Jane. Her two best friends; her only true friends. She trusted them implicitly.

A loud tut of annoyance cut through Josie's thoughts.

'By the time ye open up, me cakes will be cold,' Annie said brusquely, her nerves making her voice sharp. Then it softened. 'Look, love, why don't ye do it now? I mean, what have ye to lose?'

Josie nipped nervously on her bottom lip. The same thought had occurred to her. But something was dragging her back, and she knew what it was. For while the shop remained closed, she could hold on to her dreams of success a little longer. The moment she opened the doors, reality would set in. And as Josie knew only too well, reality could be very cruel.

'Josie! Josie!' Jane burst into the kitchen. 'There's some women outside looking at the price list in the window. And one of them tried to get in.' The young girl was breathing rapidly, as if she had been running.

'Well! What's to be done, Josie?' Annie was staring at her.

Josie's stomach was churning, and her gaze flitted from one woman to the other as if seeking guidance. Annie, bless her, looked a bundle of nerves, while poor Jane was positively trembling with excitement and apprehension. Suddenly Josie wished she hadn't scoffed down those iced buns, for they were in imminent danger of coming back up. Swallowing noisily, she smiled bravely and said over-loudly, 'Don't just stand there, Jane, open the door. We've got customers waiting.'

Jane turned away, then back to Josie.

'Will . . . will you come with me, Josie?' she asked almost piteously.

'Course I will, silly,' Josie answered with a lot more confidence than she was feeling. Glancing back at Annie, she crossed her fingers.

'Wish me luck, Annie.'

The Irishwoman laughed.

'And what d'ye think I've been doing for the last few months? Sure an' I've nearly worn me rosary beads out praying to the Blessed Virgin.'

Back in the tea room, Josie waited a few moments to regain her composure. She ran a critical eye over Jane's plain grey dress with the starched white apron tied around her slim waist, and nodded. Yet it wasn't the girl's attire that concerned Josie. She only hoped no one would make any tactless comment concerning Jane's birthmark, because if that happened . . . Josie shook her head. She had more pressing things to concern herself with. But if anyone did make a derisory remark, that person would be out of the shop before their feet could touch the ground. A wry smile touched the corners of Josie's mouth as she visualised the scene. That would be a great start to her new enterprise, wouldn't it? Especially if the offending customer landed at the foot of more potential customers about to enter the shop.

She took a last look at her own garb. The long, plain black skirt and white blouse looked smart without being too ostentatious. And like Jane, she too wore a white apron, only hers had a small frill around the edge.

Raising her eyes, she could see several faces hovering outside. Whether they were simply curious bystanders or potential customers remained to be seen.

Josie looked to Jane and nodded.

'Open the door, love. It's time to start work.'

The first hour was quiet, their only customers ordering just a cup of tea, making pleasing comments about the array of cakes on offer but declining to order any. The women in question were simple housewives, unable to afford the luxury of pastries. And with each order of 'Just a cuppa, please, love', Josie's heart had sunk a little lower; as had Annie's, who could see all her hard work and effort going to waste.

Then Jane had tentatively suggested that they put a notice in the window saying that all orders of tea would be accompanied by a free cake until eleven thirty. Within minutes of the notice going up, the tea room had been besieged. Yet even in the midst of coping with the never-ending flow of customers there had been a nagging fear at the back of Josie's mind that come eleven thirty, the tea room would once again be empty. But she had been proved wrong. Oh, the crowds had dwindled, but in their wake had come a steady stream of customers, all asking for one of the delicious cakes they had heard so much about. Jane's publicity idea had paid off.

Then Josie had an even greater boost to her morale.

Between the hours of one and two thirty, many of the stallholders came in asking if they did dinners, adding that they would have to be plain and quick as they couldn't leave their fellow market traders keeping an eye on their stall for too long. After a hurried word with Annie, Josie had been able to promise that such meals would be available from the next day.

It was five thirty before a tired but happy Josie locked the door and turned the sign round to 'Closed'. Now, an hour later, after the tea room and kitchen had been cleaned ready for tomorrow, the three women sat down to a welcome and well-deserved cup of tea – without cake. Even if there had been any left, they were all much too tired to eat.

'Begod! The lads are going to be sorely disappointed when I come home empty-handed. They were looking forward to the leftovers,' Annie commented, her tired voice tinged with pride at her achievement.

'Well then, we can tell them to come down here and wait in line like the rest of our customers.' Jane, younger and fitter than her mother and Josie, was positively glowing with happiness. Mainly for Josie's sake, but also because she had achieved her dream of having a job. She had almost resigned herself to having to depend on her family for the rest of her life, but not any more. Working for her own wage had given her an extra boost of confidence, even more so than the trip up West had done.

Josie finished her tea, her face worried.

'Are you sure you can cope with cooking dinners as well as making the cakes? I mean it's gonna be a lot of hard work, Annie. You're worn out now; just imagine what it'll be like having to cook for the stall-holders as well.'

Annie put down her cup and sighed.

'I'll not lie to ye, Josie, that same thought's been preying on me mind all afternoon. But I said I'd do it and I'll not go back on me word. And you can't either, love. You promised the stallholders simple meals and that's what we'll have to supply. After all, if we want to fit in with the other traders and shop-keepers, it won't look good if we go back on our word on our first day, now will it?'

Josie nodded, her face still etched with worry.

'I know, Annie, I know. But we should have talked it over properly instead of promising something we might not be able to do. Besides, when I first started thinking about opening me own business, I only wanted a simple place to run. Something sort of posh . . . Oh! You know what I mean, Annie. I wanted something different, something with a bit of class. And it won't have a chance in hell of being that if we start serving up pie and mash or egg and chips, will it? All I wanted was a nice clean tea shop for women to come to after they'd finished their shop-ping. And don't forget, Annie, the markets get their fair share of the upper classes as customers. But if we start catering for the traders, it'll turn into a working men's club . . .' She trailed off miserably.

Annie swivelled her head round to get a better look at Josie, her eyes narrowing.

'Well now, people say ye learn something new every day, and they're right. I'd never have put ye down as being a snob, Josie Guntrip.'

Leaning across a silent Jane, Annie patted Josie's knee none too gently.

'I'm going to tell ye something now that I've been keeping to meself, and it's this. I didn't say anything afore 'cos I didn't want to burst your bubble. I kept quiet thinking you'd realise soon enough that just selling cups of tea and cakes was never going to make ye a fortune. I just didn't think ye'd find out so soon. But the truth is, by the time ye've paid the rates, the food, and me and Jane, ye'll have precious little to show in the way of profit.' Annie leaned back, her eyes on the downcast head. 'I'm sorry if I'm being too harsh, Josie love, but it had to be said. And ye know deep down I'm right. You'll have your tea shop one day, love, I know ye will. But first ye've got to make enough money, and like I've already said, ye'll not make your fortune by serving cups of tea and fancy cakes – at least, not round these parts.'

Josie kept her head down so that neither Annie nor Jane would see the hurt and disappointment on her face. All of what Annie had said was true; even the part about knowing she would never earn a decent living from owning her own tea shop.

Annie turned to her daughter.

'C'mon now, let's be getting home afore we fall asleep right here.'

'That's all right, Mum, at least we'll get an early

start in the morning,' quipped Jane, trying to lighten the atmosphere, for she hated any form of tension or unpleasantness.

Josie reluctantly got to her aching feet.

'Mum's right, Jane. We'd best get going, I can hear me bed calling. It's a bit of supper and an early night for me. I've got a lot to think about.'

Josie was putting her coat on before she noticed the silence.

'What's up?' she asked, her forehead furrowed.

Jane and Annie looked at each other, then Jane said, 'You just said *Mum's* right, not Annie.'

Josie froze midway through buttoning up her coat.

'Oh, did I?' she said awkwardly. 'Sorry, Annie, I didn't . . .'

The plump figure walked over to the embarrassed young woman and took hold of Josie's hands.

'Don't ye be apologising to me, love. Why, there's nothing I'd like better than to be called Mum by you, 'cos I've thought of ye like a daughter for years. So if ye want to call me Mum, that's fine by me.'

Now it was Annie's turn to feel awkward as Josie just stared at her in bewilderment.

'Of course, if ye'd rather not . . .' she stammered.

A lump formed in Josie's throat as she held tight to the plump hands.

'I've thought of you as me mum for years, even as far back as me school days. I just . . . I just didn't want . . .' Her voice cracked with emotion and she dropped her head.

Annie patted Josie's hands.

'Well, now that's settled we'd best be getting ourselves home.' She pointed at the wall clock, adding,

'Would ye look at the time. Bejasus, the men'll be starving, but I'm not doing any more cooking the day. We'll pick up some fish 'n' chips on the way home.'

Out in the street, the women shivered and linked arms against the bitter chill of the evening air. There were still a few stallholders packing up their goods, and they called out a cheery good night to their new acquaintances.

'Don't forget, missus,' one of the men shouted over to them. 'Sausages an' mash tomorrow. Those little cakes ain't no good ter a working man, ain't that right, lads?'

The other men agreed and waved, and the simple words and gestures brought a feeling of warmth and camaraderie to all three women. Josie looked at Annie and squeezed her arm.

'Now that we're both working,' Jane said suddenly, 'you'll have to tell Dad and the boys they'll have to start learning to cook their own meals.'

Annie's face took on an expression of horror.

'Have ye taken leave of your senses, girl? Sure and your father's never cooked a meal in his life.'

'Well then, maybe it's time he started—'

Josie put pressure on Jane's arm, and shook her head in warning.

'Let's leave it, eh, Jane? Besides, me and your mum have a lot to talk about, haven't we . . . Mum?'

'That we have, Josie love.' Annie smiled. 'That we have.' Then, turning to Jane, she said lightly, 'Maybe ye was right, Jane . . . About your dad, I mean. If we're going to make a go of the shop, we're going to need all the cooks we can get.'

This comment brought Josie and Jane to an abrupt halt. They looked at each other and then at Annie. Seeing the stunned expression on their faces, Annie threw back her head and roared with laughter; mostly at the idea of seeing her Paddy wearing an apron. Her laughter was infectious. Without quite knowing why, Josie and Jane began to laugh too, and as they walked on, their combined laughter filled the cold evening air.

CHAPTER FOURTEEN

Christmas had come and gone, and now preparations were being made for the New Year. Josie had celebrated Christmas dinner with the Flynn family, an occasion she had both looked forward to and dreaded. But she needn't have worried, for Rory had gone out of his way to make her feel at ease, and for two glorious hours she had enjoyed his company. As usual the Flynn men had kept up a constant stream of jokes and anecdotes, and Josie had laughed so much she'd ended up with indigestion after the huge turkey dinner.

The only blight on the occasion had been the presence of Pat's new wife Freda. Poor Annie had gone through torment with the knowledge that her son was, in her eyes, living in sin, as he'd braved her wrath and, without telling anyone, married Freda in a registry office instead of the Catholic church, just a month before Christmas. Josie had been apprehensive that Freda might flaunt this fact in Annie's face, but the normally loud-mouthed, opinionated woman had been on her best behaviour. And even though Annie was still hurting terribly at what she perceived to be her son's betrayal, she had put on a brave face, determined not to spoil Christmas.

After dinner, with the crackers pulled and the last of the Christmas pudding demolished, they had sat around a roaring fire while the Flynn men continued to entertain the company. Yet even as they had laughed, there had been an underlying strain in the merriment, caused by Freda's stony-faced presence. Pat had tried his best to draw his wife into the festivities, but to no avail. So it had come as a mixture of relief and regret when Pat announced they had to leave to visit Freda's parents. It was at that point that Rory had taken the opportunity to leave too, accompanying his brother and sister-in-law from the house, much to Annie's distress and Josie's disappointment – for both women knew the reason for his hasty departure.

With Rory's leaving, the convivial atmosphere had soon fallen flat. Paddy and Shaun had tried their best, but despite their efforts they were no match for Pat and Rory's quick-witted humour. With their bellies full and the numerous tots of whisky taking their toll, both men had soon fallen asleep in front of the roaring fire. Josie had made her excuses and left not long after, politely refusing Annie and Jane's invitation to stay on for tea.

Now, as she dressed for the New Year's Eve party being held over the road, Josie stared hard at her reflection in the dressing table mirror and smiled. If she did say so herself, she scrubbed up quite nicely.

At Christmas she had deliberately dressed in a simple outfit, new but plain, not wanting to take the chance that Rory would think she was flaunting her new business stature in his face. But tonight she had no such scruples. Why shouldn't she dress nicely and make the most of herself; she'd worked hard enough for it. Her old wardrobe had slowly been replaced by new outfits, plain but quality made, until her old image had been erased for ever. Yet up until now she hadn't had the chance to wear the outfit she'd bought at that wonderful woman's shop in the summer, and she hadn't paid out all that money to let the best outfit she'd ever owned moulder away in her wardrobe.

Her hand went to her throat to make sure the jet necklace was fastened securely, then did the same with the earrings. Finally she put on the close-fitting jacket and glanced at the hat nestling forlornly on the bed. She smiled wryly. It was a pity the party was just across the street. She couldn't see any reason to wear the hat without appearing to show off. It wasn't as if it was practical, for it barely covered her head, yet it would have been nice to wear the whole ensemble.

Her stomach fluttered at the thought of appearing in front of her neighbours in the grand outfit. But Annie had promised she would wear her grey costume, so at least Josie wouldn't feel completely out of place. Her neighbours were still getting used to the new Josie Guntrip, for after watching her grow from childhood to adulthood, too timid to stand up to her tyrant of a mother, it was hard for them to accept the smart, confident woman Josie had become.

Taking one last look in the mirror, she left the house.

She shivered as the cold December air hit her in the face. Out of the corner of her eye she saw the net curtains move in next door's window and stopped. As far as she knew, the invitation to the Flynns' party was open to everyone in the street. And judging by the loud laughter and music already blasting from the house, it seemed as if it had been taken at face value by all the neighbours. Yet, knowing the history between Ida Black and Annie, Josie could understand Ida's reluctance to go over to the house on her own. On the other hand, Annie, formidable as she could be when roused, had a kind heart. Josie was sure she wouldn't want Ida to see in the New Year on her own; even if she was a miserable old cow.

Hesitating only for a few seconds, Josie knocked on Ida's door. A minute went by and the door remained shut. Josie's teeth began to chatter. Banging the knocker harder, she bent down and called through the letterbox, 'Ida! Come on, I know you're in there. Open the door, I'm freezing out here.' There was still no answer. Josie shrugged. She had tried. If Ida didn't want to answer her door, that was her look-out. She was turning to walk away when she heard the door being opened.

'Who's there?' Ida's croaky voice called out.

'Who the bleeding 'ell d'yer think it is, Jack the Ripper?' Josie answered impatiently while hugging herself tightly against the cold.

'What d'yer want?' came back the reply.

Cold and becoming increasingly annoyed, Josie pushed the door open, knocking a startled Ida into her narrow hallway.

'Stop playing silly buggers, Ida. Are you coming over to the party? If you are then I'll wait for—'

'You taking the piss, Josie? Yer know as well as I do Annie can't stand the sight of me – or the rest of the street for that matter. Did she put yer up ter this? Get old Ida over 'ere so I can kick 'er out. That'd give yer all a good laugh, wouldn't it? Well I ain't that daft, an' . . . and I know we've 'ad our differences in the past, but . . . but I'd never 'ave 'ad yer down as being spiteful.'

Josie stared in amazement at her neighbour. The lamp Ida was holding at shoulder level showed clearly the misery etched on the thin, pinched face, and Josie felt a jolt of shame as she saw the faded blue eyes glisten with unshed tears.

Her voice gentler now, she said, 'I'm a lot of things, Ida, but I ain't never been spiteful, and Annie ain't either. Now then, you coming over or not? You might as well, 'cos you ain't gonna get much sleep with that racket going on.'

A spark of hope flickered in Ida's eyes.

'You sure Annie won't mind?' The question was asked in a defensive tone and the thin body remained stiff with tension. It was as if Ida was bracing herself for rejection.

'Course she won't mind. I said so, didn't I?' Josie was taking Ida's coat off the hall stand. 'Get this on, it's bleeding freezing out. Lucky we ain't got far to go, ain't it?'

Before she could protest further, Ida found herself out in the street, walking towards her adversary's house. The nearer she got, the more she shivered; and not just from the biting wind.

The door was ajar and Josie stepped inside as confidently as if she were entering her own home, dragging Ida in with her.

A battered piano had been borrowed for the occasion from someone in the street, and an elderly man whom Josie knew by sight but couldn't put a name to was playing an off-key rendition of 'Danny Boy', accompanied by loud, raucous voices, also off key.

'Bleeding hell! What a racket,' Josie shouted at Ida, but the older woman made no comment. Josie could feel the tension emanating from Ida's thin frame and tried to put the frightened woman at ease. 'I wish I'd worn something plainer now. Talk about being dressed up like a dog's dinner. You wait, someone's bound to make a comment soon.'

Looking through the haze of smoke, Josie saw Jane pushing her way through the crowd towards them.

'Hello, Josie. Oh, you look lovely.'

Josie smiled.

'Thanks, love, you don't look too bad yourself.'

Jane ran her hand self-consciously down the front of the blue dress Josie had bought for her. Then she looked at the woman by Josie's side, and, sensing Ida's obvious discomfort, said warmly, 'Hello, Mrs Black, I'm glad you're here. Mum said if you didn't arrive with Josie I had to come over and get you. So you've saved me from having to brave the cold. Here, give me your coat.'

Ida said nothing as Jane helped her off with her coat, but when a glass of sherry was put into her hand she began to relax. Fifteen minutes later, with another two drinks under her belt, she wandered off, her gait uneven, and approached a small group of women she knew.

'Thank Gawd for that,' Josie sighed. 'I thought I was gonna have to baby-sit her all night.' Giving Jane a nudge, she asked, 'Did your mum really say she was gonna send you over to fetch Ida, or did you make that bit up?'

Jane grinned impishly.

'Well . . . I might have exaggerated a bit, but it was in a good cause. Anyway, I'm glad you decided to wear that outfit. It took me nearly two hours to talk Mum into wearing the suit you bought her, though she drew the line at the corset. She said she wasn't going to spend the evening trussed up like a turkey, especially on New Year's Eve, and I can't say as I blame her. What's the point of having a party if you can't eat, drink or have a good old knees-up?'

Jane's eyes darted over Josie's shoulder, then, leaning closer, she whispered, 'Dad said if she wore the corset it would stop her falling over like she normally does when she's had a drink. But she's been like a cat on hot bricks since we got home from work. She's really been dying for the opportunity to wear the suit again. She had hoped to wear it to Pat's wedding, but . . .' Jane smiled sadly and shrugged. 'Anyway, she wore it to Christmas Mass and you should have seen the looks she got.' She giggled. 'Even Father Murphy nearly dropped the chalice when she went up for Communion.'

Josie burst out laughing, but it was a nervous laugh. She was painfully conscious of the looks she was getting. Even after all the years she had lived in the street, she still didn't know her neighbours very well. It would have been easy to blame her mother for this fact, but the truth was, she herself had never made the effort to form friendships. She had been too wrapped up in her own misery to realise that these good, simple people could have been a comfort to her. But she'd had the Flynns, so she hadn't bothered to try and form new friendships.

Now here they all were, packed into the small terraced house, their eyes darting in her direction then sliding away uneasily. Josie knew they were thinking that she was showing off her new-found wealth, and she squirmed with embarrassment. Her face burned and she had a fleeting desire to turn round and head back home to change into something more inconspicuous.

'Are you all right, Josie?' Jane's voice had changed to one of concern, and she glanced from her friend to the gathering of neighbours. Sensing Josie's discomfort, she squeezed the satin-covered arm. 'Don't worry, Josie. Mum got the same stares when the neighbours started arriving. But you know me mum. She was scared stiff of the reaction she might get, but she braved it out, you know, made a joke about it. She even gave an impromptu fashion parade. I wish you'd seen it. She had the whole place in stitches.'

'I didn't have to see it, I can imagine Annie doing something like that. But I'm not like your mum, Jane. I don't have that gift of making people laugh.' Josie smiled wryly at Jane. 'I ain't Irish. Maybe one day I'll go over to Ireland and kiss that famous stone I've heard so much about. D'yer think it'd work on me? . . . What's so funny about that?' Josie asked as Jane put her hand to her mouth to smother a laugh.

'I'm not laughing at you, Josie, just the thought of you kissing the Blarney Stone. You could try it one day, I suppose, that's if you don't mind being held upside down and lowered into a well by your ankles.' Jane giggled at the image that had sprung into her mind. 'And even if you were brave enough to try it, you'd have to make sure you were first in the queue, 'cos by the afternoon the men in charge of the tourists have usually got a good few Guinnesses under their belt.'

Heads again turned in their direction, but this time drawn by Jane's infectious laugh.

'Come on, Janie, let us in on the joke,' Maude Cooper, the Flynns' next-door neighbour called out. Seeing an opportunity to ease Josie's discomfort, Jane gently pulled her friend towards the group, and recounted the story of the Blarney Stone.

'Bleeding 'ell!' Arthur Cooper exclaimed loudly. 'Every Irishman I've ever spoken to 'as bragged about that stone. But the way they told it, I thought it was lying on the ground an' yer just 'ad ter bend over ter kiss the bloody thing. 'Ere, yer ain't making this up, are yer, Janie love?' the grinning man asked, winking at his companions. ''Cos we all know what you Irish lot are like fer stretching the truth, don't we?'

They were all laughing now, and Josie began to relax. Then Sadie Smith nudged her, saying, ''Ere, Josie. If yer ever do go over the water, you'd better borrow a pair of my Alf's trousers if you're thinking of kissing that stone. You'd soon lose yer dignity being held upside down with yer knickers showing fer all the world ter see.'

Then Arty Jones said loudly, 'Now that's something I'd pay good money ter see.' All the men present roared, apart from Arty Jones, who was nearly knocked off his feet by a hefty clout around the head from his wife.

'Oh, yer would, would yer? Well, if you've got money going spare, yer can pay me. I'll show me knickers fer a few bob.' She glanced around the grinning group. 'Well! Any takers? Come on, I ain't fussy.'

'No thanks, Maude. I've seen yer knickers 'anging on the washing line for the past twenty years, an' they've got bigger every year,' a man shouted above the din.

Josie felt a drink being pressed into her hand and looked up to see Shaun by her side. She smiled gratefully. Too late she realised she had made a mistake in the warmth of her smile, for it bolstered Shaun's courage enough to place an arm around her waist – a gesture which didn't go unnoticed by the inebriated crowd, who gave each other knowing glances, nudges and sly winks. It was all done without malice, but nevertheless Josie felt embarrassed.

As gently as she could, she moved away from Shaun's embrace. She sensed rather than saw his disappointment and compensated for her gesture by squeezing his hand gently while giving him a warm smile. They had been out a few times, but just as friends, much to Shaun's dismay. And each time Josie vowed not to go out with him again, but he was such good company, and a much-needed balm to her bruised ego after being cast aside by Rory. Yet for the last few weeks her conscience had begun to trouble her.

Poor Shaun was the antithesis of his brother, for his feelings were so transparent, anyone seeing them together could tell he was head over heels in love with Josie. But tonight was the first time he had made such a public display of his feelings, and Josie knew she couldn't string him along any longer. She wouldn't spoil the evening for him, but first thing tomorrow she had to pluck up the courage to tell the smitten young man she could never reciprocate his love. For the longer she left him hoping, the harder it would be to sever their relationship. He would be hurt, but he was a handsome man, and kind and gentle. Many a young woman would break her neck for a chance to snare such a good catch, and he would be free to find someone who would give him the love he deserved; the love that Josie couldn't provide.

"'Ere, Josie. 'Ow about doing a turn fer us? Annie put on a good show earlier. 'Ad us in stitches she did.'

'Yeah, come on, love,' shouted another voice she recognised as Edie Sharpe. Josie also recognised the touch of spite in the tone. 'Course, now you're a woman of means, I suppose yer think yer too posh fer the likes of us.'

The laughter suddenly faded. Most of the assembled crowd averted their gaze, looking down at their feet and shuffling uncomfortably at the insidious jibe. There were also a few hard glances directed at the woman for her spiteful comment, and this gave Josie heart. If she wanted to be accepted into the close-knit community, then she would have to prove that despite her new wealth she was still one of them.

Gulping down the entire contents of her glass, Josie

shuddered and coughed as the whisky burned down her throat and body. Then, staring straight at Edie Sharpe, she said loudly, 'Posh, am I, Mrs Sharpe? Well, you just clear a space an' we'll see how posh I am.'

Striking a pose, Josie, hand on hip, sashayed across the floor, smiling as a space was cleared to allow her freedom of movement. Gathering up one side of her dress, she twirled gracefully, saying in a haughty voice, 'Here we have the latest creation in women's fashion; that is to say, for the discerning woman's taste.' Her eyes sought out Edie Sharpe, and she smiled inwardly as the loud-mouthed woman dropped her gaze.

For the next ten minutes, Josie entertained the delighted assembly, and no one watching her antics would have guessed at her inner feelings of panic and self-consciousness at being the centre of attraction. When she'd finished her display, she lifted her skirt and curtsied with all the grace of a true lady. It was this final act that brought forth a loud burst of applause, plus a few piercing whistles from the men.

Then she was being surrounded. The men were hugging her, while their wives looked on grinning.

'Gawd, Josie love, I ain't laughed so much in ages.' Arthur Cooper lifted her off her feet and twirled her around. 'I never knew yer was such a comedian, and a bleeding good sport. What yer drinking, love? An' when yer gonna give us another show? In fact, what about you and Annie doing a double act . . .'

Feeling slightly sick from the whisky Shaun had given her, and the reaction to her performance in front of the entire street, Josie swallowed loudly, praying fervently she wouldn't disgrace herself by throwing up.

When the jovial man had put her back on the ground, she summoned up a weak smile and said, 'Thanks, Arthur, but I don't think so. Maybe next New Year's Eve. I doubt whether me or Annie will be wearing our best gear until then. They're not exactly the sort of clothes people like us wear every day, are they? And we wouldn't like anyone to think we was showing off.' Josie glanced around to find Edie Sharpe, but the woman in question, knowing she had been bested, was nowhere to be seen.

Still hardly believing she had acted in a way that was completely against her nature, Josie was desperate to find somewhere quiet and have a sit-down. So when she felt a strong arm encircle her waist, she didn't pull away. Instead she sank gratefully against Shaun's side.

Ever hopeful, Shaun pulled Josie closer, and after a few minutes' banter with his guests he led her through the packed room to where his father was sitting comfortably in his favourite shabby armchair by the fire. Like the rest of the occupants of the small house, Paddy had a drink in his hand, and was in the middle of sharing a joke with Pat, who was sitting opposite. At the sight of Josie, Pat jumped to his feet.

'Hello, Josie. I didn't see you come in. 'Ere, sit yourself down.'

When Josie was seated, Paddy leaned forward, tapped her knee and grinned.

'Begod, lass, you're honoured an' no mistake. Once

we Irish find a seat at a party, we don't move from it for love nor money – though we might be persuaded for a glass of the hard stuff.'

Josie settled into the comfortable armchair and breathed a sigh of relief, knowing Paddy wasn't joking. Annie had once told her that the reason behind this was because the Irish normally consisted of large families, and even the smallest child soon learned to secure a place to sit at the earliest opportunity. With this in mind, Josie settled back further into the sagging armchair, determined not to leave the coveted seat until the party thinned out. Another drink was pressed into her hand, and this time she sipped it slowly, her eyes sweeping the room looking for Annie. Jane also seemed to have disappeared. She didn't bother looking for Rory, painfully aware where he would be, and with whom.

Taking another sip of her drink, she realised there was someone else missing. Turning her head upwards, she tugged at Pat's arm and, raising her voice to be heard over the noise, shouted, 'Where's Freda, Pat?'

Pat bent down to hear better.

'What? Sorry, Josie, I can hardly hear meself think above this racket.'

'I said, where's Freda?'

Pat's amiable face turned a dull red.

'Oh, she wasn't feeling well. It might be the flu. She wanted to come, but I put me foot down. I wasn't gonna drag her out on a freezing cold night like this, which reminds me . . .' He looked at the clock on the mantelpiece and quickly downed his beer. 'I promised her I'd just show me face an' have one drink to be sociable, what with it being New Year's Eve an' all.'

'Oh, I'm sorry to hear she's not well. Give her my regards, won't you?'

'Yeah, I will. Thanks, Josie, an' Happy New Year.' He bent over and kissed her lightly on the lips in a brotherly fashion. 'I'll just go an' say me goodbyes ter Mum, or else I'll never hear the end of it.' He smiled, but his eyes were full of sadness, and Josie's heart went out to him. It was obvious Freda was no more ill than she herself was. The woman was just being awkward. She knew that Paddy and Annie didn't regard her as Pat's lawful wife, and this was her way of venting her spite on her in-laws. But it was Pat who was suffering the most. This would be the first New Year he hadn't seen in with his family, and Josie knew he must be hurting badly. Poor Pat.

She looked across at Paddy, her expression betraying her knowledge of the true cause of Freda's absence. Paddy returned her look and shrugged, then took another swig of his Guinness, his silence speaking volumes and confirming her suspicions.

For the next two hours Josie, despite her protests, was pulled up again and again to dance. It wasn't something she was good at, having had little practice, but after a few more drinks she was kicking her heels up with the rest of the street. She was happy. She couldn't stop smiling, even though she knew it was the drink that was making her feel so confident. What did it matter? She was thoroughly enjoying herself, and it was a wonderful, euphoric feeling.

At various stages of the evening, Annie would put

in an appearance, have a dance, then vanish back into the kitchen to make sure there was still plenty of food for her guests.

'Come on, Josie love, on yer feet.' Arthur Cooper was beaming down at Josie, who by some miracle had found her seat still vacant. Tired and a little light-headed, she pleaded for mercy.

'No more, Arthur. Me feet are killing me.'

But Arthur, full of good spirits, in more ways than one, insisted.

'Aw, come on, girl. Just this one, then I'll leave yer in peace, I promise.'

Unable to refuse the likeable man, Josie got to her feet.

'All right, but just one more, all right?'

She was pulled into the centre of the room just as the pianist burst into 'Knees Up Mother Brown'. Holding her skirt up to her knees, Josie threw herself into the dance with gusto. Then just as she thought her legs couldn't support her any more, the music stopped and she staggered back to the arm-chair that was being guarded by Jane.

'Ah, so there ye are, Josie darlin'. Sure an' I was beginning to think I'd never get the chance for a chat with ye.'

Annie was standing before Josie, her rotund body lurching alarmingly, her face flushed and perspiring, thick strands of hair escaping from her tight bun. She was sporting a wide grin that was threatening to split her face in two.

'Well! Aren't ye going to . . . to get up and let a lady rest her . . . her weary bones?'

Her words slurred, she slapped Paddy on the back,

causing him to spill his beer down his best shirt.

'Will ye give me a minute, woman,' Paddy splut-
tered, then he laughed. 'Aye, go on, take me seat
afore ye fall down.' He rose slowly, like his wife grinning widely. Winking at Josie, he asked Annie, 'An'
how many have ye had, me darlin'? Sure an' ye
promised ye'd stay off the whisky so ye wouldn't
make a show of yourself.'

Flopping heavily into the still warm armchair,
Annie twisted her head round and up, her face indig-
nant.

'I'll have ye know I've just had . . . had the one.
Sure an' ye wouldn't begrudge me a drink on . . . on
New Year's Eve, now would . . . would ye?'

Paddy threw back his head and laughed.

'Begod, but that must have been a bloody big glass
. . .'

But Annie was no longer listening. Looking across
at Josie, her eyes softened.

'Ah, Josie darlin'. You're a picture of loveliness, so
ye are. An' if that stupid eejit of a son of mine didn't
keep his brains in his trousers, you'd be me daughter
by now. But then ye'll always be that to me, Josie. If
Rory doesn't realise what he's missing, that's his
look-out.'

Josie felt her face burn and quickly looked to see
where Shaun was, heaving a silent sigh of relief when
she spotted him standing by the piano with a small
group of men, all of them laughing. Annie wasn't
known for her tact, but she would never have made
such a remark if she had been sober.

Changing the subject, Josie looked at the jacket of
Annie's suit and remarked, 'You've lost a couple of

buttons, Annie. They must have popped off sometime during the evening.'

Annie looked down at her own chest, but before she could answer Paddy had bent down close to his wife and, looking at Josie, said loudly, "Tis lucky no one was standing too close when they did, else one of them could have taken someone's eye out.'

But Annie's thoughts were still on her errant son. Turning her head towards the mantelpiece she peered at the clock.

'Rory promised on the Holy Bible he'd be back to see in the New Year with us. Will ye look at the time. It's a quarter to twelve already and still no sign of him. Begod, if he's forgotten I'll break every bone in his body, that I will. It's bad enough that one son of mine won't be with us tonight. I'll not be—'

'Hello, Mum. Bet you thought I wouldn't make it in time, didn't you?'

Josie's hands began to tremble as she recognised Rory's voice above the din. Gathering her composure, she steadied herself, lifted her glass to her lips and took a long gulp of the whisky and lemonade Shaun had made for her, but she couldn't stop the pounding of her heart.

As if she had conjured up his image, Shaun appeared at her side. Perching himself next to her, he draped an arm around her shoulder and looked up at his brother.

'You cut it a bit fine, didn't yer? I didn't think yer were coming, but I'm glad yer did else Mum would've made all our lives a misery, 'specially with Pat not being here either. Well, don't just stand there, look at the time. Get yerself a drink. You can't see the New Year in without a drink in yer hand.'

But Rory was staring at Josie. Bathed in the glow of the firelight, with her hair tumbling around her shoulders, she was wearing the same beautiful red dress she had been wearing that day in the restaurant. Rory felt his heart skip a beat at the sight of her. Bewildered by his feelings, he said tersely, 'Yeah, all right, Shaun, I'll go an' get one. Hello, Josie. Glad yer could make it,' then he turned and went into the kitchen, where the array of drinks were laid out.

Throwing back a tumbler of whisky in one go, he refilled his glass and stared unseeingly into space for a few moments. The sound of raised voices brought him sharply out of his reverie and he hurried into the parlour, pushing through the merry crowd forming a circle and heading towards his parents and Shaun – and Josie. Without thinking, he slid between Josie and Shaun, his hands clasping Josie's on one side and his brother's on the other.

There was an expectant hush as all waited for the clock to strike twelve. Then someone began shouting the countdown, and it was quickly picked up by the rest of the room.

'Ten, nine, eight, seven, six, five, four, three, two, one . . .' There was a collective roar as the clock struck midnight, then everyone began to sing 'Auld Lang Syne' with gusto. The next few minutes were bedlam, with the well-lubricated crowd hugging and kissing each other, wishing all a Happy New Year.

Josie's heart was beating so fast, she was finding it hard to breathe. She had been kissed by Paddy, Annie, Jane, Shaun and all the neighbours; even Ida Black –

everyone but the one person who mattered most. Then Rory was in front of her. Without a word he pulled her close to him and pressed his lips to hers.

Josie let herself be swept up in the embrace. Her heart beating wildly, she felt a warm sensation building in her chest, and her legs turn to jelly. The noise in the room faded into the background, and Josie was transported back to the time when she and Rory were together. Then he pulled away, and the magic of the moment was rudely broken.

Holding her away from him, Rory smiled warmly. 'Happy New Year, Josie. You deserve it.'

The kiss had only lasted a few seconds, but to Josie it seemed as if the world had stood still. And she knew in that moment that she was still in love with Rory, and always would be.

CHAPTER FIFTEEN

It was gone two in the morning before the last of the neighbours staggered noisily from the Flynn household. Amidst much cheerful banter and high spirits, Annie finally managed to close her front door. Leaning her back against it, her body sagged and she gave vent to a heavy sigh.

'Jasus, but I thought they'd never leave,' she said wearily, then she beamed. 'By, but we had a grand time, didn't we? This party will be the talk of the street for a few weeks. And a good many sore heads in the morning I'll be bound.' Her eyes swept the chaos her sitting room had been left in. 'Holy Mary! Sure an' it'll take a month of Sundays to clear this lot up.'

'Oh, I don't think it'll take that long, Mum.' The affectionate term slid easily off Josie's tongue as she stifled a yawn. 'Me and Jane will help. Between us we'll soon have the place tidy.'

'Thanks, love, but ye look dead on your feet. Why

don't ye get yourself off home to your bed. I'll soon—'

'Don't be daft, I'm not leaving you and Jane to clear this lot up by yourselves. Now then, let's roll up our sleeves and get to work, 'cos it won't get done on its own, will it?'

A loud snore caught their attention.

Annie looked over to where Paddy, Shaun and Rory were sprawled over the armchairs and sofa, all of them dead to the world. She shook her head and sighed in exasperation.

'Will ye look at the lot of them, the useless lumps. Still, that's men for ye. They don't mind the eating and drinking, an' having a good time. But when it comes to the cleaning up, they're either nowhere to be seen, or have drunk themselves into a stupor.'

Josie followed her glance, her eyes lingering a little longer on the lean frame of Rory slumped in the armchair.

Despite her resolve not to get her hopes up where Rory was concerned, she had failed. For he had been charm itself. Even now, hours later, she could still feel a tingle in her spine at the memory of that kiss.

After seeing in the New Year she had expected him to stay a while to keep his mother happy, then disappear at the earliest opportunity, as he had done at Christmas. But he had stayed. Stayed and danced with her, talked to her, and made her feel the same heady sensations as he had done in the past. Josie was aware that the drink had contributed to his behaviour, but still, he hadn't had to spend so much time with her, and he could hold his drink. He never said or did anything when drunk that he wouldn't when sober.

'Right then,' Annie said briskly. 'Once we've the rubbish out of the way, we'll start on the washing-up. I'll wash, Josie can dry and Jane can put it all away.'

Too tired to talk, the women began putting the house in order. Annie set to with a heavy broom, sweeping through the house with renewed vigour. Opening the front door, she brushed the debris into the street. Normally she would empty it into the bin, but tonight she was just too tired to bother. Slamming the door shut, she saw with satisfaction that the noise had woken Paddy and Rory. Both men jumped, then groaned, letting their faces fall into their hands.

'Blimey, Mum! D'yer have to make all that racket?' Rory groaned. 'Me head feels like someone's banging a drum in there.'

'Oh, well, excuse me.' Annie looked without sympathy at her son and husband. 'If I'd known I was disturbing ye, I'd've been quieter; what with all the hard work ye've put in the day.'

Josie and Jane stood in the kitchen doorway, grinning as the irate woman berated the stricken men.

Groaning, Paddy heaved himself out of the armchair.

'Enough, woman, enough,' he whimpered piteously. 'Sure an' it's New Year's Eve. Everyone has a drink on New Year's Eve, me darlin', even you.'

'Aye, I know well enough what day it is, Paddy Flynn. I should do, 'cos we have the same conversation every year. 'Tis true I've had a drink or two, but I've never drunk meself unconscious. Now you an' Rory get Shaun up to his bed . . . No, wait a minute.'

She leaned over her youngest son, her head turned to one side as she pressed her ear against the slim chest. Satisfied he was still breathing, she straightened up.

'G'wan then; get going . . . And lay him on his belly, just in case he's sick during the night,' she shouted up the stairs after the bleary-eyed men.

'And what are you two grinning about?' she demanded of the two smiling women.

'You, Mum . . . just you!' Jane's mouth opened into a wide yawn. 'Oh, I'm sorry, Josie. Do you mind if I go to bed? I feel exhausted.'

Stirring herself, Josie said quickly, 'Yeah, me too, Mum. I keep forgetting I don't live here.' Shrugging her jacket on, Josie was doing up the buttons when Annie stopped her.

'I wish ye did, love. With all me heart, I wish ye did.' Annie's voice took on a softer tone. 'How in God's name our Rory could reject a lovely young woman like you, an' take up with that . . . that . . .'

Josie caught hold of Annie's hand.

'It's all right, Annie, it's all right. We can't help who we fall in love with.' She gave a nervous laugh. 'I should know, shouldn't I? Anyway, I'll be getting off home.'

'No, wait a while, love. I know it's late, but just stay for a cup of tea and a bite to eat. There's still some cakes left. I put them by just in case we felt peckish after cleaning up.'

Josie hesitated. There was nothing she would like better than to stay in this warm, happy household, not just for the night, but for the rest of her life. The temptation to remain a little while longer instead of

217

returning to her own cold house was too appealing to resist.

'All right, Mum. I'll just nip home and put some more coal on my bedroom fire. I meant to go over earlier, but I was having such a good time it went clear outta me mind. It'll make it nice and warm for me. I'll even put me hot-water bottle in me bed. There's nothing worse than climbing into a cold bed on a dark winter night.'

The simple words tore at Annie's heart and her eyes involuntarily looked to the ceiling above. Suddenly she realised just how lucky she was. Paddy might be drunk, which meant he'd be in and out of bed all night to relieve himself in the chamber pot, and he'd be letting off wind all night too, but what did that matter? She didn't need a hot-water bottle when she had his back to warm her feet on.

'You get off then, love. I'll have the tea and cakes on the table by the time ye get back . . . Oh! And come in by the back yard, would ye, love. I don't want anyone to see ye and think the party's still going on.'

Annie put the kettle on and unwrapped the cakes left over from the party. And they certainly wouldn't have been left if Annie hadn't had the foresight to hide them.

Her thoughts still on Josie, the older woman's face softened. She was a grand girl, so she was. The kind of woman any mother would want for a daughter-in-law.

Annie shook her head wearily. It was bad enough having one eejit for a son, without producing two, for Pat too had taken up with a flighty piece. Well! He may have married the woman, but Annie would never accept her into the family, because in her eyes they weren't married. She closed her eyes tiredly and sent up a silent prayer. Please God, don't let Freda become pregnant. It had always been Annie's wish to have a grandchild – and not just one, but as many as God sent her – but not from a marriage that was not recognised by the Church. Any children that resulted from that union would be looked upon as bastards. And what would she do then? Pretend they didn't exist? Deny them the love of their grand-parents through no fault of their own!

She could never do that, and neither could Paddy.

Realising she was becoming maudlin, Annie set about laying the table. Josie should be back soon. It didn't take that long to fill a stone water bottle, and put a few lumps of coal on the fire. But a hot-water bottle was no substitute for a warm body to snuggle up to on a winter night such as this. And Annie wasn't just thinking about a man's body. Being one of eight children, she had never had the luxury of a bed of her own; she had always had to share. And not with just one of her siblings either. As the family grew, so did the number of occupants of the bed. None of the children had ever queried the arrange-ment, simply because they had never known any other way of life.

Annie paused, one of her best china cups in her hand. In fact, come to think of it, she'd never had a pram of her own either. Looking back down the years, she could see herself crammed into the con-fines of the large pram, and from there squashed into the ever decreasing bed space. She chuckled at the memory, then a sadness came over her plump, homely face. Her family had always been so close; now she doubted if she would ever see any of her brothers and sisters again.

She and Paddy had only been back to Ireland twice since coming to England, and both times it had been to attend funerals on Annie's side of the family: Bridget, her elder sister, and Michael, the baby of the family. The rest had scattered. Two of her brothers had emigrated to Australia over twenty years ago, then her two remaining sisters had followed them over once they had settled. Now she had only the one brother left in Ireland, and she had been promising herself for years that she would save the boat fare and go over and see him. But each time she managed to put a few bob by, something happened and she'd had to break into her savings.

She let her eyes sweep around the empty kitchen and wished Josie would hurry up. Annie wasn't used to being on her own with nothing to do. For one thing, it gave her mind too much time to wander down memory lane. At least she received regular photos of her nieces and nephews every Christmas, but it wasn't the same as seeing them grow up.

'Josie gone home then?' Rory ambled into the kitchen, his unruly red hair sticking up at the back of his head, his hand rubbing his chin absently. 'Oh, good. You've got the kettle on. Give us a cup, Mum. Me mouth feels like a sailor's armpit.'

Annie struggled to her feet, tutting, hiding the feeling that washed over her every time Rory walked into a room. She loved all of her children, but there was just that extra bit of love she felt for Rory; even when she could cheerfully strangle him.

'Ye've picked up some disgusting sayings since ye started working on that building site . . . And just how d'ye know what a sailor's armpit feels like?'

Rory grinned, then, in an exaggerated affected tone said, 'Wouldn't you like ter know? Then again, it's best yer don't.'

Annie flicked a tea towel at his head.

'Ye think you're a funny beggar, don't ye . . . And get your hand off them cakes.' The towel came down across his knuckles as he reached out to the plate. 'Those are for me and Josie. She's just away across the road to make sure the fire hasn't gone out in her bedroom, and to put a hot-water bottle in her bed so it'll be nice and warm for her when she leaves here.'

Rory looked up at his mother through bleary eyes, his forehead creased.

'She's coming back! What for? It's the middle of the bleed— blooming night.'

Annie's lips pursed in annoyance.

'Is it deaf you're going? Sure, haven't I just been after telling ye . . . Oh, never mind.' She flapped her hand at him. 'It was my idea, if ye must know. With all the shenanigans going on tonight, I barely managed to say a few words to her – not that it's any of your business; or is it? Ye seemed to be paying a lot of attention to Josie tonight. And don't ye try to deny it.' She pointed a finger at him. 'Why d'ye think our Shaun drank himself into a stupor the night, the poor divil. He's mad about Josie, an' ye know it.' Pulling up a chair, she leaned over the table. 'Now look, lad. Ye know how I feel about young Josie, an' after seeing the way ye was fussing over her tonight, I thought maybe—'

Rory jumped to his feet as if he'd been scalded.

'Hang on a minute, Mum. There's nothing like that going on. I like Josie, I've always liked her. And yeah, I admit, there was a time when I thought that maybe things might become serious. But then I—' He broke off, his teeth nipping his bottom lip, now fervently wishing he'd gone straight to bed.

There was no warmth in Annie's voice now as she spat out, 'Aye, I know what changed your mind. The whole street knows about your trollop. I'll tell ye something else while I'm at it. You used to be respected around these parts, but now you're a laughing stock.'

'Mum, leave it, please. We've been over this a hundred times. I love Cathy. I wish I didn't, 'cos she's brought me nothing but trouble, but I can't stop feeling the way I do about her. Look, Mum . . . 'Ere, sit down a minute, please. At least let me have me say . . . Mum!' Rory pleaded.

After a moment's hesitation Annie sat down, but her expression remained cold.

Pulling up a chair, Rory sat down and stared at Annie across the kitchen table. Wetting his lips nervously, he tried to find the words needed to help her understand how he felt; even though he knew no words would ever endear Cathy to his indomitable mother. Still, he had to try.

The atmosphere in the small kitchen was so highly charged it could have been cut with a knife. If the two people concerned hadn't been so wrapped up in their own conversation, they would have heard the back door opening.

* * *

Josie closed her front door and hurried across the street, humming beneath her breath. The whisky she had consumed earlier, added to the memories of Rory's attentions, warmed her body against the biting cold. Her steps light, she hurried towards the Flynn household. She couldn't remember ever being so happy as she felt right at that moment. She knew the whisky had a good deal to do with her state of mind, but no amount of spirits could have made her feel this good. Still humming, she pushed open the back gate and walked the few short steps to the scullery door. As she stepped into the small room she could hear voices coming from the kitchen. Her face broke into a wide smile as she recognised Rory's deep, familiar voice. Turning the kitchen doorknob, she stepped into the room, her evident happiness shining through every pore of her body, lighting up her face from within. Then the smile faltered as she heard Rory's words.

'. . . and I'll tell yer something else, Mum. Josie's a lovely girl, and there's nothing I'd like better than if her and Shaun got together. But even if Cathy wasn't in the picture, it wouldn't change me feelings for Josie.'

Just a few steps away, Josie stood rigid, hardly able to believe what she was hearing. She knew she should make her presence known, but she had to hear what Rory had to say. Even though every fibre in her being was screaming at her, warning her it would be better if she didn't know, she stayed where she was. And with each word he spoke, it was like a knife piercing her flesh. She couldn't breathe, couldn't move. It was as if she had been turned to stone.

'I don't love her, Mum. I'm very fond of her, but I don't love her and I never did even when we were together. I'm really sorry I hurt her, but there it is. So if you've any ideas about us getting back together, you're wasting your time, 'cos—'

'Then ye shouldn't have got her hopes up, should ye?' Annie broke in, her voice bitter. 'Ye knew how she felt about you, yet ye played up to her. I never thought I'd say this, Rory, but you're a cruel bugger, God forgive me for swearing. Now get out of me sight—'

'It's all right, Annie. Don't upset yourself, he's not worth it.'

Both heads turned towards the voice, their faces registering shock at the sight of Josie framed in the doorway, her face white.

Her eyes sought Rory's as she said in a low voice, 'Don't worry, Rory. I admit tonight I almost felt that maybe . . . But I know different now, don't I? So like I said, don't worry. I'll get over you. I only hope Cathy Meadows really does love you, because I wouldn't wish what I'm feeling now on me worst enemy.'

'Josie, love . . .' Annie started to her feet, but Josie stopped her.

'It's not your fault, Annie. If anyone's to blame it's me for making a fool of meself. I won't stop for tea, thanks. I've suddenly lost me appetite.' She turned, then stopped, and without looking back said, 'I'm sorry I won't be able to visit any more. I think, in the circumstances, it's for the best. Good night, Annie.'

* * *

As the door closed quietly behind Josie, Annie slumped back on to her chair, her eyes filling with tears. Out of all that had happened, what was hurting her the most was the fact that Josie had reverted to calling her by her first name.

'Mum . . .'

Rory was staring down at his mother with concern. Then she looked up at him and he found himself backing away. For in Annie's eyes was a look he had never imagined would be levelled at him; it was a look of pure hatred.

Through gritted teeth Annie growled, 'Get out of me sight, Rory, or by Christ I won't be held responsible for me actions.'

Rory continued backing away, knocking over a chair in his haste to escape. He knew only too well what his mother was capable of.

Annie heard him running up the stairs. When she was sure no one would be coming back down, she spread her arms on the table and lowered her head into the warm flesh, and let the tears she'd held in check fall freely.

Across the road Josie lay wide awake, staring at the flickering light from the fire dancing on the ceiling. Unlike Annie, her eyes were dry. She was too hurt and angry at herself to cry. How could she have been such a fool? Every time she thought of the way she had acted she squirmed with embarrassment. But never again. Oh no, never again. There would be no more false hopes where Rory was concerned. She didn't need him. She didn't need any man. She could cope very well on her own.

Her eyes began to close and she pulled the heavy quilt up around her neck. But even with the fire alight in the grate and the hot stone bottle nestling under her feet, she couldn't stop shivering.

CHAPTER SIXTEEN

'Two eggs, sausage, bacon and chips, twice. Oh, and fried bread, for table four, please, Mum.'

Annie slipped another four rashers of bacon and two slices of bread into a huge frying pan containing half a dozen sizzling sausages and five rashers of bacon. Turning the sausages over to brown, she then broke four eggs, one at a time, into a mug before pouring them into a separate pan. When everything was ready, she wiped her hands on the print apron she wore, picked up two clean plates from the pile stacked on the draining board, dished up the order and handed it to Jane.

'Sorry, Mum. Two mugs of tea as well, please.'

'You get that to table four while it's still hot. I'll bring the tea out.'

Annie poured the tea with one hand, while filling the space left in the frying pan with more bacon and sausages. This meal was the most popular with the market traders, and Annie always made sure the pan remained full until three o'clock, that time being the latest the traders had their dinners. It all depended on how busy they were.

As Jane left the kitchen, Josie entered.

'Blimey, it's like a madhouse out there today, Annie. Still, mustn't complain. We've only been open four months and already the business is making a profit. If it carries on like this, you and Jane will be getting a pay rise. And it's all thanks to you.' Josie sat down for a moment's rest and looked fondly at the small, plump woman. 'I must have been mad to think I could run a tea shop down an East End market. I'd've gone out of business in a month, if not sooner. Which reminds me . . .' Josie smiled. 'Table seven want three cups of tea – cups, mind you, not mugs. And a selection of your delicious cakes, of course.'

Annie turned from the stove and grinned.

'Let me guess now. Could that order be for the Slater sisters, by any chance?' When Josie nodded in amusement, Annie's grin broadened. 'By, but 'tis a strange coincidence they only ever come in here on a market day, isn't it? What with them being ladies, and the place always full of men on those particular days. Lord love them, they're game women, I'll give them that. Sure and the youngest of them will never see forty again, but they're not going down without a fight.'

Annie threw back her head and roared with laughter. The infectious sound brought a chuckle from Josie's lips and she had to clap a hand over her mouth to stop herself from making too much noise.

'Stop it, Annie, please,' she pleaded with the older

woman, who was now holding her stomach as if she were in pain. Wiping tears of mirth from her eyes, Annie nodded.

'I'm sorry, love. I shouldn't make fun of them, poor souls. But truth be known, if a man did as much as put a hand on any of them, they'd probably faint clean away.'

Still chuckling, Annie reached up to the cupboard where the china was kept.

'Here, I'll get it.' Josie got to her feet. 'You've got enough to do.' Laying out a silver tray, she remarked good-naturedly, 'You're a bleeding marvel, Annie. I don't know how you do it. I mean, what with cooking for the stallholders and passing trade, you still manage to find time to bake those lovely cakes. Then when you leave here, you go home and cook dinner for the family. It puts me to shame, it really does. I haven't half your energy; how on earth do you do it?'

Annie's face flushed with pleasure.

'G'wan with ye. 'Tis nothing. Sure an' I've been cooking for a brood since I was eleven, while me dear sainted mother went out to work, God rest her soul.' She made the usual involuntary sign of the cross she always performed when speaking of the dead.

'That's as may be, but I couldn't have managed without you, and Jane of course. Which reminds me, it's about time for her break, isn't it?'

The door to the kitchen was flung open.

'What's happened to the tea, Mum? I thought you said you were bringing it out. And what were you both laughing at? It must have been something really funny; you could be heard outside.'

Annie's hand flew to her mouth.

'Lord! I nearly forgot. Here, they're poured out. Take them through, will ye, love? I'll tell ye what we were laughing at later; g'wan now.'

'And when you've done that, go for your dinner break,' Josie commanded.

Jane made a face at both women.

'It seems a bit silly going out for my dinner when I work in a café,' she said forlornly. 'Besides, it's freezing outside. I'd rather stay here in the warm.'

Josie, the tray with the china teapot and plate of selected delicacies held in both hands, said firmly, 'No! You're going out, otherwise you'll end up working, like you did yesterday, and the day before.'

Jane started to protest, looked at Josie's face and shrugged.

'All right, I'll go. Even though I'll probably freeze to death. But don't you worry about that. When the police carry my frozen corpse in, don't feel guilty. Just lay me out in front of the oven to thaw out; oh, and make sure you leave enough room to step over me. I wouldn't want to get in the way.'

Her head held high, Jane gave a loud sniff and, holding a mug of tea in each hand, turned and pushed the door open with her buttocks. She was about to let it swing shut when Josie cried out, 'Hang on a minute, Jane. I've got me hands full an' all, you know.'

Annie returned to the stove. By the time Jane returned there was a steaming bowl of soup waiting for her.

'Get that down. Ye need something hot inside ye in this weather.'

Jane raised her eyebrows heavenward but stayed quiet. It was pointless trying to change her mother's mind; as she knew from past experience.

Minutes later, as she was being dressed for the outdoors by Annie, again Jane made no protest, making do instead with a deep sigh of resignation. She stood patiently as Annie buttoned up her coat, wrapped a thick scarf over her head and mouth and around her neck, tying it into a knot which she then tucked inside the collar of Jane's tweed coat. Josie came through just as Annie said, 'Now then. You go for a nice walk and get a breath of fresh air.'

Smothering a laugh Josie said, 'You're joking, ain't you? Bleeding hell! She'll be lucky to be able to breathe at all trussed up like that. The Christmas turkey had more room to move than that poor cow.'

Out in the street, Jane wandered aimlessly through the market, stopping at various stalls to chat with the traders. It was a nice feeling, being a part of the camaraderie that pervaded the market. Plus she had the extra satisfaction of knowing that she could now afford to buy anything that caught her eye, without having to ask her mother or one of her brothers for the money.

'You warm enough, Janie?' called out one of the stallholders.

Jane waved.

'Very funny, Charlie. Will you be in later?'

'Yeah! Too right I will, just as soon as Bert gets back to keep an eye on me stall. He must be 'aving second 'elpings, 'cos he's been gone nearly 'alf an hour. Me stomach thinks me throat's been cut.'

'See you later then, Charlie,' Jane replied.

She strolled on leisurely. Despite her objections at being forced out of the café, she was enjoying her time alone. She stopped by the fruit and vegetable stall and bought six large oranges as a treat for her parents and brothers, and one for herself, of course. When she reached the end of the market she crossed over and began to make her way back. There weren't that many stalls on this side of the street, due to the presence of the rival shops. She had just passed the haberdashery shop when two men barred her way.

'Excuse me, please,' Jane said, and stepped to the side to walk around them, but they moved again, stopping her from getting past, and a tiny ripple of fear made her stomach flip over. Then, determined not to be intimidated, and safe in the knowledge that she was within shouting distance of the stallholders, she said again, 'I said, let me pass, please.'

'Course we will, darlin', just as soon as yer 'and over yer purse.'

Frightened now, Jane turned to run, but the men were too quick. One of them grabbed her round the waist while the other snatched her basket. Then she was sent sprawling, hitting first her hip and then her head on the hard ground. Dazed, she heard a man call out, then the sound of feet running and lots of shouting.

'Come on, Jane, it's all right now, they're gone. Here, let me help yer up.'

Shaken, Jane grasped the firm hand as she got to her feet.

'Thank you,' she said, her voice quavering. Then she looked at the man holding her and gasped. Pulling away, she stared at Barney Hobbs.

'It's all right, love. I ain't gonna hurt yer. You don't have ter be afraid of me, honest.'

Jane, her eyes wide, tried to walk away, then cried out as a sharp pain shot through her ankle. Immediately Barney's arm went around her shoulders.

'What's the matter, Jane? You hurt?'

Almost crying with pain and fear, Jane twisted from Barney's grasp.

'You stay away from me, Barney. I mean it.'

Barney threw his hands up and backed away.

'Look, I don't blame yer for being scared, but I ain't gonna hurt yer, Jane. I just want to get yer back to yer mum.'

Hobbling, Jane stared into Barney's face suspiciously.

'And why would you want to help me, Barney? I still remember the last time we met.'

Barney bent his head penitently.

'I know, Jane, and I'm really sorry for the way I treated yer that day. I was drunk . . . I know that ain't no excuse, but it's been playing on me mind ever since. You're a nice girl, Jane, an' yer didn't deserve what I did to yer that day. And I don't blame Rory for giving me a good hiding. I'd've done the same in his shoes.'

He moved forward cautiously, not wanting to frighten her further. 'I know I don't deserve it, but . . . well, what I want to know is, if you'll forgive me. Yer probably won't believe me, but every time I think of what happened that day I cringe. If you'd been anyone else, I'd've come round your house to apologise, but . . .' He shrugged and smiled wryly. 'The truth is, I ain't that brave. But if you'll just let me help yer back to the café, it'd mean a lot to me.'

Jane stared hard into the handsome face, remembering vividly the cruel words and the assault on her body this man had subjected her to. Looking at him now, it was hard to reconcile Barney with that same man.

Sensing her suspicion, Barney changed tack.

'All right, love. I don't blame yer for not trusting me. Look, you wait 'ere and I'll go and fetch yer mum.'

At the mention of Annie, Jane sprang to life.

'No! No, don't do that. I'll manage,' she cried anxiously. The last thing she wanted was for her mum to come face to face with Barney Hobbs. There was no telling what Annie would do.

Suddenly she was surrounded by several men.

'You all right, Janie?' Charlie was holding her gently. 'We caught the buggers. They won't be bothering any more women for a long time. 'Ere, love, we got your purse back.'

'And yer oranges.' Another man stepped forward and handed over her straw basket. The oranges, a bit dirty from the road, had been placed back inside it.

Jane looked gratefully at Charlie and the other men who had come to her rescue.

'Thanks, Charlie, and the rest of you. It was kind of you to leave your stalls to help me.'

Charlie Watson's face took on a sheepish look.

'Don't be daft, Janie. We don't put up with that sort of thing round 'ere.' Glancing down, he saw Jane was limping. ''Ere, you've twisted your ankle. Come on, girl, I'll carry yer back to—'

Embarrassed by all the attention, Jane said quickly, 'Oh, no thanks, Charlie. I don't want any fuss. It's not that bad.'

It was at that point that Charlie noticed Barney's presence. His face grim, he said sharply, 'You 'ave anything to do with this, Hobbs? We all know about the feud between you and Rory, but a man would 'ave to sink bleeding low to take it out on an innocent girl.'

The rest of the men began to move in, their faces grim. To his credit, Barney didn't flinch. He stood his ground and said firmly, 'I didn't have nothing to do with those scum. I don't attack girls.'

'Yeah! Well, that ain't what we've 'eard, Hobbs. Word travels fast in the East End, 'specially down the markets, you should know that. And if what we've 'eard's true, this wouldn't be the first time you've tried to get at Rory through Janie.'

The small group were surrounding Barney now, murmuring menacingly.

Watching, Jane began to panic. The men looked set to do Barney serious harm, and as much as she disliked the man, she couldn't let him suffer for something he hadn't done.

Grabbing one of the men's arms, she gabbled, 'It wasn't anything to do with Barney, Fred. He was trying to help me.'

The men stopped in their tracks, all looking at Jane.

'You telling the truth, Janie? 'Cos we all know what he thinks of your Rory, and he ain't worth lying for.'

'No, I'm not lying, Charlie, honestly.' She appealed to the man she knew best. 'He's telling the truth.'

The men began to disperse, still muttering and

darting menacing looks in Barney's direction. Desperate to defuse the situation, Jane said, 'Please, all of you, get back to your stalls. I'd feel awful if anything was stolen while you've been helping me.'

Barney stepped forward.

'She's right. There's a lot of thieves about. I'll help her back . . . if that's all right with you, Jane?' He stared at her, holding his breath.

Just wanting the whole unpleasant episode over with, Jane nodded. After all, there was nothing Barney could do to her, not with every eye in the market trained on him.

'Thanks, Barney. That would be fine,' then she gasped as he swept her up into his arms. She hadn't been expecting to be carried. Feeling self-conscious, she tried desperately for something to say, then she remembered, and her face became sombre.

'I'm sorry about your dad, Barney. I didn't really know him, but my mum said he was a nice man.'

At the mention of his late father, a muscle twitched in Barney's cheek. He and his father hadn't always seen eye to eye, but Barney had loved him, and the pain of his loss was still raw.

'Thanks, Jane. Your mum was right, me dad was a nice man; not like me, eh?' There was a note of self-deprecation in Barney's voice; there was also the unmistakable sound of pain, and Jane bent her head in sympathy, for the thought of losing her own father was unthinkable.

Five minutes later, despite her protests, she was being carried into the café. Her face burned with acute embarrassment as the crowded room turned to stare at the spectacle.

Then Josie was standing in front of them, her eyes burning with anger.

'Get your hands off her, Barney—'

'No, no, it's all right, Josie,' Jane pleaded. 'Some men stole my purse, and Barney helped me. Charlie and some of the other traders chased them and got it back.'

But Josie wasn't convinced and continued to stare at Barney, her eyes suspicious.

'That was handy, wasn't it? I mean, you just happen to be passing at the same time Jane gets set on. Right little knight in shining armour, ain't you? All right, you've done your good deed for the day; probably for the century, knowing you. Now put her down before Annie comes out, otherwise it'll be you needing help getting home.'

Gently lowering Jane to the floor, Barney cast his eyes over Josie, hardly recognising her. The last time he'd seen her, she had been a drab, timid drudge, looking twice her age. This angry woman was confident, unafraid and surprisingly attractive, even in the plain outfit of a waitress. Yet he couldn't resist getting a dig in.

'Don't get yer knickers in a twist, Josie. I'm going.'

Turning his eyes on Jane, who was now being supported by Josie, his gaze softened.

'I'm glad you're all right, Jane. And I meant what I said earlier. I'm sorry about what happened before.'

Jane returned his gaze, and was alarmed and confused by the strange feelings she was experiencing.

'I know, Barney. Forget it, it's water under the bridge now.'

Josie hugged Jane against her side, glaring at Barney.

'Make sure you shut the door on the way out.'

Barney gave an exaggerated bow, and grinned.

'And I'm pleased to see you too, Josie. You're looking good these days. Amazing what money can do, ain't it?'

The kitchen door opened and Annie appeared, holding two plates. At the sight of her, Barney made a hasty exit. He'd rather face the entire market than Annie Flynn, for the Irishwoman's temper was legendary.

'Jasus! What's happened to ye, love?' Annie rushed forward, slamming down the plates on the nearest table, making the occupants jump. 'Let's get her into the kitchen, Annie. She's had a bit of a shock.'

Sitting in the kitchen with her foot in a bowl of warm water, Jane let her mother's worried words and ministrations wash over her. Safe now, she found herself remembering Barney Hobbs, and the kindness he had shown her. Maybe he had changed. He had seemed genuine enough in his apologies, though she would keep those opinions to herself. Sipping a hot mug of tea, she also remembered the strong arms carrying her back to the café, and a ripple of pleasurable excitement invaded her body.

Barney rounded a corner and cut down a back alley.

Two men were waiting for him. Taking out his wallet, he handed two pound notes to one of them.

''Ere you go, two quid as promised,' he said casually.

The man looked at his accomplice, then back at the man who had hired them to give the girl a scare.

'I think we deserve more than a poxy quid each.

Look at the state of us. You didn't say nothing about getting seven bells knocked outta us. Those bastards gave us a right hiding,' whined the man.

Barney flicked his eyes over them disdainfully. Both men were bruised and bleeding; not that it mattered to Barney.

'Take the money and piss off,' he growled. 'Unless you want another pasting.'

The men looked into the hard face and dropped their gaze.

'All right, guv'nor, there's no need ter get nasty.'

Barney watched them run off and smiled smugly.

The first stage of his plan had been set in motion. He was reasonably sure he had gained Jane's confidence; if so, the rest should be easy.

Washed and ready for bed, Josie snuggled up in her armchair by the fire. In her lap lay a book she planned to finish before she went to bed, her hands were clasped around a steaming mug of hot chocolate, and her aching feet were soaking in a bowl of warm water. Taking a sip of the milky beverage, she leaned her head against the high back of the chair, gazed into the cosy glow of the fire and gave a satisfied sigh.

This was one her favourite times, especially at the end of a busy market day. Not that she ever complained; the market traders were her bread and butter after all. Still, she was glad the market only opened four times a week. She didn't think she'd be able to manage if it was a full-time arrangement. Tomorrow would be quieter, thank goodness. On Wednesdays the café relied on passing trade and the shop assistants who occasionally came in for their dinner. Without the market traders wanting their breakfast, Josie opened up later on Wednesdays and Mondays, which meant she could have a lie-in tomorrow. Smiling at the thought, she opened the book and began to read.

She had only read two pages when a loud knocking disturbed her. Startled, she glanced at the clock and saw it was nearly ten o'clock. The only people who visited her were the Flynns, and none of them would knock at this time of night; not unless something was wrong. Suddenly afraid, she jumped to her feet, knocking over the bowl of water in her haste. Sliding back the bolt, she opened the door, her heart beginning to beat with fright when she saw who her late-night visitor was.

'Sorry it's so late, Josie, but I had to see yer.' Rory stepped into the hallway and headed for the kitchen with easy familiarity.

Stunned into silence, Josie closed the door and followed the tall figure, her wet feet marking the plain corduroy carpet. Wrapping her dressing gown tighter around her waist, she asked hesitantly, 'What is it? Has something happened to your mum or dad?'

'What?' Rory turned from where he was warming his hands by the fire, his face perplexed. 'Oh! No, nothing like that. I just wanted to ask yer about what happened to Jane this afternoon. I wouldn't 'ave known nothing about it if I hadn't overheard me mum and Jane talking.' Facing her directly now he demanded, 'What really happened, Josie? And don't go giving me any of that old codswallop about Barney Hobbs just *happening* ter be passing by when

Jane was attacked. He should 'ave been at work, 'specially since his dad died and left him the business. So what was he doing down Well Street market in the middle of the day, eh?'

Josie stared at him, her mouth agape, stunned into silence at the cheek of the man; but not for long.

'Hello, Josie, how are you? Oh, fine, thank you, and what about yourself? Keeping well, I hope? Dear me, where are me manners? Do come in and make yourself at home.'

The sarcastic tone caused Rory's eyebrows to rise in surprise. Then he looked properly at Josie and felt a sudden rush of apprehension.

Lowering his gaze, he rubbed the back of his neck and said in a quieter tone, 'Sorry, Josie. I wasn't thinking. It's just . . . Well, yer know how I feel about Barney Hobbs. And it's not the first time he's had a go at Jane, that's why I couldn't believe it when I heard Jane defending him to me mum. She clammed up when she saw me, and I couldn't get anything outta Mum either. So I thought maybe you could shed some light on what went on today. I know you probably think I'm overprotective of Jane, but she's me little sister and—'

'You sure it's Jane you're thinking of, Rory?'

Josie pushed past him, her anger rising at his cavalier attitude. Barging into her home without a by-your-leave. The bloody cheek of him. Sitting back down in the chair, she picked up a towel placed in front of the fire and began drying her feet.

'What d'yer mean by that, Josie? You ain't sticking up for Hobbs, are yer?' A belligerent tone had crept into Rory's voice.

'What I do or say ain't got nothing to do with you, Rory; not any more. But I'll tell you what I meant, only because I want to, not because you've come storming into me 'ome demanding an answer. I don't know if Barney was in the market on purpose or by accident, and to tell the truth, I don't really care. Jane wasn't badly 'urt, and that's all that matters. I'm not saying you wouldn't have wanted to get your 'ands on the men who attacked her, any brother would. But that's not what's really worrying you, is it, Rory? The fact is, you're obsessed with Barney Hobbs, you always have been. You're both as bad as each other, always trying to score points off each other. The pair of you have been fighting since we was at school, but now it's different, ain't it? Ever since Cathy Meadows came back you've been terrified she's gonna dump you as soon as your money runs out . . . Oh! Don't worry, your mum 'asn't said anything to me; well, she wouldn't, would she, not in the circumstances.'

She stared up at him, enjoying his discomfort. It was comforting to have the power to make him squirm. Somehow it gave her back some of the self-respect that had taken such a battering at New Year. Concentrating on her feet, she continued to rub them, even though they were now dry.

'It ain't that difficult to work out, we did used to go out with each other, didn't we? I know all about your savings. I should do, you were always talking about the money Annie was putting by for you. You was gonna do so much with it one day, weren't you? If I remember rightly, it was a toss-up between going around the world, and starting your own business one day. You were never satisfied with being like the other men in the street, you 'ad to be something better, and I don't blame you for that. There's nothing wrong with wanting to better yourself, I should know. But there's a big difference between wanting to make something of your life and thinking you're better than everyone else. And what did you end up doing with all that 'ard-earned money, eh? You've gone and chucked it away, or as good as. All you do now is save every penny while she's back with her fancy man, just so you can act the big man when she decides to come back for one of her visits. And now Barney's taken over the family business, 'e's even more well off than he was before, and that's what sticks in your throat. I wonder what Cathy will say when she finds out 'ow much Barney's worth now.'

Rory, his face looking like thunder, said harshly, 'You're enjoying this, ain't yer? But you ain't exactly as innocent as yer make out. Shaun's been walking round like death warmed up since yer decided yer didn't need his services any more. You did well outta him while yer 'ad the chance, didn't yer? All that painting and decorating 'e did for yer, you didn't mind 'im 'anging around then. Not when there was furniture to be shifted and extra locks put on your doors.' His lip curled back over his teeth as he bent his head towards her. 'There's a name for women like you, Josie, only I never—'

Before she realised what she was doing, Josie had raised her arm and brought the back of her hand down across his cheek. Springing to her feet, she spat out, 'That isn't true and you know it. I've been honest with Shaun from the start. The reason I stopped

243

seeing 'im was to spare 'im the pain he'd feel if I let our relationship go on any longer when I knew there was no future for us; Shaun's too good a man to mess about. He's twice the man you are. Now get out of my 'ouse, you're not welcome here, not any more.'

'Don't worry, I'm going.' Rory's face was now almost as red as his hair. 'I should have known better than to come 'ere. Only I didn't think you could be so spiteful. I 'ope you're pleased with yourself,' he added childishly.

When Josie remained silent, Rory, his chin wobbling with anger and resentment, growled, 'Well! Ain't yer got nothing to say for yourself?'

Josie advanced upon his retreating figure.

'Oh, yes. In fact there's two words I could say to you, and the second one is off.'

They stood still, glaring at each other like old adversaries, neither of them wanting to back down. But the tension was too much for Rory. Flinging himself away from her, he stormed down the hall and out of the house, banging the door behind him with as much force as he could muster.

Josie ran upstairs to her bedroom. Carefully lifting the corner of the net curtain, she watched the tall, lean figure march across the road and into the house opposite. When he had disappeared from view, she let the curtain fall back into place. Her hand clenched into a fist, and she pushed it against her mouth and bit down on it.

She hated him. She did. She didn't care if she never saw him again.

She stayed by the window until she suddenly became aware of her bare feet and the coldness of them. Then, her face set, she went back downstairs and curled up in the armchair, the book she had been looking forward to reading lying open and ignored on the hearth.

CHAPTER SEVENTEEN

'Looks like you've got company, guv.'

Pat looked towards his hut and saw three well-dressed men obviously waiting for someone, and that someone had to be him.

'Cheers, Bob. Put young Johnny on the cement mixing, but keep an eye on 'im. I don't want 'im sticking 'is 'ands together like he did last week.' Pat grinned.

'Righto, guv. I'll watch him, don't worry.'

Walking towards the waiting men, Pat pulled out a grimy handkerchief from his trouser pocket and wiped his hands as best he could. As he neared the trio, he recognised the youngest of the men and groaned under his breath. Putting on a pleasant face, he approached them.

'Afternoon, gentlemen. What can I do for yer, Mister Hunter?' He directed his attention to the man he knew only by sight. 'How's yer dad? Hope he's feeling a bit better.'

Matthew Hunter, the owner of the construction site, had suffered a heart attack the week before. Fortunately it had been a mild one; nevertheless, he had been ordered to rest. Pat had visited his employer in the hospital, not just because he was the man who paid his wages, but because he was genuinely liked and respected by all the men who worked for him. Matthew Hunter had told him he would be back at work as soon as the doctors allowed. In the mean time he had asked Pat to take care of the work in progress, and keep him informed of any troubles that might arise in his absence – and Pat intended to do just that.

Robert Hunter's eyes raked over Pat as if weighing him up.

'I'm afraid my father's health has taken a turn for the worse, that's why I'm here. As from today, I'll be taking over the business.' Aware of the curious eyes trained on him, he added loftily, 'Perhaps it would be better if we continued our discussion in private, Flynn.'

The condescending tone in the man's voice immediately raised Pat's hackles. Warning himself to remain civil, he replied shortly, 'In that case we'd better talk in the hut.'

Without waiting for an answer, Pat opened the hut door and entered, going straight to his desk. Moments passed, then Robert Hunter appeared in the doorway, his boyish face clearly showing his annoyance at Pat's indifferent attitude.

Pat surveyed the well-dressed man, smiling inwardly. Snotty little git. Probably expecting me to click me heels to attention. How a man like Matthew

Hunter could have a son like this one beggared belief. Pat had worked for Matthew Hunter for nearly ten years, and had always found him to be both fair and hard-working. Over those years his employer had often rolled up his sleeves and worked alongside his men when necessary; Pat couldn't imagine the son dirtying his hands. Still, he had better be polite, until he'd heard him out.

'Take a seat, Mister Hunter, we don't stand on ceremony here.'

Robert Hunter's eyes swept over the empty chair disdainfully.

'I'll stand, thank you. What I have to say won't take long. As I've just informed you, my father's health has deteriorated. On doctor's orders and my mother's insistence, both my parents embarked on a cruise yesterday. My father would have liked to come here to tell you of his plans in person, but my mother made the arrangements so quickly, he simply didn't have the time. During his absence I'll be overseeing the work site. I see from my father's files that this building's deadline is for August; I'd like to see it moved forward to April at the latest. I've already signed a provisional contract for a further building to start the first week in May. I've also decided not to renew our contract with Barnett's. As foreman you must be aware that that contract expires in two weeks, so I've made arrangements to purchase our supplies from Murphy's; to take effect from the end of this month.'

Pat stared at the foppish figure, hardly able to believe his ears. Then he was on his feet.

'You're 'aving a laugh, ain't yer? Me and my men

work flat out every day bar Sundays. That's why we're on schedule for August. We'd be able to bring the deadline forward by about a month, six weeks top, but no way can we finish the work here any sooner. We're halfway through February already. What you're asking is impossible. Even with overtime, there's no way we can complete the work by April. And as for Murphy's . . . Huh! They're nothing more than a bunch of crooks. All their materials are shoddy. Your father would never buy any supplies from them, he—'

'But my father is no longer in charge of this project, as I've already made abundantly clear,' Robert Hunter interrupted impatiently. 'I've studied the plans carefully, and I'm aware the work can't be completed in time with the current workforce. That's why I've hired temporary help. They'll be starting work tomorrow. I'd like you to assure your men that their jobs are in no danger. Indeed, they should be grateful for the extra help. But as a concession, I'm prepared to raise their wages until the work is completed. The labourers I've hired will of course not be paid as much as your experienced crew. I'm sure if you explain the situation—'

''Ang on. Let me get this straight.' Pat leaned across his desk, his eyes hard. 'You're gonna take on unskilled navvies, and buy materials from a firm that no reputable builder would use. 'Ave I got that right?'

The face in front of him flushed, the body becoming rigid.

'I don't like your attitude, Flynn. May I remind you that you are merely an employee, and as such will do as you are told. May I also remind you who pays your wages, and those of the men under you. If your scruples are the issue, there are plenty of other men who would be only too happy to take your place. But if you wish to hold on to your job, you will treat me with respect and address me as sir in any future discussions . . .'

Robert Hunter's face took on a bewildered look as Pat began to laugh. Drawing himself up to his full height, he rocked back on his heels and said haughtily, 'I fail to see any humour in the situation, Flynn. I must also warn you that the only reason I've tolerated your behaviour so far is because my father thinks so highly of you. If you continue to behave in this manner I won't hesitate to dismiss you. Now then, what do you have to say?'

His face sombre now, Pat sat back down in his chair and said quietly, 'If you wanna bring in jerry-builders there's nothing I can do to stop yer, but I'm 'aving no part in it, and neither will any of me men. As for showing yer respect, yer can shove it. I don't call any man sir, except for me dad; and of course the King, if he 'appened to drop in. He likes to keep in touch with us commoners, does our Bertie, God bless 'im.'

Holding his gold-topped cane in both hands, the irate man stared down at Pat. Robert Hunter had expected his demands to be accepted without question; now he knew better and was in a quandary. Like it or not, he needed the Irishman more than he would care to admit. Unlike his father, Robert Hunter was motivated by money, and had no qualms as to how he could acquire it. His father's condition wasn't as bad as he had led Pat to believe. The truth was, his mother, badly shaken by her husband's heart attack, had insisted on taking him away for a complete rest. They had left on a cruise yesterday, and if his mother had her way, they wouldn't be back for a while. During that time Robert Hunter was determined to make as much money as he could. His father had already halved his allowance and delivered a warning to start pulling his weight or risk having that allowance completely withdrawn. As things stood, his heart attack couldn't have come at a better time for Robert.

Remembering his rising gambling debts, a knot of fear gripped Robert's stomach. The men he owed money to weren't the type to wait patiently. He needed money and he needed it fast. And he would have to make a lot of it, because when his father returned and found out what he had done to his good name, he would be thrown out on his ear. But to do so he needed the belligerent Irishman's help. Swallowing hard, he adopted a more conciliatory tone.

'Look here, Flynn, let's not be hasty. There's a good deal of money to be made in the building trade, as you well know.' He attempted a smile, then felt it slip as the stony-faced man remained silent. Stumbling on, he added, 'What I mean is, you won't lose by it. I'll see you all right; do we understand each other?'

Pat held Hunter's gaze a moment longer, then pushed back his chair and came around the desk.

'Yeah, we understand each other all right. I think it's what the police would call bribery. If I was you, *Mister* Hunter, I'd get going. I've got work to do.'

A wave of panic rushed through Robert Hunter's slender frame. Nothing was going the way he had anticipated. He hadn't expected a subordinate like Flynn to stand up to him. Telling himself to act as his father would do in such a situation, he tried to adopt an authoritative tone, and was dismayed when his voice came out in a high squeak.

'I think it would be a good idea if you allowed your men to make up their own minds. Unless, of course, you feel you have the right to categorically speak on their behalf.' His body relaxed slightly as he saw Flynn's sudden indecision, and he pressed home his advantage. 'I'll return tomorrow. You can let me know the men's decision then. Good day to you, Flynn.'

Pat glared at the now smug face, fighting down the urge to give the baby-smooth skin a good slap. He could, however, vent his anger and wound the young man's vanity with words.

Jerking his head towards the two burly men waiting outside, he said in a scathing voice, 'I think yer baby-sitters are getting restless. Mind you, it's nothing to be ashamed of. It can be a dangerous place, the East End, if yer are of a nervous disposition.'

Robert Hunter's face turned scarlet. He opened and closed his mouth, trying to find the words to put the smiling Irishman in his place, and salvage some pride into the bargain, but none came. His lips pursed tightly, he said, 'I'll be back tomorrow, Flynn. We'll soon see who has the last laugh then. Your men may not be as loyal as you think.'

'Yeah! Yeah! Whatever.' Pat was seated at his desk, his head bending over a pile of invoices, his hand waving dismissively.

When the hut door slammed shut, he leaned back

in his chair, his face thoughtful, all trace of humour gone as he realised the enormity of the situation he found himself in.

'So what you're saying is that this Hunter bloke is trying to make some money while his father's away, and he's offering ye a bribe to turn a blind eye. Is that the way of it, lad?'

'That's about the scope of it, Dad. Old Mister Hunter will do his nut when he gets back. He's spent years building up a good reputation, and that stuck-up little sod's going to ruin it all if he gets his way.'

Paddy looked around the table at his sons, for this affected them all.

'What's to be done, lad?' he asked of Pat.

Finding all eyes on him, Pat shifted about uncomfortably on the hard kitchen chair.

'I honestly don't know, Dad. I mean, what can I do? It's all right me blowing off steam, but he's got me . . . well, all of us, over a barrel. If we all down tools he can easily sack the lot of us and bring in more unskilled navvies. There's plenty of them about. At least if we're on the spot we can keep an eye on what goes on, and maybe minimise the damage . . . Oh, hell. It's a bloody mess all round.'

And such was the gravity of the situation that Annie, who had been listening intently, didn't reprimand her son for swearing.

'Look, I've gotta get home. Freda will be wondering where I've got to.' Pat looked longingly around him, as if reluctant to go, then he shrugged and left.

There was silence in the room, then Rory, pushing back his chair, said, 'I'll go after him. He shouldn't 'ave to take all the worry on himself. What d'yer think, Dad?'

Paddy shook his head.

'Jasus, lad, sure an' I don't know what to think. One thing I do know is that I'd never be able to live with meself if any work I'd had a hand in caused injuries or even the lives of innocent people. No amount of money's worth that, son. But you're right. Get away after your brother, let him know he's his family behind him, whatever he decides.'

Rory ran out into the street, calling out loudly, ''Ere, wait up, Pat.'

Ahead of him Pat stopped and waited for his brother. Side by side they walked on, the cold air causing their breath to billow in front of them like clouds of fog.

Choosing his words carefully, Rory asked, 'So this bloke then, just how much did he offer yer, Pat?'

Pat glanced at his brother.

'Is that all you're interested in, Rory, the money?' The contempt in his voice made Rory flinch.

'That ain't fair, Pat,' he said defensively. 'But like yer said, if we don't do the work, that fella will soon find someone else. Why shouldn't we get a few quid outta it?'

Pat stopped abruptly.

'What's 'appened to yer, Rory? We all know about Cathy Meadows; it must be the worst-kept secret in the East End. And we all know she's only after what she can get. She comes 'ome, cleans yer out, then pisses off again. And yer put up with it. You've changed, Rory. There was a time when you'd 'ave knocked a man senseless if 'e'd offered yer a bribe to build shoddy homes that might collapse. So I'll ask yer straight: just how far would yer go to keep her? Or should I say, how low would yer sink?'

Rory turned away, his hands thrust deep in his pockets.

'Oh, fuck off, Pat. You can talk. Freda only has to say jump and you say 'ow 'igh. She's got yer right under the thumb, so don't go getting all hypocritical on me.'

Pat glared at his brother's back.

'Yeah, Freda's got me in check, I won't deny it, but there's only so far she can push me, and she knows it. Now I'm off, 'cos the minute I tell her what's going on, she's gonna ask me the same question – you've got that much in common with me wife. You know, the woman yer look down yer nose at.'

There was nothing Rory could say in his defence; he just stood out in the cold street, long after Pat had gone.

'Me and some of the men are going for a drink. D'yer fancy a pint, Pat?' Rory stood in the doorway of the hut, looking at the dark head bent over a pile of papers.

'What? Oh, no thanks, mate. I've gotta sort this lot out before I leave tonight. I wouldn't mind a couple of pies though, Freda didn't do me any lunch this morning. She's got the 'ump with me, 'cos of the extra time I've been spending 'ere. It'd be different if I was getting paid overtime, but seeing as I ain't . . .' The broad shoulders lifted and he smiled. 'She'll just 'ave to like it or lump it for now.'

'Blimey! You're getting brave in yer old age.' Rory

grinned back. 'I hope old Mister Hunter appreciates all you're doing to keep 'is reputation intact while 'e's off sunning 'imself abroad. Anyway, I'll get off. I don't wanna waste time talking in me dinner hour. Me governor's a right old slave driver.'

'And don't forget me pies,' Pat shouted after the retreating figure. Rory raised his hand to acknowledge the request and quickened his pace.

Pat shook his head, then applied himself to the task in hand. After twenty minutes he put down his pen, leaned back in his chair and rubbed his eyes. Lord, but he was tired. He hadn't had a decent night's sleep for the past month. Which wasn't surprising, since he'd been doing the work of two men during that time. But he wasn't the only one who'd been putting in the extra hours without extra pay. The way his men had rallied around to help was heartwarming; he was lucky to have such a good crew, for he couldn't have managed without their support.

Pushing back his chair, he paced the small hut, remembering the days following the visit from Robert Hunter. Pat had called a meeting the next morning, and apart from a few of the newer recruits, the men had stood firmly behind him. He had been unable to prevent Hunter from bringing in his motley crew, but he had been able to make sure that the unskilled labourers had been kept from taking part in any of the specialist tasks needed to make safe the homes they were building.

Like Pat, the majority of the men were proud of their skills and craftsmanship, and didn't want to see their work compromised by a group of navvies who, in Pat's words, didn't know their arse from their elbow. Also like Pat, most of the men had worked for Matthew Hunter for years and felt they owed some loyalty to the man who had kept them in steady employment.

Unfortunately Pat hadn't been able to stop Robert Hunter from obtaining materials from Murphy's; and that, most of all, was the reason for his sleepless nights. So far he and his men had managed to use the inferior stuff where it could do the least damage, while saving what was left of the dwindling supply from Barnett's for the important structural work. But those supplies were almost gone. Soon, maybe as early as tomorrow, they would be forced into using the substandard materials; it was either that or go on strike, and neither he nor his men could afford to do that. To make matters worse, the entire Flynn family depended on Hunter's money. If it was just him, Pat would have had no compunction in handing in his notice.

Rubbing his jaw, he stared out of the small window. He didn't think he could go through with using the crumbling bricks and rotten planks that were stacked in the site's warehouse. He'd been in the business long enough to know what havoc jerry-built homes could cause, often at the cost of innocent lives. Such homes could last for anything from four months to four years; a lot of the time it was down to sheer luck. If he went ahead with Hunter's plans and anything happened to the occupants, he'd never be able to live with himself. He wasn't alone in his doubts. Each and every man on the site knew the situation, and none of them were happy with it. What the hell was he going to do? Slumping back down in his chair, he tried to concentrate on the invoices but the words and figures appeared to dance before his tired eyes.

He needed a break. If he carried on like this he'd end up in hospital. It hadn't helped when Robert Hunter had turned up this morning, demanding to know when the work would be completed, his very presence causing disquiet among the men. Pat hadn't been able to hide his disdain for the man, and his contemptuous manner hadn't gone unnoticed.

Suddenly he felt an urgent need to get away from the hut, from the site. Picking up his jacket, he shrugged it on. He would join the men in the pub. Maybe a short time away from his working environment would liven him up.

He was putting the padlock in place when he heard steps behind him. He half turned, the hairs on the back of his neck standing up in warning. His instincts proved to be sound. The last thing he remembered was seeing a stockily built man holding a steel pipe high in the air. Pat saw the pipe coming down towards him but it happened so quickly he never had the chance to protect himself. He never even felt the vicious blow, for he was rendered unconscious the second the steel pipe staved in the back of his head.

'Drink up, lads, we've still got a lot of work to get done before knocking-off time.' Rory drained his glass and reluctantly placed it on the beer-soaked table.

The men around the table groaned.

'Don't remind us, Rory. I'm bleeding knackered,

we all are. You got any idea when old man Hunter is coming back?' one of them asked.

Rory shook his head.

'Nope! I'm no wiser than you lot. It's a pity there's no way to get in touch with him. He'd be back like a shot if he knew what his precious son was up to.'

As the men left the pub, Rory clapped his hand to his forehead.

'Bleeding 'ell! I nearly forgot Pat's pies. You lot go on, I'll catch up.'

Ten minutes later he entered the yard, then stopped in his tracks at the sight of the men grouped outside the hut.

''Ere, what's going on?' he called out, a ripple of alarm rushing through his body.

Three men were kneeling on the ground, blocking his view; one of them was his father. Rory pushed through them, his breath catching in the back of his throat at the sight that met his eyes.

Dropping to his knees, he gazed first at his brother, and then at his father, who was cradling Pat's bloodied head in his lap.

'Pat! Pat! Oh God!' Twisting his body around, Rory yelled frantically, 'Someone get some help—'

'I've already sent Shaun to the hospital, Rory. There should be help coming soon.'

Hearing the quiver in his father's voice brought Rory's head up sharply. His dad was crying. He had never seen Paddy cry, not ever. Rory's nose began to tingle as tears welled up behind his eyes, and a fear such as he'd never known before struck him deep in the pit of his stomach.

Pat's head was a bloodied mess. Whoever had

attacked him had obviously meant to inflict serious harm; if not worse.

'Don't just stand there. Get back, let him breathe, for Christ's sake.' Rory's voice was pitched high with growing fear. He couldn't feel any movement inside his brother's chest, or anywhere else. To all intents and purposes Pat appeared dead.

After what seemed an eternity, a hospital cart arrived, followed by a police wagon. Rory climbed into the ambulance with Pat and his dad, leaving the rest of the men talking to the police, and Shaun with the unenviable task of informing their mother that someone had tried to murder Pat.

'It's done, Mister Hunter. That Irish bastard won't be giving yer any more trouble.' Harvey Banks, one of Robert Hunter's henchmen, climbed into a waiting carriage and sat down heavily.

Robert Hunter's mouth was drawn in a tight line. In a short, clipped tone he said, 'I hope you're right about the other brother being more amenable, Banks. I don't have time to worry about finding a new foreman; in particular one who does as he's told without question.'

Banks leered cruelly.

'Don't yer worry about that, Mister Hunter. It's common knowledge round these parts that Rory Flynn's got a fancy piece that likes the 'igh life. 'E'll do what yer want, if yer offer 'im enough money.'

Gripping his cane tightly, Robert Hunter raised it and knocked on the roof of the carriage. Immediately it began to move away from the kerb.

Banks, knowing Hunter's moods, saw the young

man had withdrawn into himself and silently shrugged. It didn't bother him if the stuck-up git didn't want to talk. As long as he got paid each week, the little bleeder could do what he wanted.

It was gone ten o'clock before Rory left the hospital. His parents, Shaun and Freda had left over an hour ago after being told there was nothing they could do but go home and wait. A distraught Annie had at first refused to leave her son's bedside, until finally, exhausted with tears, she had let herself be led away. Rory had volunteered to stay as long as the doctor allowed; or until Pat awoke, whichever came first.

Stopping on the hospital steps, Rory lit up a Woodbine and took a deep drag into his lungs before walking down the rest of the steps and out on to the street. Pat still hadn't regained consciousness, and Rory, needing a break and unable to put up with the odours that pervaded every hospital, had slipped out for a breath of fresh air. He took another satisfied drag, his mind filled with anger against the cowardly thug who had attacked his brother, and fear that Pat might die.

The night had turned cold, and Rory shivered, turning up the collar of his jacket to protect his face and neck. Throwing the cigarette butt on to the stone step, he crushed it under his heel, wishing it was the face of the man who had left his younger brother for dead. He fought the temptation to light up another cigarette, and turned and walked with heavy footsteps back to the hospital, praying that when he returned Pat would have regained consciousness.

'Mister Flynn. May I have a moment of your time?'

Startled, Rory spun on his heel to see who had addressed him.

A carriage was waiting in the road, its door open. Squinting in the direction of the voice, Rory walked slowly forward, his head bent warily to one side.

'Over here, Mister Flynn,' the same voice called again.

Rory peered at the man hanging out of the window. He looked familiar. Rory kept on walking, trying to remember where he had seen the man before.

'Mister Flynn? Mister Rory Flynn?'

Rory was now face to face with the man.

'Yeah! Who wants to know?' he asked aggressively, then looked closer. 'You're Mister Hunter's son, ain't yer? I saw yer at the site this morning.'

Putting on his most sympathetic face, Robert Hunter said gravely, 'I was deeply upset to hear about your brother's misfortune. How is he?'

'About as well as can be expected after 'aving 'is head bashed in,' Rory answered bitterly. Stepping back a pace, he stared at Hunter with suspicion. 'What yer doing 'ere anyway? And don't tell me you're 'ere 'cos you're worried about me brother. We both know there's no love lost between you two.'

'Please, Mister Flynn, I don't want any unpleasantness. I won't insult your intelligence by pretending the only purpose for my visit is to enquire about your brother's health; although please believe me, I am genuinely concerned. Nevertheless, this unfortunate incident has left me – temporarily, I hope – without a foreman. The contractors for the next building project are getting impatient. The work

262

currently in progress is way behind schedule. That being the case, I'm sure you will appreciate that I need someone to take over your brother's job as soon as possible. I thought that maybe you might be interested in filling in for him – just until he's well enough to return to work.'

Rory's eyes narrowed, a sudden thought striking him. Reaching into the carriage, he grabbed hold of Hunter's throat.

'This is all very convenient for yer, ain't it, Mister Hunter? My brother won't go along with your crooked deals, and suddenly 'e's put into 'ospital. If I thought yer 'ad anything to do with—' A movement in the carriage caught Rory's eye and he tightened his hold. 'You tell your bully boy to keep well outta this, or by God I'll throttle yer.'

There was no doubt in Hunter's mind that the maddened man meant every word. Gesturing to Banks not to interfere, he struggled to speak.

'Please, Mister Flynn. I don't blame you for being angry. I agree the whole sorry business may appear suspicious, but at least give me the benefit of the doubt before jumping to any conclusions.'

Rory's grip slackened but he remained wary.

Rubbing his sore neck, Robert Hunter swallowed hard, the movement hurting his bruised throat. Blast these Flynns. They were each as stubborn and dangerous as the other. It must be the Irish blood in them. Everyone knew the Irish were renowned for their temper; and their drinking. If there was any other way to get the current building work completed in the allotted time, he wouldn't have hesitated in letting his heavies give the arrogant man a good hiding. Yet as tempting as that idea was, suspicions would be raised if two of the Flynn men were beaten up in one day. And he would still be without a foreman. If he could persuade Rory Flynn to take Pat's place, the men would accept him more readily than they would a stranger.

'Take a walk, Banks. I wish to have a word with Mister Flynn in private.'

'Righto, guv. Me an' Benji will be around if yer need us.' Banks stepped down from the cab, casting a menacing look at Rory. But Rory held the man's gaze without flinching.

Holding the door open, Hunter said, 'Please, Mister Flynn, get in. All I ask is that you hear me out. If you don't like what I have to say, then you can be on your way with no harm done. What do you say?'

Rory stood in the street, still distrustful of Hunter's real motives, then he climbed into the carriage. Like the man said, it wouldn't hurt to listen, and it was warmer in the cab than out on the street. Pulling the door shut, he sat down opposite Hunter.

'All right, I'm listening. But make it quick. I've got to get back to the hospital. I've been gone too long already.'

Feeling more confident now, Robert Hunter began to talk.

CHAPTER EIGHTEEN

Pat lay in a coma for three days. And those three days seemed to the Flynn family like three years. Annie and Paddy stayed by their son's bedside throughout most of the long, agonising wait.

Jane, despite tearful protests, had been ordered by Annie to continue working. Not only would it spare the young girl further distress, but also, as Annie had pointed out to her daughter, Josie couldn't run the tea rooms by herself.

The doctors had long since given up trying to persuade the family to stick to the hospital's visiting times. For as soon as Shaun and Rory finished work, which could be as late as nine at night, they took their parents' places by Pat's side. This enabled Annie and Paddy to get home for a much-needed rest, and ensured there was someone with Pat at all times.

And it wasn't just the Flynns who were in constant attendance; there was also a steady stream of Pat's workmates parading in their dirty overalls through the sterile ward, each of them anxious to see for himself that their gaffer was all right.

The only good thing to come out of the horrifying attack was that it brought Freda closer to her in-laws. Annie had always believed that Freda had pushed Pat into marriage just so she could give up her job at the matchbox factory and live off his wages; now she knew differently. Freda was devastated at the thought of Pat dying, and turned to Annie for comfort. No doubt she would revert to type once Pat was back home, but witnessing Freda's grief left Annie in no doubt of the love the woman felt for her husband.

Even though Pat had regained consciousness, the doctors were still concerned, due to the severity of the blow he had suffered. Head traumas, they had explained to Pat's anxious loved ones, were unpredictable; as a worried Annie was now repeating to Josie.

'The big fellow, ye know, the one in charge, specialist so I'm told, anyway, one minute he's telling us not to worry – pshaw!' Annie tossed her head impatiently. 'Jasus, but he might as well tell the Pope to get himself a wife. Anyway, according to this specialist, Pat could make a full recovery, or he might . . . he might . . .' Her voice broke and she turned away.

Josie watched helplessly as the small, stout woman vigorously attacked the pile of dirty crockery in the sink, her shoulders heaving up and down the only sign she was crying.

Moving closer, Josie put her arms around Annie's shoulders, and this simple, kind gesture caused

Annie to drop her head against Josie's chest, her body sagging.

'I'm so sorry, Annie. I don't know what to say. Look, why don't you go home, or to the hospital, if it'd make you feel better. I can manage. Everyone's pitching in to help.' Josie gave a small laugh. 'Charlie even cooked breakfast this morning, though he didn't have a clue how to work the stove. He broke nearly a dozen eggs, burned almost a pound of bacon, and only cooked the sausages on one side. Honestly, Annie, it was painful to watch, but nobody complained.' Hugging the trembling body closer, Josie murmured, 'They're a good bunch, Annie. And they're all rooting for Pat. We'd never have got this sort of support if I'd opened a posh tea shop up West, would we?'

Her eyes reddened, Annie gave a watery smile.

'You're right enough there, Josie love. They've been a tower of strength, God love 'em.' Dabbing at her eyes with a lace handkerchief, she sniffed loudly, her body shuddering as she composed herself. Then, patting Josie's hand, she said firmly, 'I appreciate the offer, love, but I'd go mad sitting at home, and I can't go to the hospital. The doctors have put their foot down at all the comings and goings. Mind you, they've been fair, I can't deny that. But now Pat's come round, they've limited visiting times to three people in the evening, and one during the day. They say too many people at once might be too much for him. Something about him needing plenty of rest. And seeing as Jane's there, there's no point in me going. We'll know soon enough if there's any news. Thank the Lord the hospital's only fifteen minutes away from here, and ten minutes from the building site.

'Now then, enough of this doom and gloom,' she said briskly. 'Those men out there need feeding, and as understanding as they've been, they won't want to be paying out good money for Charlie's cooking, else they might find themselves lying alongside our Pat.'

'Charlie just wants to help. I expect it makes him feel he's doing something. Speaking of which . . . I think the sausages are burning.'

'Jasus! Sure and I've never burned anything in me life.' Annie rushed to the frying pan, quickly moving it away from the heat.

'Don't worry, Annie. We can always blame it on Charlie,' Josie quipped, trying hard to take Annie's mind off Pat.

She herself had taken the news very hard. Even though she hadn't stepped foot inside the Flynns' since the embarrassing débâcle with Rory at the New Year's Eve party, she hadn't stopped caring about the family. Pat was like a brother to her, and she was worried sick about him. She'd hardly slept a wink since the brutal attack and had been one of the many visitors Pat had received. When asked her connection to the patient, Josie had answered, 'I'm his sister' without a moment's hesitation. The ward sister had stared at her before saying drily, 'I know the Irish are renowned for large families, but yours seems to have outdone itself.'

Rory and Shaun had been at Pat's bedside, yet what might have been an awkward situation was overshadowed by the sight of Pat lying in the hospital bed, his head covered in bandages, looking so pale, and so still. She had known to expect the worst, but nothing could have prepared her for the awful vision that greeted her. She would have fallen if Shaun hadn't quickly helped her on to the chair he had just vacated. She had stayed for over an hour, and during that time the trio had hardly exchanged a dozen words. Yet the atmosphere had been warm, with no hint of animosity. It was as if she truly was one of the family.

She had been to the hospital every day to begin with, at odd hours, but since Pat had come round and the new visiting restrictions had been put in place, she had stayed away to give the precious time to his real family.

'Don't forget, if you want any time off, you only have to say,' she told Annie.

'That's grand of ye, love, but I'm best off working. It helps keep me mind off Pat, and what might happen.'

'He'll be fine, Annie.' Josie squeezed the plump hand reassuringly. 'He's young and strong. You told me yourself that the doctors told you that would stand him in good stead. Besides, he's a fighter, is Pat. He's his mother's son. And you wouldn't give up without a fight, would you?'

Annie patted Josie's hand.

'No! And I'll not give up on Pat either.'

All businesslike now, she returned to the stove and began dishing up the greasy food that the market traders liked so much.

'Here, take these through, will ye, Josie? And tell anyone waiting they'll have theirs in another five minutes. Oh, and Josie . . .' Josie stopped, the large tray carrying four plates of steaming food weighing heavy on her arms, and looked quizzically at Annie. Her voice quiet, Annie said, 'Will ye tell them out there I'm grateful, ye know . . .'

Josie nodded.

'Yeah, I know,' she replied sympathetically. 'I'll tell them.'

'Jane, over here.'

Jane looked to where the voice was coming from and felt a tingle race up her spine. Since the incident down the market, and the four accidental meetings since, she had found herself looking all around her when she was out alone, hoping that Barney would appear. The feelings she had for Barney Hobbs were very mixed. On the one hand she felt guilty for making friends with her adored Rory's enemy; but on the other, she found herself becoming more and more attracted to him.

Even though she knew none of her family would be visiting Pat until later, she glanced quickly up and down the street to make sure. Satisfied she had not been seen, she walked quickly to the corner.

'Barney! What are you doing here? If any of my family see me with you, I'll be locked in my room until I'm forty – and I'm not joking.'

Barney tipped his hat to the back of his head and smiled disarmingly. That smile made Jane's legs go weak at the knees. Afraid she would give her feelings away, she stared down at the pavement.

'Yer worry too much, Jane. Yer wouldn't make a very good mistress, would yer? . . . Oh, come on, love, I was only joking.' He bent his head down and gently lifted her chin with his fingers. 'You take life too seriously, Jane. You only live once, and I say make the most of it; 'cos yer won't get a second chance.'

Barney could feel the trembling of the innocent girl's body, and he smiled inwardly. This was going to be like taking sweets from a baby. Barney's gaze swept the street, for he too was not eager to meet any of the Flynn family, then he put an arm around Jane's shoulders and led her off towards a small restaurant he knew well.

When they were seated and their meal was ordered, Barney said, 'Relax, Jane. None of your lot are likely to come in here, are they?'

Calmer now, Jane looked at the handsome face opposite her, noticing the curious stares being cast in their direction. Leaning her elbow on the table, she covered her face with her hand, saying, 'We seem to be attracting attention, Barney. They're probably wondering why a man like you would want to be seen in public with a girl like me.'

Her tone was light, but Barney could detect the misery reflected in it, and was surprised to feel a moment's qualm about what he was planning to do. Annoyed with himself, he silently shrugged off the feeling. He had put too much time and effort into his plan to get to Rory through Jane to start going soft now.

This was the fifth time they had met since he had rescued Jane from her would-be attackers. On each occasion he had contrived to meet her when he was sure she was on her own, and he always expressed surprise when they bumped into each other, careful not to raise any suspicion on her part. On those occasions they had merely talked, the object being to make Jane feel more comfortable in his company. But Barney was quickly becoming bored. He was too used to having women fall at his feet to waste time chasing them. If it had been any other girl but Jane, he would have lost interest by now. It was only the desire to get one over on Rory that was spurring him on.

Barney hadn't even considered the possibility that he would fail to get Jane into bed. No woman had ever turned him down, and he couldn't see why Jane would be any different. Not that he would ever brag about it, for if Rory found out what he had done to his little sister, he would kill him; Barney had no doubt about that. It would be enough that he, Barney, would know. Besides, he thought as he looked across the table at Jane, he would be doing the poor cow a favour. No other bloke would be interested in her, not with that ugly birthmark covering half her face.

'What are you smiling at, Barney? If it's something funny, let me in on the joke. I could do with a laugh.'

Realising he had nearly let his kind façade slip, Barney warned himself to be careful. Jane might be disfigured, but she was no idiot.

'Oh no, it's nothing, love. Just remembering something that 'appened at work. The manager of one of me shops caught an old dear shoplifting. When 'e stopped 'er from leaving she laid into 'im with 'er walking cane. Poor sod took a right beating. Well, 'e couldn't fight back, could 'e? She must 'ave been well

272

into her seventies. So while me manager was rolling about in agony, she walks off with a shopping bag full of me hard-earned merchandise. Anyway, that's not important. I only came to the 'ospital on the off chance I'd see yer and find out 'ow Pat is. I know I ain't exactly a friend of the family, but Pat's a good bloke, he didn't deserve what 'appened to him. Do the police know why 'e was attacked?'

'No. The hut door was open, but nothing had been disturbed. It's a mystery why anyone would want to hurt Pat, but at least he's a lot better than he was.'

A wistful look came over Jane's face.

'He's talking more now, but he's still very weak. The doctors say he'll have to stay in hospital for at least another fortnight, and Pat's not too happy about that. He wants to come home and can't understand why he can't. Mum and Dad won't stand up against the doctor. And we can't tell him how bad his injuries are. He thinks he just got a bump on his head. If we tell him the truth, and he realises how dangerous his condition really is, it could put his recovery back; at least that's what the doctor's told us.'

'You poor love, it must be like living a nightmare right now. Here, have a drink, it'll help settle yer nerves,' Barney said soothingly as he poured some wine into the glass by Jane's plate.

Jane's eyes widened in fright.

'Oh no, Barney, I can't. I mean, I don't drink, and besides, I've got to get back to work. And my mum would throttle me if I turned up drunk.'

Barney laughed.

'Don't worry, darling. Yer can't get drunk on wine. Over in France parents give their kids wine with their meals, and not only in France. There's a lot of countries that 'ave wine with all their meals, instead of a cuppa tea like we do over 'ere.'

Jane looked at the clear liquid with trepidation, yet even as she struggled to decide whether to drink it or not, all she could focus on was the fact that Barney had called her darling. If she didn't drink the wine she would look foolish, childish, and she didn't want to upset him. Feeling gauche and out of her depth, she picked up the glass warily. Under Barney's watchful eyes she gingerly took a sip, then shuddered.

Barney laughed.

'It's all right, it takes a bit of getting used to. Tell yer what, 'ow about some champagne? I bet yer'll like the taste of that.' Turning in his chair, he called out, 'Waiter, waiter, could I have a bit of service 'ere?'

Again heads turned, making Jane's embarrassment more acute.

'Please, Barney. Don't make a fuss, everyone's looking.'

Barney's eyes swept the room.

'So what, let 'em look,' he said flippantly.

The waiter arrived with their meal.

'Your dinner, sir. Is there anything else you require?'

'Yeah! I'd like a bottle of your best champagne, at the double.'

Jane cringed. She imagined that all eyes were on her. Feeling like a fish out of water, she hesitantly picked up her knife and fork and speared the smallest chip on her plate. Within minutes the waiter had returned with a green bottle in a bucket of ice.

'Come on, Jane, tuck in. They do a lovely steak dinner here. 'Ere, let me pour yer a glass of champers.'

'Oh, no, I couldn't . . .' Jane started to protest, her words dying on her lips as she saw an impatient look come over Barney's face. Not wanting to spoil the moment, she picked up the glass and took a sip, then another. Barney had been right, this champagne was much nicer than the wine she had tasted earlier. It was almost like drinking lemonade.

'That's better. I told yer you'd like champagne, didn't I? 'Ere, get another glass down yer throat . . . Don't worry,' he said quickly as Jane made to protest. 'Yer can't get drunk on champagne. I wouldn't let yer drink it if it was gonna get yer drunk.' Refilling her glass, he topped up his own and raised it. ''Ere's to Pat. Let's 'ope 'e gets well soon and the police get the bastard who did it. Who's with 'im now, by the way?' he asked casually, wanting to know if there was any chance of bumping into one of the Flynn men while in the company of their precious Jane.

Jane lifted her glass self-consciously.

'Oh, we don't have to be with him all the time now he's come round. Mum asked me to go and sit with him awhile. He gets upset if he's left alone too long, poor thing. I can't blame him, it's not very nice being in hospital. But he sleeps a lot; the doctors keep giving him drugs to keep him calm, otherwise he'd be out of bed and heading for home, and like I said before, that could be dangerous . . .' She took a big sip of the champagne to help ward off the feelings of panic that beset her when thinking of her brother. 'Anyway, once I get back to work, Mum might come up and visit if we're not too busy. Josie's been very good, but then she's like a part of the family.'

Not comfortable eating in front of Barney, Jane took delicate mouthfuls of the tasty meal, wishing she was at home and able to do justice to the unexpected treat.

'That's it, love, eat up,' Barney encouraged her, pouring more champagne into her glass.

When they left the restaurant, Jane staggered as the fresh air hit her.

'Steady on, love,' Barney laughed as she fell against his side.

Jane gripped his arm as her head began to whirl.

'Barney! Barney, I feel strange. Sort of like my head's floating above my body . . .' She giggled suddenly. 'Oh dear, I think I might have had too much of . . . of that cham . . . champagne. I thought you said I could . . . couldn't get drunk.' She wagged a finger at him in mock anger.

Barney hugged her closer, amazed at the effect the alcohol had had on her. Despite his urgings, she had only drunk two glassfuls of the sparkling wine, yet she was acting as if she'd downed the whole bottle. Guiding her along the pavement, he was dismayed when she started to call out to strangers, then began to dance and sing at the top of her voice.

As they progressed in the direction of Barney's home, he began to feel anxious. People were stopping to stare at Jane's antics, calling attention to the odd couple. And that was the last thing Barney wanted. So far he hadn't bumped into anyone he knew, but he was taking a risk by bringing Jane to his home. For all he knew someone might be watching them from behind closed curtains. Practically carrying her now,

Barney made his way around the side streets until he was in his back garden, though he didn't breathe properly until he was safe inside the four-bedroomed house.

"'Ere we are, Jane love. You'd better 'ave a lie-down while I make some tea. I can't take yer to work in this state, can I? Your mum would have the 'ead off me shoulders.'

Quieter now, Jane allowed Barney to guide her into a large bedroom. She was so tired. Through an alcohol-induced daze she felt herself being undressed and futilely tried to ward off the strange hands that were stripping her. Something was wrong, terribly wrong, but she was too tired to prevent herself from being put into the double bed. If she could just get some sleep she would feel better. She snuggled down into the warm feather bed and closed her eyes. She was floating. Floating outside her body. It was a nice feeling; strange but pleasant. The bed sagged as a weight climbed in alongside her and a warm body pressed close to her bare skin. And that was pleasant too – at first. Then it started to hurt, and by the time the real pain penetrated through her stupefied mind, it was too late.

Barney sat on the side of the bed, looking down at the sleeping girl. Jane was lying on her side, the ugly birthmark hidden from view, and the sight of the lovely face brought a sharp breath of shock to the back of his throat. Lying there so peacefully, she looked about twelve years old.

Swearing softly, Barney got up and took a cigarette from the pack on the bedside table. Inhaling the smoke, he struggled with his conscience. All this time he had been planning, and now he had succeeded, but there was no sense of victory, just a sour taste in his mouth and a tight knot in his stomach. Cursing, he began to dress. Within minutes he was fully clothed, wanting only now to get Jane out of his house, and back to her mother. Then he swung round, startled to hear his name whispered.

'Barney! What did you do, Barney?'

Jane was looking up at him, her blue eyes filled with tears and hurt betrayal.

His voice hard now, he snapped, 'Get dressed and hurry it up. I've got work to get back to, and so do you.' His eyes were darting all round the room, anywhere but at Jane.

'Please leave me to get dressed in private, Barney. I think it's the least you can do.' Jane spoke quietly and with dignity, and it was that fact that drove the burden of guilt deeper into Barney's mind. Too ashamed to look at the girl he had used so cruelly, he left the room.

Out on the landing, he sat down on the top stair and dropped his head into his hands. He was still there when Jane emerged from his bedroom. He went to rise but Jane's voice halted him.

'I know my way from here, Barney. Please stay where you are until I've gone. And don't worry about me telling anyone what happened. I don't relish the idea of anyone finding out what a stupid idiot I am; I feel ashamed of myself enough as it is.'

Barney moved to let her pass, his guilt mixed with astonishment at the way Jane was handling the situation. He had expected her to cry and try to hold on to him; instead she was acting like a woman beyond her years.

He did as she had asked him.

And he stayed there for a long time after Jane had left the house.

CHAPTER NINETEEN

Josie shut the door behind her, grateful to be home. Kicking her shoes off, she headed straight for the kitchen and put the kettle on to boil. While she waited she removed the takings for the day from her bag and laid the cash box on the table, noticing it was markedly heavier than usual. Being Easter Saturday, the market had been extra busy. It seemed to Josie that the world and his wife had been in the tea shop today.

Emptying the contents of the cash box onto the kitchen table, Josie sorted the coins into different denominations, entering the amounts into a leather-bound ledger. The kettle whistled just as she had finished adding up the rows of figures, and with a sigh of relief she closed the book.

The tea made, Josie curled up in her chair by the empty grate, the mug clasped in her hands, for once thankful of the solitude of the empty house. She'd never thought the day would come when she would be glad she was no longer able to come and go as she pleased from the Flynn household, for that once happy home was now bitterly divided.

Taking comfort from the well-earned tea and rest, Josie mused over the past two months.

Pat had made a full recovery, but the reason behind the unprovoked attack was still unknown. At least by the police. Everyone had been so relieved when Pat had left the hospital, not least Pat himself, who was eager to get back to work, that speculation about his attacker had been pushed to the back of everyone's mind; including Pat's. He'd had to rest at home for a further fortnight, advised by the doctor and enforced by Freda and Annie, and during that period everything had been fine. Then Pat had gone back to work, and all hell had broken loose.

He had known that Rory had taken over his job in his absence, and had been immensely grateful that someone he could trust had been put in his place. That was until he'd discovered that Rory had fallen in with Robert Hunter's demands and was using the substandard materials Pat had fought so hard against. The brothers had nearly come to blows, and they would have if Paddy and Shaun hadn't stepped in and separated them.

Since then the two of them had barely spoken. Pat had resumed his position as foreman, but by then too much damage had already been done. When challenged, Rory had defended his actions by asking Pat what he would have done in his place; and to this, Pat had had no answer, for it was that same predicament he had been wrestling with when attacked. And that knowledge had caused Pat's suspicions to resurface. The assault that had left him hospitalised had been very convenient from Robert Hunter's point of view, but without proof Pat could do nothing.

The building was now near completion, but the Flynns were still a family at war, with Paddy and Annie stuck in the middle.

Josie shivered as the evening began to turn chilly. Rather than go to the trouble of lighting a fire, she ran upstairs to fetch her dressing gown and a blanket from the foot of her bed. As she turned from the bed, she couldn't help, out of years of habit, glancing out of her window to the house opposite. She paused, her expression turning to one of annoyance, as she saw the shadowy figure of Jane crossing the road towards the house. Josie bit her bottom lip and immediately felt guilty for the way she was feeling, telling herself it wasn't so long ago that she used to escape to the noisy, happy fold of the Flynn family. Now it was her house that had become a refuge.

Running down the stairs, she opened the door before Jane had time to knock.

'Oh! You gave me a fright. How did you know I was here?' Jane entered the house breathlessly. 'I'm not stopping. Shaun's going to the chip shop in a minute and Mum asked me to pop over to see if you wanted anything.'

At Jane's thoughtful words, Josie experienced another wave of shame. You selfish cow, she berated herself silently. Here she was, annoyed that her quiet night in might be invaded, and all Jane wanted was to save her friend from having to cook after a long day.

'Yeah! That'd be nice, ta. Hang on while I get me

purse.' As she went to fetch her bag, she noticed that Jane hadn't followed her into the kitchen, which was unusual.

'Here you are, love. I'll have cod and chips . . . No, I've changed me mind, I'll have a bit of skate instead, and whatever everyone else is having. It's my treat. You deserve it after the day we've had. I don't know about you, but I could go to sleep on me feet right now.'

'Oh, I don't know, Josie,' Jane said awkwardly. 'You know what Mum's like about taking favours . . .'

'Don't be daft. It ain't favours when it's among friends. Now you go on home, and if your mum kicks up a fuss, you send her over to me.'

Jane smiled, but there was sadness in her eyes, causing Josie to take a better look at her young friend.

'What's up, Jane love? You've not been your usual self lately. Is it this business between Rory and Pat?'

Jane had visibly jumped; now she relaxed.

'You're right, Josie. It is because of Pat and Rory. And it really makes me angry, because for one thing Pat doesn't live at home any more, so he can come around shouting the odds then go back to his own house. Then when he's gone, Rory starts trying to put his side of the argument, and me, Shaun, Mum and Dad are caught in the middle. We can't take sides, can we? But it is causing a lot of bad feeling. Mum won't hear a word said against Rory, but then he was always her blue-eyed boy. That's what makes Pat so mad. My dad tries to keep the peace, but it's not easy. I feel sorry for me dad and Shaun. It's bad enough at home without having to try and keep Rory and Pat out of each other's way at work.'

Josie tried hard to look sympathetic but it was difficult. She'd been hearing the same grievances every day at the tea shop from a deeply concerned Annie. But Jane was only sixteen; she shouldn't have to be involved in the bitter dispute between her brothers. Remembering her earlier uncharitable thoughts, Josie said kindly, 'Look! How about you come back here after supper? We can have a proper chat; I'll even light the fire.'

Jane's pinched face brightened.

'Thanks, Josie, I'd love to. I know it's a terrible thing to say, but I'd be glad of the chance to get out of the house for a while.'

'Well, don't just stand there, get off 'ome before Shaun goes without waiting for you to get back . . . Oh! I nearly forgot . . . Would you take the money with you? I've already counted it, but check it for me, will you? I'm bleeding hopeless at arithmetic.'

It was common knowledge that all Josie's takings from the tea room were kept at the Flynns' for safekeeping. It had been Annie's idea to continue this practice, mainly so she wouldn't have to lie awake each night worrying about Josie having large sums of money in her house.

Later, as they sat by the fire, Josie kept darting worried glances at the young girl as she talked incessantly about mundane matters. She knew Jane well enough to know there was something, other than her family troubles, weighing on her mind.

Her face set, Josie cut into Jane's ramblings.

'What's up, Jane? And don't try fobbing me off either. Something's worrying yer, and not only today neither. You've been going round like a tit in a trance for the last couple of months. At first I put it down to you worrying about Pat, which was understandable at the time, but not now.' She stared hard into the young girl's eyes. 'Look, I'm worried about yer, love. If there's something on your mind you can tell me. I promise I won't tell anyone; not even your mum. Though I can't think of anything yer could have done that would be bad enough to make yer frightened of telling your mum.'

Jane's head drooped, her fingers plucking nervously at her skirt. Josie, watching her friend struggle with her emotions, kept her counsel. Finally Jane mumbled, 'Can I ask you something, Josie?' Relieved that Jane was finally going to tell her what was worrying her, Josie smiled.

'Course yer can, you daft cow.'

Jane swallowed, took a deep breath and blurted out, 'Would you have Rory back if he asked you?'

The question was so unexpected it shocked Josie into silence.

'Oh dear, I've upset you, haven't I? I'm sorry, Josie, I shouldn't have asked such a personal question.'

Gathering her thoughts together, Josie licked her lips before replying harshly, 'What on earth made you ask me that?'

Jane hung her head, shaking it from side to side.

'Look, forget what I said, Josie. Please! Anyway, I'd better be getting home. Hopefully my brothers will have gone out for the evening, and peace will reign once more.'

She made an attempt at a laugh, but couldn't quite manage it, then went to rise from the armchair, but Josie wasn't about to let her off the hook so easily.

''Ang on a minute, Jane. You must've had a reason for asking a question like that. It didn't just come out of the blue.' She leaned forward, her expression urgent. 'Now, tell me what's going on in that head of yours. And don't bother trying any lame excuses. I want the truth, 'cos you ain't leaving here till I get it . . . Oh! Oh, don't cry, love,' Josie said quickly as tears welled up in Jane's eyes. 'I didn't mean to have a go at you, but you must admit, it was a bleeding strange thing to come out with. Look, forget what I just said. You get off home and put your feet up. It's been a long day and—'

'No! I don't . . . don't want to go home, Josie, that's just the point. I . . . I know that's an awful thing to say, but I can . . . can't help it. Mum and Dad try to keep up a front, but the atmosphere is so awful sometimes.' Her entire body heaving with sobs, Jane stumbled on. 'And . . . and I was just thinking how . . . how different things would be if you and Rory got ba . . . back together. Mum's been sending me out of the room after dinner most nights, but . . . but I can still hear them arguing from my bedroom.'

Totally lost now, Josie's forehead furrowed in bewilderment.

'Just a minute, love. I'm not with you. What on earth has me and Rory got to do with—'

Tears streaming down her cheeks, Jane valiantly strove to compose herself. Drawing in a deep, shuddering breath, she spoke so quietly Josie had to strain to hear her words.

'Because if you were still going out with Rory, he wouldn't be so desperate for money to keep that

286

Cathy Meadows happy, and he wouldn't have gone along with that man's plans to cut corners on the new building. He keeps saying he hasn't done anything wrong, but he's lying, we all know it, and he knows it too. I think he's more angry with himself than Pat, 'cos Rory's a good man, you know he is, Josie. It's that horrible woman's fault. Whenever she comes back she causes trouble, but I never thought Rory would let himself be bribed on account of her.' She stopped, her breathing rapid, her face flushed. Then she raised her head and looked Josie straight in the eyes, her own defiant. 'I hate her, Josie. I really hate her, and that scares me, 'cos I've never hated anyone before, and . . . and it's not a nice feeling.'

Josie held Jane's gaze.

'I know, love, believe me I know. If it makes you feel any better, you're not alone. I hated her for a long time, but in all fairness, nobody's forcing Rory to keep on seeing her. He knows what she's like, and if he's stupid enough to keep on spending money on her, well, that's his look-out. He's a grown man, love, and he makes his own decisions. And he has to take the consequences of his actions; we all do. Anyway, how d'yer know he's taking bribes? I mean, from what Annie's told me, Pat would've had to do the same, or face the sack. It's all very well having principles, and I admire people who do, but it's cold comfort if you've a family to support. So don't be too hard on him. For what it's worth, I don't believe Rory would ever take a bribe, 'specially if people's lives were at stake. Anyway, there's nothing we can do about it now. Best leave it to the men to sort out among themselves.'

A sudden wave of tiredness swept through her body.

'Look, love, I hope you don't think me rude, but I'm whacked. I promised meself an early night with a good book for company, but I think I'll give the book a miss, 'cos I can hardly keep me eyes open.'

Immediately Jane jumped to her feet, flustered, already regretting her embarrassing outburst. Brushing her tear-stained cheeks with the back of her hand, she mumbled, 'Sorry, Josie. I didn't mean to outstay my welcome.'

'Don't be silly, you could never do that.'

Josie walked Jane to the door, striving to keep her tone light, for after hearing yet another sordid account of Rory and that slut, she too was hurting inside. Only unlike Jane, she wouldn't afford herself the luxury of unloading her misery with tears. She'd already shed enough over those two to last a life-time.

Just as she was about to close the door, Jane stopped and turned as if about to speak.

'What's up, love?' Josie asked, hoping Jane wouldn't notice the tiredness in her voice.

Jane gave a weak smile.

'No, it's nothing. Good night, Josie, thanks for the chat.'

'Good night, love. See you Monday.'

Wearily Josie closed the door, but not before she'd seen the anxious look that flitted over Jane's face.

As she prepared for bed, she remembered that look and wondered if there was something Jane was keeping from her, apart from her worry over her favourite brother.

Her face stretched in a wide yawn as she snuggled down under the bed covers. Whatever was worrying Jane could wait until tomorrow.

Rory sat on the edge of the bed, buttoning up his shirt, wishing he didn't have to leave the woman he loved. When he was fully dressed he turned and rolled over, leaning on one elbow as he gazed down at Cathy.

'I'll have to go, darling, it's late.' He stroked her smooth skin with the back of his hand.

Cathy rolled over and smiled lazily. Catching hold of his hand, she laid it against her cheek.

'I had a wonderful time tonight, Rory. I'll be here for another few days, so when will I see you again?' she murmured seductively.

The corners of Rory's mouth lifted in the crooked smile she loved so much. Yet even loving him as she did, it wasn't enough. Pulling herself upright, she laid her head against the feather pillows, knowing how beautiful she looked with her mass of golden curls tumbling over her shoulders and naked breasts.

Rory bent down to kiss the full lips.

'Every night of me life if I could, sweetheart. And we could if you'd leave that Jonathan bloke. I—'

Cathy pulled away from him, her expression changing swiftly to one of irritation; the loving intimacy they had shared only a few moments earlier vanishing like a puff of smoke. Her voice cool, she said, 'For heaven's sake don't start that again, Rory, it's getting to be boring. Now you listen to me, and listen good, 'cos I'm only gonna tell you once more. I ain . . .' She paused, then, in the affected voice she always adopted when wanting to put Rory in his place, continued, 'I mean, I'm not going to leave Jonathan. I'm too used to the good life to throw it all away to live in some dreary hovel, like the ones you're building. I know what it's like to live from hand to mouth, and I'm not going back to that way of life. And I'm sick of having to repeat it over and over again. What will it take for you to accept the fact that I'm perfectly happy as I am? Do you want it carved in stone? Oh! Damn you, Rory. Why can't you be satisfied with the way things are? Go on, go home to your bloody family. I'm sure your mum will be waiting up for you.' Her upper lip curled back over white teeth. 'All you ever talk about is your precious family . . . and good old Josie of course.'

Rory turned away from her, his fists clenched tight, wondering how it was possible to love a person and hate them at the same time. Between clenched teeth he growled, 'Don't push me too far, Cathy.'

'*Don't push me too far, Cathy,*' she mimicked sneeringly. 'Or what?'

There was no mistaking the challenge in her voice. She had thrown down the gauntlet; now it was up to Rory to either pick it up or let it lie.

The bedsprings squeaked as Rory removed his weight.

'I'm going. There's no point talking to yer when you're in this sort of mood. But I'll tell yer this much. I'd move outta 'ome and get a place of me own if I thought it'd make things easier for us, instead of 'aving to sneak a couple of hours in some poxy hotel. But then I wouldn't 'ave as much money to spend on yer if I got me own place, and you wouldn't like that, would yer?'

Cathy's face remained mulish.

'If you really loved me, you'd find a job that paid better. Or better still, take that job Robert Hunter offered you. Just because your brother's taking the moral high ground, it doesn't mean you have to. I mean, what does it matter if you've cut a few corners here and there? Lots of builders do it all the time; what makes you so special? Besides, it's not as if those flats are being built for people that matter. In fact the sort of tenants your buildings attract are probably from the slums. They'll think they're in the lap of luxury after the hovels they've been living in.'

Rory slowly turned to face her, his emotions in turmoil. A combination of anger, fear and pain filled his eyes with mist and blotted her from his sight, and he pulled at his collar to ease the choking feeling in his throat. Then the mist cleared and he saw her as others did, the side of her that his love had blinded him to for so long.

Still he had to give her the chance to redeem herself in his eyes, for surely she couldn't hold human life so cheaply!

'D'yer know what you're asking me to do, Cathy?' His voice was little more than a whisper as they locked eyes. 'That last block of flats is little more than a death trap, and for turning a blind eye, I took a hundred pounds. Mind you, we 'ad a good time on that money, didn't we? And 'ow long did it last, eh? Two days – two lousy days, 'cos you was determined to spend it all, weren't yer? Well, I'll tell yer now, I won't be doing any more of Hunter's dirty work, not for any amount. 'Cos it's blood money. Now yer might be able to live with that knowledge, but I can't.'

Cathy's eyes never wavered. No one watching her would ever have known the emotions that were flooding through her, or the hurt she was experiencing. She'd lost him. She could see it in his eyes. The Rory she had manipulated for so long had gone, and he wasn't coming back.

Rory too was fighting with his emotions, praying for the strength to walk away from the woman who had wrought havoc with his life. Because of her, and his own weakness and stupidity, he was now shunned by everyone he knew and loved. The crew hadn't bothered to hide their feelings. Rory had gone from being one of the men to someone to be avoided whenever possible. And not only had he lost the trust and friendship of his workmates, but also the respect of his family. Except his mum, of course! And even she was wavering. He could see it in her eyes, feel the way she shied away from contact with him, and that had hurt him more than he had thought humanly possible.

The silence in the room was deafening, and Rory had a sudden wild desire to run, run fast and not look back.

Cathy stared hard into the blue eyes, desperately trying to find some softening in them, but all she could see was a man wanting to be gone from her presence. Then her head went up defiantly. No man, not even Rory, could ever intimidate her. If the relationship was over, it was she who would have the last word.

'Why should I worry about people I've never met,

nor ever will? You think I'm hard; well, maybe I am, but I'm not going to apologise for the way I am. What's the point in getting sentimental? It doesn't get you anywhere; I've learned that the hard way.'

Rory's body sagged with relief. With those indifferent words Cathy had sounded her own death knell. It was over, finally over. He was free of her at last. Pulling on his cap, he said, 'I'm sorry it had to end this way, but I'm sure yer won't 'ave any trouble getting another mug to take me place. Goodbye, Cathy.'

As he opened the door, Cathy scrambled across the bed. Leaning on her elbows, she shouted scathingly, 'You're right enough there. In fact I can think of one not very far from here who'd be only too pleased to have me back.'

Rory turned slowly, his eyes filled with contempt.

'Yeah, you're probably right. He was never short of a few bob, but now, according to gossip, he's practically rolling in it. So you go and see Hobbs, and I wish yer luck. Neither of you give a damn about anyone but yourselves; you're well suited. Yer never know, he might even marry yer. You'd be set for life then, wouldn't yer? Then again, Hobbs is no mug, not like me, he—'

'Well, that's where you're wrong, mister know-it-all. He can't marry me, no one can, 'cos I'm already married. Jonathan and me got hitched a month after we left this dreary hole.' Her voice had risen to a screech of fury, wanting only to hurt Rory, to make him feel as worthless and dirty as she felt now.

Rory's hand tightened on the doorknob. He was stunned, unable to believe his ears. He turned to face her for the last time, and what he saw sickened him to the very pit of his stomach. For the lovely face he had worshipped since the first time he had clapped eyes on her was now twisted with hate, and the sight was ugly to behold.

'Remember all those times when yer begged me to marry yer? Do you?' Holding her hands together as if in prayer, she mimicked, '*Marry me, Cathy. Marry me, darling, I'll take care of you.* Gawd, what a joke that was. I don't know how I stopped meself from laughing in your stupid face.'

Shaking his head, Rory left her lying on the bed, still shouting obscenities after him.

He closed the door quietly. Once out on the landing, he took a deep breath, then expelled the air from his lungs. He was at a loss as to what had happened. He should be gutted; instead he felt as if a great weight had been lifted from his shoulders.

Anxious now to get away, he hurried down the stairs and headed for home. He had a lot of bridges to build. He only hoped and prayed he hadn't left it too late.

'Telegram for you, sir.'

Matthew Hunter was in one of the state rooms aboard the cruise ship, a small brandy in his hand. Taking the proffered telegram from the ship's steward, he looked down at it, puzzled as to who would want to contact him. Certainly not his son. That lazy beggar hadn't even tried to pretend he was sorry to see his father go. He had been infuriated when he'd learned that his father had left written instructions transferring the running of the business to Pat Flynn. Matthew's lips twitched as he recalled the look on his son's face. Robert had fully expected to be left in charge, even knowing what his father thought of him; the boy wasn't only useless, he was stupid as well.

Thanking the steward, he opened the telegram. And what he read brought him sharply to his feet.

Downing the brandy in one go, he went off in search of his wife.

CHAPTER TWENTY

'Can I 'ave a word, Pat?'

Pat was standing by the small window of the hut overlooking the site.

'Yer can 'ave as many as yer like, but I don't think you'd like any of 'em.'

Unperturbed by his brother's terse attitude, Rory stepped inside.

'Give us a chance, bruv. It's bad enough me mates are making me feel as welcome as a fart in their dinner, without me own family turning on me.'

'If you've come looking for a shoulder to cry on, you've come to the wrong man. But while yer 'ere, I might as well tell yer you won't 'ave to work alongside me after today, 'cos I'm 'anding in me notice. It's bad enough I've gotta live with that last block of jerry-built flats, but I ain't gonna help line that snotty-nosed git's wallet on the next building. Not that he'll be bothered. Why should he, when he's got you in his pocket? Until Mister Hunter comes back I'll get another job. I ain't fussy what I do. Even if I 'ave to sweep the roads, at least I'll be able to sleep nights. And I still ain't sure it wasn't Robert Hunter who put someone up to beat the shit outta me. But if I ever find out for sure, his own mother won't recognise the bastard when I'm through with 'im.'

Rory rested his body against the desk, his arms folded.

'You'd 'ave to get past his bodyguards first, but I reckon between the two of us we wouldn't 'ave any trouble; that's if yer could stand 'aving me in your corner. I 'ope so, 'cos I reckon I'll be sweeping the streets with yer. In fact, knowing how Dad and Shaun feel, we could set up our own business.'

Rory saw Pat start, and with the movement came a slight relaxation of his taut body; but he made no gesture of acknowledgement. Encouraged, Rory pressed on.

'I've been a blasted fool, Pat, and I'll 'ave to live with what I've done, but I've gotta feeling old Mister Hunter will be cutting 'is holiday short.'

Now he had his brother's attention. Turning from the window, Pat faced him.

'What d'yer mean?'

Rory smiled and tapped his nose in the gesture he always used when pleased with himself.

'Let's just say he might 'ave received a telegram telling 'im what his precious son's been up to.'

Pat's mouth hung open, his eyes stretched wide.

'You're joking, ain't yer?'

'Nope.'

He grinned, and Pat knew the old Rory was back. Excitement etched on his face, Pat asked, 'But how d'yer find out what ship he's on? Even I didn't know that.'

Again Rory tapped the side of his nose.

'I 'ave me ways,' he said mysteriously. 'Nah! It wasn't that difficult. I just went to a couple of the shipping line offices and asked around. Luckily a girl was very obliging. I told her Mister Hunter's name and the day him and his missus sailed, and she gave me the name of the ship. Lucky I'm so irresistible to women, ain't it? It wouldn't 'ave been any use you going, not with your ugly mug.' He ducked as Pat took a playful swing at him. 'Anyway, after that it was plain sailing – excuse the pun. I sent the telegram off first thing Monday morning. That's why I was late for work. D'yer remember? Yer gave me a right bollocking.'

Pat's face became sheepish.

'Yeah, I did, didn't I?'

The brothers stared at each other with affection.

'Friends again, Pat?' Rory asked.

Pat threw out his hand and Rory grabbed it tight.

'Yeah, yer soppy git. At least until the next time we fall out.'

Rory heaved a sigh of relief. The rift between himself and Pat was over.

Then Pat, his voice awkward, asked, 'What about Cathy Meadows? She ain't gonna be very pleased, is she? I mean, with you being outta a job for a while. Or has she gone back home again?'

Rory let go of Pat's hand, and turned his face away.

'It's over. I finally saw what everyone else did under the surface. She . . .' He stopped, his head bent. 'Look, I don't wanna talk about it right now, all right,

Pat? Maybe in a few weeks, or months . . .' He gave
a low laugh, but there was pain in the sound. 'Maybe
never. But it's definitely over between us. I ended it
on Saturday. But I'll say this for Cathy, she doesn't
'ang about. Word is she's already got Barney Hobbs
in 'er bed; it's a wonder yer 'aven't 'eard. The gossipmongers 'ave been 'aving a field day, and I don't
think I've come outta it very well. Not that I'm surprised. Truth is, I don't know whether to be jealous
of the geezer or sorry for him. Still, he's got plenty
of money to keep her 'appy. And even Cathy won't
be able to go through the amount he's got.' He didn't
mention the fact that Cathy was married; that would
have been too much of a humiliation for him to take.

Pat patted Rory's shoulder sympathetically.

'I'm sorry, mate. Not because of her, but 'cos I
don't like to see yer hurt.' He saw the pain in Rory's
eyes and asked quietly, 'D'yer still love her?'

Rory shrugged and turned away.

'To tell the truth, Pat, I'm not sure. I know it's
hurting like hell, but I don't know if it's because I've
lost her, or 'cos I'm feeling sorry for meself . . . Look,
let's drop it, eh? We've got more important things
to think about – like those flats. We can't let people
move into them, Pat, they're death traps.'

Pat rubbed the back of his neck, his movements
agitated.

'What d'yer think I've been thinking about these
past few days? But what can we do? The new tenants
are moving in on Monday; that only leaves the
weekend. What the hell can we do in that time? . . .
'Ang on. If you sent that telegram on Monday . . .
Nah.' He shook his head in frustration. 'Even if he

got it the same day, Mister Hunter still wouldn't be able to get back by then – not unless he sprouts wings and flies.'

'I've thought about that. It all depends on where the ship was when he got the message. If it was still at sea, then he won't get back in time. But if it had docked, he could've boarded another ship back to England. For all we know he might be on his way back right now.'

'And he might not get back for another few weeks. We haven't got time to wait.'

Rory thought hard. He'd already come up with a way to prevent the shoddy flats being moved into, but would Pat be prepared to take such drastic measures? There was only one way to find out.

'We don't 'ave to. What if we knocked 'em down? They couldn't be moved into then, could they?'

Pat swung round, his mind already in tune with his brother. They locked eyes for what seemed an eternity, then he said sharply, 'Well, what we waiting for? They went up easy enough. It shouldn't take much to knock 'em down. Not with the entire work-force lending a hand. Let's go and ask the men, see what they think.'

Pat and Rory stood in the narrow doorway of the hut watching the crew clearing away the last of the debris. Normally, when a job was completed, this task was performed with good humour and high spirits, and most of all a sense of pride for a job well done. But today they worked quietly, their faces grim. Pat had paid off Hunter's navvies yesterday; the men left were all of his own crew.

'Stop work a minute, will yer? Me and Rory's got something ter ask yer.'

The men stopped what they were doing and began walking towards the hut. When they were all gathered, Pat's eyes flitted from one man to another. Then he cleared his throat and addressed them.

'Me and Rory's had an idea. None of us are 'appy with the way things have turned out, but it ain't too late to do something about it.'

The men looked at each other, their grimy faces bewildered, before turning back to listen to what their gaffer was saying.

'We all know that last block of flats ain't fit to live in. We did the best we could, but it ain't good enough. Now, you've all been paid, and this is your last day on this site, but me and Rory ain't gonna leave until those death traps 'ave been pulled down.'

Now he had the men's full attention. They all started to speak at once and Pat had to hold his hand up for silence. The talking died down slowly, then Paddy and Shaun stepped forward, and it was Paddy who asked, 'What exactly are ye saying, son?'

Pat grinned, but it was Rory who spoke.

'D'yer remember when we were kids, Dad? And me, Pat and Shaun used to build 'ouses outta pebbles and stones, and when we'd finished we'd knock 'em down? . . . Well! How d'yer fancy doing it for real?'

There was a moment's silence at the enormity of what their gaffer was asking them to do. They could be arrested for destroying property, or at the very least blacklisted from ever working on a building site again. It was an enormous decision to make, and yet there wasn't a man among them who hadn't thought of doing exactly what their gaffer was asking.

Pat could understand their mixed feelings, and he didn't blame them. Worse still, they had put them on the spot, and that hadn't been fair.

'It's all right, lads, and you, Dad. I shouldn't 'ave asked. You finish up 'ere then get off 'ome. I won't think any the worse of yer. You're a good bunch, the best I've ever worked with. Yer built those flats 'cos yer 'ad no choice. If there's any blame to be laid, it's down to me and Rory for knuckling under to that jumped-up little toerag Hunter. So, like I said, it's mine and Rory's fault they were built; it's up to us to make sure they're never lived in.'

Nodding his head at the silent men, Pat strode past them, Rory at his side. Stopping only long enough to pick up the heavy tools they would need, they headed towards the last block of flats. They hadn't gone more than a few yards when they heard Paddy shout, 'Hold your horses, lads, I'm not after letting you two have all the fun.'

'Nor me.' Shaun stood beside his father, his homely face lit up with pleasure at the sight of Rory and Pat united again. The rest of the men followed, tools in hand, ready to demolish the jerry-built flats they'd all had nightmares about.

'Well, don't just stand there, yer lazy bleeders.' Pat grinned. 'Let's get started'.

Entering the end building, the men climbed to the top floor.

'Right then, let's get to work. We'll start with the windows, then the outer walls . . . You listening,

Jimmy?' Pat asked the youngest of his crew. 'Whatever yer do, don't touch the inner walls; those are the ones holding up the building.'

The young man smiled sheepishly.

'I know, guv. I ain't that stupid.'

'I bleeding 'ope so, mate. Now, we can't knock 'em down completely, otherwise the roof and floors'll go and us with them. But we can do enough damage so that they'll be impossible to live in. Once we've finished with each floor, we'll knock down the stairs as we go. Now, I'll just say one more thing before we start. If any of yer are 'aving second thoughts, walk away now. Nobody will blame yer.'

His eyes swept around the eight-man crew, looking for any sign of weakening, but he found none.

'Right then. One more thing . . .' He paused. 'As gaffer, I'm entitled to the first whack.'

So saying, he swung the hammer at one of the outer walls, his face tightening as the brittle bricks crumpled with the first blow. Turning his head, he stared over his shoulder and saw the same look on the face of each man present. If those bricks had been solid it would have taken more than a whack with a hammer to knock them down.

Without a word the men set to work. It took the entire crew only fifteen minutes to demolish the top-floor two-roomed flat. Once down on to the next floor, they set about smashing the stairs, thus cutting off any remaining access to the top floor. As they made their way downwards, their progress became slower, knowing only too well that with the damage they had done, the entire building was now dangerously unstable.

With only three floors to go, Pat called a halt.

'That's it for you lot,' he said breathlessly. 'It's too dangerous now for all of us to be inside. Me and Rory will finish off the last three.' He put out his hand, shaking with each man in turn. 'Thanks for the 'elp, lads. You get off 'ome now. There's bound to be some nosy parker watching, so the law might be 'ere soon. And if they do arrive, I don't want any of you lot 'anging around. As far as anyone knows, none of you had anything to do with any of this.'

The men shuffled around, wanting to stay until the job was completed, yet worried they could be arrested if the law did suddenly turn up. One by one they drifted off, but only to the pub across the road. None of them were going home until the Flynns were safely off the site.

'Be careful, lads. Sure if anything happened to either one of ye, your mother would have me head on a plate.' Paddy stood outside, his lined face etched with worry.

'Don't worry, Dad. We know what we're doing,' Rory called out with more confidence than he was feeling. 'You and Shaun stay where you are. Once we've finished this one, we can do the other two from outside.'

Gently now, Rory and Pat dismantled the walls, working quietly and as quickly as they dared. They were just finishing the last wall when they felt a tremor from above.

'Bleeding 'ell! I don't like the sound or feel of that,' Rory said, his head raised upwards. Pat too looked up.

'Nah! Me neither. What say we get outta here while

we're still in one piece? If we knock the bottom two from outside, it'll bring this one down with it. Even if it doesn't, it won't be any use now.'

Gingerly, they began to edge their way out of the room. Watching anxiously from outside, Paddy and Shaun breathed a sigh of relief as they saw the two men emerge from the third-floor landing.

Then all hell broke loose. Behind them Paddy and Shaun heard a loud commotion and turned, their hearts skipping a beat at the sight of a group of wild-eyed men brandishing sticks and poles, racing towards them. Before they could defend themselves, they found themselves shoved aside as the men raced inside the building.

Stunned momentarily, neither man could speak, then Shaun was running after the men, shouting, 'Get away, you fools. You'll bring the whole lot down on yer 'eads if yer don't get out now.'

Paddy looked wildly around for some kind of help; instead he saw Robert Hunter standing by the hut, his face like thunder. Quickly now, Paddy ran across the site, babbling, 'You've got to get those men out. That whole side's about to come down, and . . .'

Robert Hunter glared at the older man with distaste.

'I know only too well what's happened, you old fool. Those sons of yours have deliberately sabotaged my property. I've already sent for the police. I intend to have them arrested and charged—'

At that moment a carriage galloped into the site, and Robert Hunter's eyes widened in disbelief as he saw his father jump down from the carriage before it had come to a halt. Then he was striding towards his son, looking angrier than Robert had ever seen him, and instinctively he stumbled back, but he wasn't quick enough to avoid the stinging blow his father brought down across his face.

'Get out. Get out of my sight, or so help me, I'll not be responsible for my actions.'

Knowing he was beaten, Robert tried valiantly to summon together a few shreds of respect. Drawing himself upright, he was annoyed to hear the tremble in his voice as he spoke. He had to clear his throat twice before he was able to say his piece.

'Look here, Father, I—'

Matthew Hunter raised his walking stick threateningly.

'So help me God, if you don't get out of my sight this instant, you'll be eating your food through a straw. Now piss off, you worthless piece of shit. From this moment on you're no son of mine.'

Robert knew there was no point in arguing any further. Besides which, he was becoming very frightened. His father did indeed look capable of murder. He'd go to Mother; she'd take him in and help him.

He was walking away when his father's voice stopped him.

'If you're thinking of running back to your mother, you'll be wasting your time. She's just as disgusted with you as I am. You're on your own, Robert, completely alone. May God have mercy on you, because no one else will.'

Paddy had listened impatiently, his only thought for his sons, who were fighting in a building that was about to collapse at any minute. Pulling at Matthew Hunter's arm, he pleaded, 'Please, Mister Hunter. Me lads are in there. They were about to come out when that bunch of thugs barged in brandishing sticks and heaven knows what other weapons they might be carrying. Please, for the love of God, get my lads out, sir . . . Please.'

Matthew Hunter patted Paddy's hand.

'Don't you fret, Mister Flynn. I'll soon have that rabble off my property.'

Giving Paddy's shoulder a rub of reassurance, he was off running towards the partly demolished building.

Paddy watched him go, then he too was running, running like he'd never run before, fear for his sons giving strength to his tired legs.

Matthew Hunter was standing in the entrance of the flats. At the top of his voice, he yelled, 'You lot hired by my son, get out of there before you get your-selves killed. Your employer has taken to his heels, so you won't be receiving any payment from him. If you come out now, I'll pay each man five pounds, and promise not to involve any of you in any police action.'

Before he'd finished talking, three shabby, dirty men had come to the bottom landing, their eyes shifty.

'Let's see the money then, mister.'

Matthew reached into his jacket pocket and pulled out a wad of notes. Immediately the men's eyes changed. Matthew noted the look and said casually, 'In case you've any thought of stealing this money, I feel obliged to warn you that the police are already on their way. In fact, I do believe I can hear them arriving.' Then his voice hardened. 'Get the rest of those thugs out right now, or I'll have you arrested and you'll not see a penny of this money.'

One of the men shouted, 'Come on, lads. On yer toes, the law's on its way.' Then came the sound of a scuffle as four more men ran from the building. Without a word they grabbed the wad of notes in Matthew Hunter's hand and fled.

'Thank the Lord! Jasus, but I thought me boys were going to die for sure.'

Walking nearer, Paddy called, 'Come on, lads. Ye can come out now. Mister Hunter's back,' but there was no answer, and Paddy's stomach lurched in fear. 'C'mon now. 'Tis no time for your shenanigans.'

Still there was no sound. Paddy cast a desperate look at Hunter, then both men were inside the building.

'Pat, Rory, Shaun, any of yous, answer me.' Paddy's voice was desperate.

A shower of dust fell on the two men, then the building started to sway. But it was the sound of falling masonry that turned their blood cold. Paddy hesitated for only a moment, then he was running up the rotten stairs, calling out for his sons.

Matthew Hunter knew there was nothing he could do on his own. But he knew where to find men, good, willing men to help.

Rory lay on the dust-covered floor, coughing the dirt and dust from his throat. He went to sit up then fell back as a pain like fire shot through his side.

'Pat! Shaun! Are yer all right?' There was a moment's silence, during which Rory held his breath in fear, then he heard Pat's voice.

'Yeah, I'm 'ere all right. Though I don't know what shape I'm in. Those bastards gave me a right thumping.' He too tried to sit up and groaned. 'Still, I don't care if me liver's 'anging out, I ain't going back into 'ospital. Hang on, where's Shaun?'

Rubbing the powdered dust from their eyes, they peered around the room, a collective sound of relief coming to both their lips as they saw their brother leaning against a wall in the corner.

'Shaun, yer all right, mate?'

'Yeah! I think so,' came Shaun's voice, but it sounded very weak.

'Come on, we've gotta get out of 'ere. The bloody lot's gonna cave in at any moment.'

With a supreme effort, the three battered and bruised men got unsteadily to their feet. Clinging on to each other for support, they had made it out on to the landing when they heard their father calling them. Then his footsteps could be heard running up the stairs.

With all the strength he had left, Rory screamed, 'Get back, Dad! Get back!' but the warning came too late.

Desperate to reach his sons, Paddy was crashing his way up the shaky staircase. As he reached the penultimate step, the rotten wood gave way. Instinctively Paddy reached for the banister, but that too was rotten. As he fell, he looked up at his sons and heard them scream out his name. Then there was an almighty noise such as he had never heard, or ever would again.

CHAPTER TWENTY-ONE

'Holy Mary! Sure and what ails ye, Jane? 'Tis the
fourth time you've been to the closet in the past hour.
And ye were sick this morning an' all. You're definitely coming down with something. Look, get
yerself off home and into bed. I'll call for the doctor
on me way home.'

Jane sat in the hot kitchen, her face pale and drawn.

'I'm all right, Mum, stop fussing, please.'

'Fussing indeed.' Annie turned to Josie and pleaded,
'Will ye tell her, love? Maybe she'll take more notice
of you . . . Oh, Lord! Table three's shouting for their
dinners. Look, stay here with Josie while I take these
through . . . Try and talk some sense into her, Josie.
Oh, all right, keep your hair on, I'm coming. Jasus!
You'd think they hadn't eaten for days,' she shouted
as she left the kitchen.

Josie gave the Irish stew a further stir to stop it
coagulating, then, wiping her hands slowly, she
leaned against the Butler sink and asked quietly,

'You got something you wanna tell me, Jane?'

Jane shook her head.

Josie stared at the bowed head, her stomach churning. If it was any other girl, Josie would have guessed what was troubling her; and Annie would have spotted it straight away. But this was Jane, naïve, innocent Jane. But still . . .

Realising Jane wasn't going to confide in her, and afraid that if her fears were true the young girl might do something silly, she said straight out, 'You pregnant, Jane?'

The effect of Josie's words was startling. Jane's normally pale skin turned absolutely white, as if every drop of blood had been drained from her; even the scarlet birthmark had turned pink. Her entire body shaking now, Jane lifted her head and looked through blurred eyes at Josie.

'What am I going to do, Josie?'

Even though she had expected the answer, still Josie was stunned by the revelation. It didn't seem possible. Not Jane. The girl was staring at her with huge blue eyes that seemed to fill the tiny face, eyes filled with fear, looking to her best friend for help; and Josie was lost for words. Despite her relatively senior years, she was as much in the dark about pregnancy as Jane was. There was only one person who could help Jane out of the mess she'd landed herself in, and that person was the one she feared telling the most. Another question entered Josie's mind. Who could be the father? Jane scarcely ever went out on her own, especially not at night. And even if she had, she wasn't the type of girl to give herself to just any man who happened along; not unless . . .

Hurrying now, Josie pulled up a chair next to Jane. Watching the door for Annie, she asked quietly, 'Did someone attack you, love?'

Jane shook her head miserably.

'No! No, I wasn't attacked, at least, not the way you think.'

Josie's eyes squinted at Jane in puzzlement.

'What d'yer mean? You either was attacked or yer wasn't; which is it?'

Jane wiped her cheeks with the back of her hand.

'It's . . . it's a bit complicated, Josie . . . Oh, Josie, what am I going to do? Me mum will kill me when she finds out,' she wailed. Then she clapped a hand over her mouth. 'Oh . . . oh no, I'm going to be sick again.' Leaping to her feet, she rushed outside to the closet, just as Annie came bustling back, her arms filled with dirty plates.

'It's getting busy out there, Josie love . . . Where's Jane gone now?' she asked, exasperated.

Keeping her back to Annie, Josie said lightly, 'Where she's been all morning. Look, she'd be better off at home. We can manage without her for today, can't we? After all, she's not—'

A sudden loud babble of voices from the tea room made both women jump.

'What the bleeding 'ell . . . ?' Josie gasped, her heart beginning to race with fear without knowing why.

Following Annie, she hurried through to the tea room, coming to an abrupt halt at the sight of all the men running out into the street, leaving their meals half eaten, the knives and forks thrown down on the checked tablecloths.

'What's happened? What's going on?' Josie ran, grabbing one of the men at the door.

The man's eyes darted from Josie to Annie, obviously uncomfortable at being the one to impart bad news. Eager to get away, he looked to Josie, his eyes sympathetic, and said gruffly, 'Look, don't get yerself in a state, but there's been an accident on the building site. I don't know how bad it is, no one does until we get there. I've gotta get off, Josie love . . . Like I said, don't worry . . .' The man's voice trailed off as he realised the inaneness of his words. Taking advantage of Josie and Annie's shocked reaction, he made his escape.

Josie stood rooted to the spot as the impact of the man's words sank in. Then an anguished cry brought her back to her senses.

'Mother of God! Me lads, all me lads, and Paddy. They're all working today.'

Ashen-faced, Annie tore off her apron, her gnarled hands trembling. Several women who had been enjoying a cup of tea and a cake after doing their morning shopping quickly came to her side.

'There, there, Annie love. It might not 'ave anything to do with your men. Why don't you 'ave a cuppa an'—'

Distraught, Annie threw off the comforting hands.

'Sure an' how d'ye know it's not my men, can ye tell me that?'

The women avoided Annie's question and exchanged glances, wanting to help, yet not knowing how.

'What's going on?' All heads turned as Jane wandered into the empty tea room, her eyes wary.

It was the sound of Jane's voice that stung Josie into action. Without preamble, she took hold of the girl's arm and sat her down.

'There's been an accident at the building site, love. The men 'ave gone to see if they can 'elp. Me and your mum are gonna go and see what's 'appened. You stay 'ere with these ladies; they'll look after you, till we get back. You will, won't yer?' she appealed to the hovering women.

'Yeah, course we will, love.' They spoke almost as one.

Jane struggled in Josie's grasp.

'No, I want to come with you. I want to see if my dad and brothers are all right. Let go of me, Josie.'

Josie tightened her grip. Leaning forward so their noses were almost touching, she said as calmly as she could manage, 'Look, Jane. There's nothing yer can do. You ain't well, and yer mum won't 'ave time to look after you – understand?'

Her lips trembling, Jane stared back at Josie and nodded.

Straightening up, Josie fetched Annie's shawl and wrapped it around the plump shoulders.

'Come on, Annie. Let's go and see for ourselves. The worst part is not knowing. They're probably all safe and sound; we've just gotta keep calm, all right?'

Annie nodded dumbly. She couldn't think, couldn't talk; all she could do was pray silently. Josie was by her side, holding her arm, talking in a soothing voice, but Annie didn't hear a word. All she could hear was the silent prayer going round and round in her head.

Hail Mary, full of Grace, the Lord be with ye. Blessed art thou amongst women, and Blessed is the fruit of thy

314

womb, Jesus. Holy Mary, Mother of God, pray for us
sinners, now, and at the hour of our death, Amen.

The building site was a hive of frantic activity. There
were two ambulance carts and a police wagon at the
gates, and a line of men covered in dust carefully
sifting through a small mountain of rubble. This was
bad enough, but what really brought the enormity of
the situation home to Annie and Josie was the eerie
silence that pervaded the site. Holding on to each other
for support, they spoke briefly to the police officer
standing guard and were immediately let through.

'Mother of God!' Annie breathed, her voice little
more than a whisper.

Josie felt as if she was suffocating. She let her eyes
roam over all the men present, hoping and praying
to see a familiar face. But even under all the dirt and
grime, she knew that if one of them had been one of
the Flynn men, she would have recognised him; and
although some of the faces were familiar from fre-
quenting the tea shop, none of them resembled the
men she was searching for.

'It's all right, Annie . . . it's all right . . .' she mumbled helplessly, not knowing what to do or say.

Somebody brought chairs for them to sit on, then
mugs of tea were being put into their hands. And
they gratefully accepted both, but as if in a dream.
None of it seemed real. Reality was suspended, as it
had to be, else they wouldn't have been able to stop
from screaming out their fear and frustration. So they
just sat still, staring at the line of men searching the
rubble, each of them wrapped in their own anguish
and misery.

Then a man was striding towards them, his steps purposeful, and both women's hearts skipped a beat.

'Mrs Flynn?' he addressed Annie.

Her mouth dry, Annie had to run her tongue over her stiff lips before she could answer.

'Aye, yes, I'm Mrs Flynn.' She stared at the man, some part of her mind noting his fine clothes beneath the layers of dust.

'I'm Matthew Hunter, Mrs Flynn. I can't tell you how sorry I am for what has happened. Believe me, everything is being done to get your husband and sons out unharmed.'

His words made Annie flinch; it was as if he had done the unthinkable. He had put into words what her heart and mind had been denying since the moment she had heard of the accident.

Matthew Hunter saw her reaction and hung his head. This was all his fault. When he had learned that his wife planned to whisk him off for a cruise to recuperate, he had instructed his solicitor, from his hospital bed, to draw up a contract giving Pat the authority to continue running the business in his absence. The document had been signed by himself and witnessed by his doctor; all Robert had had to do was get Pat to sign the contract, which Matthew had no doubt the man would do willingly, and return it to the solicitor. He should have known his son would have ignored his request, but at the time he had honestly thought Robert was too spineless to defy him. He must have known he would be found out. Which was why he had tried to line his pockets while he could. And because of Matthew's assumption that his son would follow his orders, the entire

Flynn family were now buried under the pile of rubble that had been meant for honest families to move into. Homes that no builder worth his salt would ever have sanctioned for habitation.

He had boarded a ship for home as soon as possible after receiving Rory's telegram. Luckily they had docked that same day in Italy. Another few days and the ship would have been heading for the Caribbean. But despite his best efforts, he had arrived too late.

Looking into Annie Flynn's terrified eyes, he lowered his, unable to meet her gaze. Instead he continued heaping recriminations on his own head. If only he had arrived back even a few hours earlier, he could have prevented the tragedy that was going on behind him. But one thing was certain: if any of the Flynn men had suffered serious injury, or even, God forbid, death, then he would personally see that his son was handed over to the full power of the law on a charge of manslaughter.

'Mister Hunter?'

Matthew's head shot up.

'Yes, Mrs Flynn?'

'Should ye be working so hard in your condition, sir? 'Tis good of ye to try and help get me men out, but sure an' there's no point in putting yourself at risk.' She paused to wet her lips again. 'I know 'twas your son who caused all this . . .' She waved an arm listlessly around the site. 'Me son Pat told us all what was going on. So . . . so, whatever happens, Mister Hunter, I'll be laying no blame at your door. Me husband and sons have always held ye in high regard, sir. So don't be taking it all on your shoulders, 'cos like I said, I know 'twas no fault of yours.'

Hearing the soft Irish lilt pardoning him from all guilt, even though she still didn't know if her family was dead or alive, brought about an unbearable wave of humbleness in him; but instead of bringing him some solace, it only served to make him heap further recriminations upon his own head.

Then a shout rang out, and Matthew Hunter pushed all other thoughts from his mind.

'I'll go and see what's happening, Mrs Flynn. You stay here. I'll be right back, I give you my word.'

Again the two women were on their feet, holding on to each other for dear life. Their heads craned to see better, they heard a joyful shout.

'He's alive, he's alive!'

Annie and Josie clasped hands. Ignoring Matthew Hunter's words, they hurried forward. At first neither woman could recognise who the man was because of the dirt and dust that covered his body. Then Annie moved closer, wiping his face with her skirt.

'Ah, Pat, thank the Lord. Are ye all right, son? Where's the others, Pat?'

A nurse and doctor appeared out of nowhere and instructed the men to lay Pat on one of the stretchers lying ready on the ground.

Unwilling to let her son from her sight, Annie hovered close as the doctor examined the still body. Then Pat began to cough, loud, harsh coughs that seemed to rack his body.

'There now, lie still, Mr Flynn. You've got a lungful of dust and your body's taken a battering, but you'll live.' Twisting his head, the doctor said to Annie, 'You're his mother.'

'Yes, I am. Will he be all right, Doctor?' The doctor winced as Annie's hand dug into his arm. 'He's not long been out of hospital. He was badly beaten up . . .'

Gently prising Annie's hand from his arm, he said, 'I know, Mrs Flynn. I'm one of the doctors who looked after him. Believe me, your son's a strong man. He'll be fine after a couple of days' rest. But I'm going to admit him to hospital for tonight, just as a precaution.'

Annie peered into the young face, but couldn't remember him from when Pat had been in hospital. Then again, all she had been concerned with at the time was her son.

'Mum?' Pat's voice rang out. 'Is that you, Mum?'

'Aye, lad, 'tis me. Now don't fret yourself, you're going to be fine. The doctor says so.'

The doctor motioned two orderlies to take the stretcher to one of the waiting ambulance carts.

Annie walked alongside the men until Pat was lifted into the cart, her hand tightly entwined with her son's. There was a question on her lips, but she dared not ask it. She didn't have to, for Pat asked it for her.

'Where's me dad . . . and the others? Are they all right?'

'I'll have to close the doors, love.' One of the orderlies was gently pushing her aside. Loath to leave her son, Annie bravely mustered up a watery smile.

'They'll be fine, lad. Ye just worry about yourself. Your dad and the others will be along soon.'

Then the doors closed. The last sight she had of Pat was the fear etched on his dirt-stained face.

As the ambulance pulled away, Annie's legs would have buckled if Josie, who had been by her side all along, hadn't caught hold of her.

'Come on, Mum.' The affectionate term came back to her lips naturally, and Josie knew she would never again call this brave, wonderful woman by any other name. 'There's nothing you can do 'ere. Let's get back, maybe they've found one of the others.'

Bemused, Annie could only hang on to Josie, letting herself be led by the hand like a child. Looking back, Josie saw the crowd of onlookers and bit down the desire to scream at them, tell them to go away, tell them anything that would get rid of them, but she knew such a gesture would be futile. Besides, she told herself, most of them were genuinely concerned for the lives of the men still buried.

Another shout galvanised both women into action. Running as fast as they could on the uneven site ground, they came to a halt as another body was lifted from the rubble. This time Annie recognised the man straight away. With a joyful cry she stumbled towards him.

'Paddy! Oh, Paddy me darlin'. Speak to me, Paddy, say something, please.' She looked down into the blue eyes of her husband and sent up another prayer of thanks. If both Paddy and Pat were alive, then surely Rory and Shaun must be as well.

'Will ye stop your gabbling, woman. Begod! Will ye give me no peace, even on me deathbed,' Paddy said tiredly.

Annie crossed herself in agitation.

'Jasus, Paddy, don't be saying a thing like that, not even in a joke.'

Again she was pushed aside while the doctor made a cursory examination, then he gave a nod of assent.

'You must have the luck of the Irish, Mrs Flynn, and here was me thinking it was just another fable.' He smiled warmly at Annie. 'I can't find anything broken, but I'll get him to the hospital anyway. I'm sure your son will be pleased to see him.'

Knowing the doctor was right, Annie reluctantly released Paddy's hand. Bending over him, she kissed him tenderly on the forehead.

'I'll see ye later, Paddy. God bless.'

Paddy tried to sit up, but the effort was too much for him and he sank back on the stretcher. But though his body was weak, he still had the power of speech.

'The others, Annie. Our lads. Are they out?'

Swallowing hard, Annie answered, 'Pat's already on his way to the hospital. The men are getting Rory and Shaun out now.' It was a small lie, but it did the trick. Paddy's body relaxed and his eyes closed in sleep.

All this time Josie had been close by. Now she was sure Paddy was safe, her gaze drifted back to the rubble and the men tirelessly pulling away the crumbling bricks as quickly as they dared without disturbing what was left standing of the block of flats.

As she watched, they stopped digging and the man at the front of the line held up a hand. Everyone held their breath. The man resumed his task, then stopped and peered down into the rubble. This time there was no joyous shout, just a dejected swing of his head.

Josie closed her eyes tight shut, not wanting to see any more. Wishing she was anywhere but here. Here, where the bodies of Shaun and Rory had yet to be pulled out.

'Josie! Josie love, what's happened? . . . Tell me, what's happened?' Annie was pulling at Josie's arm, her voice rising, unable to look herself.

A silence had fallen. Fear and despair hung heavily in the spring air, the atmosphere so strong it was almost palpable.

'Go and look, Josie love, please.' Annie was standing, her face pale, her eyes tightly shut. 'G'wan, me darlin'. Go and see for me. I'll . . . I'll wait here till ye come back.'

Josie looked again to where the men were peering down into the rubble. They appeared to be discussing their next course of action, but no move was being made to bring anyone else up.

She began to walk forward, her steps slow and faltering. Men glanced at her then quickly looked away, their silence speaking volumes. She walked on, her breath held in check, her heart hammering so hard she felt it would burst through her chest. And all the time she was inching nearer and nearer that awful hole in the ground, and she didn't want to see; didn't want to know what lay down there. She had a sudden irrational urge to pick up her skirt and flee. To run from this dreadful place, and keep on running until she could run no more.

''Ere, Josie. 'Ang on to me, love. That's it, I've got yer.'

Josie felt a strong arm around her shoulders and let herself slump against a broad chest. Glancing up, she saw Barney Hobbs' face hovering over her, and she clung to him. She would have held on to the devil himself rather than face that walk alone.

Then they were at the spot. Josie saw one of the men look at Barney and shake his head, and the emotions she had held in check for Annie's sake suddenly overwhelmed her. Her whole body convulsed, a rush of tears spurted from her eyes, and she thought she was choking, for there seemed to be a huge lump in her throat that was preventing her from breathing. She felt rather than saw Barney lean over to look down into the gaping hole, then she heard him whisper, 'God Almighty!' She felt his grip tighten around her, and still she refused to open her eyes.

After what seemed an eternity, but was only a few seconds, Barney spoke again.

'What yer waiting for? Why ain't yer getting 'em out?'

A voice Josie didn't recognise answered, 'We can't get one out without the other, it's too dangerous. Look! That section of roof is right over the pair of 'em. If we try to separate 'em, the whole lot could come down.'

'Well, what the fucking 'ell yer gonna do? Just sit there looking at them all day?'

'Look, mister, we're doing the best we can. If either of them are still alive, they won't be for long if that lot comes down. If you've got any ideas, let us know, otherwise bugger off and let us get on with it.' The angry voice was tinged with desperation.

Barney bit down hard on his bottom lip and murmured, 'Sorry, mate, I didn't mean to sound off.'

Josie heard the exchange and felt a leap of hope rise in her. Slowly opening her eyes, she braced herself and looked down, and what she saw brought a gasp of horror to her lips.

Lying motionless at the bottom of the chasm were two bodies, one on top of the other as if the upper man had tried to shield the man underneath. Both were smothered in chalky dust, but Josie would have known them anywhere. What she couldn't distinguish was which was Rory and which was Shaun. It was too much. With a moan of sheer hopelessness, she turned her face into Barney's chest. Then her mind, unable to cope with the horror of it all, shut down and she felt herself slipping away into darkness – and she didn't fight it. She let herself go, grateful to have the traumatic scene wiped from her mind.

Watching from a distance, Annie saw Josie being carried in Barney Hobbs' arms. She looked on as he laid Josie tenderly on a stretcher before taking his jacket off and joining the rescue crew. She stood alone, just watching the comings and goings as if she was looking down from on high. It was only when she saw a body being lifted out that she finally moved.

It was less than a minute's walk, but to Annie it was the longest journey of her life. The still body was lowered on to a stretcher, the same doctor kneeling on the ground beside it. Then he shook his head and covered the man with a blanket. Almost at the same time, the last man was pulled out and there was a frantic scuffle as the remainder of the building came crashing down, filling in the hole with such force it rocked the nearest men off their feet.

At last Annie was staring down at her two lads. One whose face was covered with a blanket, and the other who was showing no sign of life.

'Mrs Flynn, I'm so very, very sorry.' Matthew Hunter was standing by her side, his face and hands filthy, as were the rest of the brave men who had risked their lives to get her men out of the collapsed building.

Annie couldn't answer. She couldn't speak. Even her eyes were bone dry. Men moved aside, unable to do any more, their heads hung low, some with tears slowly rolling down grimy faces, leaving oddly shaped streaks of clean skin in their wake.

As if in a dream, she went to the uncovered man first. The doctor, his face solemn now, saw her and got to his feet. And, like Matthew Hunter, he too spoke his condolences, but Annie was no longer listening. She stood between the two stretchers, her eyes resting on the man nearest. Then she saw his chest move, and she swayed on her feet. Unknown men's arms reached out to her, but she quickly steadied herself without their help.

Glazed blue eyes stared up at her, and from cracked lips the man asked, 'Mum! Are the others all right?' And once again Annie was forced to lie.

'Aye . . . Yes, lad, they're fine. Rest now,' she murmured soothingly, her cold hands stroking his face.

This time she didn't accompany the stretcher to the ambulance. Instead she slowly knelt down by the body covered by a blanket. The men began to walk away, their shoulders hunched over, their heads down.

Annie tenderly drew back the blanket and gazed down at the dead face of her son; her beautiful child, her child whose laugh she would never hear again. Her son who would never again come through the back yard shouting for his dinner, a loving smile on his face. Nor would she ever again see the cheeky smile that had always made her want to reach out and grab him to her.

'He was a very brave man, Mrs Flynn.' Matthew Hunter was kneeling by her, his eyes bright with unshed tears. 'He must have thrown himself over Rory to protect him. They were pinned down under piles of bricks, which indicates they must have taken the brunt of the fall. If Shaun hadn't . . . Well, Rory would probably be dead too. He must have loved his brother very much.'

'You're right enough there, sir. From the day he could crawl, Shaun followed our Rory everywhere he went, bless his little heart. But Rory didn't mind; even though he moaned sometimes, he loved his little brother as much as Shaun loved him . . .'

Her voice broke and she turned and pulled the lifeless body into her arms, rocking him back and forth as she had done when he was a baby. Then she began to sing a lullaby, her chin resting on top of Shaun's head. Her face dreamy, she crooned softly, a smile on her lips, while those around looked on nervously.

A few feet away, Josie lay in a deep faint, watched over by a solemn Barney Hobbs, himself caught up in his own thoughts.

To the many onlookers, the pitiful scene appeared like a photograph, so still were the participants. It was only when the orderlies tried to take Shaun away from Annie that the spell was broken. Clutching the body of her youngest son tight to her bosom, Annie struggled to keep hold of him.

'Away with ye, let him be, I say. Let him be.'

The nurse tried to prise Annie's arms from around Shaun and was sent flying by a back-handed slap. Then the doctor took charge. Directing the orderlies to remove the body, he and the nurse coaxed and pleaded with Annie to let Shaun go. But she hung on to her child as if her own life depended on it, screaming wildly, 'Let us be, let us be. Ye'll not be taking me baby child away from me, ye divils. Sure and he's only sleeping, aren't ye, Shaun darling? Ye've always liked your sleep, haven't ye, son? Ye take no mind of them. Your mother's here, lad. I'll not let them take ye away from me. Ye rest now, Shaun . . . ye rest, me sweet, precious, darling son . . . No! . . . No! Leave us be, I tell ye. Leave us be!'

It was the screaming that roused Josie. Her eyes fluttered, then opened wide as she was forced to accept that this was no nightmare; it was real, and Annie needed her help now more than ever before. A hand helped her to her feet, and once more she felt a spark of hope that all this was indeed a dream. For surely if it was real she wouldn't be standing here arm in arm with Barney Hobbs. Then she was again distracted by a loud wail of sorrow, the awful sound similar to that a wounded animal would make when caught in a trap. She swung round to see where the sound was coming from and saw a policeman, doctor and nurse trying to take a man's body away from a demented Annie.

At last the doctor, knowing Annie was hysterical with grief, fetched a bottle of laudanum from his bag, and while the policeman and the nurse held on grimly to the grief-stricken woman, he put a few drops of the liquid on to a swab and held it over

Annie's mouth. Within seconds her struggle abated until finally she slumped over, dead to the world.

Josie's eyes flickered from Annie to the lifeless body being carried away by the two orderlies. Her first instinct was to run to Annie's side to comfort her as best she could. But she had to know whose body it was on the stretcher.

Turning to face Barney, she asked fearfully, 'Who's on that stretcher, Barney?'

Barney tried to avoid her eyes, but she wasn't to be put off so easily. Gripping him by the collar of his shirt, she demanded, 'I know it's either Rory or Shaun. Which one is it? Damn it, Barney, tell me. Don't let me have to go over on me own.'

'It's Shaun, Josie. I'm sorry. I don't know if you'll believe me, but I am,' Barney spoke in hushed tones. 'I know me and the Flynns 'ave never been what yer might call friends, but I respected them . . . all of them; even Rory.' His arm went around her once again. 'Come on, love, I'll take yer 'ome, or to the 'ospital. Wherever yer want, I'll take yer. Just say the word.'

Josie tried to speak, but her throat was too full. Instead she patted Barney's arm and walked over to the stretcher.

'Could I see him, please?' she pleaded.

The orderlies stopped and waited as Josie pulled back the blanket from Shaun's face. He looked so peaceful, and she was glad of that, for it meant he hadn't suffered. Her vision blurred, she bent down and for the last time kissed the kind, gentle man who she knew had loved her. Tears rained down on the still face as Josie laid her cheek next to Shaun's.

'Goodbye, Shaun. Oh, Shaun . . . Shaun. It's not fair, it's not fair . . .'

Barney felt his own eyes prickle, and quickly controlled his emotions. Pulling Josie away, he jerked his head at the two orderlies, and they hastened their steps, eager now to get the hospital, where they would be relieved of their duties.

Behind them they left a distraught Josie being comforted by the man who had, indirectly, been a party to the catastrophe that surrounded them.

CHAPTER TWENTY-TWO

'Morning, Josie. 'Eard anything from Annie yet? Your place ain't the same without 'er 'aving a go at us and making us laugh. Not that we don't enjoy your company, Josie,' the market trader added hastily, his face split into a wide grin.

Josie smiled back, though it was becoming an effort. She had been hearing the same question for months now, and her answer was always the same.

'Nothing yet, Charlie. But I'll let yer know as soon as I 'ear anything.'

'Cheers, Josie. D'yer know, it's 'ard to believe it's nearly a year since the accident. Seems like only a couple of weeks ago, don't it?'

Josie just nodded, and the man took the hint.

'Righto, darling. See yer later.'

'Yeah, see yer later, Charlie.' Josie waved and walked on quickly, keeping her eyes firmly on the ground so as to field off any further questions regarding the Flynns.

Opening the café, she busied herself getting it ready for the breakfast rush. Once everything was in place, she sat down with a mug of tea, enjoying the fifteen minutes she set aside for herself each morning before the traders started arriving. Blowing on the hot tea, she reflected on what Charlie had said. He was right: it didn't seem like a year ago since their world had been turned upside down. Sometimes it seemed much longer, in another time – and sometimes it seemed like only yesterday. To all intents and purposes it might well have been. The anguish she'd experienced on that and the following days was still fresh in her mind. If she were to close her eyes she could still see the coffin bearing Shaun's body being lowered into the open grave, still hear the cries of Annie as she buried her youngest son, the pitiful sound almost drowned amongst the sobs of everyone present.

But that hadn't been the end of Annie's grief. For the shock of losing his son had resulted in Paddy being rushed to hospital, his heart giving out through the trauma it had sustained. Jane too had collapsed, and had been taken with her father in the same ambulance. To the mourners attending the funeral it had presented all the makings of a theatrical play; but to Josie and the remainder of the family it had only served to heighten the nightmare of the past week – and there was a further shock still to come.

While Annie, Pat and Rory had waited to hear news of Paddy, Josie had volunteered to sit with Jane. During that time she had subconsciously prayed that the shock would bring on a miscarriage, thus saving Jane and the rest of the family from any further worry. But her prayers had gone unanswered. Looking back to that dreadful time, she felt a rush of guilt for even having thought of such a thing. Yet she had truly had everyone's best interests at heart.

She had been the one to impart the news of Jane's pregnancy to a bewildered Annie – a woman who had just buried a son and was now facing losing her husband as well. Knowing Annie as she did, Josie imagined that the devout Catholic must have wondered what terrible thing she had done to cause her God to desert her. Yet even in that, her darkest hour, Annie still clung to her faith, sitting beside her husband and her daughter in turn, her rosary beads running through her fingers as she kept up a constant vigil of prayer.

Josie didn't know what might have happened to the family if Matthew Hunter hadn't stepped in and taken control of the fraught situation. He had arrived at the hospital and immediately insisted both Paddy and Jane be removed to private rooms. He had also made certain they both had the best specialist and nursing care available.

Paddy's recovery was slow, and the family were warned not to say or do anything that might put it in jeopardy.

Jane had visited her father every day, until her condition had begun to show. Even though the doctors had given Paddy the all-clear, she had been terrified her dad would have a relapse once he knew his only daughter had been made pregnant by a man she wouldn't name. But there she had been proved wrong.

Once back home, Paddy had been told the truth,

but instead of having a relapse, he had drawn on his inner strength to help and care for his beloved daughter. That had left only the small matter of taking care of the gossips. For a woman of any age to have a child out of wedlock was considered a scandal, and the woman in question little more than a whore. In normal circumstances, Annie, once over the shock, would have stood by her daughter, defying anyone to defile Jane's name and character. But those hadn't been normal circumstances, and the usually stalwart woman had been in a very vulnerable state.

It was at that point that Matthew Hunter had again stepped in to help. He had kept in constant touch with the family during their harrowing ordeal, and such was the gratitude felt by the Flynns for his kindness and help, they had kept no secrets from him. It was his idea to send Jane and her parents to Ireland until the baby was born. This kind offer had come as a godsend to Annie, for not only would Jane be spared the looks and sly whispers, but Annie would at last see her brother Declan again.

The sound of the bell tinkling over the door brought Josie out of her reverie. She glanced at the wall clock and was shocked to find she'd been sitting daydreaming for nearly half an hour. In a panic now, she had the frying pan loaded with bacon and sausages in minutes. Pouring a mug of tea from the giant urn, she took it into the tea room.

'Sorry, Charlie, it ain't quite ready yet. My fault, I was too busy daydreaming. Look, it won't be long, and seeing as you've gotta wait, yer can 'ave this one on the 'ouse, and a mug of tea to be getting on with.'

Charlie gazed at Josie fondly. She was a lovely girl in more ways than one. There was hardly a man in the market who hadn't tried his luck, but Josie wasn't having any of it. Even if he wasn't happily married, and a good twenty years younger, Charlie knew that a girl like Josie was well out of his league. Rumour had it she was still carrying a torch for Rory Flynn. Whatever the reason, she continued to steadfastly refuse any offers from the many men who frequented the café. Yet she did it in such a way that the men still left feeling good about themselves. Now Charlie looked upon himself as a father figure and was fiercely protective of Josie. And during Paddy's absence, that protection now included Jane as well.

Opening his morning paper, Charlie smiled good-naturedly. 'Don't be daft, love. You've got a living to earn, just like the rest of us. I don't mind waiting a few minutes; besides, Jane'll be in soon, won't she?'

'Yeah, thank goodness. She had a bit of a rough night with Shaun. The poor little devil's teething.'

Charlie gave a sympathetic smile.

'Still living with yer, are they?' Then he laughed. 'That was a bloody silly question, wasn't it? Still, it must be 'ard on yer, love. I remember when my lot was that age. Didn't get a decent night's kip for years. Still, they're better off with you till Annie and Paddy get back.' His face became solemn, and he seemed to wait a bit before asking awkwardly, 'Rory still no better then?' He saw Josie flinch and took her hand. 'Sorry, love. Me an' my big mouth, always putting me foot in it. It just seems a shame he's missing out on 'aving his sister and nephew at 'ome with 'im. I'd've thought it'd do 'im the world of good 'aving Jane an' the little 'un around the place.' He absently scratched behind his ear, embarrassed now. 'Still, what do I know, eh, love?'

'It's all right, Charlie, I know yer mean well; I'll get your breakfast.'

Charlie's words had evoked images she had constantly tried to suppress since the accident. Alone in the large kitchen, she raced around in a whirl, trying to catch up on lost time, thinking that if she kept busy it wouldn't give her time to dwell on the past; but it was no good. She couldn't get thoughts of Rory out of her mind. Out of all the family, he was the one who had suffered the most. For not only had his younger brother died saving him, he still blamed himself for letting the accident happen, and the guilt had lain heavy on his mind, turning him from an easy-going, happy and confident man to one broken up inside.

Pat had tried to ease Rory's mind by pointing out that it could just as easily have been him who had overseen the building of that block of flats, for he had let the building go ahead when he'd returned to work. But no amount of words could convince Rory he wasn't to blame for Shaun's death.

He and Pat were currently working on another site for Matthew Hunter, but that was all Rory did. He went to work, came home, slept a few hours, then went back to work the following morning. On Sundays he didn't even bother to get out of bed. Josie had tried to help when Annie and Paddy set off for Ireland, but Rory had told her in no uncertain terms that he didn't need anyone's help. Then he had shut the door in her face.

She hadn't seen him again until a few days ago, when Jane and little Shaun had turned up on her doorstep. Rory had first come over to speak to her on his own. He had been unshaven and scruffy, his clothes hanging loose on the once muscular frame, and Josie had been deeply shocked at the sight of him, for Rory had always been so particular about his personal appearance. He had gruffly asked if she would take Jane and the baby in until Annie and Paddy came back, and Josie, desperately lonely without her friends, had readily agreed.

Now, even having not enjoyed a full night's sleep for the past four nights, she didn't regret her decision one iota. In fact she treasured this time with Jane and the baby, for she knew it would be short-lived. It had come as a tremendous shock to Josie to realise that Annie had let Jane and baby Shaun return to England on their own, fuelling her fear that Annie's state of mind was still frail, but Jane had soon reassured her, explaining that they had been preparing to leave Ireland when her uncle had been taken ill. Although not serious, Annie had used her brother's ill health as an excuse to stay with him a little longer, for, as she had tearfully explained to her husband and daughter, once she returned to England, it was doubtful she would ever see him again. Even so, she had balked at the idea of her precious daughter and grandson making the journey back alone.

But it was the change in Jane's character that had caused the most surprise to Josie. For the once timid girl had changed remarkably. When Josie had taken her in she had expected Jane to stay in the house behind closed curtains, but Jane would have none of it. Instead, she had wheeled her son down the street and around the market, her head held high as she pushed the pram past stunned faces, her eyes silently challenging anyone to make a scurrilous comment. Josie smiled to herself. She should have realised the depth of Jane's character by her steadfast refusal to name the father of her illegitimate son; she was indeed her mother's daughter! The support of the market traders had done much to strengthen Jane's resolve not to hide away. Like a family, they had closed ranks around the young girl, their protectiveness soon made apparent to the curious shoppers hoping for a juicy bit of gossip. One and all had been sent on their way with a curt word; some more colourful than others.

As if she had conjured them up out of thin air, Jane came in by the back door, pulling the cumbersome pram with her.

'Sorry, Josie, I've only just got him settled.' She left the pram in the doorway while she took her coat off and donned her apron. 'You can't have had much sleep either, with him crying most of the night.'

Josie gave a wry smile.

'Don't worry, I'll survive. Though if those blasted teeth of his don't come through soon, I'll buy him a set of false ones.'

Jane ignored this remark, saying, 'Anyone in yet?'

'Yeah, Charlie. I'm running a bit late today. Do the eggs for me, will yer, love, then take it through. The poor sod must be starving. I'm glad I don't have to open at the crack of dawn, not that I haven't been

337

asked plenty of times. But as much as I'm fond of all of them, I ain't getting outta my bed at five in the morning for anyone . . .' She paused, looking towards the pram. 'Well, almost anyone.' She smiled lovingly.

Jane checked the frying pan's contents, took out three sausages and two rashers of bacon, which she put on a warm plate from the oven, dropped two slices of bread into the sizzling fat, waited a few seconds, turned them over, then added them to the plate along with two fried eggs.

'The pan needs filling, Josie. When you've finished staring at Shaun, of course. Though if you wake him up, you can get him back down again, all right?'

Josie made a face at Jane, then turned back to the pram for another few precious seconds before returning to work. From the other room she heard the bell ring twice in succession, and Jane's laugh as she talked to the customers. And that sound was music to Josie's ears. There had been a time when Josie had thought never to hear it again. When Jane's pregnancy had first become known, Annie, in desperation, had asked Pat if he and Freda would consider adopting the baby. Pat would have agreed like a shot, but Freda had refused point blank. Her reason to Annie was that she wanted a family of her own, but in private she had told Pat she wasn't taking in any bastard, especially when the father could be anyone. And that fact remained a mystery, for Jane, who had always been so biddable, had refused to reveal the identity of the father.

In normal circumstances, Annie wouldn't have rested until she'd elicited the truth from her daughter, who she still considered a child herself.

But those hadn't been normal circumstances, and Annie, tired and grief-stricken as she had been, had been unable to cope with any more traumas. She had always been a strong woman, able to tackle any problem that arose in the family, but even the strong had their breaking point; and Annie had had her fair share. There had been a time during that dreadful period when Josie had feared for Annie's state of mind; not to mention her children, who had expected her to ease their pain and pull the family together again.

Then Mister Hunter had stepped in!

Remembering the kindness of the man caused Josie to pause in her cooking. That poor man. Everyone's sympathies had lain with the Flynns, yet Matthew Hunter had suffered; in a different way, but none the less painful for that. He had turned his son over to the police, an action that had nearly caused the break-up of his marriage, for his wife had wanted to give her only son the benefit of the doubt. Agreeing to meet his wife halfway, Matthew had reluctantly put up the bail money to get his son out of prison until the trial date. And how had that smarmy bastard repaid him? Only done a bunk, leaving his father with a thousand pounds' debt. Not content with that, he had also taken all his mother's jewellery, and the small amount of money Matthew had had in his safe. No one knew where he was now, but the general consensus was that he would soon be forced to return home, because he could never make it on his own wits.

'Two more breakfasts, Josie. Honest, I don't know where they put it, especially when they come back again for dinner, and puddings, though the puddings aren't as good as Mum makes; as is constantly commented on. Oh, Josie, I wish me mum and dad were back. I don't half miss them.'

Josie looked at the sad face, knowing exactly how Jane felt, for she too missed them, especially Annie; dear, larger-than-life Annie. Without her presence there was a void that could never be filled until her return. Though that in turn would create another void in Josie's life, because as soon as Paddy and Annie came back from Ireland, Jane and young Shaun would move back home; and Josie would miss them terribly.

'You daydreaming again, Josie? The place is filling up.'

Startled, Josie set to work, cooking and talking as she went.

'Sorry, Jane. I was just thinking about your mum and dad. If one more person asks me when they're coming back I'll scream.'

'I know, Josie. Some days I wish I hadn't come back early. But Mum never gave me a minute alone with Shaun. I know she meant well, and I couldn't have got through it all without her, but I had to get away. She was smothering me, Josie. To Mum I'm still her little girl, and I needed the chance to stand on me own two feet. So when Uncle Declan caught influenza, I took the chance to come back on my own. Mum nearly had a fit, but I'd made up my mind. Mind you, I wasn't quite fair. I mean, I knew how much Mum hated the thought of leaving Uncle Declan and I took advantage of the situation. I know I've only been back four days, and I know things would be a lot different if you hadn't taken me and Shaun in, but I'm learning to cope. It isn't easy, especially when I've always had everything done for me.' Holding a tray with three laden plates, Jane smiled wryly. 'Mind you, I wouldn't say no to a lie-in tomorrow if you're offering.'

'What was that yer was just saying about standing on your own two feet?'

Jane shrugged.

'Well, it was worth a try . . . By the way, those sausages are burning.'

Josie whirled round, then relaxed when she realised Jane had been teasing her. A soft gurgle attracted her attention and she looked in the pram. Two large blue eyes were staring back at her, the small mouth uttering a squeal of delight at the familiar face peering down at him, and Josie's heart melted.

'Oh, you're awake, are yer? Well I ain't picking you up, so there's no use yer looking at me like that.' As she moved away, a cry of disappointment came from the pram and she cursed herself for letting the baby see her. Pulling the pram into the kitchen, she propped the four-month-old baby up against his pillows and laid his rattle and toys in his lap.

'Now, you behave yourself, mate, or you'll get me hung. Worst still, your mum might walk out on me, and then I'd have to hire someone to help me out like I did when you lot was on holiday. Bloody useless they were an' all.'

When Jane came back she looked at Josie suspiciously.

'You woke him up, didn't you?'

Putting a puzzled expression on her face, Josie

answered, 'Who, me? I never went near him. He woke up on his own.'

Shaking her head in mock irritation, Jane kissed her son then carried on working.

The morning flew by, and it was twelve thirty before there was a lull in the café. With just five tables occupied by women shoppers wanting only tea and cakes, Josie took her break while Jane served. She normally took at least fifteen minutes for her lunch, but with Annie absent, the amount of time varied from day to day.

She had finished her sandwich and was playing with the baby on her lap when Jane came through, her face subdued.

'What's up, love?' Josie asked, concerned at Jane's obvious distress.

Jane picked up Shaun and buried her face against his belly, much to the child's delight.

'Nothing, Josie. I can manage.'

'Like hell yer can. Something's upset yer . . . Or someone.' Her eyes darted suspiciously to the door Jane had just hurried through.

Seeing the look on Josie's face, Jane said quickly, 'Look, don't get upset, but . . . but Cathy Meadows is out there. She wants a pot of tea and a menu of the cakes available.'

Josie's lips tightened.

'Does she now?'

'Josie, calm down, please. There's no point in making a scene, that's just what she wants. I shouldn't have let her upset me. I'm not a child any more. Just give me a few minutes, then I'll go out and see to her.'

'What did she say to you? And don't tell me nothing, Jane. She must have said something to upset yer.'

Jane nuzzled her baby's cheek.

'She . . . well, she asked me if it was true I'd had a baby, and . . . and she asked me who the father was. But it wasn't just what she said, it's the way she said it. You know, sort of spiteful; nasty like.'

'Oh I know just what yer mean,' Josie replied, her face grim. 'Well now, seeing as how I'm the owner, it's only right I should see to our special visitor.'

Jane's arms tightened around Shaun's squirming body, her heart racing. She knew what Josie could be like when in a temper; and boy was she in a temper. Following closely behind, Jane felt a sudden excitement course through her. If Josie was going to confront Cathy Meadows, she wanted to be there to see it; even if she was shaking all over with nerves.

Cathy Meadows was seated by the window, dressed as though she was going to the theatre instead of out on a shopping trip.

'Well, well! Josie Guntrip in person. I wouldn't have recognised you. I had heard you'd come into money, and I must say you look good on it.'

Cathy was peering up at Josie from beneath a wide, fancy hat. The hat, like her expensive silk costume, was a deep sky blue in colour. But it was the face that Josie concentrated on. It was still beautiful; beautiful but hard, cold even; and the painted lips were curved with disdain.

Waving a hand in the air as if to take in her surroundings, Cathy said with a smirk, 'So this is what

343

you did with the money. I must say, I was expecting something, shall we say, a bit more grand. I mean, with a name like The Tea Shop, one would expect a more selective clientele, instead of common market traders and bored housewives.'

An angry murmur could be heard as the women present took offence at the comment, but they remained seated, waiting with bated breath for Josie to speak.

Josie too was seething inside, but she kept her voice calm.

'If that's what you think, then I'm surprised you lowered yourself to come in.'

Cathy let out a tinkling laugh, a laugh she had cultivated to impress men; it did nothing to ingratiate herself among women.

'Oh, come now, Josie, don't get on your high horse. I simply commented that the name above the shop was slightly misleading, maybe even a trifle ostentatious, that's all.' She smiled up at Josie, but her eyes were hostile.

'I think the word you're looking for is pretentious, Cathy, not ostentatious. You really should look up the meaning of words before you use them.'

Jane looked on and listened with rising enjoyment, as did the rest of the customers, all silently urging Josie on, waiting to see the spiteful bitch taken down a peg or two.

Cathy's smile faltered, but only briefly.

'You *are* full of surprises, Josie. I didn't know you had become so educated. Anyway, as much as I'd love to stay and chat, I have a busy afternoon ahead of me. So if you'd be good enough to bring me a menu, I'll have my lunch and be on my way.'

Josie didn't move. Instead she looked hard into the scornful face and said, 'I'm sorry, Cathy, but you'll have to find somewhere else to have your lunch . . . I don't wait on whores.'

A concerted gasp reverberated around the room at Josie's words. Behind her friend, Jane hugged her baby tight with glee.

Cathy's face looked as if she'd been hit, and hit hard. Worse still, in those few, damning words, she had been forced to acknowledge the truth about herself. Gathering up her bag and gloves, she moved gracefully to the door and left without a backward glance.

As soon as the door closed behind her, Josie was surrounded by women, all laughing and congratulating her for the way she had handled Cathy Meadows. Josie received their heartfelt compliments before excusing herself. Once back in the kitchen, she sat down heavily at the table, her hands and legs shaking. She couldn't believe what she had just said; not that she regretted it, oh no, definitely not. That slag had deserved every word, yet she couldn't believe it had been her that had said it.

'You were great out there, Josie. Oh, I wish I could see it all over again. And it'll be all over the market by the end of the day, if not sooner.'

Josie tried to smile and found her teeth were chattering.

'Pour us a cuppa, will yer, Jane. Gawd, look, I'm shaking like a leaf.'

'Well, you didn't show it, Josie, and that's what counts. Here . . .' Jane put a mug of tea on the table. 'Get that down you. It's not as effective as a drop of brandy, but it'll have to do for now. We can celebrate properly when we get home.'

Josie picked up the mug and was alarmed to find she had to grip it in both hands. But though she was shaking on the outside, inside she felt a growing sense of pride in herself for having had the courage to speak out. It was a feeling that would stay with her for the rest of her life.

'Are you listening to me, Barney? You've not said a word all evening. Aren't you even a little bit annoyed at the way Josie treated me today?'

Barney was sprawled in an armchair, an empty brandy glass in his hand. Getting up to refill it, he glanced over towards the bed, where Cathy was sitting propped up by pillows, her bare arms hugging her knees over the quilt.

'What d'yer want me to do about it? Go round and give Josie a good hiding? You sort it out between yer, I ain't interested. D'yer want a drink?'

Cathy's eyes screwed up in frustration. This was the last straw. She had expected Barney to be loving and sympathetic when he heard of the way Josie had spoken to her; instead, he looked bored to tears.

'No, I don't want a drink. I want you to listen to me, unless you don't care any more.'

Barney sighed and sat back down.

'Look, Cathy, you're a big girl now. You can look after yourself. Besides, I've had a pig of a day. In fact it's been a lousy week all round. I get enough grief at work; all I want right now is a bit of peace and quiet. Look, maybe we should give tonight a miss. Neither of us is in the mood for company.'

'Company!' Cathy screeched, and her voice grated on Barney's nerves. 'Is that what I am now – just company!'

Barney sprang out of the chair and began to pace the room.

'Give it a rest, will yer? You're beginning to get on me nerves. Yer don't wanna drink, yer don't wanna go to bed, and yer don't wanna go out, so what's the point of yer stopping?'

Cathy stared at him wide-eyed, a tingle of alarm rippling down her spine. Barney wasn't as attentive as he used to be. In fact, if she didn't know better, she'd think he had someone else. Still, it wouldn't hurt her to go carefully, just in case.

Pasting a seductive smile to her lips, she said warmly, 'I'm sorry, darling. You're right, I am big enough to fight my own battles.' Patting the bed, she murmured, 'Why don't you take those clothes off and get in here with me?'

Barney downed his drink, his gaze flickering over the woman in his bed. There was a time when he would have jumped at the offer; now the sight of Cathy repulsed him. Since the accident his feelings for her had changed. It had been a gradual thing, and he had thought at first it was just a reaction to the aftermath of that terrible day. But her charms had continued to wane. Now, looking at her naked, inviting body, all he could see were the numerous other men who had enjoyed that same body. Suddenly he felt sick to his stomach. It was over. All he wanted now was to get her out of his bed, and out of his house. And he briefly wondered if this was how Rory had felt when he had walked out on her.

Turning away, he poured another brandy and said abruptly, 'Get dressed, Cathy. I ain't in the mood. Go on, hurry up, and I'll take yer home.'

Cathy flinched at the cruelty in his voice. Suddenly she felt dirty and used. But if there was any walking out to do, she would be the one to do it this time. Having one man leave her was bad enough; she wasn't going to let another one do the same.

Slowly she got out of bed and dressed, her mind trying to find a way to leave with her pride intact. She started to talk, just talk, saying the first thing that came to mind, anything rather than endure the awful silence.

'I still can't believe that Josie Guntrip had the cheek to call me a whore in front of the whole shop. Talk about the pot calling the kettle black. What does she call that scabby-faced little slag she's so fond of? Huh! Looks as if butter wouldn't melt in her mouth, don't she? Well, she didn't get that baby of hers playing marbles. Mind you, I was surprised. I mean, what man would want to—'

She screamed as strong hands grabbed her by the shoulders. Then she was being shaken like a rag doll.

'What did yer say about a baby?'

'Stop it. You're hurting me.'

Barney stopped his shaking, but kept hold of her. 'I said, what d'yer say about Jane 'aving a baby?'

Genuinely bewildered, Cathy stared into Barney's wild eyes, then a glimmer of light began to break through the mist of her mind. *No!* she thought. Never in a million years! But why else would Barney be so . . . She began to laugh, softly at first, then louder and louder until her entire body shook with merriment.

Startled by Cathy's reaction, Barney's grip loosened, his eyes instantly wary. He should have known better than to make such a stupid slip. Cathy might not be a genius, but she was as sharp as a tack when it came to sniffing out any kind of dirt.

'Shut up! D'yer hear me, shut up!'

But Cathy only laughed harder. 'I can't believe it . . . You and scarface. Bleeding 'ell, Barney, yer must have been well pissed if yer was able to give Jane Flynn one. Either that or yer bumped into her on a dark night. Oh! Gawd blimey, I can't remember the last time I had such a good laugh.'

She paused a moment, wiping tears of merriment from her cheeks. She still couldn't believe it, but the look on Barney's face was a dead giveaway. What a turn-up for the books this was. And it couldn't have come at a better time. Now she could leave him with her head held high and her pride intact.

Buttoning up her coat, she picked up her hat and gloves from the nightstand and walked, still chuckling, to the door. There she paused. Turning to face him, she giggled.

'Don't worry, Barney, your secret's safe with me. I'll keep it quiet for now. Who knows when I might be able to use it against yer? 'Cos you was going to dump me, weren't yer?' She stopped giggling, her voice becoming hard. 'Now you listen to me, Barney Hobbs. If anyone asks, I dumped you, understand! If I hear anything to the contrary, I'm sure the Flynns will be only too pleased to find out who the mystery father is. Goodbye, Barney, see you around – maybe!'

Barney stood rooted to the spot, unable to fully take in what Cathy had told him. Jane had a child.

It had to be true. Even Cathy wouldn't make up something like that. But why hadn't he heard about it? News such as this travelled like wildfire around the East End. Then again, as he'd just told Cathy, he'd been having a devil of a time at work. If he'd stuck to his usual habit of having a drink after work he would surely have heard; that is, if it were true. And if it was, then . . . God Almighty!

Grabbing up his jacket from the back of a chair, Barney left the house at a run; his steps taking him in the direction of the Flynns' address.

Rory was slumped by the cold, empty grate, a bottle of whisky in his hand. He'd already drunk half of it, but it still wasn't enough to make the nightmares go away; it was never enough. He looked across to where his father normally sat, then to the sofa where he and Shaun would sprawl out after Sunday dinner, and felt the familiar prickle of tears start behind his eyes. Would he ever be able to forget Shaun, and what he'd done for him? He laughed harshly. Yeah, look what his brother had done for him. Sentenced him to a living hell, that was what his baby brother had done. Rory poured another drink. Maybe if he finished the bottle it would blot out the images that were branded into his brain, even if only for a little while. It would be enough; just a little time of oblivion was all he asked for these days.

The drink jumped in his hand as a loud banging resounded throughout the house. Getting unsteadily to his feet, he staggered to the door.

'Yeah, what—' He was flung back against the wall, helpless to stop the man from entering his house.

'Where is she? Come on, Rory, where is she? And don't try lying to me, 'cos I know. D'yer hear me, I know!'

Rory shook his head to clear the fog from his mind. He thought at first he was hallucinating. He'd certainly been hitting the bottle lately, but no, he wasn't imagining it. Barney Hobbs was in his house demanding to see *her*, whoever *her* was.

'What yer going on about, Hobbs? There's no one here but me. And even if there was, what business is it of yours?'

Barney stopped his pacing, looking at Rory properly for the first time since barging into the house. And what he saw shocked him almost as much as the revelation that he was a father.

'Good God, man. What the hell yer done to yerself?'

Rory shambled by, leaving behind a sour, fetid smell that made Barney wrinkle his nose in distaste. This wasn't the Rory he knew. Not this broken, smelly shambles of a man. And then he realised. Nobody knew he was the father. Jane must have kept the truth to herself as she had promised. He hesitated, not knowing what to do next. He had to see Jane, but obviously she wasn't here. And if she wasn't here, then there was only one other place she could be. He looked out of the window to the house opposite. Suddenly he was afraid. He hadn't stopped to think when he'd left his house in such a hurry. All that had been in his mind was seeing Jane, and maybe having to fight Rory to get to her. Now he had to build up his courage to go over the road to see Jane . . . and his child. Even thinking the word made his

351

head spin. He had a child. The fact that it might not be his didn't even enter his mind.

Blowing out his cheeks, he started rehearsing what to say when Josie opened the door . . . if she opened the door. After hearing how she had sent Cathy packing, he wasn't too anxious to confront her.

'Hey, Barney. Why don't yer come an' 'ave a drink with me? Come on . . . I don't like drinking on me own.' The slurred voice came from the room in front of him, and Barney followed the sound.

Rory was slumped in an armchair, his mouth slack, his clothes stained and wrinkled. Barney had never imagined he would ever feel pity for Rory Flynn, but he did at this moment. The man must be going through hell to have let himself go in such a way. He looked little more than a tramp, the poor bastard. But as much as he sympathised with Rory's predicament, there was nothing he could do to help. Furthermore, he wanted to get as far away from this . . . this stranger as possible.

'Sorry to trouble yer, Rory. My mistake. I'll let meself out.'

Rory didn't even look up. Barney let himself out quietly, then, taking a deep breath, he crossed the road.

Jane had put the baby to bed, and as always, she looked over the road to see if the lights were on. She was worried sick about Rory, but he refused to let her help him. All she could do was bring him hot meals and hope that he ate something. If only her mum would come home. She would soon have Rory back on his feet. She was about to close the curtains when she saw a man's shape crossing the road. As he stepped under the lamppost she let out a loud gasp of fright. It was Barney, and he was coming this way. Cathy must have told him about the baby. Oh Lord. What was she going to do now? All hell would break out once the truth was known.

Her mind in a whirl, she flew downstairs, landing at the bottom of the stairs just as the knock came at the door. There were a few moments' silence, then the knock came again.

Josie came along the hallway and saw Jane standing there as if stuck to the spot.

'What on earth's the matter with you? Why didn't yer open the door?'

'Don't open it, Josie, please.'

Her hand on the knob, Josie paused.

'What's the matter, yer daft cow? Who's out there yer don't want to see?'

Jane sank down on the bottom step. It was no use. She couldn't pretend any more. Shaking her head, she said simply, 'Go on, then, Josie. Open the door, but you'd better brace yourself for a shock.'

Josie's eyebrows rose, then she opened the door.

'What are you doing here at this time of night?' she demanded, her glance flitting from Jane to Barney.

Jane got to her feet.

'Let him in, Josie. He's come to see his son.'

Josie reeled back in surprise.

'Barney Hobbs! He's the mystery father?'

Jane nodded and looked at Barney.

'Would you leave us for a while, Josie? We've got things we have to sort out, and I'd rather not have an audience, if you don't mind.'

Did she mind! Well, yes, she did actually. But she kept quiet and stood aside to let Barney enter.

'Thanks, Josie. Bet you're surprised to see me, ain't yer?'

'Yeah, just a bit.' She looked to where Jane was standing by the front room and asked, 'You sure you'll be all right?'

Jane smiled nervously.

'I'm sure, Josie.'

Josie shrugged and was about to go upstairs when Barney caught her arm.

'Look, I know it ain't none of me business, but I went to Rory's first. He's in a bad way, Josie. To be honest, he frightened me. He seems to be trying to drink himself to death.'

Josie pulled away.

'So? What you telling me for? I tried to help him once, and got the door slammed in me face.'

Barney rubbed his chin nervously.

'Yeah, well, I was only saying. Anyway, thanks for letting me in, Josie. I appreciate it.'

'You just treat her right, or you'll 'ave me to answer to.'

Barney bowed his head, then followed Jane into the front room. When the door closed, Josie had a sudden, frightening feeling of loss that she couldn't explain. Chiding herself for a fool, she ran upstairs and looked in on the sleeping baby. Then, like Jane had done only minutes earlier, she too looked out of the window. She stood there for a long time, biting her lip, while she tried to make up her mind to go over the road.

'And get the door slammed in yer face again? You

must be a glutton for punishment,' her inner voice mocked her.

Quickly, before she could change her mind, Josie had her coat on and was out of the house and standing in the back yard of the Flynns' house. Her breath coming in giant gasps, she forced herself to walk in the back door. Bracing herself for another load of abuse, she called out, 'Rory! You there, Rory? It's me, Josie.'

The house remained as silent as a tomb. Inching her way through the scullery, she made for the front room, and what she saw there shocked her to the very core of her being.

Rory was sprawled in the armchair, an empty whisky bottle hanging from tobacco-stained fingers, his mouth open and dribbling. Josie's hand flew to her mouth. She'd had no idea he was this bad. Why on earth hadn't Jane told her? She stepped nearer, then stopped as the stench emanating from Rory's body hit her full in the face.

Dear God! He was lying in his own filth. Her first reaction to the awful sight was pity, then her mood changed quickly, and she felt a surge of rage flood through her. Not worrying about her reception now, she fetched a bucket of water from the kitchen and emptied it over the sleeping man's head. Rory woke instantly, spluttering and coughing at his rude awakening.

'What . . . !'

'I'll give you what, yer miserable, cowardly bastard. Is this what Shaun gave his life for? Just so as yer could drown yourself in self-pity? You make my blood boil, Rory Flynn. In case you've forgotten, you've got a sister and baby nephew over the road. Jane came back from Ireland 'cos she was worried about leaving yer on yer own; and she wanted to see her big brother. Her brave, afraid of nothing big brother. That's a laugh. It's a good job she had me to come to, 'cos if it'd been left up to you to look after them, they'd be lying in the gutter. Now get yourself up and out the back. You stink like a pig. What would your mum say if she could see yer in this state?'

Stung by the harsh words, Rory staggered to his feet.

'What's it gotta do with you, Josie? You ain't a part of this family, even though you think you are. Now piss off, and take your sanctimonious preaching with yer, 'cos I don't need it.'

Unperturbed by his outburst, Josie stood her ground, her fists resting on her hips.

'I ain't going nowhere till yer clean yourself up. Oh, not for you; you don't deserve any pity, you've got enough of that to spare yourself. I may not be a member of this family by blood, but I am by friendship. And by God, I'm not gonna stand by and watch Annie and Paddy bury another son. 'Cos that's what you're trying to do, ain't it? Only you ain't got the nerve to do it properly. You're taking the coward's way out, in more ways than one. At least some people kill themselves for a reason, and they have the decency to do it quietly and quickly. But not you, oh no! You have to try and drink yourself to death, so as people will think it was just another tragic accident.' She circled him, her nose wrinkling in disgust. 'Now, you gonna get yourself washed and into some clean clothes, or do I have to get them off you meself?'

Rory was wide awake and sober now. He looked down at himself and felt waves of shame and humiliation flood through him. That Josie, of all people, should see him like this was unbearable. Brushing past her, he headed for the scullery.

'Thanks for the concern, Josie. And now you've done your good deed for the day, you can bugger off back home.'

Josie faced him, her eyes unflinching.

'I told you, I ain't going nowhere till you're cleaned up. Then you can help me get this place clean an' all. If your mum came back unexpectedly and saw her beautiful home looking and smelling like a backstreet pub, she'd have a heart attack. Then you'd 'ave another death on your conscience. You'd like that, wouldn't yer? It'd give yer another excuse to kill yourself—'

The door to the scullery banged shut, but Rory could still hear the scathing words, and he couldn't bear it any more.

'*Shut up!* D'yer hear me? Shut the fuck up!'

Rory stood in the scullery doorway, his face and hair dripping with water, wearing a pair of crumpled but clean trousers held up by braces. His eyes wild, he stared at Josie, and she held his gaze until he was forced to look away. Pushing her roughly aside, he staggered back into the front room and went to sit down in his chair, then he paused, his eyes staring down at the stained material. And suddenly he couldn't take any more. Being forced to face what he had allowed himself to become was the final straw. He stumbled, then lowered himself gently on to the sofa and dropped his head in his hands.

Josie couldn't bear to watch any longer. She had done all she could; the rest was up to him.

'Don't go, Josie, please. Stay awhile with me. I . . . I don't want to be on me own any more.'

Josie's eyes rested on his bowed head, and despite all her efforts she couldn't hide the love she still felt for this man. Even if he didn't feel the same, she would never stop loving him, no matter how many times he pushed her away. But he wasn't pushing her away; he was asking . . . pleading with her to stay. Yet could she bear to go through all that hurt again?

'He's dead, Josie. Shaun's dead, and . . . and it's all . . . all my fault. I killed him, Josie. D'yer hear what I said? I . . . I killed him. Me own . . . brother. Help me, Josie . . . Please . . . please, help me. I . . . I don't know what to do.'

His body heaved with dry sobs, and so fierce were they that Josie feared they would tear him in two. With a cry of pity, she was across the room and sitting beside him, holding his head in her lap as he continued to cry.

'Oh, Josie. I should never have let yer go. I . . . I love yer, Josie. I know yer . . . yer probably won't believe me, but . . . but I do. I always have. I've been such a fool, Josie. Will yer give me another chance? I . . . I won't let yer down again, I . . . I promise. Shaun loved yer too, Josie. And I was jealous of him, 'cos he was a . . . a better man than I could ever be. And now . . . now he's gone, and . . . and I never had the chance to tell him . . .'

Josie held him tight.

'It's all right, Rory, everything's gonna be all right. And you mustn't worry about Shaun. He knew you loved him, just like he loved you. It's just that men don't tell each other things like that. Most times, especially in families, they don't have to; they just know. You sleep now, Rory. You sleep and let me look after you.' Laying her head next to his, she whispered, 'I love you, Rory. I always have and I always will.' She felt his hand reach for hers and clasped it tightly.

Who knew what tomorrow might bring when Rory was sober? Would he still feel the same, or were his words of love simply another reaction to the whisky and self-pity? She hugged him closer. It didn't matter. She had plenty of love for both of them; it would be enough. And as his body grew calmer and inched ever closer to hers, she felt his love reach out and touch her; and she held fast to his body and the love emanating from it. She was home at last.

And maybe this time it was for good.

Time Warner Paperback titles available by post:

❏ Ragamuffins	Anna King	£5.99
❏ Luck be a Lady	Anna King	£5.99
❏ Playing with Fire	Mary Larkin	£5.99
❏ Best Laid Plans	Mary Larkin	£5.99
❏ Twilight Time	Emma Blair	£6.99
❏ Wild Strawberries	Emma Blair	£5.99

The prices shown above are correct at time of going to press. However, the publishers reserve the right to increase prices on covers from those previously advertised, without prior notice.

TIME WARNER PAPERBACKS

P.O. Box 121, Kettering, Northants, NN14 4ZQ
Tel: +44 (0) 1832 737525, Fax: +44 (0) 1832 733076
Email: aspenhouse@FSBDial.co.uk

POST AND PACKING:

Payments can be made as follows: cheque, postal order (payable to Time Warner Books) or by credit cards. Do not send cash or currency.

All UK Orders   **FREE OF CHARGE**
E.E.C. & Overseas   25% of order value

Name (Block Letters) _____

Address _____

_____

Post/zip code:_____

❏ Please keep me in touch with future Time Warner publications

❏ I enclose my remittance £_____

❏ I wish to pay Visa/Access/Mastercard/Eurocard

Card Expiry Date